The Rose in the Ring

George Barr McCutcheon

CONTENTS

BOOK ONE

BOOK TWO

BOOK ONE

CHAPTER I

THE FUGITIVE

The gaunt man led the way. At his heels, doggedly, came the two short ones, fagged, yet uncomplaining; all of them drenched to the skin by the chill rain that swirled through the Gap, down into the night- ridden valley below. Sky was never so black. Days of incessant storm had left it impenetrably overcast.

These men trudged—or stumbled—along the slippery road which skirted the mountain's base. Soggy, unseen farm lands and gardens to their left, Stygian forests above and to their right. Ahead, the far-distant will-o-the-wisp flicker of many lights, blinking in the foggy shroud. Three or four miles lay between the sullen travelers and the town that cradled itself in the lower end of the valley.

Night had stolen early upon the dour spring day. The tall man who led carried a rickety, ill-smelling lantern that sent its feeble rays no farther ahead than a dozen paces; it served best to reveal the face of the huge silver watch which frequently was drawn from its owner's coat pocket.

Eight o'clock, —no more, —and yet it seemed to these men that they had plowed forever through the blackness of this evil night, through a hundred villainous shadows by unpointed paths. Mile after mile, they had traversed almost impassable roads, unwavering persistence in command of their strength, heavy stoicism their burden. Few were the words that had passed between them during all those weary miles. An occasional oath, muffled but impressive, fell from the lips of one or the other of those who followed close behind the silent, imperturbable leader. The tall man was as silent as the unspeakable night itself.

It was impossible to distinguish the faces of these dogged night-farers. The collars of their coats were turned up, their throats were muffled, and the broad rims of their rain-soaked hats were far down over the eyes. There was that about them which suggested the unresented pressure of firearms inside the dry breast-pockets of long coats.

1

This was an evening in the spring of 1875, and these men were forging their way along a treacherous mountain road in Southwestern Virginia. A word in passing may explain the exigency which forced the travelers to the present undertaking. The washing away of a bridge ten miles farther down the valley had put an end to all thought of progress by rail, for the night, at least. Rigid necessity compelled them to proceed in the face of the direst hardships. Their mission was one which could not be stayed so long as they possessed legs and stout hearts. Checked by the misfortune at the bridge, there was nothing left for them but to make the best of the situation: they set forth on foot across the mountain, following the short but more arduous route from the lower to the upper valley. Since three o'clock in the afternoon they had been struggling along their way, at times by narrow wagon roads, not infrequently by trails and foot paths that made for economy in distance.

The tall man strode onward with never decreasing strength and confidence; his companions, on the contrary, were faint and sore and scowling. They were not to the mountains born; they came from the gentle lowlands by the sea, —from broad plantations and pleasant byways, from the tidewater country. He was the leader on this ugly night, and yet they were the masters; they followed, but he led at their bidding. They had known him for less than six hours, and yet they put their lives in his hands; another sunrise would doubtless see him pass out of their thoughts forever. He served the purpose of a single night. They did not know his name—nor he theirs, for that matter; they took him on faith and for what he was worth—five dollars.

"Are those the lights of the town? " panted one of the masters, a throb of hope in his breast. The tall man paused; the others came up beside him. He stretched a long arm in the direction of the twinkling lights, far ahead.

"Yas, 'r, " was all that he said.

"How far? " demanded the other laboriously.

"'Bout fo'h mile. "

"Road get any better? "

"Yas, 'r. "

"Can we make it by nine, think? "

"Yas, 'r. "

"We'd better be moving along. It's half-past seven now. "

"Yas, 'r. "

Once more they set forward, descending the slope into the less hazardous road that wound its way into the town of S— —, then, as now, a thriving place in the uplands. The ending of a deadly war not more than ten years prior to the opening of this tale had left this part of fair Virginia gasping for breath, yet too proud to cry for help. Virginia, the richest and fairest and proudest of all the seceding states, was but now finding her first moments of real hope and relief. Her fortunes had gone for the cause; her hopes had sunk with it.

Both were now rising together from the slough into which they had been driven by the ruthless Juggernaut of Conquest. The panic of '73 meant little to the people of this fair commonwealth; they had so little then to lose, and they had lost so much. The town of S—-, toward which these weary travelers turned their steps, was stretching out its hands to clasp Opportunity and Prosperity as those fickle commodities rebounded from the vain-glorious North; the smile was creeping back into the haggard face of the Southland; the dollars were jingling now because they were no longer lonely. The bitterness of life was not so bitter; an ancient sweetness was providing the leaven. The Northern brother was relaxing; he was even washing the blood from his hands and extending them to raise the sister he had ravished. There was forgiveness in the heart of fair Virginia—but not yet the desire to forget. The South was coming into its own once more—not the old South, but a new one that realized.

Intermittent strains of music came dancing up into the hills from the heart of S—. The wayfarers looked at each other in the darkness and listened in wonder to these sounds that rose above the swish of the restless rain.

"It's a band, " murmured one of the two behind.

"Yas, 'r; a circus band, " vouchsafed the guide, a sudden eagerness in his voice. "Van Slye's Great and Only Mammoth Shows—"

"A circus? " interrupted one of the men gruffly. "Then the whole town is full of strangers. That's bad for us, Blake. "

"I don't see why. He's more than likely to be where the excitement's highest, ain't he? He's not too old for that. We'll find him in that circus tent, Tom, if he's in the town at all. "

"First circus they've had in S—— in a dawg's age, " ventured the guide, with the irrelevancy of an excited boy. "Rice's was there once, I can't remember jest when, an' they was some talk of Barnum las' yeah, they say, but he done pass us by. He's got a Holy Beheemoth that sweats blood this yeah, they say. Doggone, I'd like to see one. " The guide had not ventured so much as this, all told, in the six hours of their acquaintanceship.

"Well, let's be moving on. I'm wet clear through, " shivered Blake.

Silence fell upon them once more. No word was spoken after that, except in relation to an oath of exasperation; they swung forward into the lower road, their sullen eyes set on the lights ahead. Heavy feet, dragging like hundredweights, carried them over the last weary mile. Into the outskirts of the little town they slunk. The streets were deserted, muddy, and lighted but meagerly from widely separated oil lamps set at the tops of as many unstable posts.

Some distance ahead there was a vast glow of light, lifting itself above the housetops and pressing against the black dome that hung low over the earth. The rollicking quickstep of a circus band came dancing over the night to meet the footsore men. There were no pedestrians to keep them company. The inhabitants of S—— were inside the tents beyond, or loitering near the sidewalls with singular disregard for the drizzling rain that sifted down upon their unmindful backs or blew softly into the faces of the few who enjoyed the luxury of "umberells. " Despite the apparent solitude that kept pace with them down the narrow street, —little more than a country lane, on the verge of graduating into a thoroughfare, —the three travelers were keenly alert; their squinting, eager eyes searched the shadows beside and before them; their feet no longer dragged through the slippery, glistening bed of the road; every movement, every glance signified extreme caution.

Slowly they approached the vacant lots beyond the business section of the town, known year in and year out to the youth of S—— as "the show grounds. " Now they began to encounter straggling, envious atoms of the populace, wanderers who could not produce the admission fee and who were not permitted by the rough canvasmen to venture inside the charmed circle laid down by the "guy-ropes. " At the corner of the tented common stood the "ticket wagon, " the muddy plaza in front of it torn by the footprints of many human beings and lighted by a great gasoline lamp swung from a pole hard by. Beyond was the main entrance of the animal tent, presided over by uniformed ticket takers. Here and there, in the gloomy background, stood the canvas and pole wagons, shining in their wetness against the feeble light that oozed through the opening between the sidewall and the edge of the flapping main top, or glistening with sudden brightness in response to the passing lantern or torch in the hand of a rubber-coated minion who "belonged to the circus, "—a vast honor, no matter how lowly his position may have been. Costume and baggage wagons, their white and gold glory swallowed up in the maw of the night, stood backed up against the dressing-tent off to the right. The horse tent beyond was even now being lowered by shadowy, mystic figures who swore and shouted to each other across spaces wide and spaces small without regulating the voice to either effort. Horses, with their clanking trace-chains, in twos and fours, slipped in and out of the shadows, drawing great vehicles which rumbled and jarred with the noise peculiar to circus wagons: tired, underfed horses that paid little heed to the curses or the blows of the men who handled them, so accustomed were they to the proddings of life.

And inside the big tent the band played merrily, as only a circus band can play, jangling an accompaniment to the laughter and the shouts of the delighted multitude sitting in the blue-boarded tiers about the single ring with its earthen circumference, its sawdust carpet and its dripping lights.

The smell of the thing! Who has ever forgotten it? The smell of the sawdust, the smell of the gleaming lights, the smell of animals and the smell of the canvas top! The smell of the damp handbills, the programs and the bags of roasted peanuts! Incense! Never-to-be-forgotten incense of our beautiful days!

Warm and dry and bright under the spreading top with its two "center poles" and its row of "quarters"; cold, dreary and sordid outside in the real world where man and beast worked while others seemed to play.

Groups of canvasmen now began to tear down the animal tent — the "menagerie, " as it has always been known to the man who pays admission. An hour later, when the big show is over, the spectators will stream forth, even as their own blue seats begin to clatter to earth behind them, and they will blink with amazement to find themselves in the open air, instead of in the menagerie tent. As if by magic it has disappeared, and with it the sideshow and its banners, the Punch and Judy show, the horse tent, the cook tent, the blacksmith shop. Where once stood a dripping white city, now stretches a barren, ugly waste of unhallowed, unfamiliar ground, flanked by the solitary temple of tinsel and sawdust which they have just left behind, and which even now is being desolated by scowling men in overalls. The crowd oozes forth, to find itself completely lost in the night, all points of the compass at odds, no man knowing east from west or north from south in the strange surroundings. The "lot" they have known so well and crossed so often has been transformed into a trackless wilderness, through which strange objects rumble and creak, over which queer, ghastly lights play for the benefit of grumbling men from another world.

Blake and his companion, standing apart from the lank, wide-eyed guide, were conversing in low tones.

"We'd better make the circuit of the tents, " said Blake, evidently the leader. "You go to the right and I'll take the other way round. We'll meet here. Keep your eye peeled. He may be hiding under the wagons where it's dry. Look out for these circus toughs. They're a nasty crowd. "

Then he turned to the guide.

"We won't need you any longer, " he said. "This is as far as we go. Here is your pay. If I were you, I'd buy a ticket and go inside. "

"Yas, 'r, " said the smileless guide, accepting the greenback with no word of thanks. A brief "good night" to his employers, and the lean mountaineer strolled over to the ticket wagon. He purchased a ticket and hurried into the tent. We do not see him again. He has served his purpose.

His late employers made off on their circuit of the tents, sharp-eyed but casual, doing nothing that might lead the circus men to suspect that they were searching for one among them. In the good old days of the road circus there were thieves as well as giants; if a man was not a thief himself, he at least had a friend who was. There was honor among them.

A scant hour before the three men came to the "showgrounds" their quarry arrived there. That Blake and his companion were man-hunters goes without saying, but that the person for whom they searched should be a hungry, wan-faced, terrified boy of eighteen seems hardly in keeping with the relentless nature of the chase.

The ring performance in the main tent had been in progress for fifteen or twenty minutes when the fugitive, exhausted, drenched and shivering, crept into the protected nook which marks the junction of the circus and dressing tops. Here it was comparatively dry; the wind did not send its thin mist into this canvas cranny. Not so dark as he may have desired, if one were to judge by the expression in his feverish eyes as he peered back at the darkness out of which he had slunk, but so cramped in shadow that only the eye of a ferret could have distinguished the figure huddled there. Chilled to the bone, wet through and through, this white-faced lad, with drooping lip and quickened breath, crouched there and waited for the heavy footstep and the brutal command of the canvasman who was to drive him forth into the darkness once more.

He had watched his chance to creep into this coveted spot. When the men were called to work at the horse tent he found his chance. It looked warm in this corner; a pleasant light on the inside of the two tents glowed against the damp sidewalls: here and there it glimmered invitingly under the bottom of the canvas. He knew that his tenancy must end in an hour or two: the big top would be leveled to the ground, rolled up and spirited away into the stretches that lay between this city and the next one, twenty miles away. But an hour or two in this friendly corner, close to the glare of the circus lights, almost in touch with the joyous, bespangled world of his ambitions, even though he was a hated and hunted creature, was better than the sopping roadside or the fields.

He knew that he was being hounded and that those who sought him were close behind. Once in the forest, far back in the hills, he had heard them, he had seen them. Off in other parts of the country men were looking for him. In the cities throughout Virginia and the adjoining states there were placards describing him ere this, and rewards were mentioned.

Resting in the bushes above the trail, late in the afternoon, he had seen Blake and his men. They had stopped to rest, and he could hear their conversation plainly. With all the wiliness of a hunted thing, he had slipped off into the forest, terrified to find that his pursuers were so close upon him.

He had learned that they were making for S—— and it was easy to see that their progress was slow and grueling. His feet were light, his legs strong; peril gave wings to his courage. Something told him that he must beat them by many miles into the town of S——. Once, when he was much younger, he had gone to S—— with his grandfather to see the soldiers encamped there. He remembered the railroad. It was imperative that he should reach the railway as far in advance of his pursuers as legs and a stout heart could carry him.

A wide *detour* through the sombre forest brought him to the road once more, fully a mile below his pursuers. He forgot his hunger and his fatigue. For miles he ran with the fleetness of a scared thing, guided by the crude sign-boards which pointed the way and told the distance to S——. Night fell, but he ran on, stumbling and faint with dread, tears rolling down his thin cheeks, sobs in his throat. Darkness hid the sign-boards from view; he reeled from one side of the narrow, Stygian lane to the other, sustaining many falls and bruises, but always coming to his feet with the unflagging determination to fight his way onward.

Half-dazed, gasping for breath and ready to drop in his tracks, he came at last to the open valley. Far ahead and below were the lights of a town—he could only hope that it was S——. Tortured by the vast oppressiveness of the solitude which lay behind him, peopled by a thousand ghosts whose persistent footsteps had haunted him through every mile of his flight, he cried aloud as he stumbled down the rain- washed hill, —cried with the terror of one who sees collapse after human valor has been done to death.

He was never to know how he came, in the course of an hour, to the outskirts of the town. His mind, distracted by the terror of pursuit, refused to record the physical exertions of that last bitter hour; his body labored mechanically, without cognizance of the strain put upon it. He had traversed fifteen miles of the blackest of forests and by way of the most tortuous of roads. A subconscious triumph now inspired him, born of the certainty that he had left his enemies far behind. It was this oddly jubilant spur that drove him safely, almost instinctively, into the heart of S——. The music of a band both attracted and bewildered him. It was some time before he could grasp the fact that a circus was holding forth in the lower end of the town. The subtle cunning that had become part of his nature within the past forty-eight hours forbade an incautious approach to the circus grounds. There, of all places, he might expect to encounter peril. To his bewildered mind every man who breathed of life was a sleuth sent forth to lay hold of him.

He gave the circus—loved thing of tenderer days—a wide berth, finding his way to the railway station by outlying streets. His first thought was to board an outbound train, to secrete himself in one of the freight cars. The sudden, overpowering pangs of hunger drove this plan from his mind, combined with the discovery that no train would pass through the town before midnight. Disheartened, sick with despair, he slunk off through the railway yards, taking a roundabout way to the circus grounds.

There was money in his purse, —plenty of it; but he was afraid to enter an eating-house, or to even approach the "snack-stand" on the edge of the circus lot. For a long time he stood afar off in the darkness, his legs trembling, his mouth twitching, his eyes bent with pathetic intentness upon the single pie and hot sandwich stand that remained near the sideshow tent, presided over by a kind-faced, sleepy old man in spectacles.

A huge placard tacked to the board fence back of this stand attracted his attention. Impelled by a strange curiosity, he ventured into the circle of light, knowing full well, before he was near enough to distinguish more than the bold word "Reward, " that this sinister bill had to do with him and no other.

Held by the same mysterious power that a serpent exercises in charming its victim, the lad stared at the face of this ominous thing that proclaimed him a fugitive for whom five hundred dollars would be paid, dead or alive.

Stricken to the soul, he read and re-read the black words, unable, for a long time, to tear himself away from the spot. A quick alarm seized him. He slunk back into the shadows, his hunger forgotten. For many minutes he stood in the grisly darkness, staring at the white patch on the fence. Curses rose to his lips—lips that had never known an oath before; prayers and pleadings were forgotten in that bitter arraignment of fate.

Then came the sudden revival of youthful spirits, carrying with them the reckless bravado that all boys possess to the verge of folly. The band was playing, the show had begun. In his mind's eye he could see the *"grand entree. "* A fierce desire to brave detection and boldly enter the charmed pavilion took possession of him. First, he would buy of the pieman's wares; then he would calmly present himself before the ticket wagon window, after which—But he got no farther in his dream of audacity. The placard on the fence seemed to smite him in the face. He drew farther back into the darkness, shuddering. With his arms clasped tightly across his chest, shivering in the chill that had returned triumphant, he dragged himself wearily away from the place of temptation.

Circling the dressing-tent, he came upon men at work. They were drawing stakes with the old-fashioned chains. For a while he dully watched them. They passed on. He crept from his place of hiding and, attracted by the lights as a moth is drawn by the candle, made his way to the sheltered spot at the joining of the tents.

After a few moments of restless vigil an overpowering sense of lassitude fell upon him. His eyes closed in abrupt surrender to exhaustion. The rhythmic beat of the quickstep leaped off into great distances; the champing and snorting of horses in the dressing-tent died away as if by magic; the subdued voices of the men and women who waited their turn to bound into the merry ring faded into indistinguishable whispers; the crack of the ring master's whip and the responsive yelp of the clown trailed off into silence. His head fell back, his body relaxed, and he slipped off into sweet unconsciousness.

A man in motley garb, with a face of scarlet and white, sitting on a blue half-barrel near the flap which indicated the entrance to the men's section of the dressing-tent, caught sight of an arm and hand lying limp under the edge of the canvas. He stared hard for a moment and then, attracted by the slim, unfamiliar member, arose and advanced to the spot. As he stood there, looking down at the hand, a woman and a young girl approached.

"Drunk, " observed the clown, with a grimace.

They stopped beside him, looking down. The woman spoke. "How long and fine the fingers are. A boy's hand, not a man's. See who is there, Joey, do. "

And so it was that the fugitive was taken.

The clown lifted the sidewall and bent over the form of the lad, peering into the white, mud-streaked face.

"He's not drunk, " he said quickly.

"He looks ill, poor fellow. How wet he is, —and *so* muddy. Is he asleep? It isn't—it isn't something else? " She drew back in sudden dread.

"He's alive, right enough. I say, Mrs. Braddock, there's something queer about this. He can't belong in this 'ere town, else he wouldn't be sleepin' 'ere in the mud. He's plain pegged out, ma'am. Like enough 'e's some poor fool as wants to join the circus. Run away from 'ome, I daresay. We've 'ad lots of 'em follow us up lately, you know. Only this 'un looks different. Shall I call Peterson? He'll wake 'im up right enough and conwince 'im that the show business is a good thing to stay out of while he can. "

"Don't call Peterson. He is a brute. Rouse him yourself, and tell him to come inside the tent. Poor boy, he's half drowned. Come, dearie, " to the girl, "go into the dressing-room. You must not see—"

"He is so white and ill-looking, mother, " said the girl, in pitying tones, her gaze fastened upon the face of the sleeper. The mother drew the child aside, an arm about her shoulder. Together they watched the clown's efforts to arouse the boy.

"He may be another Artful Dick, my child, " ventured the mother. "Your father says the pickpockets are uncommonly numerous this spring. "

"I'm sure he isn't a thief—I'm sure of it, " said the girl eagerly.

She was a pretty, brown-haired creature, whose large, serious eyes seemed unnaturally dark and brilliant against the vivid coloring of her cheeks and forehead. The blacks, whites and carmines of the make- up box had beautified her for the ring but not for closer observation. One who understood the secrets of the "make-up" could have told at a glance that underneath the thick layer of powder and paint there was a soft, white skin; even the rough, careless application of harmless cosmetics could not, in any sense, deceive one as to the delicacy of her features. The mouth, red with the carmine grease, was gentle, even tremulous; her nose, though streaked with a thin, white line, was straight and pure patrician in its modeling, with fine, quivering nostrils, now gently distended by sharp exercise in the ring; her ears were small, her throat round and slim; right proudly her head rode the firm, white neck; the warm, brown hair swept down in caresses for the bare shoulders.

A long, red Shaker cloak enveloped the slim, straight body. Dainty golden slippers, protected by the ungainly ground shoes of the circus performer, peeped from beneath the hem of the robe. A small, visorless cap of red velvet fitted snugly over the crown of her head.

Now the lips were parted and the eyes narrowed by interest in the stranger who slept against their walls.

The mother was still a young woman; a pretty one, despite the careworn expression in her eyes and the tired lines in her face. She was dressed in the ordinary garments of the street, in no way suggestive of the circus. There was an unmistakable air of gentle breeding about her, patient under the strain of adverse circumstances, but strong and resolute in the power to meet them without flinching. This woman, you could see at a glance, was not born to the circus and its hardships; she came of another world. Tall and slender and proud she was, endowed with the poise of a thorough gentlewoman. Hers was a fine, brilliant face, crowned by dark hair that grew low and waved about her temples. Deep, tender brown eyes met yours steadily and with unwavering candor. There was strength and loyalty and purity in their depths. No hardness, no callousness, no guile, no rancor there: only the clear, sweet eyes of a woman whose soul is white. There was an infinite pity in them now.

The clown had shaken the boy into partial wakefulness. He was sitting up, leaning forward on his hands, his eyes blinking in the contest between sleep and amazement.

"Get up, " said Grinaldi, the clown, shaking him by the shoulder. "What are you doing here, boy? "

The lad came quickly to his feet and would have rushed away into the darkness behind him had it not been for the restraining grip on his arm. He felt himself being dragged into the stuffy, mysterious vestibule of the tent, into plain view of a half-dozen vividly attired persons, almost under the feet of stolid, gayly caparisoned horses wearing the great back-pads.

And this creature who led him there—this grotesque object with the chalky face and coal-black eyebrows that ran up in tall triangles to meet a still chalkier pate—this figure with the red and black crescents on his cheeks and the baggy, spotted suit of red and white and blue and the conical hat—who and what was he?

The clown!

He was not dreaming—he was in the dressing-tent of the circus, enveloped by the dull, magic atmosphere that comes in the smoke of burning oils, —an atmosphere that is never to be found outside the low walls of a dressing-tent. He experienced a sudden feeling of suffocation. The whole world seemed to have closed in upon him; a drab sky almost touched his head; the horizon seemed to have rushed up to within ten feet of where he stood.

His bewildered gaze took in the horses, the boxes, the trunks, the ring paraphernalia, the "properties, " the discarded uniforms of attendants—cast in apparent confusion here, there and everywhere. Somehow, as he stared, this conglomerate mass of unfamiliar things seemed to creep away into the black shadows he had not perceived before; the drab dome of the tent began to swirl above his head, like a merry-go-round; the lights danced and then went out.

Grinaldi, the clown, caught him in his arms as he slipped forward in a dead faint.

CHAPTER II

IN THE DRESSING-TENT

When he regained consciousness, he was lying on a thick, dusty mattress, his head pillowed on a bundle of cloth that smelled of cotton and dyestuffs. Faces emerged from the gloom around him. Some one was holding a torch over his strange couch. That odd face in bismuth and lampblack was bending over him.

"He's come 'round, Mrs. Braddock, " he heard this creature say, in a far-off voice. "Only a faint, nothing more. Poor lad, he looks ill and hungry. "

Then other figures, all gaudy and bright and glittering, crowded into his vision. He tried to raise himself to his elbow, a fierce wave of embarrassment rushing over him. Some one supported him from behind. As he came to a sitting position, he turned his head to thank this person. It was with difficulty that he repressed a cry of alarm. The being who braced him with friendly arms was a glittering, shiny thing of green, with a human face that leered upon him.

Observing the youth's bewilderment and uncertainty, Grinaldi laughed.

"He's not a boa-constrictor, lad. He's the boneless wonder. He's as gentle as a spring lamb, and not hardly as tough. Signer Anaconda, the Human Snake, that's what he's called on the bills. Ed Casey is his real name. "

"Aw, cheese it, Joey, " growled the amiable Signer. "Say, young feller, what's ailing you? Where'd you come from? "

The stranger in this curious world managed to turn his body so that his legs hung over the side of the vaulter's mattress; he faced his audience, a sudden wariness in his eyes. Before venturing a word of explanation, he allowed his gaze to sweep the entire group. They mistook his deliberateness for stupefaction.

He saw perhaps a dozen people in the group before him. The colors of the rainbow were represented in the staring, curious company. There were men in tights and women in tights—in pink and red and green and blue—some of them still panting and breathless after their perilous work in the ring. He took them all in at a glance, but his eyes rested at last on the one figure that seemed out-of-place in this motley crowd: the tall, graceful figure of the woman in street clothes. He looked long at the sweet, gentle, unpainted face of this woman, and drew his first deep breath of relief and hope when she smiled. She moved quickly through the crowd of acrobats and riders, followed close behind by the slim, wide-eyed girl in the long red cloak. An instant later she was sitting beside him on the mattress, smiling with friendly encouragement as she laid her hand upon his arm. The girl stood at her knee. For the first time the fugitive noticed the face of this slender girl—no, it was the eyes alone that he saw, for the face was grossly covered with pigments.

"What has happened? " asked the tall woman gently. "Have you— have you run away from home, my boy? "

"How long have I been here? " There was a suggestion of alarm in the abrupt question.

His voice, querulous through excitement, was quite strong and musical. The tone and his manner of addressing the questioner proved beyond contradiction that he was no ordinary tramp, or show-follower, such as they were in the habit of seeing in their travels. A dozen fine old Virginia gentlemen, perhaps, one after another, had lived and died before him; down that precious line of blood had come the strain that makes for the finished thoroughbred—the real Virginia aristocrat. Six words, spoken with the mild drawl of the cultured Southerner, were sufficient to prove his title. No amount of mud or tatters or physical distress could take away the inborn charm of blood. No haggardness or pain could detract from the fine, clean movement of the lips, or sully the deep intelligence of the eyes.

His audience at once found a new interest in him. He was not what they had expected him to be; this boy was no scatter-brained country lout, with the dream of the circus at the back of his folly.

He, of course, could not have known that during the ten minutes in which he lay unconscious on the huge pad a score of these curious, sympathetic strollers, partially or wholly dressed, had come out to gaze upon him, each delivering a characteristic opinion as to his purpose, but all of them roughly compassionate. Without exception, they looked upon him as one of the show-sick youths who, in those days, as now, succumb too readily to the lure of sawdust and spangles. More than one scoffing jest was uttered over his unconscious head.

Now they realized that he was not what they had thought him to be. A deeper tragedy than this seemed to be stamped in his wan face.

"You fainted ten minutes ago. Are you feeling better now? Give him some brandy, one of you. We will put you on your feet again in a few minutes, and then you may get on to the hotel. How wet you are! You must have come far. "

He watched her face all the time she was speaking. No sign of trust or confidence came into his own as the result of her kindliness. Instead, the wariness grew.

"Only across the mountain, " he said succinctly. A half smile, quizzical and almost grotesque by reason of the mud on his chin, came to his lips. "I've been out in the rain, ma'am, " he vouchsafed. "I should say you had, " said the contortionist. "You're soppin' wet. By gum, I'll bet the green runs in these tights of mine, too. " The wet body had drenched them thoroughly.

Whereupon the newcomer undertook to support himself, not without a word of thanks to the acrobat. Once more he surveyed the mystic circle of figures. He had never been so close to men and women in tights before. Somehow they were not so alluring as when viewed from the blue seats of the circus tent. The fluffy, abbreviated tarletan skirts of two women bareback riders who stood not more than two yards away seemed tawdry and flimsy at close range; the pink fleshings of the world's greatest somersault artist looked rumpled and fuzzy; the zouave costume of the lady rope-walker lost its satiny sheen through propinquity; the clown was dusty and greasy and stuffy. An illusion was being shattered in the flash of an eye.

"I must be moving along, " he said, in quick return to apprehension. "Thank you for looking out for me. It was very kind of—" He swayed as he tried to arise. The genial contortionist caught him.

"He's hungry! " cried one of the bareback queens. He made a heroic effort to pull himself together. The innate modesty of a gentleman reproved him even as things went hazy: he was conscious that he was staring at the surprisingly large kneecaps of the speaker. He was vaguely troubled because they were dirty.

A flask of brandy was pressed to his lips. He gasped, caught his breath, and, as the tears came to his eyes, smiled apologetically.

"It's pretty strong, " he choked out.

"Puts snap and ginger into you, " said the clown, standing back to watch the effect of his ministrations. "It strikes me you're not a common tramp. Wot were you doing 'angin' round this tent, son? Don't you know you might 'ave got clubbed to death by one of the canvasmen out there? They're never 'appy unless they're kickin' some poor rube over the guy-ropes. You wasn't trying to peep into the dressing-tent, was you? "

A hot flush mounted to the boy's forehead. He arose unsteadily.

"No, " he said quickly. "I was trying to find a dry spot. I was tired out. Let me go now, please. I'm all right. " He started toward a flap in the tent wall.

"Better not go that-a-way, " said the clown. "You'll go plump into the ring. Wait a minute. Are you 'ungry? "

"No, " said the boy, but they knew he was not speaking the truth. The girl in the long red cloak, she of the wonderful eyes, stood before him.

"Please wait, won't you? " she said, half timidly, half imperatively. "I will get something for you to eat. It's—it's right over there in my corner. The cook always brings my father's supper here after the show begins. He won't mind if I give it to you. He can get more. My father owns the show. "

"No, no, " he cried. "I can't take his supper. I am not hungry. "

But she smiled and flew away, disappearing behind the flap at his left: a fluttering red fairy she might have been. He never forgot that first radiant, enveloping smile.

"It is all right, my boy, " said the girl's mother, also smiling. "You *are* hungry. We know what it is to be hungry—sometimes. "

"That we do, " said the contortionist, rubbing his narrow abdomen and drawing a lugubrious mouth.

"You must be quite frozen in those wet clothes, " observed Mrs. Braddock pityingly.

"I can't stay here, ma'am, " he said abruptly. The hunted look came back into his eyes.

"He's no regular bum, " said the "strong man, " in the background, addressing the pink-limbed "lady juggler. "

"He's got a 'istory, that boy 'as, " said the lady addressed, deeply interested. "Makes me think o' that boy Dickens wrote about. What was his name? "

"How should I know? " demanded the strong man. "You Britishers are always workin' off riddles about something somebody wrote. "

"What is your name? " asked the gentle-voiced woman at the boy's side. "Where do you come from? "

He hesitated, still uncertain of his standing among these strange, apparently friendly people.

"I can't tell you my name, " he said in a low voice. "I hoped you wouldn't ask me. I have no home now—not since—Oh, a long time ago, it seems. More than a week, I reckon, ma'am. "

"You have been wandering about like this for a week? " she asked in surprise. He gulped.

"Yes, ma'am. Since the eleventh of May. " He wanted to tell her that he had been hunted from county to county for over a week, but something held his tongue. He felt that she would understand and sympathize, but he was not so sure of the others.

Perhaps she suspected what was going on in that troubled brain, for she laid her hand gently upon his arm and said: "Never mind, then. When you are stronger, you may go. I am sure you are a good boy. "

He thanked her with a look of mute gratitude. The girl with the long red cloak came tripping back with a tray. She placed it on his knees; then she whisked away the napkin which covered it. All he knew was that he smiled up into her eyes through his tears, and that the smell of warm food assailed his nostrils. As she straightened up, the neglected cloak slipped from her shoulders. She caught it on her arm, but did not attempt to replace it. He lowered his eyes, singularly abashed. A trim, clean figure in red tights stood before him, absolutely without fear or shame or in the least conscious of her attire.

He was in her world, that was all. In his, outside that canvas crucible and between performances, she would have died of mortification if, by chance, there had been one-tenth of the exposure. Here, she was as fully dressed and as modestly as she would be an hour later, clothed from head to foot in the conventional garments of her sex, rigidly observing the strictest laws of delicacy.

A trim, straight figure she was, just rounding into young womanhood; turning fifteen, in truth. Lithe and graceful, with the sinuous development of a perfectly healthy young girl who has gone through the expanding process without pausing at the awkward stage, due no doubt to her life and training. Firm, well-rounded hips; a small waist, full chest and perfect shoulders, straight, exquisitely modeled limbs and high, arched insteps: perfect in girlhood, with promise of the divine at the height of full womanhood.

The mother arose at once. She remembered that he was in their world.

"Come, " she said to her daughter. They withdrew to the women's half of the dressing-tent, leaving him to devour his feast alone. Slowly the others, taking their cue, edged away. When next the clown approached him, fresh from a merry whirl in the ring, the tray was on the mattress at his side, every particle of food gone. The boy's face was in his hands, his elbows on his knees.

"Well, you *was* 'ungry, " said the kindly voice. The boy looked up, his eyelids heavy.

"I reckon I was almost asleep, " he said. "I haven't slept much of late. "

Suddenly it dawned on him that the clown was staring intently at his face. With quick understanding he shrank back, but did not withdraw his gaze from the eyes of the other.

"By jingo! " muttered the motley one. "You—you are the one they're 'unting for—all over the state. The reward bills! I remember now! "

The lad had risen. A look of abject misery and dread leaped in his eyes.

"Let me go! " he said, almost in a whisper, fiercely intense. "I'll get out. I haven't done any harm to you. Don't keep me here a minute—"

"Then you *are* the Jenison boy! " in open-mouthed wonder. "Well, I'll be jiggered! Here! Don't bolt like that! "

"Let go of me! " cried the boy, striking at the hand that clutched his arm. "I won't let them catch me! Let me go! "

"Keep your shirt on, my son, " said the clown coolly. "Nobody's going to 'urt you 'ere. Just you remember that. I am not going to give you up—leastwise, not just yet. So you murdered your grandfather, did you? Well, I wouldn't 'ave took you to be that kind—"

"I didn't do it! I didn't do it! " There was piteous appeal in his wide eyes. "I swear I didn't. They're trying to put it on me to save some one else. Oh, please, don't keep me here. They—they are—they must be here by this time, looking for me. Oh, if you knew how I've tried to dodge them. They had bloodhounds last Saturday. Oh! " He covered his face with his hands and shuddered as with a mighty chill.

Grinaldi eyed him speculatively.

"You say they're 'ere now? So close as that? " he demanded in a low voice.

"I passed them on the mountain. I tried to make the railroad ahead of them. There was a bridge down back there. There were two of them, officers from the county seat. They won't have any mercy if they find me. They'll take me back and I'll be hung. I can't prove anything—I can't escape. " He had dropped helplessly to the edge of the mattress, and was staring hard at the sidewall beyond as if expecting his pursuers to burst in upon him at any moment.

"And you didn't do it? " the clown asked, something like awe in his voice.

"Before God, I did not. I—I loved my grandfather. I *couldn't* have done it. Why, he was the only father I had—the only mother. He was everything to me. It was—" He caught himself up quickly in his wild declaration. "I know the man who did it. I heard them talking it over before it happened, but I didn't know what they were talking about. " His eyes grew almost glassy with the horror that surged up from behind them.

"Then why don't you tell your story? " demanded the clown. "Let the other chap clear 'imself. "

"They've got the evidence against me. Oh, you don't know! You can't know how it looked to the world. There's a man who says he saw me with a gun at my grandfather's window. He did see me there and I had a gun, but not to kill poor old granddaddy. No, no! I heard some one walking on the gallery—a thief, I thought. I crawled out of my window with my shotgun. I—but I oughtn't to tell you this. You must let me go. I'll never tell on you, I swear—"

"Wait a minute, " interrupted the clown, laying his arm over the boy's shoulder. "We'll talk it over with Mrs. Braddock. She can tell by lookin' in your eyes whether you're good or bad. As far as I'm concerned, I don't believe you did it. Yes, yes, that's all right! Don't hug me, sonny. Here she is. She's the wife of the man wot owns the show. "

Mrs. Braddock crossed over to them, smiling. It was not until she opened her lips to speak of the compliment his appetite had paid to the cook tent that she perceived the look in his eyes. Then she glanced at the serious face of the clown.

"This 'ere chap, ma'am, " said Grinaldi, in low, level tones, "is David Jenison, the boy wanted for that murder near Richmond last week. You've seen the reward bills. His grandfather, you remember —"

She drew back; her eyes dilated, her lips stiff. "You are the Jenison boy? " she said slowly, even unbelievingly. "The one who killed his grandfa—" "But I didn't do it! " he almost wailed. "You—*you* must believe me, ma'am. I didn't do it! " He stood before her, looking straight into her eyes.

"No, Mrs. Braddock, " said Grinaldi, "he didn't do it. " "How do you know, Grinaldi? How can you—" "Because he says another person did it, " said Grinaldi calmly.

The woman turned to the boy once more. She seemed to be searching his soul with her intense gaze.

"No, " she murmured, after a moment, breathing deeply, "I am sure you did *not* commit murder. You poor, poor boy! "

He would have dropped to his knees before her, had not the clown checked him by means of a warning hiss.

"Brace up! " he said sharply. Then to Mrs. Bradock: "We've got to find a way to 'ide 'im. The officers are right on his 'eels. "

She hesitated for a moment. Swift glances passed between her and the clown.

"You must keep very quiet and do what we tell you to do, " she said to the boy, who nodded his head eagerly. "You will be safe here. A circus is the safest harbor in all the world for the thief and the lawbreaker. Why should it not be so for one who is innocent? "

"Let me tell you all about it, madam, " began David Jenison, the hunted. She stopped him.

"Not now. There is no time for that. We will take you on faith and we will help you. My boy, I knew in the beginning that you were of gentle birth—I saw it in your face, in the way you held yourself. But that you should be one of the Jenisons of Virginia—why, Grinaldi, the Jenisons are the bluest—But, there, we'll talk of that another time, too. Sam! " She called to a ring attendant who stood near the entrance. The burly, rough-looking young man came up at once, respectful to a degree.

"Go out in front and tell Mr. Braddock to hurry back here as soon as he is through with the tickets! " The man slid out between the flapping walls. "Now, Grinaldi, you must make it your business to tell every one who this boy is, and what must be done for him. Don't be alarmed, David Jenison, " she said with a smile. He had opened his lips to protest. "There isn't a soul in all this company, from feed-boy to proprietor, who will betray you to the officers of the law. We stand together—the innocent and the guilty. If you are vouched for by Joey Grinaldi and—me, or by any other in our little universe, that is the end of it. Even the basest ruffian in the canvas gang, even the vilest of the hostlers, will stand by you through thick and thin. And there are real murderers among them, too. You must have faith in us. "

"I have faith in YOU" he said simply. Then, true Virginian that he was, this tired, harassed boy bent low and lifted her hand to his gallant lips. "I will give my life up for you any day, madam. It is yours. "

"Spoken like a gentleman, " said the clown, his eyes twinkling.

A couple of horses came clattering into the tent from the ring. At the entrance they were seized by waiting attendants; one of the mysteries that had always puzzled the boy was solved. He had wondered where the plunging steeds raced to after their whirlwind exit from the ring. A moment later, a swarm of men came rushing in with hoops, balloons and banners and hurdle-poles, followed by the "Greatest Living Bareback Rider of the Globe, the One and Only Mellburg. " After him came a tired ringmaster, lanky and not half so proud as he looked to be in his spike-tailed coat.

Some one in the big tent was making an announcement in stentorian tones.

"It's time for me to go in, " said the clown. "My song comes now. Just you go along with Casey 'ere, into the dressing-room. He'll get you something dry to wear out of my box. Don't forget one thing: we're all as thick as thieves 'ere, whether we're honest men or not. You'll find every man, woman and child wot appears in the ring to be absolutely square and honest. They've got to be. The bad men are not the performers. You'd find that out if you was with 'em a bit. I don't mind tellin' of it to you, as a consolation, that there is two real murderers among the canvasmen and a dozen or more pussons which are wanted for desp'rit things. Nobody peaches on 'em, mind you, and that's the way it goes. We've just *got* to stand together. Hi! Hi! "

He was off with a rush. A few minutes later he was heard singing his lay in the ring, the then popular and familiar ditty, "Whoa, Emma! " with a crude but vociferous chorus of male voices to "join in the refrain. " Casey, without further instructions, and asking no questions, led the youth into the men's section. Here all was confusion. A dozen men were stripping themselves of one set of tights to don another, for in those days the ordinary acrobat did many turns in the process of earning his daily bread.

By the time Grinaldi returned, young Jenison was completely arrayed in an extra costume of the clown's, a creation in red and white stripes, much too baggy in all directions, but dry as toast. The owner of the costume put his hands to his sides and roared with laughter.

"Casey, you serpent, " he gasped, "I didn't mean that kind of a suit. I meant my Sunday togs—the ones I go to church in, when I goes. Which I doesn't. 'Ere, boys, step right up and listen to an announcement. " The crowd gave attention. "This 'ere chap is wanted. There's a big reward for 'im. You've all seen the posters. He's the Jenison boy. Well, he ain't guilty. Get the notion? We Ve got to 'elp 'im out of the country. Mum's the word, lads. Say! " He stood back to inspect his charge. "If you're going to wear them togs, you've got to 'ave your face done over to match. "

Whereupon he began to apply grease and bismuth to the countenance of the amazed young patrician. The others looked on and laughed good- naturedly. To his surprise, no one seemed to mind the fact that he was a fugitive and an alleged slayer. They had stared at him curiously for a moment; two or three of them exchanged whispers, that was all.

In a twinkling he was transformed into a real scaramouch. A conical hat adorned the knit skullpiece that covered his black hair.

"Don't peep in the lookin'-glass, " said Signor Anaconda, now in the pale blue tights of a "ground and lofty" tumbler. "You'll keel over again, plumb dead. "

The flap at the entrance was jerked aside and a tall, black-mustached man peered in upon the group.

"Where's the kid? " he demanded sharply. "My wife said he was with you, Joey. Say, I don't like this business. They're out in front now, looking for him. Two of 'em. Have you let him get away? "

David, peering from behind the real clown, experienced an instantaneous feeling of aversion for Braddock, the proprietor. Even as he quailed beneath the new peril that asserted itself in no vague manner, he found himself wondering how this man could have come to be the husband of his lovely benefactress.

"He's here, Tom, " announced Grinaldi, shoving the boy forward.

"What's he doing in that costume? " demanded the owner, dropping the flap and staring hard at the boy.

"His clothes were wet. Besides, if they come botherin' around back 'ere, Tom, they won't be so likely to reckernise him in these —"

"Say, do you suppose I'm going to get into a muss with these people by hiding a murderer? " snapped Braddock. "Bring him out here. Come along, bub. "

"You're getting blamed virtuous all of a sudden, Braddock, " said the clown angrily. "'Ow about these dogs you are protectin' all the time? What's more, this 'ere kid's innocent. "

"There's five hundred dollars reward for this fellow, " said Braddock, jamming his hands into his coat pockets. "That doesn't sound like he's innocent, does it? Besides, the officers are plumb certain he's hanging around this show some place. I'm not going to be pestered with constables and detectives from here to Indiana, let me tell you that. It's bad business, monkeying with stray boys, ever since the Charley Ross kidnapping job last year. So you lummixes have decided to protect him, have you? Why, the whole pack of you ought to be in jail for even thinkin' of it. Come out here, boy! "

Without a word, the boy shook himself free of Grinaldi's protecting grasp, and stepped forward.

"I'm not willing to see these men get into trouble, " he said steadily, addressing the boss. "Give me time to change my clothes again, and then you can call in the officers. "

"Don't be a fool, " exclaimed the clown. A murmur of protest arose from the others.

"Thomas! " A woman's voice was calling from the other side of the low canvas partition.

"That's my wife, " growled Braddock. "I suppose she'll be beggin' for you, too. What do you want? " The question was roared through the canvas.

"Come here, please. I must speak with you. "

"Change your clothes, boy, " he said, after a moment of indecision. "See that he don't get away, you fellows. If he gives you the slip, I'll have blood, and don't you forget it. "

The man had been drinking. His eyes were bloodshot and unsteady. His face was bloated from the effects of long and continued use of alcohol. Once on a time he had been a dashing, boldly handsome fellow; there could be no doubt of that; the sort of youth that any romantic girl might have fallen in love with. He was tall and straight and powerful, despite the evidences of dissipation that his face presented. A wonderfully vital constitution had protected his body from the ravages of self-indulgence; the constitution of a great, splendid human animal, in whom not the faintest sign of a once attractive personality remained. There was no refinement there, no mark of good breeding; all of the mirage-like glamour that may have bewildered and deceived *her*, long years ago, was gone. What she had evidently mistaken for the nobility of true manhood, in her innocence and folly, was no more than the arrogance of splendid health. This man had been beautiful in his day, and frankly pleasing. That was long before the thing that was in his blood, and in the blood of his fathers, perhaps, had claimed dominion: the mysterious thing which inevitably registers the curse of the base-born, so that no man may be deceived. Blood always tells, but usually it tells too late.

But of the Braddocks and their hateful history, more anon. Let us look at this man as he now is, just as we have looked, perhaps too casually, at the woman who called him husband.

A heavy black mustache, lightly touched with gray, shaded a coarse, rather sinister mouth, from the corner of which protruded an unlighted but thoroughly-chewed cigar. His hair and eyebrows were thick and black. Thin red lines formed a network in his cheeks, telling of the habits that had put them there; on his forehead there was a perpetual scowl, a line slashed between the eyes as if laid there by a knife. The features were not irregular, but they were of the strength that denotes cultivated weaknesses. His chin was square and strong, heavily stubbled with a two days' growth of beard. Eyes that were black and sullen, stood well out in their sockets; the lids were red and thick, and there were narrow pouches below them; the whites were bloodshot and indefinite. He was flashily dressed in the mode of the day, typical of his calling. A silk hat tilted rakishly over his brow. His waistcoat was a loud brocade, his necktie a single black band, knotted once. There was a great paste diamond in his soiled shirt-front. A long checked coat, with tails and sidepockets, trousers of the same material, completed his ordinary makeup. Tonight, on account of the rain, he wore high gum boots outside of the trouser-legs.

You could hardly have mistaken his calling in those days, unless you might have suspected him of being a gambler. In which you would not have been wrong.

The line between his eyes seemed to deepen as he turned from the group to join his wife in the "green room" of the tent. As the flap dropped behind him, Grinaldi turned to the boy, who had started to unlace the striped overshirt.

"Wait a minute, " he said quickly. "Mebbe we can fix it with 'im. She'll put in a plea for you and so will Little Starbright, —that's what 'is daughter is called on the bills—if she gets a chance. Stay right 'ere, youngster. I've got to go in for my girl's act now. I wish you could see my girl. She's the queen of the air, and don't you forget it. Ain't she, boys? "

There was a combined—apparently customary—chorus of approval.

Outside, Braddock was glowering upon his wife, who faced him resolutely. There never had been a time when she was afraid of this man; even though he had mistreated her shamefully, he had never found the courage to exercise his physical supremacy. As so often is the case—almost invariably, it may be affirmed—with men of his type and origin, Braddock recognized and respected the qualities that put her so far above him. Not that he admitted them, even to himself: that would have been fatal to his own sense of justice. He merely felt them; he could not evade the conditions for the reason that he was powerless to analyze the force which produced them. He only knew that somehow he merited the scorn in which she held him. There were times when he hated her for the very beauty of her character. Then he cursed her in bleak, despairing rage, more against himself than against her; but never without afterward cringing in morbid contemplation of the shudder it brought to her sensitive face.

If any one had been so bold as to accuse him of not loving her, he would have been crushed to earth by the brute that was in him. On the other hand, if he were timorously charged with loving her, it would have been like him to call the venturesome one a liar—and mean it, too, in his heart.

"But five hundred is five hundred, " he was repeating doggedly in opposition to her argument in behalf of the boy. "You don't know whether he's guilty or not, Mary. So what's the use of all this gabble? It makes me sick. Business is bad. We need every dollar we can scrape up. I won't be a party to—"

"You harbor pickpockets and thieves and—yes, murderers, I'm told, Tom. It is a shameful fact that more sneak thieves follow this show and share with its owner than any other concern in the business. Oh, I know all about it! Don't try to deny it. They pay a regular tribute to you for privileges and protection. Artful Dick Cronk gave you half of the hundred he filched from the old man at Charlottesville last week. I—"

"Here, here! " he said in an angry whisper. "Don't talk so damned loud. Next thing you'll be telling that sort of stuff to the girl. That'd be a nice thing for her to think, wouldn't it? Say, don't you ever let me hear of you breathin' a word of that kind to her. I'd—I'd beat your brains out. Understand? "

"Oh, I'm not likely to tell her what kind of a man her father is, " said his wife bitterly. "Take care, Tom, that she doesn't find it out for herself. Be quiet! She is coming. "

The girl, cleansed of her paint and powder, her lithe body clad in a prim, navy blue frock, the skirt of which came below the tops of her high-laced boots, approached hastily from the women's section. She was tying the strings of her quaint poke-bonnet under her chin, and her eyes were gleaming with excitement.

"Where is that boy? " she asked, looking about in some anxiety. "Father, you should see him. He is so different from the boys who follow—"

"We were just talking about him, " interrupted her father shortly. "He's wanted by the police, so you see he ain't so different from the rest after all. He's a—"

"Don't, Tom, " cried his wife.

"—a murderer, " completed Braddock, rolling his cigar from one side of his mouth to the other.

The girl stared at him for a moment, dumbly, uncomprehendingly. Her lips parted and her eyes grew very wide.

"Oh, father, " she cried, in low, hushed tones. Then she turned to her mother, almost imploringly. "Is—is it true, mother? "

"Well, see here, " broke in Braddock angrily. "Don't you believe me? Haven't I said so? "

"He is the Jenison boy we were talking about last night, dearie, " said Mrs. Braddock. "I don't believe he committed that horrid crime. I can't believe it. "

"I am sure he didn't—I am sure he didn't, " cried the girl impulsively. "He is a gentleman, father. He couldn't—"

Braddock took instant offense. He hated to hear any one spoken of as a gentleman.

"What's that got to do with it? " he demanded. "Gentleman, eh? You two seem to think that these pretty gentlemen can't do anything wrong. Why, they're rottener than nine-tenths of the blokes that follow this show—every mother's son of 'em. I'm sick of having this gentleman business thrown up to me. That's all you two talk about. I suppose you think you're better than the company you live with. Let me tell you this, you're show people and nothin' more. I don't give a damn who your people are; you're my wife and my daughter, and that's all there is to it. I won't stand this sort of—"

"Tom, you *must* keep still, " said his wife firmly. He was intoxicated; she knew better than to argue with him, or to agree with him. "All this has nothing to do with the boy. We must give him a chance, the same as —you understand? "

He glared at her warningly.

"I don't protect thieves and murderers, " he said quickly.

Then he whirled about and snatched aside the flap, calling to the group of acrobats.

"Come out here, you! Step lively. I want to ask a few questions. Where the dev—Say, haven't you got out of that suit yet? Why, you little scuttle, I'll rip it off your back if you're not out of it in two minutes. Hold on! Come out here first. "

As Jenison walked past him the proprietor gave him a violent cuff on the side of the head. The boy, weak and faint, reeled away and would have fallen but for the tent pole which he managed to clutch. His face was convulsed by sudden rage. Even while his head swam, he pulled himself together for a leap at the man who had struck the wanton, unexpected blow.

Braddock was huge enough and strong enough to crush the infuriated lad, but drink had made him a coward at heart. He stooped over and picked up an iron-ringed stake from the ground.

With a little cry of terror his daughter, recovering from her sudden stupefaction, sprang forward and frantically clutched the man's arm. Her mother was no less active in putting herself in front of the boy, staying him with resolute hands. The performers who had followed David from the room leaped in with clenched fists, glaring hatefully at their employer. Others, in remote parts of the enclosure, hurried up, aroused from drowsy meditation by the sharp excitement.

"Don't, father! " cried the girl in the agony of dread.

"Damn him, he may have a gun, " exclaimed Braddock. "He's used one before. "

"Why did you strike me? " cried David hoarsely, his lips twitching, his eyes glowing like coals.

"Aw, none o' that, now, none o' that, " snarled Braddock, taking a step forward.

"Why did you strike me? " repeated the boy dully.

"Calm yourself, my boy, " Mrs. Braddock kept repeating insistently, without raising her voice, always low, tense, impelling.

The tears sprang to his eyes—tears of rage and helplessness. With a sob he turned away and leaned his head against the pole.

"Poor boy, " she whispered.

"Don't you call me a brute, Casey, " roared Braddock, turning upon the contortionist in a fury. Casey had not uttered a word, but Braddock instinctively anticipated the charge. The contortionist was afraid of him. He drew back with a scared look in his eyes.

Mrs. Braddock was speaking quietly, compassionately to the suffering boy. "We must be careful, " she said, "not to oppose him too strongly. Those men are out in front. He will turn you over to them if you resort to violence. Calm yourself, do. There is still the chance that he may change his mind. He is not really heartless. It is only his way. "

"Why did he strike me? " again fell from the lips of the fugitive.

At this moment Grinaldi came hurrying in from the ring. He took in the situation at a glance. Behind him, peering over his shoulder, was a black-haired young woman in pink tights and spangled trunks.

David was afterward to know this handsome, black-haired girl as Ruby Noakes, the daughter of Grinaldi, otherwise Joey Noakes, and known to the gaping world as Mademoiselle Roxane, the Flying Queen of the Air.

CHAPTER III

DAVID ENTERS THE SAWDUST RING

Braddock saw at once that the old clown was against him. With an ugly imprecation he directed one of the attendants to go to the main entrance with instructions to bring Mr. Blake and his friend back to the dressing-tent.

"We'll see who's running this show, " he declared, taking a fresh grip on the stake, and rolling the dangling cigar over and over between his teeth.

"Hold on, Camp, " said Grinaldi, checking the attendant with a gesture. "See 'ere, Tom, " he went on earnestly, "wot's the reason you won't give this one an even chance with the others? "

Stand aside, Christie, " Braddock said to his trembling daughter. "Don't get in the way. Oh, I'm not going to smash the cub, so don't worry. Here! Come away from him, I say. Both of you. I won't stand for any petting of a rascal like him. Well, I'll tell you, Joey Noakes, " he went on, turning to the clown, "I don't mind saying I need the money. This kid's going to be caught by somebody before long, and the man that does it gets five hundred. It might as well be me. Business is business, and just now business is bad. You people all know what this infernal weather has done for us. We haven't had a paying day since we opened, and here it is the middle of May — nearly six weeks, that's what it is. There's a lousy three hundred dollars in the big top to-night and half as much this afternoon. I tell you if these rains keep up I'll have to close. It takes more than five hundred dollars a day to run this show. I owe back salaries — all of you have got something coming to you. Five hundred dollars velvet, that's what this boy means to me — not for myself, mind you, but for the treasury. That's why I'm going to turn him over, if you want to know. "

"But he ain't guilty, " said Grinaldi sharply.

"How do you know? " snarled Braddock. "Go and do what I told you, " to the wavering attendant. Mrs. Braddock and Christine were standing beside the dejected boy, the former looking steadily at the face of her husband, whose bloodshot eyes would not meet her gaze.

Christine's eyes were wide with the bewildered stare of an intelligence that has suddenly been aroused to new aspects: she was having a glimpse of a side to her father's character that had never been revealed to her before.

She put forth a hand and drew Ruby Noakes close beside her, pressing her hand tightly in actual alarm. The Noakes girl's arm went around the slender figure, but she continued to stare curiously at the face of the stranger in their midst. She was half a head taller than Christine, and at least three years her senior.

"We ought to have a new clown to help out dad, Mr. Braddock, " ventured Miss Noakes coolly.

Braddock stared at her. He was not in the habit of accepting feminine advice.

"What's that? " he barked.

"Keep still, Ruby, " cautioned her father nervously. Ruby's lips parted quickly, and then, thinking better of it, she closed them.

David's face took on a queer, uncertain expression while Braddock was advancing his dire need of money as an excuse for turning him over. The proprietor resumed his bitter harangue against the weather, prophesying bankruptcy and sheriff's sales. The boy's face began to clear. An eager, excited gleam came into his eyes. He looked about him as if searching for some sign of corroboration in the faces of the performers. A certain evidence of dejection had crept into more than one countenance. It began to dawn on him that the man was more or less sincere in his argument; even the words of others, in conflict with his purpose, served to convince him that the money was needed, very seriously needed.

"If he's innocent, he can prove it, " argued Braddock stubbornly. "The county pays the five hundred. It's nothing out of his pocket. Why the devil shouldn't I get it? "

David had opened his lips two or three times to utter the words that surged up from his anxious, despairing heart. A sense of guilt and shame had checked them on each occasion. Whatever it was that he felt impelled to say, his honest pride rebelled against the impulse.

Now he lifted his head resolutely, and addressed the proprietor, whose stand appeared to be immovable.

"I will pay you the five hundred dollars, " said David clearly.

Every eye was turned upon him, every tongue was stilled. The tumblers who had started for the ring stopped in their tracks to gaze in open- mouthed wonder at the straight, grotesque figure that faced Braddock.

The proprietor blinked unbelievingly. Then he gave vent to a short, derisive laugh.

"You will, will you? "

David felt a hot wave of blood rush to his head. His offer had met with the rebuke it deserved!

"I thought that if it was only the money, I could let you have it. I didn't mean to try to buy you off, " he explained hastily.

"Are you in earnest? " demanded Braddock, depositing the stake on the ground, a curious glitter swimming across his eyes.

"About the money? "

"Certainly. Where are you going to get it? "

"I've got it with me, " said David, feeling at his side. A look of dismay spread over his face. It was quickly dispelled by the recollection that his own clothes were lying in the men's dressing-room. "It's in my vest. "

No one thought to oppose him as he passed hastily under the flap. He was back in a moment, carrying his rain-soaked waistcoat. With nervous fingers he drew a heavy pin from the mouth of the inside pocket, and extracted a long leather purse therefrom. It was tied up with a heavy piece of string.

"Do you mean to tell me that you've got five hundred dollars in there? " demanded Braddock incredulously.

David felt without seeing the look that went through the crowd. He knew, by some strange mental process, that they were condemning him, that they were drawing away from him. He was bewildered. Then suddenly he understood. It came like a blow. Something rushed up into his throat and choked him.

They took this money to be the profits of murder! The spoils of a dreadful sin!

Speechless, he turned to Mrs. Braddock. There was no mistaking the look of pain and distress in her dark eyes. There were doubt and wonder there, too. It seemed to him that she shrank back a step; although, as a matter of fact, she remained as motionless as a statue. Christine was glowing upon him in grateful amazement, unutterable relief in her gaze. To her, it meant only that he was rich and could save himself. It did not occur to her that he had come by the riches dishonestly, nor was she at once conscious of a feeling that her father would do wrong to accept the tribute. It was not until later that she felt the shock of revulsion.

"It is my money! " cried David, speaking to Mrs. Braddock. "Every cent of it! I—I know what you are thinking. You think I stole it. " His eyes were flashing and his chin was held high now. "I'll kill any one who says I steal. I'd sooner commit murder a thousand times than to steal. "

"How did you—come by all that money? " asked Mrs. Braddock, more than half convinced by his fervor.

"That's what I'd like to know, " added her husband. "Here! Lemme take that pocket-book. "

David jerked his hand loose and abruptly thrust the purse into the hand of the astonished Mrs. Braddock.

"Look at it, " he cried passionately. "Open the purse. It's still in the sealed envelope, just as my father left it when he went off to the war the second time—after he was wounded. He left it with my mother for me. No one has ever opened the package. It was in my mother's trunk until she died. She wouldn't put it in a bank. My uncle Frank never knew that she had it; he doesn't know that I have it now. But it is mine. My father gave it to me when I was six years old. See what it says on the envelope. It's his own writing. 'For my son David. To be used in the acquiring of an education if I should fall in this dear, beloved cause, which now seems lost. God defend us all! ' See! 'Arthur Brodalbin Jenison. ' My father's signature. Here is the seal of his ring. It is my money. "

Even Thomas Braddock was swayed, convinced by the eloquence of that fierce appeal. He stared at the boy, his lips apart, his cigar hanging limply from one corner of his mouth.

"By thunder! " he murmured, frankly surprised in himself. "I believe the tale, hang me if I don't! "

But David was waiting only for the verdict of the woman. Mrs. Braddock had not glanced at the envelope that she now clutched in her tense fingers; her eyes were only for the eager, chalk-colored face of the boy. Tears welled up in her warm eyes as he paused for breath.

"I believe you, too—yes, yes, my boy, we all believe you, " she cried, putting out her hand to him. He snatched it up and kissed it.

At that instant the ringmaster, white with rage, dashed in from the big tent.

"Say, what's the matter with you loafers? "

The crowd of tumblers jumped out of the trance as if shot.

"The show's been held up for ten minutes! Get in there all of you! " Here followed a violent explosion of appropriate profanity. "The audience is gettin' wild. They'll be wantin' their money back unless the performance goes on purty blamed — "

Braddock reached the man's side in three steps. He delivered a resounding slap on the ringmaster's cheek, almost knocking him down. The tall hat went spinning away on the ground. Tears of pain and terror flew to the fellow's eyes. He began to blubber.

"Don't you swear in the presence of my wife and daughter, —you! " snarled Braddock, his own blasphemy ten times as venomous as the other's.

"I—I beg your pardon, Mrs. Braddock, " stammered the ringmaster in great haste. If the gaping, respectful hundreds could see the despot of the ring now!

Braddock's daughter uttered a low moan of horror and amazement. Her heart swelled with pity for the poor wretch who dared not to defend himself. Ruby Noakes felt the quiver that ran through the girl's body. She promptly led her away from the spot.

"Come with me while I change, " she said quickly.

Together they passed into the women's dressing-room. Christine's look of mute surprise and shame rested on David's face as the flap dropped behind her.

A minute later, the humiliated ringmaster, Briggs by name, was cracking his whip in the middle of the ring, mighty lord of all he surveyed, although, to his chagrin, there was no clown present to receive the attention. In those good old days the circus carried but one clown. He was the most overworked man in the ring, but he had the satisfaction of knowing that he was the solitary idol of thousands.

Grinaldi did not accompany the tumblers to the ring. The lone elephant that graced the show and the horses had been led out for the "lofty somersault men" to vault over after the run down the "spring board"; that part of the dressing-tent in which Braddock stood was now clear of humanity, except for his wife, the clown and David Jenison.

"Well, he knows I don't permit swearing in front of my daughter, " said Braddock, resenting the unspoken scorn in his wife's face. "Let's see that envelope, " he added roughly.

She held the coveted package behind her back, shaking her head resolutely.

"How do I know there's five hundred in it? " he demanded.

"There's more than that, " said David nervously.

"How do you know? It's never been opened. "

Mrs. Braddock glanced at the writing on the face of the staunch, yellow envelope. She started violently. In plain figures, in one corner, she saw: "$3,000. " She realized, with a flash of shame, that it would be fatal to the boy's interests if her husband should come to know of the actual value of the package. She opened her lips to utter a word of caution to David, but he was too eager and too quick for her.

"There's three thousand dollars in it, " he said.

Braddock started. For the first time he removed the chewed cigar from his lips, all the while fixedly regarding the youth with narrowing eyes. He was thinking fast and hard. Three thousand dollars!

"You are not to break this seal, David Jenison, " said Mrs. Braddock firmly, her face very white. "Take it and go. It is your money, not ours. "

"Hold on there, " objected her husband. His befuddled brain was solving a certain problem to his own eminent satisfaction. "These officers have got to be convinced that you are not with this show. I can't afford to lie to 'em. There's only one way out of it. I can hire you under another name and you can travel with us till we get out of this part of the country. Five hundred is the reward. If I get it from you, most of it can be paid back in wages. If I turn you over to them and take their coin, I'd be doing the best thing for myself, but I'm willing to run the risk of—"

"Thomas Braddock, you are *not* to take this boy's money, " cried his wife. "It would be infamous! "

"Now, you keep out of this, " he growled, fearful for his plans. "It's one or the other, Mary. Either he antes up or they do. "

"I will not allow it! "

David broke in, with a rare show of dignity. "I said I would pay it, Mrs. Braddock. I can't break my word. If Mr. Braddock will send them away, I will pay the amount they offer. "

"Give him the envelope, Mary, " commanded Braddock.

She looked about her as if seeking means of escape with the precious package. Then, with a deep sigh, and a look of unutterable scorn for the man, she handed the envelope to David.

He broke the seal.

"Maybe it's Confederate money, " said Braddock, a sudden chill in his heart. But it was not Confederate money. There was exposed to view a neat package of United States treasury notes of large denomination, brand-new and uncrumpled, just as they had come from the treasury department.

Without hesitation, young Jenison counted off five hundred dollars. Mrs. Braddock closed her eyes in pain as he laid the notes in her husband's hand. Grinaldi turned away, suppressing the bitter imprecation that rose to his lips.

"I'll tell those scoundrels that you haven't been near the show. " He did not count the money. He had counted it with greedy eyes as David told off the bills in his nervous, clumsy fingers. "Now, you lay low. Stick close to me. Don't let anybody see much of you till we're over in Ohio. I'll guarantee to get you off safe. Don't you worry. Just lay low. I'll find work for you to do. We're headed for Indiana and Illinois. They'll never get you out there. By thunder! I've got an idea, Joey, that girl of yours is right. You *do* need a bit of help. We'll make a clown of him. We'll have two clowns. How is that, Mary? "

She did not reply. He looked away hastily.

"I couldn't be a clown, " began David in consternation.

"Sure you can, " interrupted the boss. "It's as easy as fallin' off a log. Joey can tell you all the tricks. He's the best in the world, Joey Grinaldi is. That's what I've got him for. We've got the best show in the world, too. Barnum ain't in the same class with us. Forepaugh and Van Amberg? They are second rate aggre—But, say, I'd better go out and steer those fellows away. " He started off, but stopped suddenly as if struck by a serious doubt.

"Perhaps you'd better let me take the rest of that money and put it in the safe in the ticket-wagon, " he said encouragingly. "It's likely to be nipped by some of these crooks that follow the show. 'T ain't safe with you, let me tell you that. "

"No! " cried his wife, her voice shrill with decision.

Braddock did not insist. He was too wise for that.

"Well, if it's stolen, don't blame me, " he said. "Remember, I told you so. I don't give a damn personally. It's your money, kid. "

"I reckon I'll keep it, " said David, suddenly acute. He began wrapping the string around the broken package, which he had kept sacredly inviolate for so long. "I'll stay with the show and do anything I can, if you'll only help me to get away. I—I don't want to be taken back there. Some day, I expect to go back, but not right now. I'm not afraid. But I can't go back until I've found the man that *knows*. "

"There *is* a man who—knows? " murmured Mrs. Braddock.

"Yes. I must find him. He—he doesn't want to be found. That's why it is going to be so hard. But I will find him! " His eyes were flashing, his teeth were set.

"So much the better, " said Braddock. "You can throw 'em off the track for awhile, then take your money and go to New York. You'll find him there, all right. They all go there. "

"He is a nigger, " said David.

"Umph! " grunted Braddock. "That's bad. You mustn't expect any jury in Virginia to believe a nigger in these days. "

"Oh, yes, they will. They'll have to, " declared David firmly.

"Say, " said the proprietor, his voice sinking to tones of caution. He addressed the three of them. "Better keep this quiet about the five hundred. It won't help any of us if it gets out that you've been bribing me, boy. I'll just say that I refused to take the wad. That will go, too. Don't let *anybody* know. Understand, Mary? " He looked at her with lowering eyes.

"I will not tell Christine, Tom, " she said evenly, meeting the look with a gaze so steady that he bristled for a moment, but gave way before it. He felt the scorn and laughed shortly in his attempt to convince himself, at least, that he did not deserve it.

"And just to show you that I'm honest in this business, " he went on hurriedly, "I'm going to begin by paying you the fifty I still owe on your salary, Joey. That's the kind of a man I am. I do what I say I'll do. Here's your fifty, Joey. "

"Not that kind of money for me, thank you, " said Grinaldi, with a scowl that brought his painted eyebrows together. He turned on his heel and hurried into the dressing-room, unable to restrain the words that would have cut the heart of the man's wife to shreds.

An attendant came in from the circus tent just as Christine Braddock emerged from the dressing-room alone. David was stuffing the purse inside the loose shirt that he wore. The girl hurried to her mother's side.

"Are they going to—to take him? " she whispered fearfully.

David saw the sweet, clean lips tremble. Her eyes were wide and dry with trouble. Somehow his heart swelled with a strange new emotion: he could not have ascribed it to joy, or to self-pity, or to gratitude. It was something new and pleasant and warm; a glow, a light, an uplifting. This sweet, wonderfully pretty girl was his friend! She believed in him.

"No, dear, " replied Mrs. Braddock, lowering her eyes in sudden humiliation.

The attendant was speaking. "Mr. Braddock, that feller out at the door has got tired waitin'. He says he's comin' back yere to see you. What'll I say to 'im? He's got a warrant an' he's got some of the town marshal's men with 'im now. "

"I'll go out and see him right away. The boy ain't with this show. "

With a slow, meaning look at his wife, he turned to follow the man. Over his shoulder he called to David:

"Go in there with Joey. He'll tell you where to hide if you have to. Be quick about it. "

He was gone. The tumblers began to pour in from the main tent.

Christine clutched her mother's arm in the agony of desperation.

41

"Did—did he take the money from—*him*? " she demanded tremulously.

Mrs. Braddock looked at David, an abject appeal in her eyes. He smiled blandly and lied nobly, like a true Virginia gentleman.

"No, Miss Braddock. Instead of that, he has hired me to go with the show. "

"Oh, I am so glad, " she cried. "I knew he would not take your money. "

David swallowed hard; and then, fearing to speak again or to meet her radiant eyes, he hastened after Grinaldi.

A moment later he was in the center of an excited, whispering group of performers, in various conditions of attire, but singularly alike in their state of mind. They were softly but impressively consigning Thomas Braddock to the most remote corner in purgatory. They plied David with questions. He reported the impatience of the officers, and Braddock's decision to protect him for the time being.

"I saw them chaps out there, standin' by the menagerie doors, " said the contortionist. "Spotted 'em right away, I did. "

A bareback rider looked in. His horse already had started for the ring.

"Lay low! " he whispered. "One of the boys says they won't be put off by Brad. They're going to search the tent with the town marshal. "

Grinaldi, who had been deep in thought, suddenly slapped his knee and uttered a cackle of satisfaction.

"I've got it! We'll pull the wool over their eyes, by Jinks! Follow me, boy, and do just wot I tells you. I'm—I'm going to take you into the ring with me. By Jupiter, they won't think of looking for you there. "

Attended by a chorus of approval, he shoved the stupefied David out before him and hustled him across the space that lay between them and the main top, all the while whispering eager instructions in his ear.

"You just follow behind me, keeping step all the time—about three steps behind me. Don't look to right or left. Keep your eyes on the middle of my back. Nobody knows you, so don't go into a funk, my lad. It's life or death for you, mebby. I'll get a word to Briggs, the ringmaster. He'll help you out, too. Just follow me around the ring, three steps behind. Stop when I stop, walk when I do. Look silly, that's all. I'll think of something else to tell you to do after we're out there. And *we'll stay out there till the show's over.* "

Trembling in every joint, David paused at the entrance. Mrs. Braddock came running up from behind.

"I've just heard, " she whispered. "Do as Joey tells you. Don't be afraid. "

"I'll try, " chattered David, pathetic figure of Momus.

"Wait, " she whispered, as much to Joey Grinaldi as to the novice. "David, will you trust me to take care of your money until to-morrow? "

Without a word he slipped his hand into his shirt front and produced the flat purse. He handed it to her.

"Good! " exclaimed Joey Grinaldi.

The next instant David Jenison, aristocrat, was trudging dizzily toward the sawdust ring, his heart beating like mad, his knees trembling.

Thomas Braddock, detaining the officers on the opposite side of the ring, saw the strange figure and for a moment was near to losing his composure. Then he grasped the situation and exulted. He boldly escorted Blake and the town authorities to the dressing-tent, where he assisted in the search and the questioning.

Before the expiration of half an hour's time every man, woman and child connected with Van Slye's Great and Only Mammoth Shows knew that David Jenison, the murderer, was among them and that he was to be protected. The word went slyly, by whisper, from car to ear, down to the lowliest canvasman. It spread to the throng of crooks, pickpockets and fakirs that followed the show; it reached to the freaks in the sideshow. And not one among them all would have betrayed him by sign or deed. They stuck together like leeches, these good and bad nomads, and they asked few questions. And so it was that David Jenison made his first appearance as a clown in the sawdust ring.

CHAPTER IV

A STKANGER APPEAES ON THE SCENE

An hour after the conclusion of the performance David was on the road once more; not, as before, afoot and weary, but safely ensconced in one of the huge, lumbering "tableau" wagons used for the transportation of canvas and perishable properties. The boss canvasman, not the hardened brute that he appeared to be, had stored him away in the damp interior of the ponderous wagon, first providing him with dry blankets on which he could sleep with some security and no comfort. There was little space between his mountainous, shifting bed and the roof of the van; and there would have been no air had not the driver of the four-horse team obligingly opened a narrow window beneath the seat on which he rode.

With considerable caution the fugitive had been smuggled into the van, under the very noses of his pursuers, so to speak. Somewhat dazed and half sick with anxiety, he obeyed every instruction of his friend the clown.

Blake and his men had watched the tearing down of the tent, the loading of the entire concern and its subsequent departure down the night-shrouded country pike. That Blake was not fully satisfied with the story told to him by Thomas Braddock, and somewhat doubtfully supported by his own investigations, is proved by the fact that he decided to follow the show until he was positively assured that his quarry was not being shielded by the circus people. With no little astuteness he and his companion resolved that they could accomplish nothing by working openly: their only chance lay in the ability to keep the circus people from knowing that they were following them. In this they counted without their hosts. At no time during the next three days were their movements unknown to the clever band of rascals who followed the show for evil purposes, and who, with perfect integrity, kept the proprietor advised of every step taken and of every disguise affected. Blake was not the first nor the last confident officer of the law to more than meet his match in the effort to outwit an old-time road circus. He was butting his head against a stone wall. Consummate rascality on one hand, unwavering loyalty on the other: he had but little chance against the combination. The lowliest peanut-vender was laughing in his sleeve at the sleuth; and the lowliest peanut-vender kept the vigil as resolutely as any one else.

Despite his uncomfortable position and the natural thrills of excitement and peril, David was sound asleep before the wagon was fairly under way. Complete exhaustion surmounted all other conditions. He was vaguely conscious of the sombre rumbling of the huge wagon and of the regular clicking of the wheel-hubs, so characteristic of the circus caravan and so dear to the heart of every boy. His bones ached, his stomach was crying out for food, and his body was chilled; but none of these could withstand the assault of slumber. He would have slept if Blake's hand had been on his shoulder.

Out into the country rolled the big wagon, at two o'clock in the morning, following as closely as possible the flickering rear lantern of the vehicle ahead. The rain had ceased falling, but there was a mist in the air, blown from the trees that lined the road. Those of the circus men who were compelled to ride outside the wagons were clothed in their rubber coats; their more fortunate companions slept under cover on the pole wagons, on top of the seat wagons, or in stretchers swung beneath the property wagons or cages. Others, still more fortunate, slept in property or trunk vans, or in the band chariots. The leading performers and officials, including all of the women, traveled by train. The gamblers, pickpockets and fakirs got along as best they could from town to town by stealing passage on the freight trains. Times there were, however, when the entire aggregation traveled with the caravan. On such occasions the luckless roustabout gave up his precarious bedroom to the "ladies" and sat all night in dubious solitude atop of his lodging house. These emergencies were infrequent: they arose only when railroad facilities were not to be had, or—alas! when the exchequer was depleted.

On this murky night the performers remained over in S—, to take an early train for the next stand. The railroad show was then an untried experiment. Barnum and Coup and others were planning the great innovation, but there was a grave question as to its practicability. Later on Coup made the venture, transporting his show by rail. Such men as Yankee Robinson, Cole and even P. T. Barnum traveled by wagon road until that brave attempt was made. The railroad was soon to solve the "bad roads" problem for all of them. Short jumps would no longer be necessary; profitable cities could be substituted for the small towns that every circus had to make on account of the distances and the laborious mode of transportation. Still, if you were to chat awhile with an old-time showman, you would soon discover that the "road circus" of early days was the real one, and that the scientifically handled concern of to-day is as utterly devoid of the true flavor as the night is without sunshine.

Three times during the long, dark hours before dawn the chariot was stalled in the mud of the mountain road; as many times it was moved by the united efforts of five or six teams and the combined blasphemy of a dozen drivers. Through all of this, David slept as if drugged. Daybreak came; the ghostly wagon train slipped from darkness into the misty light of a new "day. " Cocks were crowing afar and near, and birds were chirping in the bushes at the roadside. Out of the sombre, crinkling night rolled the red, and white, and golden juggernauts, gradually taking shape in the gray dawn, crawling with sardonic indifference past toll-gate and farmhouse, creaking and groaning and snapping in weird, uncanny chorus.

Early risers were up to see the "circus" pass. It was something of an epoch in the lives of those who dwelt afar from the madding crowd.

The elephant, the cages of wild beasts, the horses, the towering chariots, the amazing pole wagons—all slipped down the road and over the hill, strange, unusual objects that came but once a year and seemed to leave the countryside smaller and more narrow than it had been before.

Hunched-up drivers, sleepily handling a half-dozen reins, looked neither to right nor left, but swore mechanically for the benefit of the tired horses, and without compunction in the presence of roadside spectators, male or female. Wet, sour, unfriendly minions were they, but they sent up no lamentations; their lives may have been hard and unpromising, but lightly in their hearts swam the blissful conviction that they were superior to the envious yokels who gaped at them from fence corners and barnyards since the first dreary streak of dawn crept into the skies. A shadowy, ungainly, mysterious caravan of secrets, cherished but unblest, it straggled through the dawn, resolute in its promise of splendor at midday. Wild beasts were abroad in the land, and mighty serpents, too; but they slept and were scorned by the men who slumbered above or below them.

The country people looked on and wondered, and shuddered at the thought of the terrific creatures at their very door-yards. Then they hitched up their teams and flocked to town in the wake of the peril, there to marvel and delight in the very things that had awed them in their own province. And all through the land people locked their doors and put away their treasures. The circus had come to town!

It was eight o'clock before David was routed from his strange bed by the boss canvasman. They were in a new town. He rubbed his eyes as he stood beside the wagon wheel and looked upon the amazing scene before him. Dozens of huge wagons were spread over the show-grounds; a multitude of men and horses swarmed in and about them; curious crowds of early risers stood afar off and gazed. The rhythmic pounding of iron stakes, driven down by four precise sledge-men came to his ears from all sides; the jangling of trace-chains; the creaking of wagons and the whine of pulleys. Here, there, everywhere were signs of a mighty activity, systematic in its every phase. Men toiled and swore and were cursed with the regularity of a single well-balanced mind. Already the horse tent and the cook tent were up. A blacksmith shop was clanging out its busy greetings.

For a moment David forgot his own predicament. He stared in utter bewilderment, vastly interested in the great transformation. Under his very eyes a city of white was about to spring into existence.

Some one touched his shoulder, not ungently. He started in sudden alarm. A rough-looking fellow in a soiled red undershirt was standing at his elbow.

"The boss says you'd better come to the cook-top and get somethin' to eat, young feller. " That was all. He jerked his head in the direction of the long, low tent in the corner of the lot and started off. David followed, sharply conscious of a revived hunger.

A score of men were seated at the long tables, gulping hot coffee and bolting their food. From the kitchen beyond came the crackling of fats, the odor of frying things and the aroma of strong coffee. The clatter of tin pans and cups, the rattle of pewter knives and forks and the commands of hungry men to the surly lads who served them assailed the refined ears of the young Virginian as he stopped irresolutely at the mouth of the tent.

"Set down here, kid, " said his escort, pointing to a place on the plank, stepping over it himself to take his seat at the board. If the stranger expected a greeting or comment on his appearance among these men, he was happily disappointed. They looked at him with sullen, indifferent eyes and went on bolting the breakfast. Some of them were half naked; all of them were dirty and reeking with perspiration. There was no effort at general conversation. David had the feeling that they hated each other and were ready to hurl things at the slightest provocation, such as the passing of the time of day.

A half-grown boy placed a huge tin cup full of steaming coffee on to the table and said in a husky, consumptive voice: "'Ere's your slop, kid. "

Another boy jammed a panful of bacon and corn-bread across his shoulder and advised him to hurry up and "grab it, you. "

David ate in shocked silence. The man at his left laughed at his genteel use of the knife and fork and the dainty handling of the bacon. Sugar and cream were not served. He was hungry. The coarse but well-cooked food pleased his palate more than he could have believed. He ate his fill of the "chuck, " as his neighbor called it. Then he was hurried back to the wagon in which he had slept. It was empty now, cavernous and reeking with the odor of damp canvas lately removed.

"Git in there, kid, " said his guide briskly. "You gotta keep under cover fer a spell. Stay in there 'tel Joey Grinaldi says the word. Them's Braddock's orders. "

David hesitated a moment. "Where is Mrs. Braddock? " he asked.

"Train ain't in yet. You don't suppose the highlights travel this away, do you? Well, nix, I should say not. Say, are you goin' to learn the business? If you are, I got some fishworm oil that's jest the thing to limber up yer joints. In two weeks, if you rub this oil of mine all over you reg'lar, you c'n bend double three ways. " It was an old game. David stared but shook his head.

"I'm not going to be a performer, " he said, with a wry smile at the thought of "fishworm oil. "

"Well, that bein' the case, have you got any chewin' about yer clothes? "

"Chewing? " murmured David.

"Fine cut er plug, I don't care. "

"I don't chew tobacco, " said David stiffly.

"Oh, " said the man in amaze. "A reg'lar little Robert Reed, eh? Well, hop inside there. I gotta shut the door. Don't you cry if it's dark, kid. "

David crawled into the chariot and the door was closed after him. A thin stream of daylight came down through the narrow slit beneath the driver's seat. For a while he sat with his back against the wall, pondering the situation. Then, almost without warning, sleep returned to claim his senses. He slipped over on his side, mechanically stretched out his legs and forgot his doubts and troubles.

He was aroused by the jostling and bouncing of the huge, empty wagon. With a start of alarm he leaped to his feet, striking his head against the roof of his abiding place, and hurried to the end of the wagon to peer out through the slit. Bands were playing, whips were cracking and children were shrieking joyously. It was a long time before he grasped the situation. The "Grand free street parade" was in progress; he was riding, like a caged beast, through the principal streets of the town!

From the security of his position he could look out upon the throng that lined the sidewalks, without danger of being seen in return. After the first great wave of mortification and shame, he was able to consider his situation to be quite as amusing as it was fortunate. He found himself laughing at the country people and their scarcely more sophisticated city brethren with something of the worldly scorn that dominated the "profession. " Even the horses that drew the "Gorgeous chariots of gold" eyed the gaping crowds with profound pity. There is nothing in all this world so incredibly haughty as a circus, from tent-peg to proprietor. Perhaps you who read this have felt your own insignificance while gazing at an imperial tent-peg that happened to lie in your path as you wandered about the grounds; or you have certainly felt mean and lowly in the presence of a program-peddler, and positively servile in contact with a boss canvasman. It is in the air; and the very air is the property of the circus.

In time the twenty wagons, with their double and quadruple teams, attended fore and aft by cavaliers and court-ladies, *papier mache* grotesques, trick mules and "calico ponies, " came once more to the grounds, still pursued by the excited crowd. Far ahead of the parade a loud-voiced "barker" rode, warning all people to look out for their horses: "The elephant is coming! " Just to show their utter lack of poise, at least fifty farm nags, in super-equine terror, leaped out of their harness and into their own vehicles when "Goliath, " the decrepit old elephant, shuffled by, too tired to lift his proboscis, thus exemplifying the vast distinction between themselves and the circus horses which only noticed Goliath when he got in the way.

David had a long wait in the dark, stuffy chariot. Finally the door was opened and Braddock looked in. Directly behind the proprietor was the dirty sidewall of a tent. David blinked afresh in the light of day, —although, alas, the sun was not shining.

"Hello, " said Braddock shortly. His cigar bobbed up and down with the movement of his lips. "Come out. You can duck under the canvas right here. Lift it up, Bill. "

The boy slid from the chariot to the ground and made haste to pass under the wall which had been raised by a canvasman. Braddock followed him into the huge tent. A small army of men were erecting the seats for the afternoon performance. David realized that he was in the "main top. "

A stocky, bow-legged man, his hands in his pockets and a short briar pipe in his lips, advanced to meet them.

"Well, 'ow are you? " asked this merry-eyed stranger, his face going into a hundred wrinkles by way of friendly greeting. "Oh, I say, David, don't you know your old pal and playmate? Hi, there! 'Ere we are! "

David stared in astonishment. It was Grinaldi, the clown, without his make-up or his wig! Never was there such a change in human face.

They clasped hands, David laughing outright in the ecstasy of relief at finding this whilom friend.

"Keep shady, you, " said Braddock, finding no pleasure in the boy's change of manner. "Those pinchers came over on the train with us. And say, we might just as well settle what's to be done about you. I've thought it over seriously. I'm taking a risk in havin' you around, understand that. But if you want a job with the show, I'll give you one. Tell you what I'll do: I'll give you two and a half a week and your board. That's good pay for a beginner. You to do clown work and— "

"But I can't be a clown—" began David.

"Well, what do you want? " roared Braddock, apparently aghast. "Do you expect to ride around in carriages and live on goose liver? Say, where do you think you are? In society? Well, you can get that out of your head, lemme tell you that, you—"

"'Ere, 'ere, Brad, " put in Joey sharply, noting the look in the boy's pale face. "Don't talk like that. 'E's not used to that sort o' gaff. Let me talk it over with 'im. "

"Well, the offer don't stand long. He either takes it or he don't. If he don't, out he goes. Say, you, where's all that money you had last night? I'm not going to have anybody carryin' a wad around like that and gettin' it nabbed and then settin' up a roar against the show, gettin' us pulled or something worse. I insist on taking care of that stuff, for my own protection, just so long as you stay with this show. "

David looked helplessly to Joey Noakes for succor.

"I'll talk that over with 'im, too, Brad, " announced the clown briefly.

"And let me add something else, " resumed Braddock, with an unnecessary oath. "I'm not going to have you hangin' around my wife and daughter if you *do* stay with us. Remember one thing: you're a cheap clown, and you've got to know your place. My daughter's a decent girl. She's got good blood in her, understand that. *Damn' fine blood.* I'm not going to have her associatin' with a—"

"'Old on, Brad! " interrupted the old clown, glaring at him. "Cheese it, will you? I won't stand for it. You got five 'undred from this boy and you ought to treat 'im decent. He's got just as good blood in 'im as Christie's got—and better, blow me, because it's probably good on both sides—which is more than you can say for her, poor girl. Thank God, she don't show that she's got your blood in 'er veins. "

"Here! Do you mean to insinuate that she's not *mine*? " gasped Braddock, suddenly a-tremble. Much as he trusted to the virtue of his wife, he was never able to comprehend the miracle that gave him Christine for a daughter. There was no trace of him to be seen in her.

"You know better than that, " said the clown coldly.

"Well, " said Braddock, nervously shifting his cigar and lowering his gaze. If he had intended to say more, he changed his mind and walked off toward the center of the tent where men were throwing up a circular bank about the ring.

"He's a drunken dog, " said the clown, glaring after him. "She's the finest woman in the world. And to think of 'er bein' the wife of that bounder. "

David had been thinking of it and puzzling his tired brain for hours.

"How did she happen to marry—"

"No time for that now, " said Grinaldi briskly. "Mebby I'll tell you about her some other time, not now. You'd better keep away from her and Christine for a couple of days. Brad will forget it in no time, 'specially if he thinks he can scrape some more o' that money out of you. Oh, he's a slick one. He's got 'is eye on that wad. Now, let's get down to business. I advise you to stick to the show for awhile—at least until we're a good ways off. Take up 'is offer. It ain't bad. You can 'ave chuck with me and Ruby. I'll look out for that. You just do wot I tell you, and you'll be a clown. Not a real one, but good enough to earn two and a 'arf. I'm not doin' this for you, my boy, because I think I need an assistant. Joey Grinaldi has been a fav'rit clown in two hemispheres for forty years. Some day I'll show you the medals I got in London and Paris and—but never mind now. You start right in this afternoon, doin' just wot I tells you. You'll be all right and them blokes as is 'untin' for you won't be able to twig you from sole leather. Wot say? "

"I'll do just as you say, " said David simply.

"Good! Now come over 'ere by the band section and I'll tell how we'll work it out. Of course, we'll improve it every day. All you needs is confidence. We 'ave dinner at twelve-thirty in the performer's end of the cook-tent. It's all right there. I'll fetch yours into the dressin'-tent for you, so's you won't be seen. There's my daughter over there. Ain't she a stunner? Say, she's a gal as is a gal.

Best trapeze worker in the business, if I do say it myself. And 'er mother was the best columbine that ever appeared in a Drury Lane pantomime, poor lass. " He abruptly passed his hand across his eyes.

"The columbine? " said David, his eyes beaming. "I remember the columbine and the harlequin and the pantaloon in Drury Lane one boxing week when I was in London with my grandfather. Was a columbine really your wife? "

"She was, " said Joey proudly. "But, " he added hastily, "it ain't likely you saw *her*. She died when Ruby was born. "

That afternoon David appeared in the ring, once more clad in the striped suit and besmeared with bismuth. He was even more frightened than at his first appearance, when he was driven by another fear. Ruby Noakes, black-eyed and dashing, winked at him saucily from her perch on the high trapeze, having caught his eye. When she slid down the stout lacing and wafted kisses to the multitude, he was near enough to catch her merry undertone:

"You have no idea how funny you are, " she said, passing him by with a skip.

"There's your friend, the detective, " remarked Joey, later on, jerking his head in the direction of the animal tent. Sure enough, Blake was standing at the end of the tier of seats, talking with Thomas Braddock. "But he doesn't reckernize you, David, so don't turn any paler than you are already. "

The new clown, wretchedly unsuited to his new occupation, managed to get through the performance without mishap. He followed instructions blindly but faithfully, barking his shins twice and tripping over an equestrian banner once with almost direful results. The audience laughed with glee, and Grinaldi congratulated him on the hit he was making.

"Hit? " moaned David, rubbing his elbow in earnest. "Good heaven! Was that a hit? "

"My boy, they'd laugh if you were to break your neck, " said the clown gravely.

Christine Braddock came on for her turn early in the program. David was told that her mother, who persistently though vainly opposed a ring career for her loved one, compromised with Braddock on the condition that she was to appear early in the performance.

"Brad was a circus rider in his younger days, before he took to drink, " explained Joey, as he and David sat together at the edge of the ring while Briggs, the ringmaster, announced the approach of "the world-famed child marvel, Little Starbright, and Monseer Dupont, in the great-est eques-trian feats evah attempted by mor-tal crea-tuah! "

"When Christie was a wee bit of a thing he took 'er into the ring with 'im. She sat on 'is shoulder and the crowd thought it wonnerful. Arter that he took 'er in reg'lar. Mrs. Braddock almos' lost 'er mind, but Brad coaxed 'er into seein' it 'is way. It was before he took to drinking steady. That gal 'as no more business being a circus rider than nothink. But you can't make Brad see it that way now. He says she's got to earn 'er bread and keep, and that she's no better than wot 'er father is. If circus riding is good enough for 'im, it's good enough for 'is offspring, says he. Her mother just had to give in to 'im. Well, when she was about ten, Brad took to drinking. That was before he bought old Van Slye out. One day he fell off the 'oss with 'er and broke 'is arm. Fort'nitly, the younker wasn't 'urt. So, then he had sense enough to listen to 'is wife. He quit riding 'isself, but he put big Tom Sacks into the act in 'is place. Tom is the present Mons. Dupont—a fine feller and as steady as can be. He's powerful strong and a fairish sort of rider—but nothink like wot Brad used to be in his best day. Christine's getting a bit biggish for 'im to 'andle; I daresay this is the last season for their double act. But for four seasons she's been doing amazing fine work with old Tom. She seems to like it, and she's as daring as the very old Nick. Don't know wot fear is, I might say. She's so fairy-like and so purty that the crowds just naterally love 'er to death. She's going to be a wonnerful 'ansome woman, David, that gal is, take it from me. 'Ere she is! "

"She's like a rose, " said David, following the slim, scarlet creature with his eyes.

"And a rose she is, my heartie, " said Joey. "When I was a lad at 'ome, there was a chap named Thackeray writing wonderful clever tales. I remembers one of them particular. It was called 'The Rose and the Ring. ' I never see Christine in them togs without thinking of the name of that book—The Rose and the Ring, d' ye get my idea?

Mr. Thackeray was a well-known writer when I was a boy. That was thirty year ago. I daresay he's dead and forgotten now. "

David smiled. "He'll never die, Mr. Noakes. He's more alive now than ever. 'The Rose and the Ring. ' Why not 'The Rose *in* the Ring'? "

"Hi! Hi! " cried Joey approvingly, "Right you are. "

During the entire act of Little Starbright and Monsieur Dupont David gazed entranced. He followed Grinaldi, but his eyes were not always leveled against the spotted back of his mentor; they were for the lithe, graceful figure in scarlet riding atop of the sturdy Tom Sacks, sometimes standing upright on his shoulders, again leaning far out from his thigh, or even more daringly dancing on his broad back while he squatted on the pad. First on one foot, then the other, then clear of his back with both of them twinkling in merry time to the quickstep of the band, her dark hair fluttering from beneath the saucy cap, her hands waving and her eyes sparkling. Kisses went wafting to every section of the tent, and with them smiles such as David had never seen before.

He was standing near when she leaped from the horse's back and skipped to the center of the ring to blow her final kisses to the multitude. It occurred to him all at once that he was staring at this wonderfully graceful, fairy-like little creature with the eyes of a delighted spectator and not as a clown. He guiltily looked for a reprimand from Grinaldi. To his surprise and disappointment she passed him by without a sign of recognition, slipping her tiny feet into the ground shoes and shuffling off to the dressing-tent with the stride peculiar to ring performers. For a moment he felt as if she had struck him in the face, so quick was his pride to resent the slight.

"This ain't a parlor, my lad, " said Joey, shrewdly analyzing the feelings of his *protege*. "You mustn't expect the ladies to stop and chat with you in the ring. It ain't reg'lar. She didn't mean nothink— nothink at all, bless 'er 'eart. "

When the performance was over, David was whisked into the men's section of the dressing-tent and told to stay there until further orders. He changed his clothes and "washed up, " listening meanwhile to the congratulations and the good-natured chaffing of the performers who were there with him. Despite their ribald scoffing, he knew they were his friends: there was something about these careless, inconsequent knights of the sawdust ring, in spangles or out, that warmed the cockles of his sore, despairing heart.

He came before long to laugh with them and to take their jibes as they were meant—good-naturedly. Joey Grinaldi beamed with congratulation. He laid himself out to make the going easy for his "gentleman pardner, " appreciating the vast distinction that lay between these men and the kind David had known all of his life. And David saw that he was trying to make it easy for him. His heart swelled with a strange gratitude; he unbent suddenly and met the rough kindnesses more than half way. They were not the kind of men he was used to, —they were not gentlemen; but they stood ready to be his friends, and something told him that they would ring true to the very end if he met them half way.

They had their own undeviating regard for what they called honor: honor meant loyalty and fairness, nothing more. Simple, genial, unpolished braggarts were they, but their word was as good or better than a gentleman's bond. David was soon to fall under the spell of this bland comradeship: he was to see these men in a light so bright that it blinded him to their vulgarities, their quaint blasphemy and their prodigious lack of veracity as applied to personal achievements. He was to find in them a splendid chivalry, almost unbelievable at first: their regard for the women in the troupe was in the nature of a revelation to him, who came from the land of gallantry itself.

"Say, kid, " said Signor Anaconda, "the human snake, " suddenly adopting a serious mien, —which did not become him, —"you gotta change your name. What'll we call him, fellers? Now, le' 's give him a reg'lar story-book name. Prince Something-or-other. What say to—"

"That's all settled, " said old Joey, his eyes full of soap and water and squeezed so tightly together that they looked like wrinkles. "Christine Braddock named 'im this morning. I forgot to tell you, David. Your name is Snipe—Jack Snipe. "

David flushed. "Why did she call me *that*? " he asked.

"Because you were lonesome, and there is nothink so lonesome as a jack-snipe. Leastwise, that's wot she says. She asked me if I'd ever seen a jack-snipe on a wet, dreary day, a-standing on a sandbar, all alone like and forlorn. She said she always felt so sorry for the poor little cuss—no, she didn't say cuss either. What was it she said, Casey? You was there. "

"She said 'thing, '" said Casey briefly.

"Right, my lad. Thing it was. Well, wot she says goes in this 'ere aggergation, so from now on you are just Jack Snipe. " He lowered his voice. "There won't nobody call you David or Jenison after this, my boy. It's too dangerous. "

David was thoughtful. "Do you mean to say, " he said, after a pause, "that every person in this show knows who I really am? "

"You bet your life they do, " said Casey.

"And what I am wanted for? "

"Certain. Wot's that got to do with it? "

"Do they think I'm—I'm guilty? "

"Well, I reckon most of 'em do, " said the contortionist blandly. "But, " he added in some haste, "they don't give a dang for a little thing like that. "

"But, " said David fiercely, "I don't want them to think I am guilty. I can't bear to think that every one is looking upon me as a criminal. Why—why, what must the ladies of the—of the show think of me? I—I— "

Joey Grinaldi put his hand on the young fellow's shoulder: "They don't think you done it, Jack—not one of 'em. I heard 'em speaking of you last night as if you was a reg'lar angel. For the fust time since I've knowed all of them women, they are all agreed on one thing: they *all* agree that you are the sweetest kid they've ever seen and that you never done anything naughty in your life. Come on, now. Mrs. Braddock wants to see you a minute. "

David's heart leaped. He followed the old clown into the open tent, his eyes bright with the eagerness to look once more upon the strange, lovely friend of the night before, —his true guardian angel.

She was standing near the entrance to the main tent, talking with half a dozen of the women performers, all of whom were in street attire. As soon as she saw him she smiled and motioned for him to join the group. He was not slow to obey the summons. To the amazement of the interested group the young Virginian lifted her hand to his lips. Mrs. Braddock flushed warmly, an exquisite smile of appreciation leaping to her rather sombre eyes.

"You must let me introduce you to these ladies, " she said, after a few low words of greeting. "This is Jack Snipe, our new clown, " she said, naming for his benefit the riders, the ropewalker, the snake-charmer and the boneless wonder. David was profoundly polite, almost old-fashioned in his acknowledgment of the introduction. The women were suddenly conscious of a new-found glory in themselves. The "boneless wonder" talked of his elegance for weeks, and always without resorting to slang.

"Where is Miss Christine? " asked David, turning to Mrs. Braddock with a shy smile.

She did not answer at once. When she did, it was with palpable uneasiness. "My daughter usually takes her sleep at this time, Dav— Jack. "

David's cheek slowly turned red. He remembered what Braddock had said to him.

"You are all very good to me, " he murmured, for want of anything better to say. His sensitive heart was thumping quickly, driven by humiliation. She looked steadily into his eyes without speaking and then walked away from the group, directing him to follow. They sat down upon the tumbler's pad, just where they had been seated the night before.

"My husband is hard sometimes, David, " she said gently. "It will last for a few days, that is all. We must not aggravate him now. In a little while he will forget that he has—has said certain things. Then, I hope that you and Christine will be good friends. I—I want her to know you well, David. I want her to be with—with some one who is different from the people here. You understand, don't you? "

"Yes, " said David, suddenly enlightened. "I know what you mean. I shall be very happy, too. "

59

"Ah, how gently you did that, " she cried, a wistful gleam in her dark eyes. "How the blood tells its story! Yes, David, I want her to know you; I want her to—to be with her own kind. " Her face flamed with sudden fervor; he was struck by the almost pathetic eagerness that leaped into her eyes, transfiguring them. "I have tried so hard to give her something of what I had myself, David, when I was a girl. Everything depends on the next year or two. She is thinking for herself now. It is the turning-point. You must know, David, you must see that she is not like the others here. "

"She is like you, " he said, very simply.

The blood surged once more to her cheeks; her lips parted with the quick breath of joy and gratitude. She thanked him very gently, very gravely. No word was uttered against the man who was Christine's father.

"I prayed last night, David, that you might stay with the show until the end of this season. I am determined that it shall be her last, no matter what it may cost both of us. "

"Cost both of us, " thought he, and at once knew what she meant. The cost, if necessary, would be the husband and father.

Then she told him, in hurried sentences, that she had watched him in the ring, and that her daughter had come back to her with glowing reports of his composure and cleverness. David's pride, at least, was appeased. She *had* looked at him, after all, and was interested.

He was struck by the sudden, curious change that came over Mrs. Braddock's face. She was looking past him toward the entrance to the circus tent. All the color, all the eagerness left her face in a flash; the warmth died out in her big brown eyes and in its stead appeared a look of positive dread and uneasiness—it might have been repugnance. Her lips grew tense, and he could see that she started ever so slightly, as if in surprise.

He glanced over his shoulder. Thomas Braddock was approaching, his face red with anger and drink. At his side walked a tall, exceedingly well-dressed stranger, who carried his silk hat in his hand and was smiling blandly upon the proprietor's wife.

"Oh, that man again! " he heard her say between her stiff lips. There was a world of loathing in the half-whispered sentence, which was so low that it barely reached his ears. He looked up quickly, and saw her face go darkly red again—the red of humiliation, he could have sworn.

"Go! " she said to David, quietly but firmly.

He turned away, vaguely conscious that the newcomer was more to be feared than Thomas Braddock himself. Instinctively the boy experienced a singular, instantaneous aversion to this immaculate intruder.

"Get out! " he heard Braddock roar after him as he paused at the partition to look once more at the stranger.

The man was bowing low before the straight, motionless figure of Mary Braddock. Her chin was high in the air, and David could almost have sworn that he saw her nostrils dilate.

From a place beyond the flap in the partition he surveyed this disturbing visitor.

CHAPTER V

SOMETHING ABOUT THE BRADDOCKS

He was not long in supplying a reason for the sudden antipathy he felt toward this man whom he had never seen before.

A somewhat prolonged study from the security of the dressing-room had the effect of settling the aversion more firmly in his mind. In the first place, the man's face was a peculiarly evil one. His dark eyes were set quite close together under a bulging forehead. His eyebrows were straw-colored, and so thin that they were almost invisible. A broad, flat nose, with spreading nostrils, not unlike that of an Ethiopian, gave to the upper part of his face a sheep-like expression. His lower lip, thick and blue and loose, protruded with flabby insistence beyond its mate, which was short and straight. The chin receded, but was of surprising length and breadth. His ears sat very low on his head and were ludicrously small. Above them rose a massive dome, covered with thick, well-brushed hair of a yellowish hue, parted exactly in the middle. His cheeks were white and flaccid, and there was a fullness in front of the jaw-point that suggested approaching bagginess. He smiled with his lips closed, and broadly at that. The picture was even less alluring than when his face was in repose. In the subdued, gray light of the tent his complexion was singularly colorless; David thought of a very sick man he had once seen.

But this man was apparently in the best of health. He was spare, and his sloping shoulders did not suggest breadth or strength; yet there was that about him which made for force and virility. His hands were long and slim and very white. A huge diamond glittered on one of the fingers of the left hand; another quite as large adorned the bosom of his shirt. It required no clever mind to see that he was not an out- of-doors man. One would say, guessing, that he was thirty six or eight years of age. As a matter of fact, he was fifty-five.

David noticed that he never allowed his gaze to leave the face of Mary Braddock, except to occasionally traverse her figure from crown to foot. The boy's dislike grew to actual resentment. He experienced a fierce desire to rush out and strike the man across the eyes.

He could not hear what they were talking about. Broddock, tipsy as usual, was urging something on her in low, insistent tones. His manner was that of one who espouses a forlorn hope; he argued with the insinuating, doubting earnestness so characteristic of the man who knows that he is operating against his own best interests in the face of one who fully understands the weakness that impels him. Mrs. Braddock stood before him, cold, passive, unconvinced. Her greeting for the newcomer had been most unfriendly. She deliberately turned her back on him, after the first short "good afternoon. " As for the stranger, he did not take part in the conversation. He stood close to her elbow, the trace of a smile on his lips.

Suddenly her tense body relaxed. Her chin dropped forward and she nodded her head dejectedly. Braddock's next remark, uttered with considerable gusto, came to David's ears.

"Good! " he said, biting his cigar with approving energy. "We can talk it over there. I think you will see it my way, Mary. You'll see if I'm not right! Come on, Bob. This is no place to talk. "

She preceded them without another word, an air of utter weariness characterizing her movements. The stranger smiled his bland, hateful smile. When Braddock, in genial relief, essayed to take his arm, the tall man coldly withdrew himself from the contact, displaying a far from mild aversion to the advances of the tipsy showman. Braddock dropped back, like a cowed dog, permitting the other to pass through the sidewall ahead of him, a step or two behind the unhappy Mary Braddock on whose back his steady gaze was leveled with unswerving intentness.

David hurried to a rent in the canvas and peered out into the sunlight of the waning day. The stranger had come up beside Mrs. Braddock, talking to her as they crossed the lot in the direction of the street. She apparently paid no heed to his remarks. Braddock made no effort to keep up with them, but loafed behind, simulating interest in the most conveniently propinquitous of his possessions, with now and then a furtive glance at the couple a half-dozen paces ahead.

David was sorely puzzled and distressed. He knew that something was going cruelly wrong with his friend and supporter, but what it was he could not even venture a guess, knowing so little about the people and conditions attached to his new world.

"So, he's 'ere again, is he? "

He whirled quickly to find Grinaldi peering over his shoulder, his erstwhile merry face as black as a thunder cloud.

"Who is he? " demanded David.

The clown did not answer at once. His eyes were glittering. It was not until the trio passed from view beyond a "snack-stand" that he sighed mightily and jammed his hands into his coat pockets, still clenched. Even then, he stared long at David before replying.

"That man? " he said harshly. "That's Colonel Bob Grand. "

"What has he got to do with the show, Mr. Noakes? "

"Call me Joey. Everybody does, my lad. " He looked around cautiously. No one was near them. Nevertheless, he lowered his voice. "That's just wot all of us would like to know ourselves, Jacky. He's a race-horse man and a gambler. Oh, don't you get it into your 'ead that he follows the show in *them* capacities. Not he. He's too big a guy for that. No, sirree. He pinches the dollars by the thousands, that chap does. No ten-dollar rube games for 'im. But I'll tell you all about 'im at supper. There's Ruby waiting for us at the door. I'm 'aving supper brought over 'ere for us three and Casey. He's a nice chap, Casey is. Brad says you are not to go to the cook-top until we're out of the woods. " Before starting off to join his daughter, Grinaldi looked again through the hole in the canvas, muttering a dejected oath.

Ruby Noakes, very pretty and quite demure in a simple frock of brown, without the prevailing bustle and paniers, was directing the contortionist in his efforts to construct a table out of three "blue seats" and a couple of property trunks, or "keesters, " as they were called.

"I insist on having a table that I can put my legs under, " she said when he argued that the trunks alone would make an "elegant" table. "We can sit on the boxes. Here, dad, you and Jack get the boxes up. The boys will be here with supper in a minute or two. Oh,

I say, isn't it going to be fun? Just like a supper party in Delmonico's—only I've never been to one there. Goodness, how I'd love to eat at Delmonico's! "

"You wouldn't like it a bit, Ruby, " announced Casey. "You got to understand French to eat what they have there. If you can't understand French, you're sure to eat something that won't agree with you, not bein' able to tell soup from pickled pigs' feet. "

"How do you know? You've never been there. "

Casey gave her a cool stare. "I haven't, eh? My dear, I'd have you to know that I've et there a hundred times. "

Her eyes popped wide open.

"Of course, " he explained, "I allus had to wake up and find I'd been dreamin'. But, by ginger, them was great dreams. I allus had 'em after my wife's cousin had been up to our shack of a Sunday to get a good square meal. He was a waiter at Delmonico's. He was allus tellin' what gorgeous things he had to eat at Del's, and then, blow me, I'd dream about 'em the livelong night. "

Presently the food came in from the cook-tent. The four sat down, David beside the girl, who generously took him in hand at this unusual banquet. In the menagerie tent beyond wild beasts were growling and roaring and snarling a weird interlude for the benefit of the banqueters, sounds so strange and menacing that David looked often with uneasy interest in the direction from which they came.

"I like this, don't you, dad? I wish we could have a runaway boy with us every night or so. " She gave David a warm, enveloping smile.

But Joey was not listening to the idle chatter of his daughter. He ate in silence, his brow corrugated with the intensity of his thoughts.

"Say, Casey, 'ave you seen 'im? " he asked at last, interrupting a tale that Ruby was telling for David's especial benefit.

"I like that! " she exclaimed indignantly.

"Seen who? " from Casey, also ignoring her.

"Grand. "

"Is that skunk here again? "

"Big as life, dang 'is bloody 'eart. He's bothering 'er, too. Makes love to 'er right afore 'er 'us-band's eyes. It's—it's *out-rage- ious*"

Miss Noakes forgot her story and her resentment. She leaned forward, her black eyes fairly snapping, her fingers clenched. David recalled the muscular bare arms he had seen during the trapeze act, and wondered how so slight a person as she now seemed to be could be so powerfully developed.

"I *knew* something awful was going to happen, " she said. "I saw a cross-eyed man in the blues to-day. It never fails. "

Circus people, from the beginning of history, have been superstitious. Not one, but all of them, carry charms, amulets or lucky pieces, and they recognize more signs than the sailors themselves.

"Some of these fine days I'm going to paste that guy on the nose, " said the contortionist heatedly.

"You'll get a bullet in your gizzard if you do, " said the clown gloomily. "He carries a gun, and he'll use it, too. And if he didn't, Tom Braddock would beat you to jelly for insulting 'is best friend. "

"Do you mean that Mrs. Braddock is in love with that man? " demanded David, his heart sinking.

The three of them glared at him—positively glared.

"Nobody said that, sir, " said old Joey angrily. "She despises 'im. I said as 'ow he was in love with 'er. There's a big difference in that, my friend. "

"I knew she wasn't that kind of a woman, " cried David joyously.

"What do you know about women? " demanded Casey

"I'll tell you about 'im and 'er and all of them, " said Joey, looking about to see that they were quite alone in their corner. "You can tell by looking at 'er, Jacky, that she ain't no common pusson. She's quality, as you Virginians would say. And for that matter, so is Colonel Grand, after a fashion. That is to say, he comes of a very good old New Orleans family. He spoilt it all by being a colonel in the Union army during the war. He wasn't for the North because he was patriotic, but because he knowed the North would win and he saw 'is chance to get rich. He's just a nateral-born gambler. Of course, he ain't been back to New Orleans since the war. I understand 'is own brothers intend to shoot 'im if he does go back. He went to Washington to live, and he made a pile of money promoting carpet-bagging schemes through the south. He's got a big gambling-house in Baltimore at present, and an interest in one in New York, besides 'aving a string o' race-horses.

"Well, Tom Braddock comes from Baltimore. His father was a hoss trainer and trader there for a good many years afore he died — w'ich was about two years ago. I've 'eard it said by them as knows, that he sometimes traded hosses in the dead of night and forgot to leave one in exchange for the one he took away. However that may be, he never got caught at it and so died an honest man. It seems that he borrowed one of Colonel Grand's riding hosses to go after a doctor one night, some years ago, and didn't return it for nearly eighteen months. He wouldn't 'ave returned it then if the Colonel 'adn't seen 'im riding it in Van Slye's street parade out in a little Indiana town during county fair week. I was with the show at the time, w'ich was afore old Van Slye sold out to Tom Braddock. Well, Tom and Mrs. Braddock begged so 'ard for the old scamp that the Colonel not only let 'im off but took 'im back to Baltimore to train hosses for him. That was about five seasons ago, and it was the first time any of us ever laid eyes on the Colonel.

"Tom Braddock and 'is wife lived in Baltimore in the winter time, where she kept little Christine in school from November to March. The rest of the year she teaches 'er 'erself. I might say that Christine is a specially well-edicated child and well brought up. You can see that for yourself. Tom wanted 'er to learn 'ow to sing and dance so's she could be earning money all winter, but 'er mother said nix to that, very proper like. In course o' time, Tom's father worked it so's Tom could practice 'is bareback acts at Colonel Grand's stables. He was the best rider in the country at that time. The Colonel got 'im to drinking and gambling. That was the beginning. The poor cuss 'adn't been such a bad lot up to that time. Him and Mary had always got on fairly well until he got to drinking. It wasn't long afore the Colonel took a notion to Tom's wife. He 'as a wife of 'is own, but that didn't stop 'im. He just went plumb crazy about Mary Braddock, who was the purtiest, loveliest woman he'd ever seen—or any of us, for that matter. I'll never forget how nice she's allus been to my gal 'ere, and to every gal in the show, for that matter. She's an angel if there ever was one. Don't interrupt, Casey. I've said it. You keep still, too, Ruby—and don't sniffle like that, either.

"I won't go into the 'istory of 'ow the Colonel tried to get 'er away from Tom. I daresay that's the very thing that makes 'er stick to Tom so loyal-like in spite of wot he is now. Just principle, that's all. Well, for more 'n two year the Colonel 'as been pestering 'er almost to death, and she 'as to stand it because he's got such a terrible 'old on 'er 'usband. You see, the Colonel lent Tom a good bit of money when he bought old Van Slye out season afore last. I will say this for Tom, he paid 'im back dollar for dollar. We 'ad a good season and he got the show cheap. Tom give up riding because he was tight all the time, nearly killing Christine once or twice. Every once in awhile, come so the Colonel would turn up and travel with the show for a week or so, inducing Tom to play poker and drink. Tom allus lost and then the Colonel'd stake 'im for a month or so to run the show on. This 'as gone on for two years, Tom getting wuss all the time and the Colonel more persistent. Tom 'as lost all sense of honor and decency. He knows the Colonel is trying to get 'is wife away from 'im, and he ain't got spunk enough left to object to it. He don't even try to protect 'er from the old villain. They say Grand 'as promised 'er a fine 'ome in Washington and will edicate Christine abroad, besides offering enough diamonds to fill a 'at. But she just despises 'im more and more every week. He'll never get 'er—no sirree! Why, she just *couldn't* do it! 'T ain't in 'er!

"Early this season he lent Tom five or six thousand, and Tom can't pay it back, I know, business 'as been so bad. He's come on this time, I daresay, to bulldoze 'em into 'is way of thinking. He's wonderful persistent. Like as not he'll help Tom out some more afore he leaves, just to draw the web closer. He'll stay a few days, 'anging around 'er like a vulture, paying no attention to 'er rebukes, and then he'll go off to return another day. He's wrecked Tom Braddock, just as a stepping-stone. Some day he'll be through with Tom for good and all, and you'll see what 'appens to Thomas. "

Grinaldi's voice was hoarse with emotion; his brow was damp with perspiration. Casey was the only one who ate; he ate sullenly.

"What beasts! " cried David, his fine nature in revolt.

"Brad 'as got to this point in 'is love for drink and cards, " said Joey. "He'll sacrifice anything for whiskey. He's got to have it. We've all talked to 'im. No good. I—I don't like to say it, Dav— Jacky, but he's slapped 'is wife more 'n once when she's tried to plead with—"

David sprang to his feet, his face quivering with rage and horror.

"I'll kill him! " he cried shrilly. "If the rest of you are afraid to stand up for her, I will show you how a Virginia gentleman acts in such matters. I'll—"

"My boy, " said Joey, very much gratified by his *protege's* attitude. "I like to hear you talk that way. But don't you go 'round gabbing about killing people. A word to the wise, my lad. You see wot I mean? "

David turned perfectly livid and then sank back to his seat with a groan of despair.

"You mean that my—that I've got a bad name already? "

"So far as the law is concerned, yes, " said Joey gently. "You see, you are David Jenison and—well, it's a fine old name, my 'eartie, but these ain't very gallant days. It's too soon after the war, I take it. "

The boy looked from one to the other, his eyes dark with the pain of understanding.

"But, " he said bravely, "he must not be allowed to strike her. Why doesn't she leave him? Why not get a divorce? No woman should live with a man who strikes her. God doesn't intend that to be. He—"

"God put us all into the world and he'll take us all out of it, " said the clown, philosophizing. "That's about all we ought to expect 'im to do. I don't think God 'as anything to do with matrimony. He says, 'you takes your choice and you trusts to luck, not to me. If it turns out all right, ' says he, 'you can thank me, but if it goes wrong, don't blame me. ' So there you are. It strikes me that God don't intend a good many things, but they 'appen just the same. As for 'er getting a divorce, she's too proud. She made 'er bed, as the feller says, and she's going to lie in it as long as there's room. She made 'er bed sixteen years ago, she did, against 'er father's wishes, and she ain't the kind to go back and say it's too 'ard for 'er to sleep in and she'd like to come 'ome and sleep in one of 'is for a change. No sirree, my lad. "

"How did she come to marry such a beast as Braddock? "

"Well, that's another story. I 'ope, Casey, I'm not boring you. "

"I wasn't gaping, " said Casey testily. "I was coolin' my mouth. Try that coffee yourself if you don't think it's hot. "

"I wish she would leave him, " said Ruby, more to herself than to the others.

"She's got some of 'er own money in the show—all of it, I daresay. Money 'er grandmother left 'er a couple of years ago. Brad promised he'd buy 'er share in a year or two and let 'er put the money away for Christine. But he'll never do it, not 'im. You see, Da—Jacky, it all 'appened this way. She was going to a young ladies' boarding-school up in Connecticut w'en she fust saw Tom Braddock. Her father lived in New York City and he was a very wealthy guy. She was 'is only child and 'er mother was dead. The old man, whose name was Portman, —Albert Portman, the banker, —was considering a second venture into matrimony at the time. Mary was eighteen and she didn't want a stepmother. She raised such a row that he sent 'er off to school so as he could do 'is courting in peace and plenty. She was a wayward gal, —leastwise she says so 'erself—and very impetuous-like. One day a circus comes to the town where she was attending school. The young ladies were took to the afternoon performance by the—er—school-ma'ams. They all perceeded to fall in love at first sight with a 'andsome young equestrian. He was very good-looking, I can tell you that, and he 'ad a fine figger. As clean a looking young chap as ever you see. Well do I remember Tommy Braddock in them days. He was twenty-two and he rode like a A-*rab*. Well, wot should 'appen but 'is hoss, a green one, must bolt suddenlike, scairt by one of the balloons that 'it 'im on the nose. Brad fell off as the brute leaped out of the ring, terrified by the shouts of the ring-men. The hoss started right for the seats where the school misses was setting. Up jumps Brad and sails after 'im. The hoss got tangled in some ropes and stumbled, just as he was about to leap into the place where Mary Portman sat. Brad grabs 'im by the bit and jerks 'im around, but in the plunging that followed, the hoss fell over on 'im, breaking 'is leg—I mean Brad's. Of course, there was a great stew about it. He was took to a 'ospital and the papers was full of 'ow he saved the life of the rich Miss Portman. Well, she used to go to see 'im a lot. When he got so's he could 'obble around, she took 'im out driving and so on. He was a fair-spoken chap in them days and he 'ad a good face. So she fell desperit in love with 'im. He was an 'ero. She told 'er father she was going to marry 'im. As the old gentleman was about to be married 'imself, he 'ated to share the prominence with 'er. So he said he'd disown 'er if she even thought of marrying a low-down circus rider. That was enough for Mary. She up and run off with Tom and got married to 'im in a jiffy, beating 'er father to the altar by about two weeks.

"As soon as Tom was able to ride again, they joined the show. Her father disowned 'er, as he said he would. He said he'd 'ave the butler shut the door in 'er face if she ever come to the 'ouse. They went up to ask for forgiveness, and the butler *did* shut the door in 'er face. So she turned 'er back on 'er father's 'ome and went to the little one Tom made for 'er in Baltimore. She never even wrote to 'er father after that, and she won't ever go back, no matter wot 'appens. Not even if he sends for and forgives 'er, I believe. She's stood it this long, she'll stick it out. Mr. Portman got married right enough and I understand he's 'ad a 'ell of a time of it ever since. Married a reg'lar tartar, thank God.

"Well, in a year Christine came. After a couple of years they went to England and the Continent, where Brad rode for several seasons very successful. When Christine was seven, he insisted that she should work with 'im in the ring. He 'ad 'is way. They made a sensation with Van Slye's show and stuck to 'im for six years straight, allus drawing good pay. Mary went with them everywhere, never missing a performance, allus scairt to death on account of the gal. I think nearly all of the last five years of her life 'ave been spent in wishing that Tom would fall off and break 'is own neck, but he couldn't do it very well without breakin' the kid's, too, so she didn't know wot to do. Then he got to drinking so 'ard that he did fall off, 'urting 'imself purty bad. After that he give it up, buying a share in Van Slye's show, and letting Christine do 'er work with Tom Sacks. Mrs. Braddock would give anything she's got in the world if she could get Christine out of the business and settled down in their own 'ome in Baltimore. Just to show you wot drink does for Brad, he pays Christine a good salary every week for riding and then insists on taking it back so's he can put it in the savings bank for 'er. He spends every penny of it for drink and he—"

"Sh! " came in a warning hiss from Ruby Noakes, whose quick, black eyes had caught sight of a figure approaching from the big top. "Mrs. Braddock is coming, dad. My, how white she is. "

The proprietor's wife moved slowly, even listlessly. Something vital had gone out of her face, it seemed to David, who knew her only as a strong, courageous defender. A wan smile crept into her tired eyes as she carne up to them and asked if she might sit down at their board. The hand she laid caressingly on Ruby's shoulder shook as if with ague.

"Jerk up a keester for Mrs. Braddock, Casey, " cried old Joey with alacrity. The contortionist found a small trunk and placed it between Ruby Noakes and David. Mrs. Braddock thanked him and sat down.

"Have you had your supper, Mrs. Braddock? " asked Ruby.

"I am not hungry, " said the other quietly. "A cup of coffee, though, if you have enough for me without robbing yourselves. You work so hard, you know, my dears, while I am utterly without an occupation. I don't need much, do I? "

"You need a snifter of brandy, " announced Joey conclusively. He went off to get it.

Ruby rinsed her own tin-cup and poured out some hot coffee. Casey called up a boy and sent off to the performer's cook top for a pitcher of soup, some corned beef and potatoes, ignoring her protests.

"And how is the new clown faring? " she asked, turning to the silent David with a smile.

"Very well, thank you, " he replied. "I have been very hungry, you know. I have never known food to taste so good. "

"The hotels in these towns are atrocious. I can't eat the food, " she explained listlessly.

Joey handed her a drink from his flask. She swallowed it obediently but with evident distaste. There was a long, somewhat painful silence.

"I think it's started to sprinkle again, " ventured the contortionist, looking at the top with uneasy eyes.

"Yes, " she said appreciatively, "it means another wretched night for us. " She toyed with the tin-cup with nervous fingers for a moment and then turned to the expectant Grinaldi. "We have been obliged to borrow more money, Joey. "

"So? " he said, nodding his head dumbly.

"Five thousand dollars. I—I signed the note with Tom. Oh, if we could only have a spell of good weather! " It was an actual wail of despair.

"It's bound to come, " said the clown. "It can't rain allus, Mrs. Braddock. "

Again there was silence. The three performers were absolutely dumb in the presence of her unspoken misery.

"Would my money be of any service to you? " asked David at last, timidly.

"You dear boy, no! " she cried warmly. "You do not understand. This is our affair, David. You are very, very good, but—" She checked the words resolutely. "We can lift the notes handily if the weather helps us just a little bit. "

"I don't like that man, " announced the boy, his dark eyes gleaming.

The others coughed uncomfortably. Mrs. Braddock hesitated for a second, and then laid her hand on his.

"He is a very bad man, David, " was all that she said. He would have blurted out an additional expression of hatred had she not lifted her finger imperatively. "You must not say indiscreet things, my friend. " It was a warning and he understood.

"Come on, Jacky, " put in Grinaldi hastily. "I've got to rehearse you a bit. You've got to learn 'ow to tumble and you've got to—"

"Just a moment, Joey, " said Mrs. Braddock nervously. "David, I can't keep your money for you. Do you object to Mr. Noakes taking it for awhile? Until we can get to a town where you can deposit it in a bank. It isn't safe with me. I—"

"It *is* safe with you, " he cried eagerly.

"No! If anything were to happen to me you would never see it again. " He was struck by the increased pallor of her face. "It's quite safe with Joey. "

He waited a moment before replying. "I know that, Mrs. Braddock. You may give it to him. But—but I want you to know that if *you* ever need any of it, or all of it—*for yourself or Christine*, you are more than welcome to it. "

Her eyes were flooded. "Thank you, David, " she said softly. Then she quickly withdrew the flat purse from the bosom of her dress and handed it to Joey, not without a cautious look in all directions.

The clown put it in his inside coat pocket without a word.

"You must deposit it in a bank at N—, " she went on hurriedly. "All but an amount sufficient to help you if you are obliged to suddenly fly from arrest. You understand. Joey will attend to it for you. You may depend on him and Casey to stand by you. In a few days we will be in Ohio. The danger will be small after that, Dav—I mean, Jack Snipe. I—I have worried about this money ever since—well, ever since last night. You *must* not have it about you, nor is it safe with me. It is too large a sum to be placed in jeopardy. Perhaps, my boy, it is your entire fortune, who knows. The Jenison estate seems lost to you, cruelly enough. I am so very sorry. "

"I only want to think that none of you believe I committed the crime I am accused of, " said David simply. "The money isn't anything. "

"We are not accusers, " she said gravely.

"Where is Brad? " demanded Grinaldi, his patience and diplomacy exhausted.

"He is up in Colonel Grand's room at the hotel, " she answered, as if that explained everything.

"Talking business, I suppose, " he said sarcastically.

"Yes, they are settling certain details. " She spoke in such a way that Joey looked up in alarm.

"You don't mean to say you are—you are going to—"

"No, not that, my friend, " she said, quite calmly.

"I didn't think so, " said Joey fervently.

Mrs. Braddock arose abruptly.

"I must go to Christine. Will you come, Ruby? "

Ruby followed her out of the tent, exchanging a quick glance with her father as she left the improvised table.

"Come on, Jacky, " said Joey. "Strip them clothes off and get to work. You've got a lot to learn. Ta, ta, Casey. Don't stay out in the rain. You'll melt your bones, if you've got any. "

David, somewhat depressed and very thoughtful, got into a portion of his clown's dress under the direction of his instructor, who was unusually cross and taciturn.

As they started for the deserted ring, Joey took the boy's arm and said, with a diffidence that was almost pathetic:

"Jacky, I—I want you to be nice to my gal. She's never 'ad no chance to associate with a real toff. It ain't 'er fault, poor gal; it's the life we leads. These 'ere circus people are as good as gold, Jacky; I'm not complaining about that. But they ain't just exactly wot I want my gal to grow up like. Not but wot she's growed up already so far as size is concerned. But she's not quite eighteen. She's been in the show business since she was two. Her mother and 'er grandmother afore 'er, too. But the business ain't wot it used to be. I want 'er to get out of it. I don't want 'er marrying some wuthless 'Kinker' or even a decent 'Joy. ' Mrs. Braddock 'as done worlds for 'er, mind you, but it's the men she's associated with that I objects to. They're—they're too much like me. That's wot I mean, Jacky. Would you mind just conversing with 'er friendly like from time to time? Just give 'er a touch of wot a real gentleman is, sir. It ain't asking too much of you, is it, Dav—Jacky? I ain't ashamed to ask it of you, and I—I kind of hoped you wouldn't be ashamed to 'elp tone 'er up a bit, in a way. She's more like 'er mother than she is like me. And 'er mother was as fine a columbine as ever lived, she was that refined and steadfast. "

David gave his promise, strangely touched by this second appeal to the birthright that placed him, though helpless and dependent, on a plane so far above that of his present associates that even the most scornful of them felt the distinction. He recalled the profane respectfulness of the boss canvasman earlier in the day—a condition which would have astonished that worthy beyond description if he had had the least idea that he *was* respectful.

CHAPTER VI

DAVID JENISON'S STORY

David's first week with the show was a trying one. In the first place, he was kept so carefully under cover, literally as well as figuratively, that he seldom saw the light of day except at dawn or through the space between sidewall and top. At night he rode over rough, muddy roads in the tableau wagon, stiff and sore from the violent exercise of the day, —for he was training in earnest to become a clown. He was learning the clown's songs, and singing with the chorus in such pieces as "I'll never Kiss my Love again behind the Kitchen Door, " "Paddle your own Canoe, " and others in Joey's repertory.

Throughout the forlorn, disquieting days he stayed close to the dressing-tent, always in dread of the moment when Blake or some other minion of the law would clap him on the shoulder and end the agony of suspense. Blake, as a matter of fact, more than once came near to finding his quarry. Twice, at least, David was smuggled out of sight just in time to avoid an encounter with his stubborn pursuer.

At last, after five days, Blake gave it up and turned back to Virginia, hastened somewhat by the cleverly exploited newspaper strategy of George Simms, the show's press agent. Simms managed it so that a press dispatch came out of Richmond in which it was said on excellent authority that the boy had been seen in the neighborhood of his old home within the week, and that posses were now engaged in a neighborhood hunt for him. Blake was fooled by it.

After it became definitely known to Simms that Blake was back in Richmond with his assistant, David was permitted to emerge gradually from his seclusion. The first thing he did was to go with Joey Grinaldi to a savings bank where, under the name of John Snipe, he deposited two thousand dollars, retaining five hundred for emergencies. Part of this he turned over to the clown, part to Ruby and the rest to the trusty contortionist. Twice during the week Braddock bullied him into giving up twenty-five dollars to "fix it" with town officials. At least once a day he was importuned to deliver the "leather" into the safe keeping of the proprietor, who solemnly promised that it would be returned. Moreover, in drunken magnanimity, he guaranteed to pay three per cent interest while the money was in his ticket-wagon safe, sealed and inviolate if needs be. On the subtle advice of Joey Noakes David did not tell Braddock that he had deposited the money; it would have been like the "boss" to fly into a rage and deliver him up to the authorities.

Braddock drank hard during the days following the departure of Colonel Grand, who stayed with the show no longer than twenty-four hours—an unusually brief visit, according to Joey.

The rainy weather continued and business got worse and worse. There was an air of downright gloom about the circus. Men, women and children were in the "dumps, " a most unnatural condition to exist among these whilom, light-hearted adventurers. When they lifted up their heads, it was to deliver continuous anathemas to the leaden skies; when they allowed them to droop, it was to curse the soggy earth.

The new clown saw but little of Mrs. Braddock and Christine. Braddock's failure to extract money from him made that worthy so disagreeable that his wife and daughter were in mortal terror of his threats to turn the boy adrift if he caught them "coddling" him.

David's close associates were the Noakeses, the contortionist and two or three rather engaging acrobats. As for the women of the company, he had but little to do with them, except in the most perfunctory way. He was always polite, gallant and agreeable, and they made much over him when the opportunity presented itself. They were warm-hearted and demonstrative, sometimes to such an exaggerated degree that he was embarrassed. He was some time in getting accustomed to their effusive friendliness; it dawned on him at last that they were not graceless, flippant creatures, but big-hearted, honest women, in whom tradition had planted the value of virtue. He was not long in forming an unqualified respect for them; it was not necessary for Joey Grinaldi to tell him over and over again that they were good women.

If Christine saw him while she was in the ring, David was never able to determine the fact for himself. He tried to catch her eye a hundred times a day; he looked for a single smile that he might have claimed for his own. Once he caught her in his arms when she stumbled after leaping from the horse at the end of her act. It was very gracefully done on his part. She whispered "Thank you, " but did not smile, and therein he was exalted. There was no day in which he failed to perform some simple act of gallantry for her and Mrs. Braddock, always with an unobtrusive modesty that pleased them. Sometimes he left spring flowers for them; on other occasions he bought sweetmeats and pastry in the towns and smuggled them into their hands, not without a conscious glow of embarrassment and guilt. He was ever ready to seize upon the slightest excuse to be of service to them, despite the fact that they resolutely held aloof from him. The entire company of performers understood the situation and cultivated a rather malicious delight in abetting his clandestine courtesies.

It was no other than the queen of equestrians, Mademoiselle Denise (in reality an Irish woman with three children who attended school and a husband who never had attended one, although he was an exceptionally brilliant man when it came to head balancing)—it was Denise who, one rainy evening, brought Christine and David together between performances in a most satisfying manner by taking the former to visit a fortune-teller whose home was quite a distance from the show lot, first having sent David there on a perfectly plausible pretext. The young people met on the sidewalk in front of the house bearing the number Mademoiselle Denise had given to David. To say that he was surprised at seeing Christine under the same umbrella with the older woman would be putting it very tamely; to add that both of them were shy and uneasy is certainly superfluous. Moreover, when I say that David was obliged to inform Mademoiselle Denise that she had given him the wrong number; that a hod-carrier instead of a sorceress dwelt within, — when I say this, you may have an idea that there was no fortune-teller in the beginning. And then, when the head-balancing husband suddenly appeared and walked off with Denise, leaving the embarrassed youngsters to follow at any pace they chose, you may be quite certain that there was a conspiracy afoot.

Christine walked demurely beside David, under a rigid umbrella. They were seven blocks from the circus lot; it was quite dark and drizzly. For the first two blocks they had nothing to say to each other, except to venture the information that it was raining. In the second block, a very lonely stretch indeed, David, whose eyes had not left the backs of the wily couple ahead, regained his composure and with it his natural gallantry.

"Perhaps you had better take my arm, Miss—Miss Christine, " he said stiffly.

She took it, rather awkwardly perhaps but very resolutely.

"I thought I heard something in the bushes back there, " she said in extenuation.

"It was the wind, " he vouchsafed, but his thoughts went at once to Blake. Involuntarily he looked over his shoulder and quickened his pace. She felt his arm stiffen.

"I'm quite sure it was a cow, " she said.

"Are you afraid of cows? "

"Dreadfully. "

"And you're not afraid of elephants or camels? "

"Oh, dear, no; they're tame. " She seemed in doubt as to the wisdom of expressing aloud the thoughts that troubled her. Twice she peered up into the face of her companion. Then she resolutely delivered herself. "I *do* hope father won't see us, David. "

"You poor girl, " he cried gently. "I'm sorry if this gets you into trouble. Denise didn't tell me. She—"

"Oh, Denise did it on purpose, " she said, quite glibly. "I suppose she thinks we're going to fall in love with each other. "

David was grateful to the darkness. It hid his blush of confusion.

"But that's perfectly silly, " went on the soft voice at his elbow. "I just want to be your friend, David. My mother adores you. So do I, but in just the same way that she does. I—I couldn't think of being so ridiculous as to fall in love with you. "

He resented this. "I don't see why you say that, " he said, rather stiffly. "But, " very hastily, "I'm not asking you to do it. Please don't misunderstand me. I—"

"Mother and I are so sorry for you, David, " she went on earnestly. "We—we don't believe a word of—of—well, you know. " She was suddenly distressed.

"How do you know that I'm not guilty? " he cried bitterly. "You have only my word for it. Of course, I'd deny it. Anybody would, even if he was as guilty as sin. I—I might have done it, for all you know. "

"Oh, don't—don't talk like that, David! "

"Nearly every one with the show thinks I did it. It doesn't matter to them, either. They like me just as well. It's—it's as if I were a friendless, homeless dog. They're tender-hearted. They'd do as much for the dog, every time. I like them for it. I'll not forget everybody's kindness to me and—and their indifference. "

"Indifference, David? "

"Yes. That's the word. It doesn't make any difference what I am, they just say it's all right and—and—that's all. "

She caught the intensely bitter note in his voice. Christine was young, but she had fine perceptions. Her lip trembled.

"*Nobody* thinks you did it, " she cried in a vehement undertone. "Even father—" She stopped abruptly, a quick catch of compunction in her breath.

"If he thinks I'm innocent, why is he so set on keeping me from talking to you or your mother? " he demanded quickly, a sudden fire entering his brain. "That doesn't look as if he thinks I'm all right, does it? I'm—I'm not a low-down person. If I was, I could see a reason. But I'm a gentleman. Every man in my family has been a gentleman since—oh, you'll think I'm boasting. I didn't mean to say this to you. It sounds snobbish. No, Christine, your father thinks I'm guilty. "

"He does not! " she whispered. "I know he doesn't. I've heard him argue with mother about you. He has told her that he does not believe that you killed your grandfather. I've heard him say it, David. He—he is only thinking of—must I say it? Of the disgrace to us if you should be caught and it came out we were your friends. That's it. He's thinking of us, David. It is so foolish of him. We both have told him so. But—but you don't know my father. " There was a world of meaning in that declaration—and it was not disrespectful, either.

David was discreetly silent. He was quelling the rage that always rose in his heart when he thought of Thomas Braddock's attitude, not only toward him but toward his wife.

"I wish he wouldn't look at it in that way, David, " she resumed plaintively. "We—we would be so happy if you could be with us, — that is, more than you are. " She was stammering, but not from embarrassment. It was in the fear of saying something that might touch his sensitive pride.

"I—I love your mother, " he cried intensely. "She's the best woman I've ever known—except my own mother. She's better than my aunts— yes, she is! Better than all of them. I could die for her. "

She clutched his arm tightly but said nothing. The words could not break through the sobs that were in her throat. Neither spoke for a matter of a hundred feet or more. Then he said to her, rather drearily:

"Did you read what the papers said about the—the murder, and about me? "

"No. Mother will not let me read the things about crime. But, " she said quickly, "she has told me all about it since you came. "

"They made me out to be a vicious degenerate and an ingrate, " he said. "Oh, it was horrible, —the things they said about me. Just as if they knew I was guilty. But, Christine, I am going to make them take it all back. I'm going to make them apologize some day, see if I don't. " The fierce agony in his voice moved her greatly.

"Oh, if I could help you! " she cried tremulously.

He apparently did not hear the eager words.

"It all looked so black against me, " he went on, looking straight ahead unseeingly. "Perhaps I shouldn't blame them. I have thought it all out, lots of times, Christine, and I've tried to put myself in their place. Sometimes I think that if I were not myself I should certainly believe myself guilty. It *did* point to me, every bit of it, Christine. And I am as innocent as a little baby. If—if they catch me they'll hang me! "

"No, no! " she shuddered.

"Doesn't it look to you as if I really had done it? " he demanded. "Tell the truth, Christine. From what you have heard, wouldn't you say it *looked* as if I were guilty? "

She hesitated, frightened, distressed. "The papers did not tell the truth, David, " she said loyally.

"They hunted for me with bloodhounds, " he went on vaguely. "If they had caught me then, I would have been strung up and shot to pieces. You see, " turning to her with a gentle note in his voice, "my grandfather was very much beloved. He was the very finest man in all the state. I have sworn to avenge his death. I swear it every night— every night, Christine. First, I'm going to clear myself of the—the hideous thing. And then! " There was a world of promise in those two words.

"You have said that there is a man who can clear you, " she ventured. "Who is he, David? Where is he to be found? Why doesn't he step forward and clear you? "

"I—I don't know where he is. In New York, I think. He—he was sent out of the country by—by some one. Do you want to hear my side, Christine? "

"Do you—care to speak of it, David? "

"Yes. You will understand. You are good. I want you to tell your mother, too. " He slackened his pace. Both forgot that the hour for the "tournament" was drawing perilously near. "I lived with my grandfather, Colonel Jenison. My father was killed at Shiloh. My mother died when I was nine years old. I had one uncle, my father's younger brother. He was an officer in the Southern army, just as my father was. He gave my grandfather trouble all of his life. They say it was his wild habits that drove my grandmother to her grave. I knew him but slightly. When the war was two years old, he was court-martialed for treason to the cause. The story was that he had been caught trying to sell some plans to the enemy. He was sentenced to be shot. It was very clear against him, my mother told me on one of the rare occasions when his name was mentioned. But he escaped during a sudden, overwhelming attack by the Yanks. They never caught him. My grandfather, who had been a colonel in the war with

Mexico and had lost an arm, disowned him as a son. He disinherited him, leaving everything to my father. When my father was killed I became the heir to Jenison Hall and all that went with it, —a vast estate.

"A year ago my uncle Frank turned up. He came to Richmond with proof that cleared him of the charge of treason in the minds of his old comrades. Three men on their deathbeds had signed affidavits, showing that they were guilty of the very thing of which he was accused, he being an innocent dupe in the transaction. I don't know just how it all came about, but he was exonerated completely. With this to back him up, he came to the Hall to plead for my grandfather's forgiveness. He came many times, and finally it seems that grandfather believed his story. Uncle Frank took up his residence at the Hall. I hated him from the beginning. He was a wicked man and always had been. I don't believe what the affidavits said.

"Well, he soon learned that I was to be the heir. Everybody knew it. I was at the University. Grandfather had sent me there. It was my second year, for I had gone in very young. When I went home for the Christmas holidays, Uncle Frank was practically running the place. Grandfather didn't really trust him, I'm sure of that. They had a couple of violent scenes New Year's week up in the library. It was something about money. Grandfather told me a little about it, but not much. He said Uncle Frank wanted him to change his will, claiming it was not fair to him, who had been so wrongfully accused. My grandfather told me that he would never change it. He might leave a certain amount in trust for Uncle Frank, but Jenison Hall was not to go to any Jenison whose name had ever been blackened.

"One day I went up to Richmond to spend the night with some college friends. My uncle Frank was already there, on business he said. Well, I found out what his business was—accidentally, of course. He was there to see a nigger lawyer! Think of that, Christine. A Jenison having dealings with a nigger lawyer. This lawyer had once been a slave on the Jenison place, a yellow boy whose name was Isaac—Isaac Perry. When the war broke out he went with my uncle as his body- servant. He was a smart, thieving fellow, — always too smart to be caught, but always under suspicion. My grandfather had given him some schooling because Isaac's father was *his* body-servant and he would have done anything for old Abraham. After the war Isaac was made a lawyer, 'way down in

South Carolina. The judges were darkies, they say. Later on he went to Richmond and did some business for the darkies there, besides conducting a barber shop.

"Well, I happened to go into his shop the evening I reached Richmond. He was shaving Uncle Frank. They did not observe me as I sat back along the wall. I heard him tell Uncle Frank he would surely come to the hotel that night to see him. Uncle Frank said it was important and asked him to be sure and bring the papers. He left the shop without seeing me, and Isaac had forgotten me, I reckon. I wondered what business he and my uncle could have to discuss. That night I made it a point to be at the hotel. I saw Uncle Frank standing out in front. When Isaac came up he took him off down the street. I heard him say to Isaac that the hotel was not a good place for a nigger to be seen, except as a servant, even if he did come as a lawyer. So they went back to the barber shop, which was closed. Isaac opened the doors and they went in. The blinds were shut. I waited until Uncle Frank came out, an hour later. He said to Isaac, who came no farther than the door, that he would be up again in about ten days to see how he was 'getting on with it. ' Isaac said he'd have it fixed up 'so slick that it would fool the old man hisself.'

"When I went back to Jenison Hall I tried to tell grandfather about all this, but I didn't do it. I couldn't bear the thought of carrying tales. I went back to school, but I couldn't get the thing out of my head. "

Christine interrupted him, intense almost to breathlessness.

"They—they were fixing up a new will! " she whispered, vastly excited.

He smiled wanly. "I wish I could prove that. About three weeks ago I had a message from Uncle Frank, saying that grandfather was quite ill. I was to come home. When I got to the Hall grandfather was much better, and seemed annoyed because my uncle had brought me home unnecessarily. That very night he was murdered. "

"Oh! " she whispered.

"He was shot by some one who fired through the parlor window. It happened at half-past eleven o'clock, a most unusual time for grandfather to be about. He was fully dressed when they found him a few minutes after the shooting. A heavy charge of buckshot had struck him in the breast. I—I can't tell you any more about that. It was too horrible. "

"I know, I know! Poor David! "

"I was studying in my room up to a short time before the shot was fired. The house was very still. Uncle Frank was downstairs with granddaddy. I couldn't imagine what kept them up so long, talking. Finally I heard Uncle Frank go upstairs to his room. Grandfather was pacing the parlor floor; I could hear the stumping. Finally he came out in the hall and called to me. I hurried downstairs. He was very much agitated. 'David, ' he said, 'do you remember a darky we used to have named Isaac? ' I was startled. 'Well, he has become a lawyer up in Richmond. He has done very well, and I want you to know what I have done for him. You are to own this place some day — soon, I fear. I have signed a paper to-night, deeding over to Isaac the little five-acre patch on the creek where he was born and where his father and grandfather were born. He saw your uncle Frank in Richmond recently and asked him if it would be possible for him to buy the ground. He wants to put up a building to be known as the Old Negroes' Home. I have thought it over. I did not sell it to him, David. I *gave* it to him. It is all quite regular and legal. The paper is in that drawer there. You are taking the law course at the university. I want you to look over the agreement to-night or to-morrow morning, before it is taken over to the county seat. It is just as well that you, who are to be the next master of Jenison Hall, should understand all that there is in it. '

"'Has Isaac Perry been here? ' I asked, for I was strangely troubled. 'He has, ' said granddaddy, 'he brought the document over this evening. Isaac seems likely to make something of himself, after all. ' 'I will read it in the morning, ' I said, and then I told him that I was glad that he had given the ground. 'Your uncle Frank advised me to tell you of it to-night, ' said he.

"I went upstairs to my work, leaving him below. Soon afterwards I went down again to get the paper, feeling that I might as well read it before going to bed. He was reading in the back parlor. I got the envelope out of the drawer in the front room and went back upstairs without disturbing him. A minute afterwards I heard the shot. My own gun was standing in the corner. I grabbed it up and crawled through a window on to the gallery, running down the back steps. As I reached the bottom I saw a man climbing over the fence to the right. Not dreaming that a tragedy had occurred, I rushed after him. He easily got away in the darkness. Then I returned to the house. As I came near I saw Isaac Perry—unmistakably Isaac Perry—at the corner. He turned and ran the instant he saw me. When he crossed in front of the lighted parlor windows I distinctly saw that he did not carry a gun. The man I chased had one. Just then a great cry came from the parlor. I rushed up to the window to look within. One of the panes of glass had been broken.

"My grandfather was lying on the floor. Two of the servants were standing near, looking at him as if paralyzed. There was blood on his white shirt front. Oh! I can't tell you how it—"

He could not continue for a full minute or more. The girl was scarcely breathing.

"I just stood there and stared, the gun in my hand. Suddenly some one leaped upon me from behind. It was my uncle Frank and he was out of breath, very much excited. 'You little devil! ' he yelled two or three times. Then he called for help. Servants came running from all directions. I didn't know what he meant. Soon I was to learn. "

"He—he thought you killed him? " whispered Christine.

"He *said* I killed him. I was dazed—I was crazy. It was a long time before I realized what was happening to me. The—the servants and the neighbors who came in wanted to lynch me—but Judge Gainsborough, who rode over in his night-clothes from his plantation, prevailed upon them to wait—to give me a hearing. My uncle Frank would have let them hang me. I began at last to realize how badly it looked for me. They laughed at my story of the man who ran away. My uncle Frank deliberately denied that Isaac Perry had been there. I was stupefied. It came over me suddenly that—that Uncle Frank had done the shooting. He had killed his own father! "

"The monster! "

"How wonderfully everything worked out against me. The gun, with one barrel empty, for I had fired it that very day in the woods; my presence at the window; the servants who saw me looking in; my uncle Frank's tale of how he came out on the gallery above and saw me hiding in the dead lilac bushes, and afterwards creep up to the window to look in upon the thing I had done. He told of my attempt to run and of his straggle to hold me. One of the servants had seen me go down when granddaddy called to me, and again he had seen me go down quietly to the library after the paper. I did go quietly, it is true, so as not to disturb the old gentleman.

"They all rushed upstairs to search my room. Lying on my table was the long envelope. Judge Gainsborough opened it, so he says. They came downstairs and I shall never forget the look of horror in the Judge's eyes as he stood there staring at me. 'David, ' he said, 'this is a terrible, terrible thing you have done. ' I couldn't speak. 'How did you know that your grandfather had made this new will? ' Christine, the—the paper was a new will, giving everything to my uncle Frank, excepting a small bequest in money and a house and lot in Richmond, which, however, was to go to Uncle Frank in case of my death. The will looked genuine—everybody said so—even Judge Gainsborough. It had been drawn three weeks before and had been witnessed by George Whitman, who died ten days after signing, and Mortimer Simms, who, strangely enough, died three days later. "

"It was a forgery—a false will? " she cried, trembling violently in her excitement.

"I know it was—I know it. My grandfather had told me of the deed. This was the envelope and the paper. There was no such deed to be found. That makes me half believe that he did sign the will, thinking it was something else. My story about the deed was not believed. As for Isaac Perry, my uncle said that he left for New York soon after my grandfather's visit to Richmond, doubtless when the will was drawn and signed. He could not have been near Jenison Hall at the time of the shooting. Uncle Frank produced a letter from Isaac, received that very day from New York, in which he said that he was going to Europe as the body-servant of a New York gentleman who had helped him to secure an education.

"They locked me in the cellar and put a guard over me until the sheriff could come up in the morning. Christine, there wasn't a single chance for me to prove my innocence. I knew that Uncle Frank and Isaac Perry had arranged the whole devilish plot—how nicely they arranged it, too! It worked out even better than they expected, for I unwittingly damned myself. I never can tell you of my feelings when the whole thing became clear to me. I must leave that to your imagination. I was as innocent as a babe, and yet, in the eyes of every one, as guilty as ever any murderer has been in this world. My only chance to escape certain hanging lay in escape. It was after three o'clock in the morning when I began to think of flight. I made up my mind that I could never hope for acquittal. I thought only of getting away from them and then devoting my whole life to finding the proof of my innocence. Isaac Perry can prove it—or my uncle. But, my uncle will not do it—and Isaac is not to be found. I discovered that when I reached Richmond two nights afterwards. He had left nearly three weeks before, never to return, it was said.

"Well, to make it short, I hit my darky guard over the head with a chunk of stove-wood. I hated to do it, but it was the only chance. You can't kill a nigger by hitting him on the head. Then I crawled through a small hole in the cellar wall into the potato bins beyond. From there I could easily get into the back yard, provided no one was watching. They were all on the other side of the wing, discussing the murder—and me. They said I'd surely be lynched the next night. Oh, it was awful. I crawled out of the window hole and sneaked off toward the hen-houses, below the old slave building. I don't know when they missed me. I only know that I reached the woods and ran and ran till I thought I should drop. Some other time I will tell you of all I went through during the next week. You won't believe a lot of it, I know, — it was so dreadful. There were a good many times when I was ready to give up, and a good many times when they almost had me. God helped me, though. He heard my prayers. I'll never again think there is no God, as a lot of us used to think at the University. You don't know the agony of dread and fear in which I'm living now. Something tells me that they will get me and that I'll never have the chance to find Isaac Perry, to force him to tell the truth. "

"I am sure you will find him, David, " she said, but her heart was very cold.

The circus tents were just ahead of them now. The band was playing and people were hurrying along the poorly lighted streets, sheltered by umbrellas, all bound for the "grounds. "

David's lips were rigid; his eyes saw nothing of the scene ahead, nor were his ears conscious of the music.

"Christine, I am going to kill my uncle Frank, " he said, quite calmly.

"Oh, David! "

"If I find I can't clear myself, I am going back there and shoot him down like a dog—just as he shot his poor old fa—father. " His body shook with the racking sobs that choked him.

"You must not do that, " she implored, terrified. "Then they would surely hang you. "

"Ah, but I wouldn't mind it then, " he said between his teeth.

"David, you must let mother talk with you. She can tell you what to do. Don't think of—of that, please, please don't. "

He turned upon her, amazed. "Don't you think that he *ought* to be killed? " he demanded.

"Can't a judge order him to be hung? " she asked encouragingly.

"But they'd never be able to prove it on him. Christine, I—I wouldn't be surprised if he has also killed Isaac Perry. I've thought of that, too. Isaac is too dangerous to be left alive, don't you see. He drew the will and perhaps forged granddaddy's name, and also that of George Whitman, after Whitman's death. Maybe granddaddy really signed the will, thinking it was the transfer. I—"

"Do you think your uncle wanted you to be hanged for something you didn't do, —for a murder he committed himself? "

"Why not? I was in the way. If they lynched me at once, he could feel very secure. Besides, he knew of the other will, dated years ago, which is in the bank at Richmond. Of course, the fraudulent will takes the place of the old one. "

David did not then tell her of his stealthy return to Jenison Hall two nights after his flight and before the funeral. On this occasion he not only secured the envelope containing the three thousand dollars, hidden in his mother's black leather trunk, but from a place of concealment he was forced to hear such damning talk regarding himself that he again stole away, fully convinced that his wild design to charge his uncle with the crime would be absolutely suicidal.

A sharp exclamation from the girl brought him out of his last fit of abstraction. They were quite near to the tents.

"We are late, " she cried nervously. "I didn't think of the time. The band is playing the waltz—that's the second piece before the tournament. We must hurry. Oh, I *do* hope father has not missed us! "

There was abject terror in her voice.

"I'm so sorry, " he murmured, apprehending the outcome for her alone. "We must make for the rear of the dressing-tent. Hurry, Christine. "

They broke into a run, intending to make a wide circuit of the main-tops. She was breathless with anxiety. He grasped her arm to help her across the rough ground.

"If he knew, he would drive you away, " she cried. She was not thinking of herself.

Near the dressing-tent they were met by Mrs. Braddock, who had started out to look for them.

"Hurry, " she whispered. "Go in on the other side, Jack—quickly. Come this way, Christine. Your father is coming back through the main-top. Mr. Briggs and Professor Hanson are detaining him near the band section—talking of a change in the music. Oh, I've been so nervous! "

"Good-by, David, " whispered Christine, as she flew to the sidewall. An instant later she disappeared, casting a quick glance up into his face as he gallantly lifted the canvas for her to pass under.

"I'm sorry, " he murmured impulsively to Mrs. Braddock as she followed. Then he raced around the tent and bolted under the wall into the men's section.

Joey Grinaldi simply glared at him.

In two minutes he was out of his clothes and beginning to slip into the stripes.

"Here's Brad, " hissed a friendly "Courtier, " calling in through the flap, beyond which a dozen men and women were waiting to make the *grand entree*, or "tournament. "

Braddock came in, his cigar wallowing in the throes of a vacuous but conciliatory smile. Every one stood ready for a shocking display of profanity.

"Jacky, " he said, with amiable disregard for the novice's tardiness, "would you mind letting me take fifty dollars until to-morrow? There's a guy out here that threatens to attach us if I don't settle an outrageous bill for feed and provisions. I'm just forty-eight fifty short. "

No one spoke. David did not even glance at Grinaldi or the others. He knew and they knew that there was no such claim against Braddock. He hesitated for an instant only. Then it was borne in upon him that Braddock may have heard of his walk with Christine and was demanding tribute.

He picked up his coat and deliberately drew from the lining a thin, folded bit of paper. It contained all the money that was in his possession at the time. He counted off five ten-dollar bills, replaced the remaining thirty dollars inside his striped shirt, and handed the tribute to Braddock.

"You're a damn' fine boy, Jacky, " said the man. "I'll not forget this. "

Later on he demonstrated the sincerity of the remark.

He came back when the show was half over, and with vast good nature took David over to where Mrs. Braddock and Christine were standing with wonder and doubt in their faces.

"I guess it's all right for us four to see a little more of each other, " he said, but he did not look at his wife. "Jacky, you rascal, you *are* a gentleman, and as such I introduce you to my family. Let's all be friends. "

Mrs. Braddock's face went white. She understood the motive of the man. He meant to follow new methods in the effort to secure possession of David's money.

Christine beamed with delight. She kissed her father's stubbly cheek and called him a darling!

CHAPTER VII

THE BROTHERS CRONK

"Don't you tell 'im you've stuck that money away in a bank, " was all that Joey Grinaldi said when David told him of Braddock's sudden change of front. It was a sentient bit of advice, showing that the wool was not to be pulled over Joey's eyes.

"I think I understand, " said David gloomily. "But what am I to say to him? "

"Don't peep. Leave it to me. I'll tell 'im that you're talking of putting most of it into the business after you get safely over into Indiana or Illinois. That'll stave 'im off. But he's going to 'ave that money, one way or another, my lad. That's wot's on 'is mind. "

The next morning, just after the parade, David went off for a walk in the town. His thoughts were of the evening before and the half-hour he had spent with Christine. He was thinking of her wonderfully sympathetic eyes, of the live touch of her hand on his arm, of the soft music in her voice, of the delicious words of faith and confidence she had whispered. He could still feel the tight clasp of her fingers on his arm; he could still hear the tremulous note in her voice.

And how gravely she had smiled at him in the ring! What a profession of deep loyalty there was in the glance she gave him when he passed her in the dressing-tent! The world seemed to have grown brighter for him all of a sudden. For the first time in weeks he whistled, —and it was a blithe air that he lilted, for, by nature, he was a blithe lad.

His reverie was abruptly disturbed. Turning a corner he came upon a group of town boys. They were making faces and hooting at a strange figure that crouched against a high board fence. David recalled this figure at once: a squat, hunchback lad who was to be seen at times behind the counter of the "snack stand. " More than once had the strong, straight Virginian gazed with a certain pity upon the pale- faced cripple. He had been struck by the look of patient suffering in the boy's face.

But now that look was gone. The hunchback, who could have been no more than fifteen, was convulsed by rage. He was showing his teeth like a vicious dog. The most appalling flow of profanity came shrieking through his white lips. David was shocked. Never in all his life had he heard such unspeakable names as those which the tormented boy was screaming back at his tantalizers.

Suddenly he spat upon the biggest of his scoffers, following the act with a name so vile that the other leaped forward and struck him a heavy blow in the face.

This was too much for David. He dashed in and planted a stinging right-hander on the jaw of the enraged bully, sending him to the ground beside the hunchback, who was writhing there with blood on his lips.

For a second or two the fellow's companions, four in number, stood undecided. Then, with one accord, they rushed at David Jenison.

The Virginian was not skilled in the art of self-defense, but he was brave and cool and strong. He met the rush staunchly. To his own surprise his wild swings landed with amazing precision and the most gratifying effect. Two of his assailants reeled away under the savage impact of his blows. A stone, hurled by one of the young ruffians, struck him on the shoulder; another reached his face with a cutting blow of the fist. He felt the hot blood trickling down his cheek. But he stood squarely in front of the hunchback, his fists swinging like mad, half of his blows failing to land on the person of any one of his crowding, cursing adversaries.

Suddenly a new element entered into the one-sided conflict. A whirlwind figure dashed out of an alley hard by and came crashing into the thick of the fray.

"Dick! Dick! " shrieked the cowering cripple, the fiercest glee in his shrill voice.

"Always on hand, " sang out the newcomer, slashing out right and left. "Old Nick-o'-time, my lads. So you'd jump on a cripple, would you? Here's a Christmas gift for you, you hayseed! "

Singing glibly after this fashion, the tall recruit laid about him with devastating effect. Three of the surprised town boys were sprawling on the ground; another was trying to scale the fence ahead of an expected boot-toe; the fifth was being soundly polished off by the exhilarated David. In less time than it takes to tell it, five terrified hoodlums were "streaking it" in as many directions, their chins high with a mighty resolve, their legs working like pinwheels, their eyes popping and their mouths spread in speechless endeavor. Five seconds later you couldn't have found one of them with a telescope.

The hunchback had leaped forward and was clasping a leg of the tall, angry rescuer, whining petulantly: "Why didn't you come sooner, Dick! You never look out for me. One of them struck me. See! "

"Struck you, did he? I'd—I'd have killed him if I'd knowed that, Ernie. But, say, who's your friend? Looked as if he was doing business all right when I came up. Hello! They got to you, did they? Bleeding like a pig, you are. Say, young feller, never—*never* put your nose where it can be hit. I hates the sight of blood, and always did. "

David was wiping the blood from his cheek. The tall young man came over and inspected the break in the cuticle.

"Just peeled it off a little, " he announced. "No harm done. Oh, I say, you're the new clown, ain't you? I saw you last night. Put it there, kid. You're a brick. I'll not forget what you did for Ernie. "

The two shook hands. The satirical grin had left the stranger's face. He was regarding David with keen gray eyes, narrowed by the odd intentness of his gaze. David had the feeling that his innermost soul was being searched by the shrewdest eyes he had ever looked into.

"I came up just in time, " explained the Virginian, still somewhat out of breath. "They were teasing him, and then one of the brutes struck him. I like fair play. I couldn't help taking a hand. They might have hurt him severely. "

"He's my brother, " said the other, putting his hand on Ernie's misshapen shoulder. "No, I won't forget this, " he went on. "You didn't have to interfere, but you did. Plucky thing to do. They say you come from Virginia. Well, you've proved it. Thank you for doing this. My name's Dick Cronk. I'm from New York. Ernest, I haven't heard you say anything that sounds like 'much obliged. ' Speak up! "

The hunchback looked sullenly at the ground, his black eyebrows almost meeting in a straight line above his nose.

"He couldn't have licked 'em if you hadn't come, Dick, " he protested.

"See here, Ernie, " said Dick, "that's no way to act. Mr. —er—this young gentleman defended you until I—"

"I saw him looking at my—my hump yesterday. He laughed at me, " cried the boy fiercely.

David's hand fell from his bloody cheek. "Laughed at you? " he cried. "I *never* did such a thing. You are mistaken. "

"What were you laughing at, then? " demanded the unfortunate boy, made over-sensitive by his dread of ridicule.

"I don't remember that I laughed, " said David, perplexed and distressed.

"Well, you did, " defiantly.

David caught the look of profound embarrassment in Dick Cronk's face. He felt a sharp pity for him, though he could not have explained why.

"I'm sorry you think that of me, " he said. "And I am happy to have come to your assistance just now. Let's be friends. "

Dick pushed Ernie forward, gently but firmly. The hunchback extended his hand grudgingly.

"All right, " he said sulkily.

"Come on! " said Dick, suddenly alert. "The cops will be along here directly. Let's get back to the lot. I'm not particularly anxious to get pinched just now. "

He winked at David in a most mysterious way, and then grinned broadly. David looked puzzled. Then a deep flush spread over his unstained cheek.

"You mean because you are with me? " he demanded.

Dick Cronk stared. "What's that got to do with me? Oh! " He appeared to recall something to mind. "I didn't mean anything like that, " he hastened to explain. "As far as that goes, I guess you're in worse company than I am at the present moment. "

With this enigmatic rejoinder he proceeded to collect three trophies of the battle and toss them over the high board fence. Three of their late enemies had neglected to pick up their hats as they scuttled off the field of carnage.

"None of them worth keeping, " was his contemptuous remark as he started off briskly in the direction of the circus lot.

For the first time in many days the sun was shining. David announced that he would proceed on his walk toward the distant hills.

"Better come along with me, " advised Dick, halting abruptly. "The cops will get wind of this. They jerk up a circus man on the slightest excuse. It's something of an honor, I believe, to land one of us in jail. The darned rubes talk about it for weeks afterwards, telling how they nailed a desperate character. Everybody connected with a show is a regular devil in their eyes. And that reminds me. I had my lamps on a couple of blue boys down the street as I came up. We'd better go up this alley. "

The three of them turned into the narrow alley and walked briskly along, Dick Cronk regaling the perplexed David with airy comments on the methods employed by rustic police in their efforts to preserve the city from the depredations of circus followers and scalawags. He was a revelation to the young Virginian.

Despite his jaunty, casual manner, there was a certain keen watchfulness in his face, an alert gleam in his lively eyes. He seemed to be taking in everything as they ambled through the alley. When they approached the intersecting street his gaze seemed to project itself far ahead, even to the scouring of the thoroughfare in both directions.

"I think those two cops are still at the corner below, " he remarked. " We'll turn to the left without looking to the right. "

They turned to the left.

"Yes, " said Dick, who, so far as David could see, had not glanced to the right, "they're still there. Let me tell you one thing, pardner. If a cop ever stops you and begins asking questions, just you tell him you're a performer. You can always prove it, whether you are one or not. " He drew forth a short black pipe. "Heigho! I'm glad to be back with the show. " There was a world of satisfaction in the way he said it.

"Are you a performer? " asked David, glancing out of the corner of his eye at the long, supple figure. The fellow was filling his pipe.

Dick Cronk laughed softly. "Yes. I've been performing on the perpendicular bars for the past two weeks. Not the horizontal bars, mind you. Banks and Davis do that act. Climbing up and down the bars has been my job lately. "

"You mean? "

"Even the innocent must suffer sometimes, " quoth the nonchalant philosopher. It was sharply revealed to David that he had been in jail.

Three abreast they moved down the main street of the town, soon mingling with the throngs of country people in the neighborhood of the public square. Dick Cronk's hands were in his trouser pockets; his shoulders were thrown back, his chin elevated, his long legs stepping out freely, confidently. His stiff black hat was cocked airily over his right ear. He was rather flashily dressed, but he had the ease of manner that enabled him to carry his clothed with peculiar unobtrusiveness. They were threadbare and untidy, if you took the pains to look closely; but you never thought of looking closely; you merely took in the general effect, which was rather pleasing than otherwise.

The face of this debonair knight of Vagabondia was curiously attractive, though not what you would call handsome. The features were too pronounced, the lips too prone to twist into satirical grimaces. His dark hair grew rather low on his wide forehead; it always looked straight and damp. The nose was long and pointed. When he whistled— which was almost incessantly—the tip of it appeared to protrude at least half an inch farther out from his face and to assume a new elevation. His chin was square and his neck was long. Swift-moving gray eyes twinkled good-humoredly under a frank, open brow.

"Are you going to be with the show the rest of the summer? " asked David hesitatingly, at one stage of their conversation.

"I don't know, " said the other, pursing his lips. "I can't say that I like Braddock's greedy ways. He wants too much in the divvy. There's plenty of shows nowadays that don't ask anything off of us. But Brad's got to have a slice of it. See? I've been thinking a little of Barnum or Van Amberg. "

Ernie spoke up shrilly. "You bet your life he ain't going to leave the show. " Dick turned pink about the ears.

"Never mind that, kid, " he said uneasily. David instinctively knew that there was a girl in the balance.

Dick had the wonderful knack of "spotting" a policeman two blocks away. At times this quality in him was positively uncanny.

"I can see 'em through a brick wall, " he said to David. "I guess it must be second sight. "

"It's second smell, " said Ernie briefly.

They came at length to the show grounds. Here, to David's amazement, every one they met greeted the tall youth with a shout of joy. He shook hands with all of them, from the hostler to the manager, from the "butcher" to the highest-priced performer, without any apparent distinction.

"Hello, Dick, old boy! " was the universal greeting.

"Hello, kid! " was his genial response, to young and old alike. Women, sunning themselves, waved their hands gayly at him; some of them wafted kisses—which he gallantly returned. Old Joey Noakes took his pipe out of his mouth, crinkled his face up into a mighty smile, and exclaimed:

"It's good for sore eyes to see you again, Dicky. How was it this time? "

"I liked the stone pile better than the chuck they gave us. Gee whiz, I'll never get pinched in that burg again. "

David turned away for a moment to speak to some one. When he looked again, Dick Cronk had disappeared.

"Where is he? " he asked of old Joey.

"He's 'arf-way uptown by this time, " said the clown quizzically.

"Who is he, Joey? "

Joey looked surprised. "Don't you know Artful Dick Cronk? " he demanded. "Why, Jacky, he's the slickest dip—that's short for pickpocket—in the United States. He's the king of all the glue-fingers, that boy is. My eye, 'ow he can do wot he does, I can't for the life of me see. " He then went into a long dissertation on the astonishing accomplishments of Artful Dick Cronk.

"And you all associate with him? " cried David, openly surprised.

"Certain sure. Why not? He's the most honest dip I ever see. He wouldn't touch a thing belonging to one of us—not a thing. He works only on these 'ere rich blokes wot thinks we're scum and vermin. But, I say, Jacky, " he interrupted himself to say sagely, "I wouldn't be seen with 'im too often if I was you. He *does* have to make some very sudden escapes sometimes, unexpected like, and I doubt if you can dodge as well as he can. If that feller was to give up lifting pocket- books, he could be the grandest lawyer in ten states. Wot he don't know about the law nobody else does. Experience is a wonderful teacher. He comes by 'is name rightly, he does, —Artful Dick. I've larfed myself sick many a time listening to 'ow he lifted things. Once he actually took a feller's pocket-book out of 'is inside westcut pocket, removed the bills, signed a little receipt for 'em, and then returned the leather to the gent's westcut. Later on he 'eard the chap was going to use the money to pay off a morgidge and that he 'ad a sick wife. Wot did Dick do but 'unt him up again and put the money back, removing the receipt and substituting a fifty-dollar bill be'd filched from a wise guy in a bank, all wrapped up in a little note telling the chap to give it to 'is wife with the compliments of Old Nick. I've larfed myself to sleep wondering wot the feller thought when he found the note! " "I've never seen any one just like him.

He's a very odd person, " said David. "I think I should like him in spite of what he is. "

"Everybody likes him. He's so light-'earted he almost bursts with joy. He's followed us for two seasons, and I've never knowed 'im to do a mean or dishonorable thing, " said Joey with perfect complacency. And yet Joey Noakes was the soul of integrity! David could not help laughing; whereupon the clown hastened to add: "Except to steal. "

"I'm sorry he's that kind, " deplored David.

"He's about twenty-one, " said Joey, a retrospective light in his eye. "He first joined us as a sleight-o'-hand man in the side-show. That cussed little brother of 'is got a job taking tickets. Dick 'ad been in jail a couple of times and he decided to turn over a new leaf. He'd 'a' been all right if it 'adn't been for Ernie. Ernie didn't think he was making enough money by being honest, so he just naturally drove 'im to picking again. That boy is a little devil. You see, the trouble with poor Dick is, that he's set 'imself up to protect and provide for Ernie all 'is life. It seems that he's responsible for the deformity. When Ernie was five years old, Dick, who 'ad a wery disagreeable temper in them days, kicked the little cuss downstairs. The kid was laid up for months and he came out of it all twisted up—just as you see 'im now. Well, Dick never got mad at anybody after that. He wery properly swore he'd take care of Ernie and try to make up for wot he'd done to 'im. He said he'd beg or steal or kill if he 'ad to, to provide for 'im. He's never 'ad to beg or kill, I'm thankful to say. So, you see, he ain't altogether to blame for 'is occupation. Ernie's a miser. He wouldn't be satisfied with 'arf of a decent man's wages, if Dick minded to go to honest work; he must have 'arf of all Dick can steal, and he sets up a 'orrible rumpus if Dick don't make some good pulls. Ernie's excuse for 'is greediness is this: he says he wants to 'ave plenty to fall back on if Dick 'appens to get a long term in the pen. Who's going to support 'im, says he, while Dick's doing time? Wot do you think of that for brotherly love? "

"It's unbelievable! "

"He curses Dick in one breath and sweeties 'im in the next, " went on Joey. "Wheedles 'im, don't you see. Once Dick was in the jug for two months. Ernie wanted to kill 'im afore he got out, he was that enraged at 'im for being so inconsiderate as to get caught. They say

Ernie has several thousand dollars in a bank in New York, every nickel of which Dick stole for 'im. Dick spends 'is own share freely, or gives it away for charity, or—ahem! lends it to needy persons as 'appens to know 'im. "

"Poor fellow! What a life! What is to become of him? " cried David, genuinely concerned.

"Oh, he's got all that set down in 'is book of fate, as he calls it. He says he's going to be 'anged some day. He's just as sure of it as he's sure he's alive. "

"Just a morbid notion. "

"Well, it's his antecedents, as the feller would say. In the family, so to speak. His father was 'anged for murder when Dick was eleven years old. I daresay it's got on 'is mind, poor lad. "

"His father was hanged? " cried David, in a lowered tone. A swift shudder swept over him.

"He was, " said Joey, refilling his pipe and preparing to scratch a sulphur match on his bandy leg. "And a good job it was, too. He was a 'ousebreaker, and he 'ad a wery gentle wife who prayed for 'im every night and tried to get 'im to give up the life on account of the children. One night he got drunk and shot a perfectly 'elpless old man whose 'ouse he was robbing. That's wot they swung 'im for. I daresay that's why Dick 'as never took to drink. He says it takes the polish off from a chap's ambition. "

All this time, at the back of the "snack-stand" across the lot the Cronk brothers were engaged in earnest conversation, low-toned and serious, irascible on the part of the one, conciliatory on the part of the other.

"You know I give you half *always*, Ernie, " said tall Dick, almost plaintively. "I never hold out on you. "

"You say you don't, " snarled the other between his teeth. "You got more than twenty dollars out of that guy last night, didn't you? I know you did. "

"S' help me God, Ernie, I didn't get a—"

"He had nearly fifty dollars in the saloon. "

"I don't know where it got to, then. I nipped only two tens, I swear, Ernie. Why, I wouldn't do you a dirty trick like that for the world. "

"You done me a dirty trick once, " grated the misshapen lad. "If it hadn't been for you I'd be as straight as anybody and I—"

"Don't begin on that again, Ernie, " pleaded Dick. "Ain't you ever going to give me a rest on that? Ain't I trying to make up for it, the best I know how? "

"Yes, and didn't you let 'em catch you back there in Staunton? Is that the way you make it up? Letting me starve—almost. " He glared at the ground. "Yes, if I was straight she'd look at me, too. She wouldn't look the other way every time I come around. Oh, you don't know how it feels! She'd go out walking with me instead of that Virginian smart aleck who killed his grandpa. But just see how it is, though! She won't look at me! She won't even look at me! "

A whole world of bitterness dwelt in that cry of despair.

"If I was straight like you, she'd—she might love me. She might marry me. Just think of it, Dick! I might get her. " With the inconsistency of the selfishly irrational he added: "I've got plenty of money. I could give her fine clothes and—But, oh, what's the use? She hates to look at me. I—I hurt her eyes—yes, I hurt her eyes! "

It was pitiful. Greed and avarice had made a hateful little monster of him, and yet a heart of stone would have been touched by the misery in his eyes, the anguish on his lips. Dick murmured helplessly:

"May—maybe you can get her anyhow, Ernie. Maybe you can. Maybe— maybe. "

But Ernie's emotion underwent a sudden change. Spitefulness leaped into his eyes; the wail of misery left his voice and in its place came shrill blasphemy. After he had cursed Dick and David Jenison to his heart's content he came to a standstill in front of his unhappy brother. Sticking out his lower jaw angrily he snapped:

"Where's the sapphire ring you got from the feller in Charlottesville? "

"I—I still got it. "

"Oh, I see! " sneered Ernie, drawing back. "You're saving it to give to Ruby Noakes, eh? That's it, is it? Cheating me out of it to give to her. An engagement ring, eh? Say, you—"

"Hold on, Ernie, " said Dick sternly. "I'm not going to do anything of the sort. Why—why, I couldn't give Ruby anything I'd stole. I couldn't! "

"Aw, but you don't mind giving me things you've stole. I'm different, am I? I'm not as good as she is, am I? Well, say, lemme tell you one thing: Ruby Noakes ain't going to hook up with a sneak thief. "

"Ernie, " said Dick, going very white and speaking very slowly, "you sometimes make me wish you'd 'a' died that time. "

"I wish I had! Then they'd 'a' hung you. "

"I was only nine, " murmured Dick, trying to put his arm around his brother, only to have it struck away with violence.

"And I was only four, " scoffed the other. "Say, let's see that ring. "

Dick produced the sapphire. It was most unusual in him to carry the smallest part of his gains on his person. The circumstance struck Ernie at once.

"So you *were* going to give it to her, " snapped he.

"She wouldn't take it if I were fool enough to offer it, " said Dick quietly, dropping the ring into his brother's hand. It immediately found a new resting place in the latter's pocket.

"Maybe the other one will take it from me, " he grinned.

"You'd better not try it, Braddock would kick you to death. "

"Everybody wants to kick me, " whined the other, taking a new turn. "But, say, he didn't offer to kick me last night when I told him she'd been out walking with that guy. I seen 'em—I seen 'em sneaking in. I told Brad. I bet he raised thunder with 'em. "

Dick was looking out past the stand in the direction of the big tents.

"I'm not so sure, " he said dryly. "I see Brad and Christine and the guy you mean talking over there by the entrance. They seem to be in a specially good humor. "

Ernie sprang forward, his eyes dilated. He stared for a full minute without blinking. Then his grip on Dick's arm suddenly relaxed.

"Oh, God, how I wish I was straight and handsome like him! " he cried brokenly.

Dick did not look down, but he knew that the tears were standing in the boy's eyes.

"Don't think about it, Ernie, " he began.

Ernie shook off his hand and angrily rubbed his eyes with his bony knuckles. He sobbed twice, and then burst forth in a shrill tirade of abuse. Quivering with ungovernable rage, he called Dick every vile name he could lay his proficient tongue to.

Poor Dick offered up no word of protest, no sign of resentment. When Ernie stopped for sheer exhaustion, not only of his lung power but in the matter of epithets, the tall martyr took his hands out of his pockets, stretched himself lazily, and announced, as if it were expected of him as a duty:

"Well, the crowd is beginning to gather at the ticket-wagon. I guess I'd better be strolling among 'em, Ernie. So long. "

Ernie looked up eagerly, his mood changing like a flash.

"Good luck, Dick, " he said, his eyes sparkling.

CHAPTER VIII

AN INVITATION TO SUPPER

That same night Artful Dick Cronk had a long conversation with Thomas Braddock. David was the principal subject of discussion. The airy scalawag was not long in getting to the bottom of the fugitive's history, so far as it could be obtained from the rather disconnected utterances of the convivial Thomas. They had come upon each other in a bar-room, but Dick had succeeded in getting the showman away from the place before he reached the maudlin stage. The day's business had been good. Braddock was cheerful, almost optimistic in consequence. He vociferously thanked his lucky sun, not his stars. Convinced that this was an uncommonly clever bit of paraphrasing, he repeated it at least a dozen times with great unction, always appending a careful explanation so that Dick would be sure to catch the point—or, you might say, the twist.

"If we only had sunshine like this, " he announced with a comprehensive wave of his hand, regardless of the fact that it was ten o'clock at night, "I'd clear a million dollars this season. We've got nearly fifteen hundred dollars in that tent to-night, Dick. Twenty-one hundred on the day. A week of this beautiful sunshine and we'd be doing three thousand a day. I'd make old Barnum look like a two-spot. Did you ever see more beautiful sunshine, Dick? Now, did you? "

"That's not the sun, Brad, " said Dick, removing his pipe from his lips. "That's a canvasman with a torch. " They had arrived at the lot.

Braddock swore a mighty oath, and with jovial good-humor chucked Dick in the ribs, not very gently, it may be supposed. Dick, with responsive good-humor, seized the opportunity to deliver a resounding thump on Braddock's back, almost knocking the breath out of him. If one could have looked into the brain of the grinning pickpocket, he might have detected a vast regret that policy made it inadvisable to thump the showman on the jaw instead of the back. He had the satisfaction, however, of hearing the other cough violently for some little time.

"Don't be so rough, " growled Braddock, taking a fresh cigar from his pocket to replace the one that had been expelled by the force of the blow.

"Excuse me, " apologized Dick promptly. "Say, " he went on, without waiting for or expecting forgiveness, "tell me something about this new clown of yours. "

Whereupon Braddock lowered his voice and told him as much as he knew of the story. They sat on a wagon tongue at some distance from where the men were tearing down the menagerie tent. Dick Cronk puffed his pipe thoughtfully during the recital. One might have imagined that he was not listening.

"I don't believe he killed him, " said he at the end of the story.

"Neither do I, " said Braddock. "But it won't hurt to let him think that we're all still a leetle bit doubtful. "

"I heard all about the murder in Staunton. The sheriff was trying to head the kid off if he came through that county. We were expectin' to see him landed in jail any day. They had bloodhounds after him, I hear. " Dick Cronk's body quivered in a sharp spasm of dread.

"Say, Dick, listen here, " said Braddock, leaning closer and dropping his voice to a half-whisper. "I've been wantin' you to turn up ever since he joined us. What will you say when I tell you he's got more 'n two thousand dollars with him? "

Dick started. "What! "

"He has. I've seen it. He's lousy with it. "

"Well, he came by it honestly, " said Dick after a moment.

"How do you know? " demanded the other insinuatingly.

"Honest men are so blamed scarce, Brad, that I can always tell one when I see him. "

Braddock rolled his cigar from one side of his mouth to the other and back again before venturing the next remark.

"It would be no trick at all to get it away from him. "

Dick Cronk looked at his averted face. "What do you mean? "

"Think of what a haul it would be. "

"I suppose you want me to lift the pile. Is that it? "

"Not unless we come to a thorough understanding beforehand, " said Braddock quickly. "It's my plan, so I get the bulk of it, understand that. "

"I do the job and you get the stuff, " sneered Dick, still looking at his companion. Braddock felt that look and moved uncomfortably.

"It's too much money to let get away, " he explained somewhat irrelevantly.

"Then why don't you pinch it yourself? Why ask me to do it? "

Braddock turned upon him angrily. "Why, I'm no thief! I'll break your neck if you make another crack like that. "

Artful Dick arose. "I'm not so easily insulted, " he said with a queer little laugh. "But, say, Braddock, let me tell you one thing. I'm not going to touch that kid's wad, and you ain't either. I'm a friend of his'n, after what happened to-day. Put that in your pipe, Brad, and smoke it. "

Braddock gulped painfully. "See here, Dick, don't be a fool. We can clean up a—"

"You'd take the pennies off a dead nigger's eyes, " interrupted the pickpocket scathingly.

"I'd do anything to keep the show from busting, " said the other with the air of a martyr. "Anything to save my wife's little fortune, and anything to keep my performers from going broke. "

"I suppose your wife thinks it's all right to get this kid's money away from him, " said Dick sarcastically.

"She—why, of course, she wouldn't know anything about it. She's so blamed finicky. "

"Of course! " scoffed Dick.

"But she'd stand for it, if she ever did find it out. She needs the money just as much as I do, only she likes to appear sanctimo—"

"I hate a liar, Brad, " said Dick coolly.

Braddock arose unsteadily. "You mean ME? "

"I do, " said the thief to the liar. "You know you lie when you say she'd back you up in a game like that. "

"I've a notion to smash you one. "

"Here's your watch, Brad, and your pocketbook. I nipped 'em just now to see if I'm in practice. Oh, yes, and your revolver, too. " He laughed noiselessly as he laid the three articles on the footrest of the wagon and turned away.

Braddock blinked his eyes. As he replaced the articles in their places, he said admiringly: "Well, you do beat the devil! "

When he turned, the pickpocket was nowhere to be seen. It was as if the earth had swallowed him.

Five minutes later Dick appeared quite mysteriously in the dressing-tent, coming from the skies, it seemed to David, who found him filling a space that had been absolutely empty when he stooped over an instant before to adjust his shoe-lacing.

"Hello, kid, " said Dick easily. "Say, do you know there's a warrant for your arrest right now in the hands of the town marshal of this burg? "

David's heart almost stopped beating.

"How do you know? " he demanded.

"I just piped him and a Pinkerton guy I know by sight hunting up Braddock. Not three minutes ago. They were talking it over between 'em out there by the road. The detective's got a picture of you, he says. Somehow they've dropped on to it that the new clown is you. Evening, Mrs. Braddock. "

The proprietor's wife came up, followed closely by Christine and Ruby, dressed for the street. In an instant David repeated the startling news.

"What is to be done? " cried Mrs. Braddock, aghast.

"They sha'n't take you, David, " cried Christine.

"Where is my father? " fell from Ruby's frightened lips.

"Not a second to be lost, " said Dick. "I've got a scheme. Come in here, kid, and let me get into the tights you've got on. Tell Joey, and put the rest of the crowd on to the game, " he added to Ruby.

When the town marshal and the detective deliberately stalked into the dressing-tent a few minutes later, a nonchalant group of performers greeted them, apparently without interest.

The new clown was partly dressed, but he had not washed the bismuth and carmine from his lean face. Braddock, perspiring freely, came in behind the officers. He saw in a glance what had transpired. His cigar almost dropped from his lips.

"We want you, " said the marshal, pushed forward by the detective. The new clown looked up, amazed, as the hand fell on his shoulder. "No trouble now, " added the local officer, nervously glancing around him. He knew the perils attending the arrest of a circus performer in his own domain.

"What's the matter with you? " exclaimed Dick Cronk, jerking his arm away.

"I want you, David Jenison, for murder in—"

There was a roar of laughter from the assembled crowd of performers.

"Come off! " grinned Dick Cronk. "You're off your base, you rube. Let go my arm! "

"None of that now, " said the detective. "I've got your picture here. The jig's up, young feller. It's no—"

"My picture? " ejaculated Dick in surprise. "Let's have a look at it. I never had my picture taken in my life. "

The man held out a small solar print of a daguerreotype that David Jenison sat for the year before at college. While the marshal, in some trepidation, regained his grip on the prisoner's arm, the crowd of performers looked at the picture with broad grins on their faces.

"Wash up, Jacky, " said Grinaldi, stifling a laugh.

"Let the rubes see what you really look like, " added Signor Anaconda.

Dick Cronk proceeded to scrub away the make-up. When he lifted his face for inspection, the two officers glared at him in positive consternation.

"I guess I'm not the guy you're after, " said Dick coolly. "A blind man could see that I don't look like that picture. My, what a nice-looking boy he is! A reg'lar lady-killer. "

"You're not the man, that's dead sure, " said the Pinkerton operative, perplexity written all over his face. "We've had a job put up on us, " he explained, turning to Braddock. "Some smart aleck sent word to our branch that the real Jenison boy was a clown in this show. We got a note from some one who said he belonged to the show. They sent me up here on a chance that it was true. We had this picture in the office. The note says David Jenison joined the show three weeks ago. How long have you been with it? "

Dick Cronk was very cunning. "That's funny. I've been with it just three weeks. Say, I bet I know who put up this job on you. " He turned to his friends. "It was that darned Jim Hopkins. He's always up to a gag of some sort. "

"Where is he? " demanded the detective.

"The Lord knows, " said Dick. "He ducked a couple of days ago. Gone to Cincinnati, I think he said. He works the shell game, and it got pretty hot for him after we left Cumberland. Well, say, this IS great! I guess the drinks are on the Pinkerton office. Thaw out, mister. Charge it to the Molly McGuires. "

In the mean time David Jenison, attired in a street gown belonging to Madam Bolivar, the strong lady, was on his way to the hotel, accompanied by Mrs. Braddock, Christine and others of the sex he represented for the time being.

An hour later he stole away from the hotel, in his own clothes, and boarded a rumbling tableau wagon at the edge of the town, considerably shaken by his narrow escape, but full of gratitude to the resourceful pickpocket.

In the railroad yards Dick Cronk hunted out his brother Ernie, and, standing over him in a manner so threatening that the astonished hunchback shrank down in fear, he bluntly accused him of informing on David Jenison.

"I know you did it, Ernie, " he said, when the other began to whimper his denials. "You've done a lot of sneakin' things, but this is the sneakin'est. If you ever peach on anybody again, I'll—well, I won't say just what I'll do. It'll be good and plenty, you can be I on that. "

"What'll you do? " sneered Ernie, but cravenly.

"Something I didn't do the first time, " announced Dick with deadly levelness. Ernie turned very cold.

"You wouldn't hurt me? " he whined.

"I'm through talkin' about it, " said Dick, turning away. "Just you remember, that's all. "

Colonel Bob Grand descended upon the show the following afternoon. His customary advent was always somewhat in the nature of a hawk's visitation among a brood of chickens: it was quite as disturbing and equally as hateful. Moreover, like the hawk, he came when least expected.

"Oh, how I loathe that man, " whispered Christine to David. She was waiting for her turn in the ring, just inside the great red and gold curtains at the entrance of the dressing-tent. Tom Sacks was peeping through the curtains at the haze-enveloped crowd in the main tent. David and the slim girl in red were standing at the big gray horse's head and she was feeding sugar to the animal. The youth in the striped tights was a head taller than his companion—for David was then but an inch or two short of six feet and broadening into manhood.

Colonel Grand had just entered the dressing-tent with Christine's father, and was paying his most suave devotions to Mrs. Braddock across the way.

"When did he come? " asked David, filled with a sharp pity for the girl, who, as yet, could hardly have suspected the real object of his visits.

"An hour ago. David, why does he come so often? "

"I—I suppose he has business in these towns, " he floundered uncomfortably.

"My mother hates him, —oh, how she hates him. I don't see why he can't see it and stay away from us. Of course, he's very rich, and he's a—a great friend of father's. They say Colonel Grand gambles and—and he leaves his wife alone at home for weeks at a time. I can't bear the sight of his face. It is like an animal's to me. Have you seen that African gazelle out in the animal top? The one with the eyes so close together and the long white nose? Well, that's how Colonel Grand looks to me. I've always hated that horrid deer, David. I see it in my dreams, over and over again, and it is always trying to butt me in the face with that awful white nose. Isn't it odd that I should dream of it so much? "

"It's just a fancy, Christine. You'll—you'll outgrow it. All children have funny dreams, " he said with a lame attempt at humor.

"I'm fifteen, David, " she said severely. "I don't like you to say such things to me. But, " and she beamed a smile upon him that fairly dazzled, "I do love the way you pronounce my name. No one says it just as you do. I hate being called Christie. Don't you ever begin calling me Christie. Do you hear? "

"I've always loved Christine, " he said frankly. Then he felt himself blush under the paint.

She hesitated, suddenly shy. "I've never liked David until now, " she said. "I've always liked Absalom better. Reginald is my favorite name, —or Ethelbert. Still, as you say, I will doubtless outgrow them. Besides, you are not David. You are poor little Jack Snipe. "

Her warm smile faded as she turned her eyes in the direction of Colonel Grand. The troubled look came back to them at once; there was a subtle spreading of her dainty nostrils.

"How I hate his smile, " she said in very low tones.

Without looking at David again she passed through the curtains after Tom Sacks and made her way to the ring, a jaunty figure that gave no sign of the uneasiness that lurked beneath the joyous spangles.

David looked after her for a moment. He became suddenly conscious of the fact that Colonel Grand was staring at him across the intervening space. Turning, he met the combined gaze of the three persons who formed the little group. There was a comprehensive leer on the face of the Colonel.

In that instant there flashed through David's mind the conviction that Colonel Bob Grand was to play an ugly and an important part in his life. Again there came over him, as once before, the insensate desire to strike that gray, puttyish face with all his might.

He had been kept out of the ring during the early part of the performance, while Artful Dick and other cunning scouts were satisfying themselves that the Pinkerton man actually had given up the chase. As a matter of fact, the disgusted operative had been completely fooled, and was well on his way to Philadelphia, cherishing the prospect of a laugh at the expense of the superintendent who had sent him on the wild-goose chase.

David kept a wary eye open for the danger signal, which, however, was not to come. He saw the Braddocks and Colonel Grand leave the dressing-tent and pass into the open air. This time Braddock walked ahead with his unyielding wife. Apparently he was expostulating with her. She looked neither to right nor left, but walked on with her face set and her eyes narrowed as if in pain. Colonel Grand, the picture of insolent assurance, sauntered behind them, a beatific smile on his lips.

The Virginian was sitting on a property trunk, dejectedly staring at the ground when Christine returned from the ring. Thunders of applause had told him when the act was over; the change of tune by the band announced the beginning of the next act—that of the strong man and his wife. How well David remembered these sudden transitions. He almost longed to be out there now, in the thick of it, with good old Joey Grinaldi at his side, dodging the ringmaster's lash and grinning at the jokes of the veteran.

The girl came straight up to him, her anxious gaze sweeping the interior. She was about to speak to him, but changed her mind and hurried on to her dressing-room. An instant later she was back, greatly agitated. "Where is my mother? " she asked.

"They went away a few minutes ago, " replied David, as unconcernedly as possible.

"Where? Where did they go, David? " she cried, her voice low with alarm.

"To the side-show, I think, " prevaricated he.

He saw the look of relief struggling into her face.

"She—she always cries when she goes out with them together, " she murmured piteously. "Oh, David, I'm so worried. I don't know why—I don't know what it is that causes me to feel this way. But I am frightened—always frightened. "

He took her little hand between his own; it was trembling perceptibly. Very gently he sought to reassure her, his heart so full that his voice was husky with the emotion that crowded up from it.

"Nothing ever can happen to your mother, Christine—nothing. Please don't worry, little girl. Colonel Grand can't—won't do anything to hurt her. Your father won't let that happen. He won't—"

"David, I am not so sure of that, " she said slowly, looking straight into his eyes and speaking almost in a monotone. He started. For a moment he was speechless.

"You must not say that, Christine, " he said.

"I don't know why I said it, " she responded, nervously biting her nether lip. Then she smiled, her white teeth gleaming against the carmine. "She'll be back presently, I know. I'm so silly. "

"You are very young, you'll have to admit, after this display, " he chided. She left him.

Joey Grinaldi came in a few minutes later and took his *protege* off to the ring, with the assurance that "the coast" was clear. All the rest of the afternoon David's heart ached with a dull pain. He could hardly wait for the time to come when he could return to the dressing-tent. At last, he raced from the ring, pursued by the inflated bladder in the hand of Joey Grinaldi, their joint mummery over for the afternoon.

Christine was sitting on the trunk that he had occupied so recently; Mrs. Braddock was nowhere in sight.

"David, " she said slowly, as he drew up panting, "they did not go to the side-show. "

He was spared the necessity of an answer by the providential return of the girl's mother. She came in alone from the main tent. A glance showed them both that she had been crying. Christine sprang forward with a little cry and slipped her arm through her mother's.

As they passed by David the mother's stiff, tense lips were moving painfully. He heard her say, as if to herself:

"I cannot—I will not endure it any longer. I cannot, my child. "

David stood before her the next instant, his face writhing with fury, his hands clenched.

"Is—is there anything I can do, Mrs. Braddock? Tell me! Can I do anything for you? " he cried.

She stared for a moment, as if bewildered. Then her face lightened. The tears sprang afresh to her eyes.

"No, David, " she said gently. "There is nothing you can do. "

"But if there should be anything I can do—" he went on imploringly. She shook her head and smiled.

As soon as he could change his clothes David hurried out to the menagerie tent. For many minutes he stood before the cage containing the African gazelle, fascinated by the nose and eyes of the lachrymose beast. He stared for a long time before becoming aware that the animal was looking at him just as intently from the other side of the bars. It was as if the creature with the broad white muzzle and limpid eyes was studying him with all the intentness of a human being. An uncanny feeling took possession of the boy. He laughed nervously, half expecting the solemn starer to smile in return—with the smile of Colonel Grand. But the deer's eyes did not blink or waver, nor was there the slightest deviation of its melancholy gaze.

A voice from behind addressed the lone spectator.

"Attractive brute, isn't he? "

David turned. Colonel Grand was standing a few feet away, gazing with no little interest at the occupant of the cage.

Young Jenison did not reply at once. He was momentarily occupied in a mental comparison of the two faces.

"It is our latest curiosity from the wilds of Africa, " he said, his eyes hardening. A Jenison could not look with complacency on a man who, first of all, had fought against his own people, even though one Jenison had been a traitor to the cause.

"The only one in captivity, " quoted the Colonel. He had the smooth, dry voice of a practiced man of the world.

"That's what they say on the bills, sir. " He was walking away when the other, with some acerbity, called to him.

"What's your name? "

"Snipe, sir, " said David, after a second's hesitation.

"I've seen you back there in the dressing-tent. You don't look like a circus performer. "

"I am a clown, " observed David coolly.

Colonel Grand came up beside him. They strolled past several cages before either spoke again.

"You are new at the business, " remarked the older man. David felt that the Colonel was looking at him, notwithstanding the fact that they seemed to be engaged in a close inspection of the cages.

"I am a beginner. Joey Grinaldi is training me. "

Thomas Braddock was watching them from beyond the camel pen.

"It may interest you to know that I am accustomed to civility in all people employed by this show, " said Colonel Grand levelly.

"Do you always get what you expect? " asked David, stopping short.

The Colonel faced him.

"Young man, " said he, after a deliberate pause, "let me add to my original remark, I *always* get what I expect. "

"Then I suppose you expect me to sever my connection with this show, " said David, looking straight into his eyes.

The Colonel smiled. "Your real name is Jenison, isn't it? "

"Yes, " said David defiantly. The Colonel was startled. He had not expected this, at any rate.

"And you are wanted for murder, I understand. "

"Yes. "

"By George, you take it coolly, " exclaimed the other, not without a trace of admiration in his voice.

"Why should I equivocate? " demanded David coldly. "You are in possession of all the facts. What do you intend to do about it? "

The Colonel's eyes narrowed. There was not the slightest trace of anger in his manner, however.

"I intend to have your wages increased, " he said quietly.

David could not conceal his surprise, nor could he suppress the gleam of relief that leaped to his eyes.

"I don't understand, " he muttered.

"I expect you to remain with this show until the end of the season, " said the Colonel grimly.

David pondered this remark for a moment.

"I may not care to stay so long as that—" he began, puzzled by the Colonel's attitude toward him.

"But you *will* stay, " said the other, fastening his gaze on David's chin—doubtless in the hope of seeing it quiver. "If you attempt to leave this show, I will—Well, a word to the wise, young man. "

"You don't own this show! " flared David. "And you can't bully me! "

Not a muscle moved in the face of the tall Colonel. In slow, even tones he remarked: "I am not cowardly enough to bully a wretch whom I can hang. "

In spite of himself, David shrank from this cold-blooded rejoinder.

"See here, Jenison, " went on Colonel Grand, noting the effect of his words, "I have a certain amount of respect for your feelings, because you are a Southerner, as I am. You have pride and you have courage. You are a gentleman. You are the only gentleman at present engaged in this profession, I'll say that for you. There is a probability that you may not be so unique in the course of a week or two. I am already a part owner of this concern. You know that, of course. It is pretty generally known among the performers that I have a creditor's lien on the business. I wish you would oblige me by announcing to your friends that I have taken over a third interest in the show in lieu of certain notes and mortgages. From to-day I am to be recognized as one of the proprietors of Van Slye's Circus. Do you grasp it? "

David, a great lump in his throat, merely nodded.

"Considerable of my time henceforth will be spent with the show. I intend to elevate you to better associations. You are of my own class. I'm going to give you the society that you, as a Jenison of the

Virginia Jenisons, deserve. It won't be necessary for you to mingle with pickpockets and roustabouts and common ring performers. There will be a select little coterie. I fancy you can guess who will comprise our little circle—our set, as you might call it. There are better times ahead for you, Jenison. Your days of riding in a tableau wagon are over. I shall expect you to join our exclusive little circle— where may be found representatives of the best families in the South and North. Portman, Jenison and Grand. Splendid names, my boy. Ah, I see Mr. Braddock over there. We are dining this evening at the best restaurant in town. Will you join us? Good! I shall expect you at six. "

He had not removed his eyes from the paling face of his auditor at any time during this extraordinary speech. He saw surprise, dismay, perplexity and indignation flit across that face, and in the end something akin to stupefaction. Without waiting for David's response to the invitation—which was a command—he smiled blandly and walked away in the direction of the camel pen.

For a full minute Jenison stood there, staring after him, his heart as cold as ice, his arms hanging nerveless at his sides. The real, underlying motive of the man was slow in forcing itself into his brain.

He was to be used! He was to be made a part of the ugly web Colonel Grand was weaving about the unhappy Braddocks!

All the innate chivalry in the boy's nature sprang up in rebellion against this calm devilry. A blind rage assailed his senses. For the moment there was real murder in his heart; his vision was red and unsteady; his whole body shook with the tumult of blood that surged to his brain. Impelled by an irresistible force, his legs carried him ten paces or more toward the object of his loathing before his better judgment revived sufficiently to put a check on the mad impulse. Instead of rushing on to certain disaster, he conquered the desire to strike for his own pride and for the honor of the woman in the case; he had the good sense to see that he could gain no lasting satisfaction by physical assault upon the man nor could he expect to help matters by reproaching Thomas Braddock for the miserable part he was playing in the affair.

Covered with shame and anger, he abruptly hurried away from the scene of temptation, making his way to the dressing-tent, where he hoped to find Joey Grinaldi.

The clown met him at the entrance to the main tent. It was apparent that he had been waiting there for his *protege*.

"Joey! " cried David, all the bitterness in his soul leaping to his lips, "do you know what has happened? "

Joey's quaint old visage was never so solemn. His pipe was out; it hung rather limply in his mouth.

"Mrs. Braddock 'as told me, " he said. "They 'ad to do it. They owed 'im nearly seventeen thousand dollars. "

"What is to become of her—and Christine? " cried the boy, his face working.

"The good God may take care of 'em, " returned the clown slowly. He puffed hard at his cold pipe. "I'm not surprised at wot's 'appened, Jacky. It's part of 'is game. Some day afore long he'll kick Braddock out of the business altogether. That's the next step. She can't do anything, either. All she's got in the world is in this 'ere show. If —if she'd only go back home to her father! But, dang it, she swears she won't do that. She'll work in the streets first. "

"She can have all I've got, " announced David eagerly.

"She ain't the kind to give up this 'ere property without a fight, Jacky. They'll 'ave to make it absolutely impossible for her to stay afore she'll knuckle to 'em. She's got pluck, Mary Braddock 'as. I know positive she 'as more 'n twenty thousand in this show. She put most of it in a couple of years ago when Brad swung over the deal with Van Slye. Since then she's put the rest in to save the shebang. I say, Jacky, I observed you a-talking to *him*. Wot is he going to do with you? Give you the bounce? "

"No, " said David, clenching his hands. Then he repeated all that had taken place in the menagerie tent.

"I will not sit at table with that beast, " he exclaimed in conclusion.

Joey led him off to a less conspicuous part of the tent. He appeared to be turning something over in his mind as they walked along.

"Jacky, I know it goes 'ard with a gentleman like you to sit down with a rascal like 'im, but I fancy you'll 'ave to lump your pride and do wot he arsks. "

"I'm—I'm hanged if I do! " cried the other.

"Well, now, just look at it from another point, " said Joey earnestly. "You can't afford to oppose 'im right now. Besides, there's others as needs you. There's got to be some one in the party to look out for Mrs. Braddock and Christine. Brad won't, so you're the one. Stick to 'em, Jacky, and if needs be, the whole show will back you up. You just go to supper with 'em. "

"You're right, Joey, " said David, his face flushing. "They stood by me, I'll stand by them. "

"The restaurant is down the main street near the 'otel, " explained the old clown. "Ruby and me will walk down with you. And, by the way, I've been talking with Dick Cronk about you. He arsked me to tell you to be mighty careful of that wad o' money. " Joey winked his left eye. "He's a terrible honest sort of chap, Dick is, so I told 'im you'd put it in a bank. Which relieved 'im tremendous. He's took a fancy to you, and he says he's working on a scheme to get you out of all your troubles at 'ome. "

"Oh, if there is only a way to do it! " cried David fervently. "If I could go back to dear old Jenison Hall, Joey! I could give them a home—for all their lives. I would do it. And you could come there, Joey—you and Ruby. Oh, you don't know how I long to be there. My old home! I—I—"

"Don't get excited now, laddie, " warned old Joey. He spent a minute in calculation. "That there Dick Cronk is a mighty cute chap. You never can tell wot he's got in that noddle of 'is. No, sir, you never can tell. "

CHAPTER IX

A THIEF IN THE NIGHT

That supper was one of the incidents in David Jenison's life always to stand out clear and undimmed. The party of five sat at a table in a remote corner of the dingy little eating-house. At no time were they free from the curious gaze of the people who filled the place, a noisy bumptious crowd of country people making the most of a holiday. The glamour was over them. Some one had recognized "Little Starbright" in the simply clad, demure young girl; the word was passed from table to table. She was stared at and whispered about from the time she entered the place until she left.

David, alert and dogged, soon forgot the boorishness of the country-folk, however, in the painful study of conditions near at hand. Colonel Grand, the host, was most affable. More than that, he was tactful. While there was an unmistakable air of proprietorship in his manner, he had the delicacy or the cleverness not to allow it to become even remotely oppressive. He managed it so that the conversation was carried on almost entirely by the two men. Now and then the three palpably unwilling guests were drawn into it, but with such subtlety on the part of their host that they were surprised into a momentarily active participation. Thomas Braddock, cleanly shaven and rather uncomfortably neat as to the matter of linen, was garrulous to the point of noisiness. He confined his remarks to the Colonel, or, in a general way, to the tables near by, with an occasional furtive glance at his wife's set, unsmiling face by way of noting the effect on her. The topics were commonplace enough: the weather, the prospects ahead, the improvements to be made in the show as business got better.

Mrs. Braddock, who sat at the Colonel's left, was so noticeably pale and repressed that David wondered if she would be able to go to the end of the wretched travesty without fainting. Unutterable despair hung over her lowered eyelids; it stood out plainly in the lines at the corners of her mouth. Christine seldom looked up from her plate. She sat next to David. He felt the restraint and embarrassment under which the girl suffered. Her cheek went red on more than one occasion when her father's coarse humor offended her delicate sensibilities; she paled under the veiled, insinuating compliments of the other. Once David's hand accidentally touched hers, below the edge of the table. His strong fingers at once closed over hers and for many minutes he held them tight, unknown to any but themselves. The dark lashes drooped lower on her cheeks; he could almost detect the flutter in her throat.

The ghastly meal drew to a close. The Colonel, leaning forward, was gazing through half-closed lids at the profile of the woman beside him. His long, white fingers fumbled with an unused spoon beside her plate. Once she had hitched her chair a little farther away from his, —an abrupt proceeding that had not failed to attract David's attention.

"Well, we will have many of these jolly little spreads, " he was saying in his oiliest tones. "Birds of a feather, you know. Ha, ha! That's rather a clever way of putting it, eh, Jack? "

Braddock laughed boisterously. He had lighted a cigar regardless of the waiter's polite announcement that smoking was not allowed.

"Yes, we will dine together frequently. I like these gay little affairs, " went on the Colonel, not even attempting to conceal his shrug of disgust for Braddock. "I am leaving for home to-night, but I expect to return in two or three days. You must all join hands in breaking me into the circus business. Don't let me be a—what is it you call it? A rube, that's it. We'll be the show's happy family. Every circus has a 'happy family. ' Yes, 'pon my soul, I like the life. I *do* enjoy these quiet, impromptu little suppers. "'

David was suddenly conscious that Braddock's eyes were upon him. He met the gaze, curiously impelled. The man's face was almost purple; the look in his eyes was not of anger, but of a shame that sprung from what little there was of manhood left in him. Braddock looked away quickly, and an instant later announced that it was time to get back to the "lot. "

In front of the restaurant they came upon Artful Dick Cronk. The pickpocket made no attempt to speak to them, but when his eye caught David's, he closed it slowly in a very expressive wink.

Braddock hurried on ahead, explaining that he was obliged to look after something at the grounds.

"I'll look after them, " said the Colonel affably. "With Jack's assistance, " he supplemented. Christine clutched her mother's arm. The Colonel and David dropped behind, for the narrow sidewalk was crowded. In this fashion they made their way to the show grounds. Mrs. Braddock and Christine did not once look behind. Colonel Grand chatted amiably with his young companion, but never for an instant was his gaze diverted from the straight, proud figure of the woman ahead.

He entered the dressing-tent with them. There he quietly said good-by to the three of them. The tears of indignation were still standing in Christine's eyes. He willfully misinterpreted their significance. A hateful tenderness came into his voice, but it did not disturb the sneer on his lips.

"Don't cry, little one; it is only for a few days, " he said.

Christine's face flamed.

"It's—it's not because you are going away! " she cried in angry astonishment. "I wish you would never come back! Never! "

He smiled broadly. "Dear me! And I thought we were getting on so nicely. Pray control yourself, my dear. I had no idea you could be so ferocious. Who does she get it from, Mary? "

Mrs. Braddock started as if stung. Her eyes dilated. It was the first time he had called her by her Christian name.

"How dare you? " she cried, her breast heaving with suppressed anger.

He shook his head dejectedly. "I have much to learn, it seems. "

She opened her lips to say more, but reconsidered, and abruptly turned away, drawing Christine after her into the women's section.

Colonel Grand turned to David. "Young man, " he said sharply, "I don't like the way you look at me. Stop! Not a word, sir! I have taken up the show business seriously. I find that our animal tamers are entirely competent. What we need here is a tamer for vicious and ungentle bipeds. There is a way to tame them, just as there is a way to break the spirit of the lion or the tiger. It shall be my special duty to deal with these unruly human beings. I hope you grasp my meaning. It would not be to my liking to begin my experiments on a young gentleman of Virginia. "

"Sir, you've already begun! " cried David in a choking voice. "You may do what you like with me, but you've just got to let *her* alone. You—"

Colonel Grand held up his hand. David seemed to be gasping for breath.

"That's the very thing I like about you, Jack, " said his late host derisively. "I can always depend upon you to look after the ladies. They will be absolutely safe while you are with them. There is a distinct advantage in having a real gentleman about. You see, I can't always be on hand to—to protect them from such bullies as Thomas Braddock. "

His allusion to Braddock was strikingly impersonal.

"I am making you my first lieutenant—no, my aide-de-camp, Jack. All you are required to do is to obey orders. Don't run the risk of a court-martial, my lad. It occurs to me that an uncle of yours has had an experience of that—but, never mind. Your first duty, sir, is to convince the ladies that I shall expect them to be in better humor when I return from the East. "

The words came from his lips with biting emphasis; the smooth oily tone was gone. There was no pretense now; he was showing his fangs.

David could only glare at him, white to the lips. He could not speak. He could only look the hatred that welled in his heart. But down in that heart he was telling himself that some day he would crush this monster.

Colonel Grand studied the clean-cut, aristocratic face for a moment. A conciliatory smile came to his lips.

"Don't forget that I am doing you a good turn, " he said. "Christie is a very pretty girl. She's fond of you. If you're smart, you'll make the most of her. You ought to thank me instead of—ah, but I see you do thank me. " He willfully misjudged the expression on David's face. "

I see no reason why you can't spend a most agreeable season with us. Jack. "

"Colonel Grand, " said David very slowly, controlling himself admirably, "if it were not that I now regard it as my sacred duty to stay with this show, I would defy you, sir, and denounce you, let the consequences be as disastrous to me as you like. I am not afraid of you. I *can* go back home—to jail—with my head up and my heart clean, if you choose to send me there. I am not afraid of even that. But I *am* afraid of something else. That is why I am ready to bear your insults, to humble myself, to submit to your—your commands. Not for my own safety, but for the safety of others. Permit me, sir, as a gentleman, to assure you that you can depend on me to carry out at least a part of your instructions as faithfully as God will let me. I mean by that, sir, your instructions to *protect the ladies!* "

He turned on his heel and left the Colonel standing there, a flush mounting to his flabby cheek.

"Braddock, " he said, a few minutes later, " I'm going to break that Jenison boy if it takes me a year—yes, ten years. "

"What's up? " demanded Braddock, rolling his cigar over uneasily. "Been sassing you? "

"People of his class do not sass, as you call it, " said Colonel Grand shortly.

"Well, shall I kick him out of the show? " asked the other, perplexed. Remembering David's money, he supplemented quickly: "Say in a week or two? "

"No. That is just what I don't want you to do. He stays, Braddock. Understand? "

"All right, " agreed the other hastily. "I like the kid. He's good company for Christie, too. *Tony* sort of a chap, ain't he? I can tell 'em every pop. I said to my wife that first night—"

"Yes, yes, you you've told me that, " interrupted Grand impatiently. "You keep him here, that's all. When I'm through with him you may kick him out. There won't be much left to kick. "

For a long time after the departure of his new partner, Thomas Braddock's attitude of extreme thoughtfulness puzzled those who took the trouble to observe him. At last, when his cigar was chewed to a pulp and the night's performance was half over, light broke in upon him. He fancied that he had solved the Colonel's designs regarding David Jenison. His face cleared, but again clouded ominously; he conversed with himself, aloud.

"By thunder, if he thinks I'm going to let him gobble up that kid's money, he's mistaken. Why didn't I think of this before? I might have known. It's the long green he's after. I wonder who told him about the two thousand. " He scratched his head in sudden perplexity. "I wonder what's got into Dick Cronk. He's too blamed good, all of a sudden. That brother of his might try the job, but—no, he'd bungle it. Besides, he'd probably stick a knife into Davy if the kid made a motion. " He began chewing a fresh cigar; his pop-eyes were leveled with unseeing fierceness at a certain patch in the "main top"; his brain was seeing nothing but that packet of banknotes. How to get it into his possession: that was the question that produced the undiverted stare and the lowering droop at the corners of his mouth.

"I've got to get that wad, " he was saying to himself, over and over again, with almost tearful insistence. Driven by the value of propinquity, he finally made his way to the dressing-tent. The performers were surprised to find him unnaturally sober and quite jovial. A certain nervousness marked his manner. He chatted amiably with the leading men and women in his company; the fact that he removed the cigar from his lips while conversing with Ruby Noakes and the Iron-jawed Woman, created no little amazement in them. He was especially gentle with his wife, and superlatively so with his daughter, both of whom were slow to show the slightest sense of responsive warmth. He proudly, almost belligerently, proclaimed Christine to be the loveliest creature that ever stepped into the sawdust ring. In spite of that fact, however, it was his plan to have her retire at the end of the season, when, if all went well, she was to go to a splendid school for young ladies.

Mrs. Braddock eyed him narrowly. She was searching for the cause of this sudden ebullience, this astounding surrender to her own views regarding their daughter. As for Christine, she was more afraid of him than she had been in all her life. This new mood suggested some vague, undefinable trouble for her mother. The girl's rapidly developing estimate of her father was taking away all the illusions she had been innocently cherishing up to the last few weeks. To her horror, she was beginning to look for something sinister in all that he undertook to do or say.

Unable to face the speculative anxiety in the eyes of his wife and child, Braddock edged off to the men's section of the tent. His furtive, nervous glances about the small apartment escaped the notice of the men who were changing their apparel. To his own disgust, a cold perspiration began to ooze out all over his body — the moisture of extreme nervousness and indecision. He took a stiff pull at his brandy flask.

His shifting gaze ultimately rested on David Jenison's neatly deposited clothing. The boy was in the ring. His "street-wear" lay on a "keester" somewhat apart from the heterogeneous pile of men's apparel on the adjacent boxes. David's "pile" was close to the outside wall of the tent. Braddock marked its location in respect to a certain side pole. He began to tremble; a weakness fell upon him; the resolution partly formed in the big tent, and which had drawn him resistlessly to this very spot, gained strength as his blinking eyes swerved their gaze from time to time in the direction of the "pile. " All the while he was talking volubly and without a sentient purpose.

After fifteen minutes he sauntered from the section, cold with apprehension but absolutely determined on the action which was to follow. Leaving the tent, he strolled off toward the ticket wagon, carefully noting the position of the men who were loading the menagerie tent for the trip ahead. A cautious *detour* brought him back to the dressing-tent, and directly in front of the spot where David's clothing was deposited.

The trembling increased. His mouth filled with saliva. He felt of his hair. It was wet. As he stood there shivering and irresolute, the band struck up the tune that signified much to his present venture, — the tune heralding the approach of the entire company of male performers in the "ground and lofty tumbling act. " It meant that the men's section would be entirely deserted for five or ten minutes.

Thomas Braddock was not a thief. He never had stolen anything in his life. He did not intend to steal now. Before he entered the dressing- tent, half an hour ago, he had justified himself unto himself: he was not going to steal David's money. His purpose was an honest one, or so his conscience had been resolutely convinced. He meant to surreptitiously borrow the idle money, that was all. Toward the end of the season, when he was vastly prosperous—as he was sure to be—he would go to David and restore the money, with interest; whereupon the grateful young man would fall upon his neck and rejoice. He needed the money. David did not need it.

What would his wife say if she came to know of this? What would Christine think of him? They were harsh questions and they troubled him. But above these questions throbbed a still greater one—the one that made his body damp with fear: was the money still in the boy's pocket, or was he carrying it with him in the ring?

Of one thing he was sure: David trusted to the integrity of his fellow performers. As for that, so did Thomas Braddock. In all his experience with circus performers he had never known one of them to steal; somewhat irrelevantly he reminded himself that circus women were notably chaste. No; David's money was quite safe in that dressing- tent.

Two full minutes passed before he could whip the conscience into submission. It was, as it afterwards turned out to be, the last stand of the thing called honor as it applied to whiskey-soaked Tom Braddock. Then he shot forward across the black shadows to the side pole he had been glaring at for a quarter of an hour. Through the lacings in the sidewall he saw that the section was empty.

When David put his hand inside the lining of his waistcoat an hour later, he turned pale and his eyes narrowed with suspicion. For an instant he permitted them to sweep the laughing, unconscious group of men surrounding him.

"Joey, " he said a moment later, taking the clown aside, "my pocketbook is gone. "

"Wot! " gasped Joey. "'Ave you lost it? "

"It has been stolen. "

Joey's face grew very sober. "Don't say that, Jacky. It was in your ves'cut—as usual? "

"Yes. The lining is slashed with a knife. "

"Jacky, are you sure? " almost groaned the clown. "Why—why, there ain't nobody 'ere as would steal a pin. No, sir, not one of—"

"I know that, Joey, " said David. He was very white and his eyes were heavy with pain. "I know who stole it. "

Grinaldi looked up sharply. Something darted into his mind like a flash of lightning.

"You—you don't mean—"

"I won't say the name. And you mustn't say it either, Joey. But I am as sure of it as I am sure my heart beats. Casey said he—the man came in here for half an hour—I can't believe he is a thief! Joey, *they* must never know. We must not mention this thing to any one. I don't mind the money. It is nothing—"

Joey wiped the perspiration from his forehead.

"Right-o! Not a blooming word. I see your meaning. By Gripes, he's sinking pretty low. But, " hopefully, " mebby he didn't do it. "

"I hope he didn't, but—" The boy shuddered. "Joey, I passed him as I came from the ring awhile ago. He was leaning against a quarter pole. The look he gave me was so queer, so ferocious, that I turned away; I couldn't understand it. But I do now, Joey. It's as clear as day to me. He had discovered that instead of twenty-five hundred dollars, there were but six ten-dollar notes in that pocketbook. Do you understand? He was black with rage and disappointment—"

"I see! Well, blow me, I—I—" Here Joey began to chuckle. "He's wondering where the balance of it is. He was trying to look through your shirt, Jacky. He—"

"Do you remember that he followed us in here and watched us change clothes? Well, I noticed that he never took his eyes off me. He was watching to see if I had anything hidden about me—a belt, a package, or—anything. Joey, it's as plain as day. "

"And he did kick that little property boy a minute ago. I remember that. He is mad! He's crazy mad, Jacky, we've got to keep our eyes peeled, you and me—and another pusson, too. We got to stand by tonight to protect 'er. He probably thinks that pusson can tell 'im where it is. "

But Thomas Braddock was not thinking of his wife in connection with the disappointment that had come to him in that last hour of degradation. He was thinking of Colonel Bob Grand and wondering what magic influence he had exercised over the boy to compel him to deliver so much money into his hands. Down in the darkest corner of his soul he was cursing Bob Grand for a scheming thief, and David Jenison for a hopeless imbecile.

Before the wagons were well under way for the next stand he was dead drunk in the alley back of the hotel bar, having first thrashed a porter who undertook to eject him from the place.

Mrs. Braddock and Christine waited for him at the lot until the men began to pull down the dressing-tent. David was with them. Not far away was Joey Noakes, the center of a group of performers, held together by his wonderful tale concerning the sensational bit of pocketpicking that had occurred early in the evening. A congressman had been "touched" for his purse and three hundred dollars while waiting for a train at the depot. The town was wild over the theft.

In the midst of the narrative, Artful Dick sauntered up to the group, coming, it seemed, from nowhere. The gossiper abruptly stopped his tale.

"They say it's going to rain before morning, " said Dick airily. "You guys will get rust on your joints if you stay out in it. Ta-ta! I'm looking for my brother. Seen him? "

He strolled on, as if he owned the earth.

"That feller'll be as rich as the devil some day, if he keeps on, " said one of the group.

That was the mild form of opprobrium that followed Artful Dick into the shadows. As he passed by the Braddocks and David, he doffed his derby gallantly. To this knowing chap there was something significant in the dreary, half-hearted smile that the mother and daughter gave him. At any rate, he took a second look at them out of the corner of his eye.

"Brad's up to something, " he thought.

The smile he bestowed upon Ruby Noakes, who stood near by with several of the women, was all-enveloping. Ruby's dark eyes looked after him until his long, jaunty figure disappeared in the darkness.

"Too bad he's a thie—what he is, " ventured the Iron-jawed Woman pityingly. She addressed the reflection to Ruby, who started and then positively glared at the speaker.

David escorted Mrs. Braddock and Christine to the hotel, where he also was to "put up" under the new dispensation. They had but little to say to each other. A deep sense of restraint had fallen upon them. He understood and appreciated their lack of interest in anything but their own unexpressed thoughts. As for himself, he was sick at heart over the discovery he had made. Not for all the world would he have added to their unhappiness by voicing the thoughts that were uppermost in his mind, rioting there with an insistent clamor that almost deafened him.

Christine's father was a thief!

From time to time, as they walked down the dark, still street, he glanced at her face, half fearing that his thoughts might have reached her by means of some mysterious telepathic agency. Even in the shadows her face was adorable. He could not see her dark eyes, but he knew they were troubled and afraid. He would have given worlds to have taken her in his arms, then and there, to pour into her little sore heart all the comfort of his new-found adoration.

For days it had been growing upon him, this delicious realization of what she had come to stand for in his life. She had crept into his heart and he was glad. Innate gallantry and a sense of the fitness of things had kept him from uttering one word of love to this young, trusting, unconscious girl. He was very young—stupidly young, he felt—but he was old enough to know that she would not understand. He was content to wait, content to watch. The time would come when he could tell her of the love that was in his heart; but it was not to be thought of now.

He walked between them, carrying Mrs. Braddock's handbag. Christine refused to burden him with hers. As they neared the business section of the town—one of the Ohio River towns—they encountered drunken men and merry-makers. A particularly noisy but amiable group approached them from the opposite direction. Christine nervously clutched David's arm. She came very close to him. He was thrilled by the contact. After the revelers had lurched by them, she gave an odd little laugh and would have removed her hand. He pressed his arm close to his side, imprisoning it. She looked up quickly, a sharp catch in her breath. Then she allowed her hand to rest there passively.

They were nearing the hotel when David impulsively gave utterance to the hungry cry that was struggling in his throat:

"Oh, Mrs. Braddock, if I were free to go back to Jenison Hall! I could ask you and Christine to come there and stay. You'd love it there. It's the finest old place in—"

"Why, David! " cried Mrs. Braddock in surprise.

"Forgive me! " he cried abjectly.

"Oh, I should love it—I should love it, David, " cried Christine in a low, wistful voice. It seemed to him that there was a strange, mysterious wail at the back of the words.

Mrs. Braddock uttered a short, bitter laugh. "How good you are, David. What would your friends think if you took circus people there to visit you? "

He replied with grave dignity. "My friends, Mrs. Braddock, include the circus people you mention. I am not likely to forget that you took me in and—"

"And made a clown of you, " she interrupted. He was gratified to see a smile on her lips. The light from a window shone in her face. Her eyes were wet and glistening.

He held his tongue for a moment, wavering between impulse and delicacy. His gaze went to Christine's half-averted face. He was moved by sudden apprehension. Was she beginning to suspect the real attitude of Colonel Bob Grand toward her mother? Was it something more than mere antipathy that filled her heart?

"See here, Mrs. Braddock, " he began hastily, "I'm right young to be saying this to you, but I want you to know that I am terribly distressed by what has taken place in—in your life. I know you hate Colonel Grand. I know he is a bad man. His new interest in this show is the outgrowth of an old one. "

She started. Her eyes were full upon his face.

"You are not likely to know any more peace or happiness here. Why don't you give it up? Why don't you leave the show? Why—"

"David, " she said, laying her hand on his arm, "you don't know what you are saying. "

"You could go back to your father, " he went on ruthlessly. "I know it would be all right. He would not—"

She interrupted him quickly.

"Who has been talking to you of my affairs? "

He bit his lip. "Why, I—well, Joey Grinaldi. He is your best, truest friend. He told me all—"

Christine was leaning forward, peering past him at her mother's averted face. The girl's clutch on his arm tightened perceptibly.

"Mother, " she said wonderingly, "what does he mean? Isn't—isn't your father dead? What is it that Joey Noakes has told you, David? "

David realized and was dumb with a sort of consternation. Mrs. Braddock hesitated for a moment, and then said to him, drear despair in her voice:

"Poor David! You don't know what you have done. No, Christine, my father is not dead. Be patient, my darling; I will tell you all there is to tell. "

"To-night? " half whispered Christine, dropping David's arm, moved by the horrid fear that there was some dark secret in her life which was to put a barrier between him and her forever.

"Yes, my dear. "

CHAPTER X

LOVE WINGS A TIMID DART

The circus encountered vile weather from that time on. Day after day, night after night, during the last two weeks in June, there was rain, with raw winds that chilled and depressed the strollers. The route of the show ran through the Ohio River valley, ordinarily a profitable territory at that time of the year. July would see the show well started for the northern circuit, where the floods were less troublesome and the weather bade fair to turn favorable. So bad were the floods in one particular region that the concern was obliged to cancel dates in three towns, lying idle in a God-forsaken river-place for two wretched days and traveling as if pursued by devils on the third. The horses, overworked and half starved, obtained a much-needed rest.

Performers and employees alike grew taciturn and absorbed in speculation as to the immediate future. No one believed that the show could continue against such distressing odds. At no performance were the receipts half adequate to the requirements; each clay saw the enterprise sink deeper into a mire of debt from which there was no apparent prospect of escape. The characteristically ebullient spirits of the performers surrendered at last to the superstitions that persistently obtruded themselves upon the notice of individuals. All manner of "bad luck" signs cropped out to sustain this multitude of beliefs. Every one was resorting to his luck stone or an amulet. Even David Jenison, sensible lad that he was, fell under the spell of superstition. He carried a "luck piece" given him by Ruby Noakes, and not once but many times was he guilty of calling upon it for relief from the general misfortune.

A bloody fight on the circus grounds between the showmen and an organized band of town ruffians came near to bringing the concern to a disastrous end. The riot happened in one of the hill towns along the river, and was due to the ugly humor of the unpaid canvasmen and the roustabouts who went searching for trouble as an outlet for their feelings. Guy ropes were cut by an attacking force of half-drunken rowdies; the canvases were slashed and wagons overturned. The oldtime yell of "Hey, Rube! " marshaled the circus forces. There was a battle royal, in which the local contingent was badly used up, more than one man being seriously injured.

David Jenison fought beside his fellow performers, who rallied to protect the dressing-tent and the terrified women. In the darkness and rain, after the night performance, the opposing forces mingled and fought like wild beasts. The young Virginian, vigorous as a colt, was a hero among his comrades. For days afterwards, every one talked of the stubborn stand he made at the rear of the dressing-tent, where he swung a stake with savage effectiveness in combat with half a dozen rioters who had cut the ropes, allowing the sidewalls to drop while many of the women were dressing.

He was fighting for Christine Braddock, who was waiting in the tent for him, instead of going to the hotel with her mother earlier in the evening. He glorified himself forever in the eyes of the terrified girl; he was never to forget the soft, tremulous words of loving anxiety she used, quite unconsciously, while she went about the task of bandaging the cuts on his face half an hour later in her mother's room, where many of their intimates had gathered for attention.

"We must find Dick Cronk and attend to his wounds, " protested David, addressing the others who were there. "He came to my assistance before any one else arrived. I think he dropped from the sky. "

Ruby Noakes closed her eyes suddenly to hide the telltale gleam that had leaped into them. She knew that Dick Cronk was fighting for her, and her alone.

"I saw him just now, " she said after a moment. "He didn't have a scratch and he is perfectly mad with joy over the whole thing. "

"He could fall out of a balloon and not even get a lump on his head, that feller could, " grumbled the contortionist, who had two very black eyes and several "lumps. "

Braddock, partially sobered by the serious consequences likely to arise from the riot, spent an uncomfortable day in the town. The circus manager succeeded in half-way convincing the authorities that his people had been set upon and were in no way responsible for the affray. Threats of suit against the town for damages had the desired effect: the authorities were eager to let the aggregation depart.

But in that sanguinary conflict David Jenison had won more than his spurs; these volatile, impressionable people, in disdain for their own positions in life, were saying, "Blood will tell. " Down to the lowliest menial the sentiment regarding him underwent a subtle but noticeable change. He was no longer the guileless outsider: he was exalted even among those who once had scoffed.

Anxiety, worry and a mighty craving for exoneration, with a glorious return to the land of his people, triumphant in his innocence, were telling on the proud, high-spirited youth. A gauntness settled in his face; there was a hungry, wistful look in his eyes; his ever-winning smile responded less readily than before; sharp lines began to reveal themselves, flanking his nostrils. His heart was bitter. The weeks had brought him to a fuller realization of the horrid blight upon his fair name; he had come to see the wreck in all its cold, brutal aspects. The realization that he was a hunted, branded thing, with a price on his head, sank deeper and deeper into his soul. Hunted! Chased as a criminal! He, a Jenison of Virginia!

Nor was he permitted at any time to feel that he was safe from arrest. Thomas Braddock, savagely disappointed on that shameful night, made life miserable for the young clown. Only a sodden hope that there was still a chance to secure the treasure kept him from actually doing bodily harm to David, to such an extent that he might be forced to leave the show. That hope, and the ever-present dread of the still absent Colonel Grand, moved Braddock to tactics so ugly that a constant watch was being observed by those who sought to shield not only the Virginian but the man's wife and child.

The proprietor was sinking lower and lower in the mire of dissoluteness. There was no longer any pretense of sobriety. He drank with vicious disregard for the common aspects of decency. He was ugly, quarrelsome, resentful of any effort on the part of his friends to guide him out of the slough in which he was losing himself. More than one kindly disposed person had been knocked down for his "interference, " as Braddock called it. David Jenison shrank from contact with him, revolting against the language he used, despising him for the threats he held over him, distressed by the snarling requests for money. No day passed that did not bring to David an almost irresistible impulse to escape this loathsome man by deserting the show. A single magnet held him: Christine. He endured torment and obloquy that he might always be there to defend her and the sad-eyed, broken woman who had defended him.

If it had not been for the plight of these loved ones he might have persuaded himself to go back to Virginia and give himself up for trial. Time had encouraged him in the belief that his innocence would prevail. He had talked it over with Joey and Dick Cronk. Both of them had advised him to stand to his original determination to find Isaac Perry before putting himself in jeopardy.

Colonel Grand's prolonged absence was the cause of much speculation and uneasiness. The entire company lived in dread of his return, yet each individual was eager to have it over with. No man liked the new partner; every one knew where his real interest lay. Thomas Braddock cursed him in secret for remaining away while the show was tottering on its last legs. Mrs. Braddock never spoke of the man, but it was not difficult to interpret the anxious, daunted expression in her eyes as, day after day, she appeared at the tent; nor was the temporary gleam of relief less plain when she convinced herself that he was not on the grounds.

There was method in Colonel Grand's aloofness. He held off resolutely, with almost satanic cruelty, while Thomas Braddock and the weather brought the show to the last stages of desperation. At the psychological moment he would present himself and exact his pound of flesh.

Christine's attitude toward her father changed forever on the night of David's luckless appeal. She had the whole story of her mother's life before she went to bed that night. From that unhappy hour of truth she gave all of her love to the abused gentlewoman whose willfulness and folly had resulted in her own appearance in the world. The knowledge that David knew the story, with all others, at first raised a sombre barrier between them, which was broken down by the young man's tender consideration and devotion.

She was no longer the gay, sprightly creature he had known at first. Now she lived well within herself, a curb on her spirits that seldom relaxed except when she was happily alone with her mother and David. Then she breathed freely and cast off the weight that oppressed her.

There was no mistaking David's attitude toward this dainty, bewitching comrade of those troublous, trying days. The whole company saw, approved, and was delighted.

Joey alone spoke to him of what was in the minds of all. "Jacky, " he said one blustering evening, "I see how it is with you now; but is it going to endure? Don't blush, my lad, and don't flare up. We all know you're terrible took with 'er. It's nothink to be ashamed of. Wot I'm going to say is this. She's a puffect child yet and you are still a schoolboy. Are you going to be man enough when you gets older and more mature-like to stick by this 'ere puppy love that means so much to 'er now? Are you going to love 'er allus, just as I dessay you'll find she will do by you? "

"But—but Joey, " stammered David in confusion—"she doesn't care for me in that way. "

Joey closed one eye and puffed thrice at his pipe.

"Jacky, it's not to your credit as a gentleman to be so blooming stupid. "

"She's so very young, " murmured David.

"Well, love grows up, my lad, just the same as folks does, " said the old clown wisely.

"If—if I thought she'd love me when she's old enough to—" began David, his eyes gleaming.

He stopped there, confused and awkward.

Joey eyed him. "You mean by that, that you'd go so far as to marry 'er? "

David flushed. Then his eyes flashed with resentment: "See here, Joey, that's not the way to speak of her. She's a lady. She's not a—" He checked himself suddenly.

"Virginians are very 'igh and mighty pussons, I've been told, " said Joey, leading him on with considerable adroitness.

"Perhaps you have also been told that we require no lessons in chivalry, " announced David, somewhat pompously.

Joey chuckled softly. "Don't get 'uffy, Jacky. Let's get back to the fust subject. 'Ow is it going to be with you two when you've really growed up? You're a couple of babes in the woods just now. "

David was silent for a moment. Then he faced the old clown proudly. "She's perfect, Joey; she's wonderful. I expect to love her always. When she's old enough, I am going to ask her to be my wife. "

"Provided you escape the gallows, " remarked Joey sententiously.

"Yes, " said the boy, setting his jaw, but turning very white. "But she knows I am innocent. Even though I should always live under this shadow, and under another name, I would not feel that I was doing her a wrong in asking her to share my lot with me. Nothing could be worse than what she has to bear now. But, Joey, " he concluded firmly, "I am going to clear my name, as sure as I live. "

The old clown nodded his head, eyed his *protege* furtively and lovingly, and lapsed into silence. For a long time neither spoke. It was David who broke the strain.

"Joey, I wonder if you know how much Dick Cronk loves Ruby? " He put the question tentatively.

"I do, " responded Joey promptly. "He loves her so much and so honestly that he won't tell 'er about it. "

"I feel very sorry for him. "

"So do I. He's often told me that he's mad in love with 'er. But he says she can't haf—afford to 'ave anything to do with a pickpocket. He says it wouldn't be right. So he's just going on loving 'er and saying nothink. That's the way it'll be to the end. "

"And Ruby? "

"Well, she knows 'ow it is with 'im. I daresay that's why she's allus trying to get 'im to give up wot he's doing now and go out West where he could begin all over again. "

"If he did that, would you let her—"

"That's the question, my lad, " interrupted Joey very soberly. "I don't think I could let 'er marry a chap as 'ad been a thief. I—I, well, you see, Jacky, I want my gal to marry a gentleman. "

His lip twitched and he fell to studying the ground. David did not smile. He looked away, for he understood the longing that was in the heart of this lowly-born jester who did not even pretend to be a gentleman.

"No, " said Joey after a long time, "he won't even ask 'er, 'Ow can he, feeling as he does about hisself? You see, he says he's going to be 'anged some day afore he gets through. He's that positive about it I can't talk 'im out of the idee. He says it won't do no good to reform if he's sure to be 'ung in the end. He says it's destiny, wotever that is. "

He got up and strolled away, saying it was time to dress for the performance, adding lugubriously that there'd be more people in the band-stand than there'd be in the "blues. "

When the night's performance was over, Thomas Braddock came back to announce to the performers that they would have to travel by wagon from that time on, unless they chose to pay their own railroad fare.

"What's good enough for me and my wife and daughter is good enough for the rest of you, I reckon, " he said. "We travel by wagon to-night. Mary, you and Christie take the car of Juggernaut. You can take anybody else in with you that you like. I've noticed you don't want me around any more. Maybe you'll take this Jacky boy in with you. "

He left the tent, laughing boisterously.

"Now is the time for me to use some of my money, " said David, hastening to Mrs. Braddock's side. "I'll get back what Joey and Casey have. You shall not travel in those wagons. I protest against it. The rest of the performers have some of their wages left. They can tide over these bad times. But you have nothing. You are at his mercy. Don't say no, Mrs. Braddock. I mean to do it. "

He had his way. Joey and Casey and Ruby produced, between them, nearly four hundred of his precious dollars. The generous boy promptly put the entire amount in Mrs. Braddock's hands.

"It is a loan, " she murmured.

"Certainly, " he said gravely.

"Ruby, you will go with us, " she went on. "My husband must be made to understand that we are to thank you and Joey for this bit of luxury. "

Joey Grinaldi sought out Braddock and told him of his determination to share his little store of savings with Mrs. Braddock and Christine. There was a scene, but the clown stood his ground.

"I suppose I can sleep in the gutter, " raved Braddock.

"I don't give a 'ang where you sleep, Tom Braddock, " shouted Joey, angry for the first time in years.

"Where's that Snipe kid? "demanded the other.

"He's to stay with me, " announced Joey.

"The damned little sneak, he could save us a lot of trouble if he'd thaw out and hand over some of the money he's hiding. I'm going to have it out with him. He can't stay on here and let—"

"I wouldn't talk so much, Brad. Better keep a close tongue in that 'ead of yours, " said the clown meaningly. Braddock looked at him in sudden apprehension. He began to wonder what the old clown suspected.

He changed his tactics. "If Dick Cronk was only here, I could borrow enough from him to get a place to sleep, " he growled petulantly. "But, curse him, he hasn't been near us since that job in Granville, ten days ago. "

When Joey left him he was cursing everything and everybody. On the way to the hotel Christine and David walked together. She clung very tightly to his arm. Leaving the grounds, she had whispered in his ear:

"David, I adore you—I just adore you. "

"I'd die for you, Christine. That's how I feel toward you, " he responded passionately.

A sweet shyness fell upon her. The chrysalis of girlish ignorance was dropping away; she was being exposed to herself in a new and glowing form. Something sweet and strange and grateful flashed hot in her blood; the glow of it amazed and bewildered her.

"Oh, David, " she murmured timorously.

"My little Christine, " he breathed, laying his hand upon hers. She sighed; her red lips parted in the soft, luxurious ecstasy of discovery; she breathed of a curiously light and buoyant atmosphere; she was walking on air. Little bells tinkled softly, but she knew not whence came the mysterious sound.

An amazing contentment came over them. They were very young, and the malady that had revealed itself so painlessly was an old one—as old as the world itself. Their hearts sang, but their lips were mute; they were drunk with wonder.

They lagged behind. Far ahead hurried the others, driven to haste by low rumbles of thunder and the warning splashes of raindrops. The drizzle of the gray, lowering afternoon had ceased, but in its place came ominous skies and crooning winds. Back on the circus lot men were working frantically to complete the task of loading before the storm broke over them. Everywhere people were scurrying to shelter. David and Christine loitered on the way, with delicious disdain for all the things of earth or sky.

A vivid flash of lightning, followed by a deafening roar of thunder in the angry sky, brought them back to earth. The raindrops began to beat against their faces. Sharp, hysterical laughter rose to their lips, and they set out on a run for the still distant hotel. The deluge came just as they reached the shelter of a friendly awning in front of a grocery store. The wide, old-fashioned covering afforded safe retreat. Panting, they drew up and ensconced themselves as far back as possible in the doorway.

She was not afraid of the storm. Life with the circus had made her quite impervious to the crash of thunder; the philosophy of

Vagabondia had taught her that lightning is not dangerous unless it strikes. The circus man is a fatalist. A person dies when his time comes, not before. It is all marked down for him.

Of the two, David was certainly the more nervous. His arm was about her shoulders; her firm, slender body was drawn close to his. His clasp tightened as the timidity of inexperience gave way to confidence; an amazing sense of conquest, of possession took hold of him. He could have shouted defiance to the storm. He held her! This beautiful, warm, alive creature belonged to him!

"Are you afraid, —dearest? " he called, his lips close to her ear.

"Not a bit, David, " she cried rapturously. "I love it. Isn't it wonderful? "

She turned her head on his shoulder. His lips swept her cheek. Before either of them knew what had happened their lips met—a frightened, hasty, timorous kiss that was not even prophetic of the joys that were to grow out of it.

"Oh, David, you must not do that! " cried the very maiden in her.

"Has any one ever kissed you before? " he demanded, fiercely jealous on a sudden.

She drew back, hurt, aghast.

"Why, David! " she cried.

He mumbled an apology.

"Christine, " he announced resolutely, "I am going to marry you when you are old enough. "

She gasped. "But, David—" she began, tremulous with doubt and perplexity.

"I know, " he said as she hesitated; "you are afraid I'll not be cleared of this charge. But I am sure to be—as sure as there is a God. Then, when you are nineteen or twenty, I mean to ask you to be my wife. You are my sweetheart now—oh, my dearest sweet-heart! Christine, you won't let any one else come in and take my place? You'll be just as you are now until we are older and—"

"Wait, David! Let me think. I—I *could* be your wife, couldn't I? I am a Portman. I *am* good enough to—to be what you want me to be, am I not, David? You understand, don't you? Mother says I am a Portman. I am not common and vulgar, am I, David? I—"

"I couldn't love you if you were that, Christine. You are fit to be the wife of a—a king, " he concluded eagerly.

"I have learned so much from you, " she said, so softly he could barely hear the words.

"It's the other way round. You've taught me a thousand times more than you ever could learn from me, " he protested. "I'm nobody. I've never seen anything of life. "

"You are the most wonderful person in all this world—not even excepting the princes in the Arabian Nights. "

"I'm only a boy, " he said.

"I wouldn't love you if you were a man, " she announced promptly. "David, I must tell mother that—that you have kissed me. You won't mind, will you? "

"We'll tell her together, " he said readily.

"We—perhaps we'd better not tell father, " she said with an effort.

The words had scarcely left her lips when a startling interruption came. A heavy body dropped from above, landing in the middle of the sidewalk not more than six feet from the doorway. Vivid flashes of lightning revealed to the couple the figure of a man standing upright before them, but looking in quite another direction. Christine's sharp little cry came as the first flash died away, but another followed in a second's time. The man was now facing the doorway, his body bent forward, his white face gleaming in the unnatural light. David had withdrawn his arms from about Christine and had planted himself in front of her. Pitchy darkness returned in the fraction of a second.

146

Distinctly they heard a laugh. Then out of the clatter and swish of driven water came the cheerful cry:

"Hello, Jack Snipe! "

"Who are you? " called out David.

"Ha! Who goes there, you mean. Always use the correct question, kid. How can I give the secret password unless you put it up to me right? Oh, I say! I didn't see you, Miss Christine. Geminy! Ain't this a pelter? "

"Why, it's Dick, " cried David. "Where in the world did you drop from? The sky? "

The pickpocket laughed gleefully.

"Did I scare you? I guess it must have surprised you, me popping in here like a Punch and Judy figure, eh? You kind o' surprised me, too, I'll say that for you. Gee whiz, I didn't know anybody was here. Say, do you mind if I get back in there out o' the wind to light my pipe? I'm perishin' for a smoke. "

They drew back into the corner, and the jovial rascal proceeded to strike match after match in the futile attempt to light his pipe, all the while standing directly in front of David and facing the street instead of sensibly turning his back toward it. With the flare of each match his face was illuminated briefly but clearly.

A more experienced observer than David would have grasped the significance of these maneuvers. But how was he to know that Ernie Cronk had been crouching in a sheltered doorway across the street, standing guard while his artful brother entered and ransacked the store whose awning now afforded him a comfortable refuge? And how was he to know that Ernie had glared out upon their tender love scene with eyes in which there was the most pitiable jealousy, the most implacable hatred? Dick Cronk, however, knew that his brother was over there and that he must have seen these two together in the flashes. Moreover, he knew that Ernie had been carrying a small derringer ever since his experience with the hoodlums earlier in the season.

That is why he stood before David and vainly tried to light his pipe.

"Why, you are perfectly dry, " exclaimed Christine, touching his coat sleeve.

"Have you been here all the time? " demanded David indignantly.

"What do you call all the time? I was here before you came, if that'll help you any. But, " he hastened to say, "I reckon I went away before you dropped in. Now don't ask questions. If you axes no questions I'll tell you no lies. "

With the next flash of lightning he cast a furtive glance in the direction of the show window to their left. The heavy shutter was still open and banging noisily against the casing. A particularly brilliant flash a few moments later revealed to this sharp-eyed young man a huddled, black thing with a ghastly patch of white that he knew to be a face, in the doorway opposite.

"Where have you been for the past ten days, Dick? We've missed you. I've asked your brother time and again—"

"Do you no good to ask Ernie, Jack, " said the pickpocket grimly. "He ain't his brother's keeper, remember that. I've been taking my vacation, that's all. My work was likely to become too confining, so I took a notion for a change of air. "

A curious note of nervousness sounded in his voice. They were conscious of the fact that he was peering up and down the drenched, black street with quick, apprehensive eyes. Far below there was a lonely street lamp; another stood quite as far away in the opposite direction.

"The rain's lettin' up a bit, Jacky, " he said in hurried tones. "You've got an umbrell'. Say, if I was you and Miss Christine I'd dig out for the hotel. It's only a block and a half. "

"We'll wait a few minutes—"

Dick pressed his arm instantly and said: "Better go now, kid; better dig. "

Christine's sharper wits grasped his meaning. The secret of his sudden appearance was revealed to her in a twinkling. She clutched David's arm once more.

"Yes, come, Dav—Jack. I don't mind the rain. Mother will be so anxious. "

And then David understood.

"Why, Dick, you haven't been in—"

"Sh! You'll wake the guy that sleeps up there and he'll throw a bucket of water out on us for disturbin' him, " said the other with quiet sarcasm. "Besides, this is no place for a young lady. "

"You're right, " cried David in no little trepidation. "Come, Christine! " He had looked uneasily down the street. "We can't stay here. If some one should happen to shout from the windows upstairs, we'd be mixed up in—"

"Say, Jack, " said Dick, detaining him an instant, "come to Joey's room in half an hour. I've got something important to tell you. Goodnight, Miss Christine. Sleep tight. "

"Do be careful, Dick, " she cried anxiously, over her shoulder.

He laughed jerkily. "The devil takes care of his deputies. Look to yourself. God don't always take such excellent care of his angels. "

David and Christine hurried off down the street. They looked back once during a faint glow of lightning. Dick had disappeared.

While they were explaining their plight to Mrs. Braddock at the hotel entrance, Dick Cronk was leading his frenzied brother by back streets to the railroad yards. He had rushed across the street just in time to restrain Ernie in his blind rage. The hunchback, sobbing with jealousy, had started out to follow David, his pistol clutched to his misshapen breast.

All the way through the dark streets the cripple was moaning: "I'd have shot him only I was afraid of hittin' her. I couldn't stand it, Dick. He's got her. "

"Don't be a fool, Ernie, " his brother kept on repeating, greatly disturbed. "He'll be leaving the show before long. He won't stay after the truth comes out about that murder. Then maybe you'll—"

"Oh, she'll never look at me! Don't lie to me. I wish I'd 'a' shot when I had the chance. "

"You'd ha' got me in a nice mess by doing that, Ernie. The police would ha' nabbed me coming out of the store and they'd ha' said I pinked him. "

"I don't care. They couldn't ha' proved it on me, " raged the hunchback triumphantly. "I'll get him some time, and don't you forget it. Say, " with a sudden change of manner, "what did you pick up in there? "

CHAPTER XI

ARTFUL DICK GOES VISITING

Half an hour later, Dick Cronk was admitted to Joey Noakes' room at the Imperial Hotel. He came in jauntily, care-free and amiable, as if there was no such thing in the world as trouble.

Joey and Ruby Noakes and the faithful Casey were there. Mrs. Braddock and Christine had just gone to their room, David accompanying them down the hall for a private word with the mother.

He returned a few minutes after Dick's arrival, his eyes gleaming with a light they had never seen in them before. His voice trembled with an exaltation that would have betrayed him to even less observing people than these.

"Sit down, Jacky, " said Joey, putting down his mug of beer on the window sill. "I understand you've met Dick to-night afore this. Well, he's got something important to tell you—and all of us, for that matter. "

David, in no little wonder and apprehension, tossed his hat on the bed and sat down upon its edge. Ruby was sitting at the little table in the center of the room, her elbows upon it, her chin in her hands. She was gazing fixedly at the nonchalant outsider who leaned back in the only rocking-chair and puffed at his pipe. He had declined the mug of beer that had been tendered by the opulent Joey.

A big, greasy kerosene lamp hung from the ceiling almost directly above Ruby's head. She had removed her hat. Her hair gleamed black in the glow from above. Casey sprawled ungracefully on a couch near by.

"I've seen that precious uncle of yours, " announced Dick, in his most *degage* manner.

David started up. "My uncle? "

"Yep, " replied Dick, enjoying the situation.

"Where? Is—is he in town? " cried the other.

"Squat, Jacky. Don't flop off your base like that. Always keep a cool head. Look at me. If the ghost of my own dad was to pop out of that lamp chimbley there, noose and all, I wouldn't bat an eye. "

"Tell me! What has happened? " demanded David, sitting down. He observed that the others wore very serious expressions. Joey was frowning.

"Well, 't is a bitter tale, " observed Dick, in his most theatric drawl. "Don't look so solemn, Ruby. It's all going to turn out beautiful, like the story-books do. No, kid, he ain't in town, — leastwise he's not in this rotten burg. Gawd knows where he is right now. Last I saw of him was in Richmond four days ago. "

"Go on, Dick. For heaven's sake, don't you see—"

"You're anxious to know how your dear relative is, I twig, as Joey would say. Well, you can take it from me, he's very poorly. If I was him I'd—"

"Get to the point, Dick, " growled Joey.

"Don't be kidding, " added Ruby eagerly.

"All right, " said he resignedly. "Well, I've been to Jenison Hall, Jacky. It's quite a place. If you ever want to sell it give me the first chance at it. "

The others drew up to the table, David and Casey standing. The pickpocket had lowered his voice.

"I got an idea into my nut a couple of weeks ago, " went on Dick, squinting at the lamp reflectively. "I let it soak in deep and then I proceeded to act on it. I hopped on a freight one night about ten days ago, and lit out for Richmond, without sayin' a word to anybody. You had told me a good bit of your own story, David, and Joey had told me the rest, adding his confidential opinions as to what really happened on the night of the murder. Thinks I, if I can get my hooks on that uncle of his, I can make him squeal. Well, I went out and hung around Jenison Hall for a night or two, gettin' the lay o' the land. To be perfectly honest with you, I inspected the interior from top to bottom one night. That's a very nice, comfortable room of yours, David.

"Next day I walked up, bold as you please, to the front door and asked for Mr. Jenison. I had found out in the village that he was drunk three-fourths of the time and raisin' he—Cain with everybody on the place. Gawd, how they hate him down there! Up I walks, as I said before. He was having a mint julep in the gallery, the nigger said. So I walked right around where he was and introduced myself as Robert Green, of New York. He said he didn't know me and didn't want to. What a mean thing drink is! He ain't a bad lookin' feller, as fellers go. The only thing against him, I'd say, is that he looks about half crazy—sorter dippy, off his nut, batty.

"To make the story short, seeing's it's so late, I up and told him I wasn't there to be monkeyed with. I wanted five thousand dollars out o' him mighty quick or I'd tell all I knowed about the murder of his father. Well, you's orter seen him set up! I thought he was going to die on the spot. He upset his glass. Say, is there anything that smells nicer than a mint julep? There's the most appealin' odor to it. If I was a drinkin' man I'd surely go daft over—but, excuse me. I notice you are yawning, Jack, and Ruby's half asleep. "

"Go on, " said she, her bright eyes glistening.

"Then he said he'd have me kicked off'n the place. But I just mentioned having seen that nigger lawyer on the night of the murder, right out in front of the house. What's more, said I, I heard the shot that was fired. Being at that time unfortunately engaged in walkin' from Richmond to Washington, I was makin' for the nearest town when night came on. So I had to sleep in that barn down the road. I had all the dates right in my mind, and the hour, and the whole business pictured out puffect, as Joey'd say. I didn't give him a chance to do much talkin'. I sees I had him guessin', so I just sailed in and told him just how it happened, claimin' that the nigger told it to me after I had jumped out and grabbed him as he run past me in the road, thinkin', says I, there had been some skullduggery goin' on or he wouldn't be chasin' his legs off. Well, sir, that uncle o' your'n, for all his bluff, was sweatin' like a horse. Somehow, he forgot to have me kicked out.

"My story was, that after I'd grabbed the nigger he told me he hadn't done the shootin', and begged me to let him go. He said the shootin' had been done by the old man's son, and a lot more stuff like that. To clinch the business, I said the nigger, scared half to death, told me about getting a deed signed that night and about a will that had been substituted, and so on and so forth. I was just repeatin' what you said, David. Well, by gum, he was knocked silly. He saw that I did know all about everything. I could tell that by the way he swallowed without having anything to swallow.

"He kind o' got control of himself after a while, though, and began to question me sarcastic-like. First, he wanted to know where the nigger was now, and what woodpile he was in. I told him I didn't know anything about the rascal, except that he'd promised to give me five hundred dollars if I'd let him off and on condition I was never to tell his employer of what had passed between us. 'Well, ' says your uncle, 'did he give you the five hundred? ' 'No, ' says I, 'he said he couldn't do it until you had got control of the old boy's money. ' Then your uncle laughed. He said I was a fool. 'But, ' says I, 'he gave me some valuable trinkets he'd stolen from a cabinet in the house when you were not looking. He said they were heirlooms and would easily bring a thousand. ' 'You infernal liar, ' said your uncle, but he got a little paler. 'Would you like to take a peek at what's in this little bag? ' says I, pulling a leather pouch from my inside pocket. He sort of nodded, so I took out a wonderful gold snuff-box with the picture of a gorgeous French lady and a big letter 'N' engraved on it and held it up. His eyes almost popped out, but he managed to sit still. Then I showed him a magnificent gold watch, a couple of rings set with rubies and diamonds and—"

"How did you get them? " cried David, his eyes wide with amazement. "I remember them. They once belonged to my father. My grandfather gave them to me a few weeks before he was killed. But—but I did not have time to get them that night. They were left—"

"Right where you put 'em, " said Dick coolly. " In the secret drawer of that old wardrobe in your room. Kid, you've got an awful memory. Don't you recollect tellin' me they were there and that you'd give anything in the world to have your father's watch, your mother's rings and your great grandfather's snuff-box that had belonged to Napoleon Bonaparte? Well, I just went in and got 'em for you, that's all. "

"A regular magician, by cricky! " gasped Joey.

"Don't interrupt, Joey, " commanded Dick, vastly pleased with himself. His audience was fairly hanging on his words. "Well, sir, you'd orter seen him then. I thought he'd bust. He said something about his brother and his brother's watch. I didn't wait for him to get collected. I then proceeded, with a great deal of caution, to take out of another pocket a long, frayed, yellow envelope. 'This, ' said I, 'was given to me by the nigger that night. It had once contained a large sum of money, he said, but you had taken most of it, leaving him just fifty dollars. Do you recognize the envelope? '

"I held it out, but beyond his reach. He sat there for three minutes gazin' at the handwritin' on the thing, his lips moving as if he didn't know they were doing it. 'My God, ' he says, 'it is Arthur's handwriting. I'd know it among a million. ' Then he jumped up and began to curse. 'Three thousand dollars! ' he yelled, forgettin' himself. 'Did that black scoundrel say I had taken it? He lied. He took it himself. I've never seen this before. I didn't know it existed! ' Suddenly he sees that he was giving himself away, so he flops down and pants like a horse with the heaves.

"I put the things back in my pocket, and calmly says, 'I reckon you'll pony up the five thousand, won't you? ' Well, sir, what do you think he does? He pulls himself together and politely asks me to have a julep. I never did see such nerve. He says he'll go and ask the servant to make it. He has an old darky named Monroe on the place, says he, who makes the best julep in Virginia. 'No, ' says I, putting my hand on my hip pocket in a suspicious manner, 'I guess not. You fork over the five first. ' Well, he gets to thinking hard. Finally he says he'll be hanged if he'll be blackmailed. 'All right, ' says I, 'you'll find me at the tavern in the town over there if you want to change your mind. Think it over. I'll give you two days to get the coin together. '

"With that I got up and walked away, just as calm as you please. I knowed he was done for. He killed your grandpa sure, David, and he knowed he was found out. I walked right pertly, though, so's he couldn't have a chance to go in and get a gun before I was safely down the road to where my saddle horse was tied. I went back to the tavern, paid my bill, and took a train out of town. But I got off at the first station and doubled back, sleeping that night in a barn. The next day, up he comes to town. He was a sight, he was so pale and shaky. I could see he'd been drinkin' all night most. They told him at the tavern I'd gone away, up to Washington to consult the President about something, but that I'd be back in two days. I never saw a man

155

look so white as he did when he rode past the place where I was hiding, on his way back home. I hung around the post-office all day, knowing just as sure as shootin' that he'd write to the nigger, wherever he was. Sure enough, about two o'clock up comes the darky that had admitted me the day before, bringing a couple of letters.

"He stuck 'em in his pocket while he hitched his horse to the rack. I bumped into him accidental-like. 'Nough said. A minute later he was lookin' everywhere on the ground for his letters, and he was scairt, too, I'll tell you that. I went back and asked him if he was lookin' for his letters. He said he was. I said 'you dropped 'em in the wagon. ' I reached in and made believe to pick 'em up. I'd had 'em long enough to see that one was addressed to I. Perry, 212 Clark Street, Chicago. "

"Chicago, " cried David excitedly. "You must give me that address, Dick. "

"The other was to John Brainard, Richmond, " went on Dick imperturbably. "Know him? "

"He runs a gambling house there. "

"I'm not fool enough to monkey with Uncle Sam, so I didn't attempt to open the letters. It's a bad game, fooling with the government. They always get you. Anyway, I had found out all I wanted, so I let him drop 'em in the office. I took the first train to Richmond and hung around Brainard's place for a day and a half, playing a little but watchin' the boss most of the time. The second day, your uncle came in, loaded for keeps. Him and Brainard went into a side room. When they came out later on, I was standin' close by. Your uncle says this to him: 'Let me know the minute he gets here, that's all. He's sure to come, sooner or later, curse him. ' Then he went away. My job was over. I'd laid the fuse. Nothing more for me to do but to take a train for the 'great and only' Van Slye's. Here I am, and, Joey, here's that envelope you took from David and hid so carefully in the lining of your satchel. Also, David, permit me to restore to you your father's watch and your mother's—Hey, don't blubber like that! "

The tears were streaming down David's cheeks. He had snatched up and was kissing the precious bits of metal the narrator had dropped upon the table.

Ruby looked up into the face of the audacious Richard. Their eyes met and his fell, after a long encounter.

"You are perfectly wonderful, Dick, " she said. "Shake hands! "

"It wasn't anything much, " he muttered, as he clasped her hand. "Humph! " was an added bit of contempt for his prowess.

"But, Dick you blooming idiot, don't you see wot you've done? " cried Joey in perplexity. "You've put the villain on 'is guard —you've queered everything for David. He'll—"

"Sure, " put in Casey, kicking the leg of the table viciously. "He'll get hold of that nigger and find out you've lied like a sailor, that's what he'll do. Then he can tell you to go to the devil. Dick, I didn't think you was so foolish. "

"I must go to Isaac Perry in Chicago before it is too late, " said David.

"Now, just hold your horses, all of you. I know more about this particular line of business than you do. In the first place, Frank Jenison is scairt stiff. I bet he's been lookin' for me to drop in on him every day, to claim the swag, or fetch an officer from Washington. He don't know just where he stands. If I'd ha' stayed around there, he'd have a chance to get me. He could even go so far as to give me the money. Or he'd probably put a bullet in me. But don't you see my idea? I'm lettin' him worry. Worry is the greatest thing the guilty man has to fight against, lemme tell you that. It nearly always breaks 'em down. He finds I'm gone. He waits for me to come back. I don't come. He goes nearly crazy with anxiety and dread. See? Well, in time, his nerves go kerflop. He'll see ghosts and he'll see scaffolds. 'Cause why: *he knows there's a feller wandering around somewhere that's on to him.* See? "

"By cricky, you're right, " cried Joey, leaping to his feet. "I can just see 'im now. "

"But when he sees Perry and finds out, " protested Ruby, twisting her fingers.

"I'll leave it to David, who knows Isaac Perry in and out, and ask if he thinks his uncle Frank will believe a word the nigger tells him, after all I've laid up before him. Isaac Perry can tell the truth from now to doomsday and Jenison won't believe him. I've fixed Isaac proper. What Jenison wants now is to get hold of Ikey and beat his brains out. And, lemme tell you this, on the word of an experienced gentleman, that is just about what is going to happen. You let two skunks like that get wise to each other and something desperate is bound to come off. Yes, sirree, I've fixed Isaac. It's in the air. If he escapes alive he'll be lucky. "

"But I need him to establish my innocence, " cried David.

"You just trust to your uncle Frank to do that, sooner or later. I'll bet my neck, he's actin' so queer these days, and sayin' so many foolish things that everybody in the township is wonderin' what ails him. Here's a little piece of rogue's philosophy for you all to remember: A guilty man is never so guilty as when he realizes that somebody is dead sure and certain he *is* guilty. That's why they confess. "

"Dang me, I believe you, " said Joey, puffing at his empty pipe.

"Now put it this way, " went on the philosopher, turning to David: "supposin' you actually had killed your grandfather. Would your eyes be bright and your lips moist? Would you be sleepin' well? Would you be thinkin' about a gal? Now, just put yourself in that position. No, sirree, David: you'd be a wreck—a mental, physical wreck, because you'd know that your uncle knowed that you killed his father. I tell you it makes a terrible difference when you know that some one else knows. Your uncle Frank understands now that two men know—me and Perry. He knows I'm hangin' around somewhere in this world, ready to spring on him. Yep; there's no more peace for him, no more sleep. He'll blow his brains out, perhaps. But he'll also do this first: he'll write a confession. They never fail to do that, these guys that have remorse. "

David Jenison placed his hands on the other's shoulders as he arose from the chair. The Virginian's eyes were glowing with a light that dazzled the pickpocket. "Dick Cronk, " said he, hoarse with the emotion which moved him, "I would do anything in the world for you. You are the best fellow I know. I don't care what you are, I want to be your friend as long as we live. I mean that. Some day I may be able to do something half as great for you. I'll do it, no matter what it costs. "

Dick was abashed. He was not used to this. His eyes wavered.

"Oh, thunder, " he said in a futile attempt to sneer. "Let's say no more about it. It was just fun for me. Besides, David, " he continued, meeting the other's gaze fairly, "you stood by Ernie that day. Don't forget that, kid. You didn't have to, you know. "

"You chaps can settle all this some other time, " said Joey sharply. "Wot we want to get at now is this: Wot's to be done next? Is David to set down and wait or is he to go back there and wait? "

"Go back there? " gasped Dick. "Why, Joey Noakes, ain't you got a mite o' sense? You old noodle! Of course, he ain't to go back there. You mark my words, purty soon his neighbors will be advertisin' for him to come home and forgive 'em. No, sir! Wait here until something drops. Read the *Cincinnati Enquirer* every day, kid. You'll find something to interest you every little while about the Jenison murder case. You see, my buck, they're still lookin' for you. "

"I hope it all turns out as you think, Dick, " cried David fervently. He was weak with excitement. "Oh, how I long to be cleared of this awful thing! How I long for the sight of Jenison Hall! And, say, Dick! If I should go back there as master, I want you and Ernie to come there and stay—all the rest of your lives. I—"

But Dick raised his hand; his eyes had narrowed. "I couldn't do that, David, " he said, a harsh note in his usually pleasant voice. "Thank you, just the same. Ernie and me are not cut out for places like Jenison Hall. We—we'd have all the silver inside of a week—and maybe the furniture. " His face flushed as he made this banal excuse for jest.

Ruby cried out in protest. "Don't say that, Dick Cronk! You *could* be different. Oh, why don't you try it, Dick? "

He looked down. His lips worked in the effort to force a grin of derision. His hand was trembling. No one spoke; somehow they felt the struggle that was going on within him. At last he lifted his eyes to hers.

"Can't do it, Ruby, " he said quietly. "I don't think I'm naturally a thief, but it's got hold of me. If I thought there was a chance, maybe I'd—oh, but what's the use! Let's change the subject. Jacky, before we part for the night, I want to say something more to you. It hurts like the devil to say it, but I got to. You said you'd like me and Ernie to—to come down there. Well, I may as well tell you right here in front of these friends of our'n that Ernie—my brother, don't like you. Now, don't say anything! You can't understand. He's terrible bitter against you. You'll excuse me if I say there's a—a girl at the bottom of it. "

"A girl? " fell from David's lips. "You—Great heaven, Dick, you don't mean—Christine! "

Dick nodded, a rueful smile flickering about his lips. "Poor boy, " he said apologetically, "he can't help it. But it's so, just the same. And I want to ask you to be on the lookout for him always, kid. He's liable to get you some time if he can. It's dirt mean of me to say this about my brother, but I don't want him to do anything like that. He—he might get desperate, don't you see; and—well, just keep your eye skinned, that's all. You—you got to remember, David, that his dad swung for killin' a man. Mebby it's in Ernie's system, too. He's had such a horrible, unhappy life, I—I somehow can't blame him for having it in for us fellers that are strong and straight. "

David had sunk into a chair, appalled by his words.

"But he must know that Christine doesn't care for him, " he said mechanically, his eyes on Dick's face.

"Sure he does. That's the hard part of it. He's bitter jealous of you. Course she wouldn't think of a cripple like him. But he's got it into his nut that she wouldn't look at you either if you was disfigured or your back was smashed or something like that. I keep arguing with him and he's sensible when he takes time to think. But, just the same, I wish you'd keep your eye peeled. "

"I am very sorry he feels as he does about—"

"Oh, I'm not asking you to give her up, kid—not for a minute. Cop her out if you can. She's a little Jim-dandy. And, say, " he said, turning to the others, who had listened to him with grave uneasiness, "speaking of her reminds me that you may expect the new partner to- morrow. "

"Bob Grand? " growled Joey.

"Yep. " Dick had cast off his repressed air and was grinning once more, with all the delight of a teasing boy. "Old skeezicks was on the train with me this evening, but he's gone on to the next stand. He looks more than ever like a fat, satisfied slug. "

"Well, " said Joey reflectively, "we don't need him, but we do need 'is money. I 'ope, Dicky, you didn't deprive 'im of it. "

"Joey, " said Dick reproachfully, "do you think I'd take the bread right out of your throat? "

David lay awake until nearly dawn, his mind whirling with the disclosures of the night. That sweet encounter in love still lingered uppermost in his thoughts, its fires fed afresh by the brand of hope that Dick had tossed upon them, but disagreeably chilled by the prospect of new trouble in the shape of Ernie Cronk. He fell asleep, thinking of those blissful moments under the awning when he held her slim, unresisting body close to his own and they were all alone in the blackest of nights with a tempest about them. In the background of his thoughts lurked Ernie Cronk and still farther back was the ominous figure of Colonel Bob Grand.

For the first time in many weeks he did not think of the detectives — and the bloodhounds!

CHAPTER XII

IN WHICH MANY THINGS HAPPEN

With all the irony of luck, Colonel Grand brought fair weather. It was as if he had ordered the sun to shine and it obeyed him.

When the mud-covered wagons rumbled into town after their tortuous twenty-mile journey, the sun was high and the skies were clear and all the world seemed to be singing with the birds.

David had prepared Mrs. Braddock and Christine; they looked for the Colonel on the station platform as the train rolled in. He was there, waiting, as if directed by Providence, at the foot of the steps which Mrs. Braddock was to descend. He had eyes for no one until she appeared in the car door. Then his ugly smile projected itself; his silk hat came off and he bowed low. One knowing the innermost workings of Colonel Grand's mind would have understood the profoundness of that bow. He was giving her time to collect herself; he was, on his own part, deliberately evading the look of repugnance he knew so well would leap into her eyes at the first glimpse of him.

She did not see the hand he extended, but with a cool nod of her head, stepped unaided to the platform. Another man would have felt the rebuke. Colonel Grand, with the utmost deference in his manner, quietly relieved her of the traveling bag, his hat still in his hand. He sent a smile of greeting up to David and the angry-eyed Christine.

"Bring Christine's bag, Jack, " he called out. "I have a hack waiting on the other side of the depot. It is too muddy for walking. "

Mary Braddock drew herself up, her eyes flashed and her lips parted to resent this easy proprietorship. But she saw that a group of performers were staring at them in plain curiosity. She closed her lips in bitter determination, and walked off at his side. Close behind came her daughter and the young Virginian.

Joey Grinaldi addressed himself to the little knot of strollers.

"I never did see such a look as she gave 'im, " said he. "My eye! It was a stinger. Take my word for it, she's going to take the bit in 'er mouth afore you know it, and show that hyena wot she's made of. "

"Hyena, dad? " scoffed his daughter. "He's not even that. He's a rep-
tile. "

"Well, he brought the sunshine, " said one of the women half-
heartedly.

"But it's still muddy, " retorted Joey with dogged pessimism. They
trooped off after him, each one lighter hearted in spite of a dull
reluctance, simply because Colonel Grand had brought not only the
sunshine but a life-saving opulence.

Thomas Braddock, muddy, unkempt and sour, had managed to
sleep off some of the effects of the liquor he had poured into himself
the night before. True to his word, he had traveled by wagon. The
treasurer of the circus had seen to it that he was tossed like a bundle
of rags into the ticket wagon, there to roll and jostle from wall to wall
over twenty miles of oblivion.

He was waiting at the show grounds for the return of the street
parade when he saw his wife and Christine approaching, followed at
some distance by Colonel Grand and the faithful David.

"Well, " said he harshly, as the women came up to him, "you were
too good to travel as I did, eh? Had to borrow money to ride in
palace cars, eh? Fine thing for you to do, you two, —setting an
example like that. I suppose Bob Grand put up for you. I notice you
didn't mention his name to me, you—"

Christine and her mother had talked long and earnestly together on
the train coming down. The girl's cheeks had burnt during that
serious conference, to which no outsider was admitted. Her mother
had listened to an eager, piteous appeal from the lips of the girl; it
was the cry of a maiden who suddenly realizes that she is conscious
of a modesty heretofore dormant. Together they were now taking up
a very portentous question with Thomas Braddock, with small hope
of having him see the matter from their point of view.

Mary Braddock had no retort ready for his ruffianly insinuation.
"Are you too busy, Tom, to come over to the cook-tent with us for a
few moments? I want to speak very seriously about something that
has been on my mind for some time. "

Colonel Grand and David were sauntering off in the direction of the animal tent.

"Why ain't that loafer in the parade where he belongs? " demanded Braddock, glaring red-eyed at the retreating David.

"How should I know? Ask Colonel Grand. He appears to be giving directions nowadays, " said his wife bitterly.

"Well, what do you want of me? Let's have it, please. I'm busy. "

"Not out here, Tom. Come over to the cook-tent. "

Braddock glanced at her sharply. It occurred to him that she was unusually calm and serious. He turned after a moment and led the way to the cook-tent, which was always unoccupied at this time.

There, in sullen amazement, he listened to the plea of his wife and daughter. He raged back at them as they pleaded; he met Mary's calm, patient arguments with sneers and brutal laughter; he put a stop to Christine's supplications with an oath that shocked and distressed her more than anything that ever had happened to her in all her life.

"What do you take me for? " he roared, time and again, for want of better weapons to meet his wife's determined assault. In the end, he struck the table a mighty blow with his clenched fist, but he was very careful to have the table between them. More than once he had followed the impulsive movement of her hand in a sort of craven alarm, born of the conviction that he might have driven her at last to the point where a pistol would put an end to his wretched dominion. "Now, this ends it, " he shouted. "I won't hear anything more about it. She's got to wear tights as long as I say so. What the devil's got into you two all of a sudden? Lookee here, Christine, don't ever let me hear you make such a fuss as this again. By thunder, I'll—I'll lick you, that's what I'll do. I've never laid a rough hand on you yet. I've allus treated you as a kind father should. But don't drive me to forget myself. You got to wear tights and do this act as long as we run this show. We—"

"But, father, please, I—I am getting too big, " sobbed Christine.

"Too big! " he roared. "Great Scot! Why, you little whipper-snapper, you're just beginning to get big enough to look well in 'em. Too big! Say, you're just getting a shape that's worth noticin'. I suppose that peanut aristocrat friend of yours has told you it ain't swell or proper to wear tights. He'll get his back broke some of these days, if he puts ideas into that silly head of yours. Too big! Say what's the matter with you, Christine? Why, they're just beginning to talk about what a fine shape—"

"Thomas Braddock! " exclaimed his wife furiously. The girl had dropped down on one of the seats, burying her flushed face in her arms.

"Well, confound it, " he mumbled, vaguely conscious of a shamed sense of the old manhood. "I didn't mean to upset her like that. But, lookee here, Mary, I don't want no more of this nonsense about her doing a side-saddle menage act. She's a world beater at the other thing. I won't listen to this guff. That ends it. You go on doing this work with Tom Sacks, Christie. I don't give a rap whether the Jenison 'Joy' likes it or not. "

Christine sprang to her feet, her face convulsed.

"I shall ask Colonel Grand to help me. He owns part of the show. His interest and mother's together are greater than yours—"

"Christine! " cried her mother, stunned.

His face went grayish white; the cigar hung loosely in his parted lips, and a thin stream of saliva oozed from the opposite corner. He tried to speak but could not. She unconsciously had struck a blow that hurt to his innermost, neglected soul.

"I'll show you who's boss of this show, " he managed to articulate at last. Suddenly his knees gave way under him. He sagged heavily forward, dropping to the board seat. With one last desperate, stricken glare in his eyes, he lowered his head to his arms. A mighty sob of utter humiliation rent his body.

Mary Braddock hesitated for an instant, then impulsively laid her hand on her husband's shoulder. A wave of pity for this wretch surged into her heart.

"Don't, Thomas! Be a man! Everything will be well again, boy, if you'll only make a stand for yourself. I will help you—I will always help you, Tom. You know I—"

He shook off her pitying hand and struggled to his feet. Without a glance at her or at their terrified daughter, he flung himself from the tent and tore across the lot as though pursued by demons. By the time he found Colonel Grand and David in the animal tent, however, his blind rage had dwindled to ugly resentment; the overwhelming shame his own child had brought to the surface shrank back into the narrow selfishness from which, perhaps, it had sprung.

Five minutes before, he had wanted to kill. Now he was ready to compromise.

"Grand, " he said hoarsely, "I'm going to sell out—I'm going to get out of this. I'm going to Cincinnati to-night and look up Barnum's man. He's ready to buy. "

Colonel Grand eyed him shrewdly. He could see that something had shaken the man tremendously. The Colonel believed in strong measures. He knew precisely how to meet this man's impulses. In his time he had seen hundreds of desperate men.

"Tom, you're drunk, " he announced coldly. "When you are sober you'll kick yourself for the thought. Go and lie down awhile. I won't talk with you while you're in this condition. "

"Drunk? " gasped Braddock. "Bob, so help me, I'm not drunk, " he almost whined.

"Then you must be crazy, " observed the other, walking away.

David saw an opportunity to escape the company of both. He was edging away when Braddock stopped him.

"Say, you! I want to give you a bit of advice. If you go to putting high-sounding notions in Christie's head, I'll break every bone in your body. If you don't like the way she dresses in the ring, why do you look at her all the time? "

Further utterance on his part, or any effort David may have contemplated in resenting his attack, was prevented by the appearance of Ruby Noakes, who came running up from the main-top, waving a newspaper in her hand and crying out in the wildest excitement:

"David! David! Have you heard? Have you seen it? We've been looking for you everywhere. Here! Look! It's to-day's *Enquirer!* See what's happened! Your uncle! "

The vanguard of the "parade" had reached the lot. Cages came creaking through the wide aperture at the end, and were wheeled skillfully into place by expert drivers. Gayly dressed horsemen trotted through. Every one was shouting to David.

His ears rang, everything went black before him. He could not seize the paper that Ruby held before his eyes, nor were his eyes quite capable of reading the sharp, characteristic headlines that stood out before him in the first column of the *Enquirer*. The letters danced impishly, as if to confuse him further. Jenison—Jenison— Jenison everywhere! That was all he could see, all he could grasp.

Dick Cronk's prophecy had been fulfilled.

His uncle Frank Jenison was dead. Some one was shouting it in his ear. There had been a deathbed confession. He was no longer a fugitive! He was exonerated—he was free!

He laughed hysterically and pressed the damp sheet to his lips. Ruby Noakes threw her arms about his neck and kissed him for joy. The voices of the half hundred people crowding about him buzzed in his ears. They were shaking hands with him, slapping his back and laughing with him, although he did not know that he laughed.

Above the hum of eager voices rose one that was discordant, hoarse with passion.

"Clear out! Skip, I say! All of you! "

Thomas Braddock was shoving the glad performers about as if they were tenpins, raging like the lions which roared their surprise at this unseemly hubbub in front of the cages.

From sheer excitement, David's head was reeling; his senses began to slip away; his legs were tottering.

Suddenly the crowd fell away. One man was facing him. The unconscious smile was still on the boy's lips as he looked into the convulsed face of Braddock. The power to dodge the blow aimed at his face had gone with his wits. He only knew that Christine's father was striking; he could only wait, with hazy indifference, for the blow to land.

"I won't have any disobedience here, " roared the frantic manager, as he struck out in his bestial rage.

"I guess that'll stop it. "

David was lying at his feet, stunned by the savage blow.

"When I say a thing I mean it, " shouted Braddock, turning to the stupefied crowd. "He can't hold a jubilee in this here animal tent. Who owns this show, anyway? "

He drew back his foot to kick the prostrate boy. Half a dozen women screamed in terror.

"Don't do that, Braddock! " cried a level voice in his ear.

He whirled to face Colonel Bob Grand.

"If you kick that boy I'll shoot you, " said the Colonel almost impassively.

"Do I own this show or not? " was all that Braddock could howl.

"Get him out of here, " said Grand, turning to the angry circle of men. "Sober him up or turn him over to the police. "

"What! " choked out Tom Braddock, his eyes bulging. "You say this to me! "

"See here, Braddock, I kept your wife and daughter outside. They didn't see this cowardly trick of yours. You may have to explain to them why you did it. You can't explain to the rest of these people. We don't like brutes. "

A dozen men crowded forward with threatening mien. Tom Braddock shrank back in mortal terror.

"Don't jump on me, boys—don't! I—I'll go out. I'll go peaceable. Let me get out where there's air. I must have been crazy. "

He almost ran to the sidewall and crept into the open air. As he slunk off among the wagons, he felt himself overwhelmed by a sudden sense of desolation, a sickening realization that he had no friends, and, worse than all this, —that no one feared him!

A curious acknowledgment of his own degradation came with the stealthy impulse to go back later on and search for the stub of cigar that had dropped from his mouth during the encounter.

In the dressing-tent, a few minutes after the proprietor's brutal exhibition, David Jenison sat in the center of a wondering, superstitious group. Not one, but nearly all of them attributed his good fortune to the working of some spell peculiarly brought about by the influence of certain "signs. " The champion bareback rider recalled that David had found a horseshoe no longer ago than ten days. The Iron-jawed woman substituted the black cat charm, while Mademoiselle Denise held out for the virtues of occasional encounters with Ernie Cronk, the hunchback, whose hump he must have touched surreptitiously, no doubt.

Only Joey and Ruby and Casey looked wise and said nothing. Dick was the luck-piece that brought it all about.

David sat on a trunk, holding a wet towel to his red, swollen cheek. He had been steadied by the advice of these good friends, all of whom urged him for the sake of others to attempt no violent return for the blow Braddock had given him. Never was mortal so sore at heart as he, but he read wisdom in their argument.

"He ain't responsible, " said Joey, putting the whole of his summing up in a single phrase.

The great news had finally found a clear lodgment in David's brain. He had listened to the reading of the newspaper story by Ruby Noakes. It was now very plain to him that his present vicissitudes were at an end. The joy and relief that filled his soul were counterbalanced to some extent by the fact that Mrs. Braddock and Christine had not come up to congratulate him. He could not understand this and was hurt.

It is not necessary to repeat the newspaper account in full. The sensational story took up columns in the paper; the history of the case was repeated from the murder of old Mr. Jenison to the final tragedy. Considerable space and speculation were given to the unhappy accusation of the grandson, who had disappeared as if from the face of the earth. It was the opinion of the paper, as well as of the officers of the law, that the proud young man, unable to face the cruel disgrace and injustice, had made way with himself.

It was announced in heavy black type that his county would not rest until the body of the last of the Jenisons was found and laid away with the greatest ceremony. David laughed with the others at this laudable but tardy appreciation.

As for the story of Frank Jenison's death, it was, according to the newspaper, "so strange that fiction paled by contrast. " Jenison and his negro accomplice, Isaac Perry, had quarreled in one of the private card-rooms at Brainard's place in Richmond, where they had met by appointment. The negro, driven desperate and in great fear of the white man, finally drew a revolver and began firing wildly at his employer, who returned the shots. Perry was killed by a bullet which found his heart. One of the negro's shots, however, had penetrated the abdomen of Frank Jenison. He was mortally wounded. On being informed by the surgeons that he had but a few hours to live, the miserable wretch directed that his confession be written out at his dictation, that he might put his signature to it and thereby set his unhappy nephew straight in the eyes of a condemning world.

The full text of this confession was printed. The reader of this tale has heard enough of it, in one way or another, to determine for himself the chief facts in connection with the murder of old Mr. Jenison. It was Frank Jenison who shot him, deliberately laying his plans so as to direct suspicion to David. The nephew played into his hands in a most startling manner. A more convincing set of circumstances could not have been imagined, much less prepared.

Isaac Perry was the first to propose the plan of substituting a forged will, but at the time neither of them contemplated the assassination of the old gentleman. It was not until it became known to them that Mr. Jenison intended to deed over a great part of his estate to David before his own death that they saw the necessity for hastening the end. The will was prepared in Perry's room at Richmond. The names of the witnesses belonged to men who were dead and could not repudiate the signatures. Then came the signing of the quitclaim deed which provided an opportunity to substitute the will, and which, as far as Isaac Perry was concerned, was a *bona fide* transaction. The little plot of ground was in truth a portion of his own compensation exacted in advance of the murder.

Perry was to have done the shooting. At the last minute his nerve failed him. Frank Jenison then coolly directed his henchman to stand guard while he committed the diabolical deed. To use his dying words, his father "was ready to die anyway, so it was a kindness to end life suddenly for him. "

We know how David walked into the trap, and how he crept out of it only to become an outlaw, hunted and execrated. Perry went to Chicago, where he was to remain for a few months before coming back to receive his promised share of the money which Jenison was to realize on the sale of certain properties as soon as he was clearly established as heir to the estate.

Remorse began to gnaw at the heart of the murderer. He could not sleep without dreaming of his slain father, nor could he spend a waking hour that was free from thoughts of the innocent boy who would be hanged if the law laid its hands upon him.

Then, one day, there came a stranger who told him of Isaac Perry's treachery. The thing he feared had come to pass—Perry's defection. He made up his mind to kill this dreaded stranger, and to follow that deed with another of the same sort which would deliver him of Isaac Perry. But the stranger disappeared. He did not come to claim his blood money. The terror which fell upon Frank Jenison was overpowering. He sent for Isaac Perry, hoping against hope that the stranger had lied and that with the negro's support he could defy him. Perry came to Richmond, expecting to receive his promised reward in coin of the realm. The half-crazed white man accused him of treachery. The negro lawyer vehemently denied every allegation, but, becoming alarmed by the other's manner, fell into a panic of fear and began shooting.

At the end of his confession, Frank Jenison said:

"My soul is black. It is already charred by the fires of hell. I was a traitor to our beloved cause, although acquitted of the charge by fraud and deception. I killed my own father. I would have killed others. My nephew has long borne the stain of guilt that is going with me to a dishonored grave. I go with the brand of Cain on my soul. There will be no rest for me in the hereafter. I have not the courage to ask God to be merciful. But I believe in God. I have tried not to believe in him. I have denied him all my life. To-day, for the first time in memory, I can say—and it is with my last breath—I can say that I thank God for one great act of mercy. He has permitted me to live long enough, with this bullet in me, to say to the world that my nephew, David Jenison, is as innocent as I am guilty. "

"Well, " said Grinaldi the clown, his voice doleful in contrast to the cheery smile he assumed, when it came time for all to go to the cook-tent for dinner, "I dessay we'll 'ave to stop calling you Jack Snipe. Wot's more, David, you'll be going back to Virginia at once and settling down to be a genuine gentleman. Afore you think of going, my lad, let it be fully impressed in your 'eart that we all love you and we all wish you the greatest 'appiness in the world. You 'ave been a very poor clown, but I dessay 't is more the fault of your bringing up than anything else. A clown 'as to be born, David, just the same as any other genius. I suppose it's too soon yet to talk about your plans—wot you intend to do fust. "

"First of all, Joey, " said David, his face aglow with the fervor that was crowding up from the depths of his grateful soul, "I want to say to you and to all of you, that if I live to be a thousand years old I shall never forget how good and how kind you have been to me. My home will always be yours, my friends, just as your home has been mine. Jenison Hall will bid you welcome, come what may. You will find Joey Grinaldi there. My home is his, when he chooses to forsake the ring. And Ruby's, too. God bless and reward all of you! "

"When are you going to leave us, David? " asked one of the women.

David put his finger to the bruised spot on his cheek.

"My career as a clown in Van Slye's show ended when that blow was struck. You know quite well that I could not have stayed after that, even though other conditions were unchanged. I cannot eat of that man's bread; I cannot serve him. I have no trunk to pack, you know. Just that old satchel of Joey's, in which my linen is carried. So I am walking out of this tent now, free in more ways than one. When I come again I shall pay my way at the main entrance. No! Don't ask me to go to the cook-tent! It is impossible. As for my plans, I—"

He stopped, stilled by a sudden, overwhelming sense of desolation. All this meant that he would have to leave Christine! His days with the show were over. His sweet, throbbing hours with her were at an end. Life for him had changed as with the blinking of an eye. Nothing could be the same. All the loneliness of despair he had known during those weeks of fear and trembling was as naught compared to the outlook that now confronted him, so bleak and so barren that his young soul sickened. For the moment it seemed to him that she was about to go out of his life forever.

His heart revolted. There surged up the fierce impulse to cast away his patrimony, his name, his pride and honor. He would not desert her, even for a day.

"As for my plans, " he began once more, and again stopped.

Joey understood the struggle that was going on within him. The old clown, in his own capricious life, had been called upon a hundred times to give up the things he loved, the associations he cherished.

"We'll talk 'em over later on, David, " he said, putting his arm over the boy's shoulder. "Come along with me and Ruby. We'll go to a restaurant and 'ave a bite together. I—I suppose you'll be saying good-by to them striped tights and the spotted trunks. "

"I should like to buy them, Joey, " cried David eagerly.

"They are yours, my lad; take 'em. They belong to me. Now, let's get out of this. I don't think it's best for Brad to find you 'ere. "

As they left the lot, David carrying all of his possessions in the unwieldy satchel, they were met by Colonel Grand.

"David, " said he, falling in beside them, "have you sufficient funds to carry you back to old Virginia? If you need money, I will gladly let you have it—as a loan. "

They were surprised by the offer.

David hated him. "No, Colonel Grand, I can't take your money, even as a loan. It will be easy for me to raise the amount. "

The Colonel gave him an ugly smile.

"As you like, " he said. He lifted his hat to Ruby and abruptly turned back.

Far ahead were two figures that they knew well. Mrs. Braddock and Christine were hurrying away from the grounds as if desirous of avoiding a meeting with the young man.

David urged his companions to a more rapid walk. They overtook the Braddocks at the corner of an avenue which led off to the residence section of the town.

"You have heard? " asked David, as they turned in response to his call. "You know what has happened? "

He could see that the girl had been crying. Mrs. Braddock's face was white and set.

"Yes, " said the older woman. "And you are going home, David? " She spoke quietly.

"I—I don't know yet, " he stammered. Christine's face had been averted. Now she looked at him.

"You—oh, David, you don't really think of staying with us? " she cried, her eyes glowing.

"You must not think of it, David, " whispered her mother hastily. "Your place is at Jenison Hall. You belong there. Lose no time, my dear boy, in returning to your home. "

They had come to a little park adjoining a church-yard where there were benches. He led them to one of the seats farthest removed from the pavement. Joey and Ruby strolled into the churchyard.

"I suppose I shall have to go back, " said David gloomily. "For a few days, at least. They will be expecting me. And the property is mine now—and all that. But, Mrs. Braddock, " he went on feverishly, "I am coming back. In a week, yes, or less than that. I am coming back to be with you—to help you. I can't stay away now, Mrs. Braddock. It would make me too unhappy. I must be near Christine. She's more to me now than anything else in all this world. "

Mrs. Braddock smiled wanly. "You are very young, " she said, "and very impulsive. Do you think it would be kind to Christine if you were to follow the show for no other reason than to be near her? Would that be the act of a sincere friend? She would be compromised, I think you will admit. It was different before. You were one of us. Now you are an outsider. Even the easiest-going of the performers would resent your attitude if you were to follow us now. It is an unwritten law among us that an outsider is always an outsider. We are like gypsies. Even you, who have been one of us, can have no future standing in our tribe—for that is what we are, David. You must take your place among those who look on from afar. As individuals we will always greet you and give you the best of our love; collectively we cannot take you among us. That is over. You are—"

"But I may still be a performer, " he cried insistently. He had taken Christine's hand in his, only to have it gently withdrawn by the girl.

"No, David, " said Mary Braddock firmly, "it is out of the question. You are no longer a soldier of fortune. You are a Jenison of Jenison Hall. We can't build a bridge for that. "

"But I won't stand it! " he exclaimed passionately. "I *will* come back. "

"As a clown? " said she, smiling.

"I'll buy a part interest in the show, " he said stubbornly.

"You are not of age, " she reminded him. "The courts will name a guardian for you, I fancy. No, my boy, we must face the thing squarely. We shall be glad to see you if you happen to be where we may meet naturally. "

"But I love Christine, " he protested. "You told me last night that you would put no obstacle in our way to—"

"I told you last night that I would put no obstacle in your way, David, if you came to me in five years and still could say that you love her and would make her your wife. "

"But we thought then that I might always be near her—with the show, perhaps, " he argued.

175

"Quite true. But all that is blotted out, don't you see. "

Christine was weeping silently.

"You think I'll forget her! " he cried angrily.

"Oh, David! " moaned Christine.

"You think I'll not care for her always—"

"Listen, David, " said the mother patiently. "I can think of no greater joy that could come to me than to see Christine your wife—some day. But we must face the true conditions. She may always be a circus rider. I hope to take her away from this life—yes, soon, may it please God. You think now that you will always care. But I know the world. I know youth too well. I—"

"But you were not much older than Christine when you were married, " he blurted out. He regretted the unhappy remark almost before it left his lips. She turned away her face, and no word came in response for a full minute. Then she ignored the tactless announcement.

"You must go your way, David. We will go ours. If God is good to us, we may come together again, and we may still be happy. You are eighteen, Christine is fifteen. You do not know your minds, my children. I have thought it all out. You must be content to wait. Christine must come to you from a different sphere, David. It is not as it was. She must not be of the circus. "

"Mrs. Braddock, " said he, rising to his full height, "I only ask you to believe that I love her, and that I, at least, will not change. Will you change, Christine? "

"No, " said the girl, giving him her hand as she rose to look into his eyes with the whole of her young heart glowing in hers. "I will not change, David. "

"Then, Mrs. Braddock, as a Jenison of Jenison Hall I formally ask you for the hand of your daughter. A gentleman may keep his word of honor for five years—for a hundred years. I pledge my love, my name, my fortune to her. "

"David, " cried the mother, twisting her fingers in the agony of a despair that could no longer be concealed, "how can we know what the next five years may bring to us? What will they be to my darling child? Oh, if I only knew the way to save her—to preserve her, to give her what belongs to her by all the laws of nature! "

"You must leave the show, " he cried. "Give up everything. It is no place for either of you. Let me help you. Mrs. Braddock, give it up before it is too late. I know that harm will come to you here. "

He pleaded long and earnestly with the silent, depressed woman. In the end she held up her hand, and he waited.

"Time will tell, David, " she said. "When it becomes too heavy to bear I will cast off my yoke. That is all I will say. " She hesitated for a moment, and then went on, holding out her hand: "Good-by, David. You are going to-night? " "I suppose so, " he said dejectedly. "But, listen; I am coming back very shortly for a few days. I insist on that. If all is not going well with you and Christine, I shall know it. I mean to watch over her in spite of everything. "

"We will see you again before you leave, " said the mother. "I am sure we understand each other. Come back, David, if you will, but only for a day. Let us walk home. You may walk with Christine. Say your good- bys now. Joey! Are you coming? "

When the train for the East pulled out at eleven o'clock that night David was aboard. He positively had refused to take back any of the money he had lent to Mrs. Braddock, preferring to borrow from Joey and Casey. Christine kissed him good-by at the station.

"I know that my father struck you, David, " she whispered, as she put her hand to his cheek. "That won't prevent your coming back, will it? You will come, won't you? "

"As surely as I am alive, " he said fervently.

There were tears in his eyes as the train rolled away. He had said good-by to all of them—to Joey and Ruby and Casey, and they had wished him good luck with that complaisant philosophy which was theirs by nature.

Some one sat down beside him in the seat. He looked up.

"I guess I'll go part ways with you, " said Artful Dick Cronk comfortably. "I want you to do me a favor. Take this money and step into the little inn there in your town and pay the woman what I owe her. I forgot to settle when I left. She was a very good woman. I never trim a woman, good or bad. "

Primarily, Dick Cronk was traveling with David because his brother had disappeared from the snack stand early in the evening. The watchful pickpocket scented trouble. Before joining David in the coach, he traversed the length of the train to assure himself that Ernie had not slipped aboard in the darkness for the purpose of doing evil to the Virginia boy when least expected. He was satisfied that Ernie was not aboard, but it was now necessary for him to go on to the next station before leaving the train.

"I owe her five dollars and sixty cents. Tell her to keep the change. I hear you're coming back soon to visit the—er—show. Let me put you onto Colonel Grand. He's a good loser, that old boy is. He's terrible disappointed because you've squared yourself with the law. He had something up his sleeve for you, but this spoils it all. But you noticed that he took it very pleasantly—polite and agreeable cuss, he is, when he has to be. Maybe you'd like to know what his game was. "

"I think I know, Dick. "

"Nix. I guess not. You were to do him a great favor before long. You were going to run away with Christie Braddock! "

David started. "You are mistaken, " he cried indignantly. "I wouldn't think of such a thing. "

"Just the same, kid, that's what he had it fixed for you to do, and you couldn't ha' got out of it. He's a wonder, he is. That's the only way he could get rid of Christie; and, with Christie gone, Mrs. Braddock's spirit would be smashed. He's going to get rid of Tom Braddock purty soon. Tom don't know it, but his days with this show are numbered. "

"What a cold-blooded devil he is! " cried David.

"Hot-blooded's what I'd call him. "

CHAPTER XIII

THE SALE

We will forsake David Jenison for the time being. He is well started on his journey to the home of his forefathers, where complete restoration and the newspaper reporters await him. Let the imagination picture the welcome he is to receive; if possible, let it also describe the attitude of the community which had hunted him with dogs and deadly weapons, but which now stood ready to cast itself without reserve at the feet of the boy who had been so cruelly wronged.

Picture Mr. Blake's disgust at learning from David's own lips how he had been outwitted by the circus people, and contrast it with his sincere relief in contemplation of the fact that he had not captured the boy in those days of prejudice.

We leave all these details to the generous intelligence of the reader, for he knows that the heir to Jenison Hall has come unto his own again; and he also knows that in spite of all that can be done to make life bright and cheerful for David, there is still a shadow in the background that turns the world into a bleak and desolate waste for him.

Two weeks passed over his head before he was able to turn away from the bewildering mass of legal requirements and look once more to the West, whither his heart was forever journeying. Not all the excitement that filled the fortnight to overflowing, nor all the homage that came to him, could ease the dull, insistent pain of separation from interests so vital to his young heart.

He stole away one night, accompanied by a single servant—for now he was "lord of the manor" and traveled only as a true gentleman of the South should travel. Half-way to his destination he stopped off to draw from the savings bank the money he had placed there. With this small fortune in his possession he resumed the journey, now closely guarded by old Jeff, who always had been a slave to the Jenisons and would be till he died, Abraham Lincoln to the contrary.

David's constant prayer was that he might not be too late.

He was destined to find many changes in Van Slye's Great and Only Mammoth Shows.

Let us go back to the night after the one which saw David's departure from the show. For two days Thomas Braddock had slunk about the show grounds, morose, ugly, taciturn. He avoided every one except those with whom he was obliged to consult. His wife and daughter caught fleeting glimpses of him; Colonel Grand and the others saw him but little more. He held aloof, brooding over his wrongs, accumulating a vast resentment against the world and all of its inhabitants, obsessed by the single desire to make some one else suffer for the ignominy that had come to him.

Strangely enough, his most bitter resentment was lodged against the wife who had stood by him all these years, through thick and thin, through incessant storm and hardship, with a staunchness that now maddened him, because, down in his heart, he could see no guile in her. She was too good for him; she held herself above him; she made him to feel that he was not of her world—from the beginning. She was loyal because it would have put her in his class if she had lifted her voice in public complaint. He knew that she loathed him; he hated her for the virtue which gave her the right to despise him and yet to remain loyal to him. His sodden, debased soul resented the odious comparison that his own flesh and blood justly could make. There had been bitter moments when this maudlin wretch almost convinced himself that he could rejoice in the discovery that Christine was not of his flesh and blood, that this too virtuous woman was not pure, after all.

His sullen despair brought him to even lower depths. In half-sober moments he began to realize that his daughter feared and despised him. She had come to feel the distinction between her parents, and she had done the perfectly obvious thing in following the instincts of the gentle blood that was in her: she had cast her lot with her mother. He forgot his own aspirations and hopes for her in this bitter hour. He wanted to hurt her, so that she might cry out with him in ugly rage against the smug, serene paragon. If he only could bring Mary to his level, so that Christine might no longer be so arrogantly proud of the blood that came through the Portmans.

He drove himself at last into such a condition of hatred for all that was good and noble that he would have hailed with joy the positive proof that his wife had been untrue to him!

All day long he had been singularly abstemious. His brooding had caused him to forget or to neglect the appetite that mastered him. Toward evening he resumed his drinking, however, mainly for the purpose of restoring his courage, which had slumped terribly in this estimate of himself.

When the time came to go over the receipts with the ticket-sellers he pulled himself together and prepared to assert his authority. He tossed away the empty bottle and advanced upon the wagon, his face blanched by self-pity. He was confounded by the sight of Colonel Grand, sitting inside and going over the cash with Hanks, the seller.

"What do you want? " demanded Colonel Grand, when Braddock, after trying the locked door, showed his convulsed face at the little window. Hanks looked uncomfortable.

"Let me in there, Grand! " grated the man outside.

"I'll attend to this. We can't have you bothering with the finances — "

"I'll kick that door in, " roared Braddock; "and I'll kill somebody! "

Colonel Grand picked up the treasurer's revolver. He smiled indulgently.

"I'm taking care of the money after this, Brad. "

"I own this show, damn you! I-I-I'll fix you! " sputtered the other. He began to cry.

"Get away from that window! " snapped Grand, his eyes glittering.

"Oh, say now Bob, treat me fair, treat me right, " pleaded Braddock, all at once abject.

"I'll talk to you later on. Get away! "

"Don't throw me down, Bob. I've always done the square thing by you. Didn't I pay up everything I owed you by — "

"Are you going to leave that window? " demanded Grand.

The miserable wretch looked into the deadly eyes of the man inside, and realized. A great sob arose in his throat. He held it back for a moment, but it grew and grew as he saw no pity in the steely eyes beyond.

"My soul! " he groaned, with the bursting of the sob. He withdrew his ghastly face and rushed away in the night, stumbling over ropes and pegs, creating no end of havoc among the men who happened to toil in his path. They ran from him, thinking him mad.

Half an hour later Ernie Cronk came upon him. He was sitting on the curb across the street from the circus lot, his elbows on his knees, his chin in his hands—staring, staring through dry, hot eyes at the tented city that was slipping away from him.

"What's the matter? " asked the hunchback, in his high, querulous voice.

The older man did not respond. He did not alter his position when the questioner spoke to him.

"What are you looking at? " asked the other.

"Ernie, " began Braddock in a voice that sent a shiver across the boy's crooked back, it was so sepulchral, "let me take your pistol a second. "

Ernie Cronk drew back a step. He eyed Braddock narrowly.

"Who are you going to kill? " he asked after a moment.

"Myself, " said Braddock, lifting his haggard face.

Again the hunchback looked long at the man. Then, without a word, he handed a new revolver to Thomas Braddock. It was not the small derringer he was wont to carry.

Braddock seemed surprised by the boy's readiness. He received the weapon gingerly. A sudden spasm shook his big frame.

"Is—is it loaded? " he inquired, less lugubrious than he had been before.

"No, " said Ernie shortly. Braddock's chest swelled suddenly. "I suppose you think I'm fool enough to let you kill yourself with my gun and me right here where they could nab me. It's got blank ca'tridges, that's all. Somebody changed 'em on me last night—just before that— that sneak went away on the train. "

Volumes could not have told more than that single sentence.

Braddock handed the weapon back to him.

"But if you really want to shoot yourself, " went on Ernie maliciously, "I've got a round of real ca'tridges here. While you're loadin' the gun I can make a sneak. If I was you, though, I'd go up that alley there, Brad. It's terrible public here. "

"You wicked little brute, you! " cried Braddock in horror, coming to his feet and drawing away as if from a viper. "You cold-blooded whelp! I—I never heard of such—"

"Ain't you going to kill yourself? " demanded Ernie, grinning.

Braddock appeared to ponder. "No, " he said with eager finality; "not just now. I've changed my mind. I'm going to have it out with her first. Then, maybe I won't do it at all. "

Without another glance at the hunchback he swung off toward the dressing-tent. Ernie's scoffing laugh followed him into the shadows. It was the last straw. He was an object of derision to this thing of jibes and sneers.

The flush of anger had come back into his bloated cheeks by the time he had slipped under the sidewall into the dressing-tent. A sense of loneliness struck him with the force of a blow as he paused to survey the conglomerate mass of gaudy trappings: the men, the women, the horses, the dye-scented paraphernalia of the ring. The very spangles on the costumes of these one-time friends seemed to twinkle with merriment at the sight of him; the tarletan skirts appeared to flaunt scorn in his face. There was mockery in everything. His humiliation was complete when this motley array of people disdained to greet him with the eager concern that heretofore had marked their demeanor. No one appeared to notice him, further than to offer a curt nod or to exchange sly grins with the others.

Christine was in the ring. Mrs. Braddock stood over by the tattered red curtains, peering out into the "big top. " He knew just where to look for her; she always stood there while her daughter was performing with old Tom Sacks. Not Tom Braddock, but all the others, noted the weary droop of her shoulders.

She started violently when he came up from behind and spoke to her.

"Well, how does it look without the gentleman in stripes? " he asked coarsely. "It ain't so refined, eh? "

She faced him, hesitated an instant, and then said, without a trace of emotion in her voice:

"Tom, do you think Colonel Grand would be willing to buy out my share in the show? "

He stared. Then he laughed sardonically.

"What are you givin' us? Buy out your share? I should say not. He might buy you, but not your share. "

"You are a beast, Tom Braddock, " she said, the red mounting slowly to her pale cheek. "Why do you say that to me? "

"Say, don't you suppose I know how it stands with you and him? " he retorted. "Come off, Mary. You're both trying to freeze me out. I'm on to the little game. "

"Don't speak so loudly, " she implored, clasping her hands.

"Oh, I'm not tellin' any secrets, " he snarled. "It's common property. Everybody's on. I should think you'd be ashamed to look Christine in the face. "

"God forgive you, Tom Braddock, " she cried, abject horror in her eyes.

"Say, I've got to have an understanding with you, " he went on ruthlessly. "I'm going to find out just how I stand in this here arrangement. Grand's taken charge of the money box. He says it's you and him against me. He's going to—"

"He lies! He lies! "

"Oh, let up—let up! I'm no fool. "

"Tom Braddock, are you—are you *accusing me?* " she cried, all a-tremble.

He opened his lips to utter the words which would have ended everything between them. His eyes met hers and the words slipped back into his throat. The spark of manhood that was left in him revolted against this wanton assault upon the pure soul that looked out upon him.

His gaze was lowered. He began fumbling in his pocket for a cigar.

"Course not, " he said reluctantly. He peered hard at the opaque sidewall uncomfortably conscious of the scornful look she bent upon him. Neither spoke for a long time.

"How much lower can you sink? " she asked in low tones.

"Don't you turn against me like this, " he returned sullenly.

"I have endured too long—too long, " she said lifelessly.

"Now, shut up, Mary. Shut up your trap. I'm sick of having you whining all the time—"

"Whining! " she cried. "God in heaven! "

"Well, belly-achin', then. " Her bitter laugh irritated him. "Say, I got to talk this business over with you. We've got to understand each other. "

"We *do* understand each other, " she said, a note of decision in her voice. "You are ready to prostitute me for the sake of worming money out of that horrid beast. I loathe him. You know it, and yet you force me to meet him. I am going to end it all. Either he leaves this show, or I do. I will not endure this unspoken but manifest insult a day longer. Do you understand me? "

"I'd like to know how you're going to help it, " he said, glaring at her with half-restored belligerence. "You can't get out without losin' what you've got in the business, and he *won't* get out. "

"Are you going to permit him to continue paying his odious attentions to me—to your wife? " she cried.

"I don't care what he does, " roared Braddock. "That's his business. You don't have to give in to him, do you? If he thinks you've got a price, that's his lookout, not mine. "

"Not yours? " she gasped. "Oh, Tom! Tom! What manner of man have you come to be? "

"Well, I'm just tellin' you, that's all. " "You—

you surely are not in your right mind. "

"You bet I am! Now, you listen to me. You are going to stick right with this show—you and Christine. And you're going to do what I tell you to do. You got to treat Bob Grand half-way decent. He's liable to leave us in the lurch any time. How'd you suppose we'd get on without his help right now? Just as soon as we get on our feet I'll put an end to his funny business. I'll show him what's what. He'll get out of the show business a heap sight wiser man than he is now. But we need him now. We got to stand together, you and me. No flunking, see. We—"

"Stop! " She stood before him like an outraged priestess. This time he did not shrink, but glared back at her balefully. "This is the end! We have come to the parting of the ways. I will never call you husband again. If you even speak to me, Thomas Braddock, I shall ask any one of a dozen men here to beat you as you deserve. Oh, they will be only too happy to do it! Now, hear me: I am going to take Christine away from you—forever. Don't curse me yet! Wait! I am not through. This very night I shall offer my share in this show to Colonel Grand. He may have it at his own price. If he will not buy, then I shall go forth and look for another purchaser. I—"

"You're my wife. You can't sell without my consent, " he exclaimed.

"Then I will ask the court to give me the right. Now, go! I—"

"You can't take Christine. She's as much mine as she is—"

"I will hear no more. I have given you the last chance to be a man. This ends it! "

She turned and walked away from him. He knew that it was all over between them.

Considerably shaken, he went over and sat down on a trunk near the wall. Suddenly he sprang to his feet with a curious half-laugh, half-sob. He glared at the flap through which she had disappeared. A cunning, malevolent expression came into his pop-eyes.

"Sell out, will you? " he muttered. "I'll block that game. I'll sell out to him myself. That's what he wants. "

He lifted the sidewall and passed out into the open air, directing his footsteps toward the ticket-wagon. Colonel Grand was leaving it as he came up.

"Hello, Brad, " he said quite genially. "If I was a bit rough awhile ago, I apolo—"

"Say, I want to talk privately with you, right away. I've got a proposition to make. It's final, too, —and it's friendly, so don't look as if you're going to pull a gun on me. Come on to the hotel. Oh, I'm not as drunk as you think! "

"Mrs. Braddock expects me to escort her to the hotel—"

"No, she don't, " rasped the other. "She's all right. Leave her alone. Are you coming? "

Colonel Grand was struck by the man's behavior. He shrewdly saw that something vital was in the air.

"All right, " he said. "I'll go with you. "

They were soon closeted in the room back of the hotel bar, a bottle between them on the table. The door was locked. Their conversation lasted an hour. When Colonel Grand arose to depart he stood a little behind and to the left of Braddock's chair, a soft, sardonic smile on his lips. He held a sheet of paper in his hand. Pen and ink on the table, alongside the more sinister bottle, told of an act of penmanship.

"We'll have the night clerk and some one else witness the signatures, " he said quietly.

"All right, " said Braddock hoarsely. He was staring at his fingers, which he twiddled in a nerveless, irresolute manner.

"The inside conditions are between you and me personally. You'll have to live up to them, Braddock. "

"Oh, I'm a man of my word, don't fret. "

"You are to get out at the end of the week. That's plain, is it? "

"If the cash is passed over. Don't forget that. Say, Bob, I swear, you're treating me dirt mean. I ought to have five times more than you are payin' me, and you know it. Five thousand dollars! Why, it's givin' the show away, that's what it is. I've built up this hereshow—"

"It is your own proposition. I didn't suggest buying you out. You came to me to sell. If you don't want to let it go at the price we've agreed on I'll tear up this bill of sale. "

"I've got to take it, so what's the use kicking? I'm going to get out of the business. My wife's against me. Everybody is. Damn them all! "

Colonel Grand knew quite well that Mrs. Braddock, as the man's wife, could interpose legal objections to the transfer, but he was not really buying Tom's interest in the show; he was deliberately paying him to desert his wife and child. That was the sum and substance of it. Braddock was not so drugged with liquor that he could not appreciate that side of the transaction quite as fully as the other.

Down in his besotted soul there lurked the hope that some day, in the long run, through the wife whom he was selling so basely, he might succeed in obtaining the upper hand of Bob Grand, and crush him as he was being crushed!

"It will be a week before the currency can get here from Baltimore. I refuse to draw on my banker in the regular way. This money, being evil, must come from an evil source. My dealers will send it from the 'place. ' Now, again, you understand that I can put you in the penitentiary if you go back on your word. You *did* take the boy's money out of the dressing-tent. My man saw you. "

"I don't see why you hired a canvasman to watch me, " growled the other, pouring another drink. "Mighty cheap work, Bob Grand. "

"I always go on the principle that it isn't safe to have business dealings with a man until you know all that is to be found out about him. In your case I had to choose my own way of finding out. "

"I'll knock off a couple of hundred if you'll tell me the name of that sneaking—"

"You need the two hundred more than I do, Brad, " said Grand with infinite sarcasm—and finality.

"Well, I'm a Jonah in the show business. I guess it's the best thing I can do to get out of it. You'll do the right thing by Mary and—and—" he swallowed hard, casting a half glance at the other out of his bleary eyes—"and the young 'un. They'll get what's coming to them, Bob? "

"Certainly. "

"I wouldn't sell out like this if—if Mary had acted decent by me, " he said, trying to justify his action. He was congratulating himself that he had sold her out before she had the chance to sell him out. He closed his eyes to the real transaction involved in the deal. It gave him some secret satisfaction, however, to contemplate the futility of Colonel Grand's designs upon Mary Braddock.

"Of course, " said Bob Grand.

"I am going to California, " said Tom Braddock, for the third time during the interview.

"I've asked you not to mention that fact to me, Braddock. You are supposed to stay with the show as manager and overseer. "

"Humph! " grunted the other. "You want to be as much shocked as the rest of 'em when I skip by the light of the moon, eh? "

"We'll sign the paper, " was the only response of the purchaser.

Ten minutes later, after two men had witnessed their signatures, the document reposed in Bob Grand's pocketbook.

The next morning Mary Braddock appeared before the master of Van Slye's Circus and offered her interest for sale. He calmly announced that he could not afford to put any more money into the concern.

"I must sell out, " she said. "All the money I have in the world is in this show. "

"It could not be better invested, " he said. She shrank from the look in his eyes.

"But I need it for Christine's education, " she began.

"I will see to it that Christine is given the best of everything, Mary. Leave it to me. She shall be sent abroad next year, if you think best. "

"I am asking no favors of you, Colonel Grand. "

"It may interest you to know that I have purchased your husband's entire interest in this show, " he said softly.

She stared, spellbound.

"He—he has sold out to you? " she murmured, going white to the lips.

"You seem surprised. "

"He could not do it! It is necessary to have my consent. I—I—" Her brain was whirling.

"I understood that he was a perfectly free agent. I can send him to the penitentiary if he has swindled me. If you and Christine care to take that sort of stand against him, I'll have to do it. I should be terribly sorry on the girl's account, but—Oh, well, I'm sure it won't come to that. "

"He—he has sold me out? " she cried weakly.

"Oh, hardly that! "

Unable to speak another word to him, she turned and blindly made her way to the women's dressing-room. The Colonel smiled comfortably as he lifted his hat to her retreating back.

Late that night four or five persons slipped out of the hotel by the rear doors. At the mouth of the dark alley a hack was waiting. With the utmost caution this small, closely huddled group approached the rickety vehicle. Three women climbed in, followed by numerous valises and small bags; their two male companions mounted the seat with the driver. Off through the still night rattled the mysterious cab, clattering across the cobbled streets for many minutes until at last it drew up at the darkest end of the railway station platform. Three trunks stood against the wall of the station building. One of the men attended to the checking of these heavy pieces, presenting two railway tickets for the guidance of the sleepy agent. The other stood guard over the cab and its occupants.

A train thundered in. The station platform was quite deserted except for the few belated revelers who had remained in town for the night performance of Van Slye's circus. When the train pulled out, a woman and two men stood beside the hack, where tearful farewells had been uttered and Godspeed spoken. Toward the east sped a tall woman and a slim, beautiful girl. In the outskirts of the town the train swept past a string of huge, cumbersome, ghostly wagons, all of them slinking away into the night-ridden pike that led to another city where the young and curious were already dreaming of the morning hours that were to bring the "circus to town. "

"Good-by—good-by! " sobbed the girl, who had been peering intently through the window of the car. The tall woman did not look forth, but sat with her eyes riveted on the seat ahead.

"Yes, it is good-by, my darling, " she said in very low tones.

Back at the railway station, after the rear lights of the train had disappeared, the lone woman turned her tear-stained face to the man whose arm was about her shoulder.

"Do you think we'll ever see them again, daddy? " she moaned.

"Yes, " said the man huskily. "She said she'd let me know, one way or another, when it is safe to do so. Don't cry, Ruby. They're better off. They couldn't 'ave stayed on, God knows. And God will take care of 'em. "

"I wish she'd said just where she's really bound for, " muttered the other man, a tall ungainly fellow. "She's mighty near dead-broke, and I'm—I'm uneasy, Joey. "

"She'll get on, Casey, confound you! "

"If she'd only make up her mind to go back to her father, " said the girl.

"That's just it. If she's going back to 'im, it's best nobody knows yet—not even us. I've got their two letters for David, if he ever comes looking them up, as he said he would. Well, God bless 'em. I—I 'ates to think wot the show will be without 'em. Come on; let's get back to bed. "

And so it was, many days afterward, that David Jenison came "looking them up, " only to find that they were gone and that no one could tell him whither they had fled. It was significant that Colonel Bob Grand was not with the show; he had gone away in a great rage when the discovery of the flight became known to him. Tom Braddock, strangely sobered and bleached out by a tardy remorse, went about mechanically in the management of the show which he no longer owned.

Joey Grinaldi delivered two precious, carefully preserved missives into the hands of the distracted Virginian.

One of these letters said that the writer would wait for him to the end of time, loving him always with all her heart. The other, much longer, came to its conclusion with these words, written by a wise, far-seeing woman whose heart was breaking:

"... And now, David, good-by. We love you. Be content to let us go temporarily out of your life, if not from your thoughts or your heart. Always think of us with love and tenderness, my dear boy, as we shall never cease to think of you. You are young. Christine is young. You are not so wise now as you will be five years hence. I shall try to mold Christine into the kind of woman you could take as a wife to

Jenison Hall. In five years, God willing, the circus ring and its spangles will be so remotely removed from her that no one can find the trace of them. In five years, David. That may seem ages to you and to her, who have youth and all of life ahead of you. When five years have gone by, David, I shall let you know where we are to be found. If you still care for her then, and she for you, no matter what the circumstances of either may be, no human power can keep you apart. You will come to her and say it all over again, and you will be happier because of this brief probation. If you should find, through the mature workings of a man's heart, that you have grown to love another, then you will both see for yourselves that my present course is right, and that your ways must continue, as now, along absolutely separate paths. Do not attempt to find us. Your own futile efforts, dear David, in that direction might be the means of bringing other and unkind searchers to our place of refuge. I know you would not bring greater trial and tribulation to us, who love you, than you have seen us suffer in the past. "

BOOK TWO

CHAPTER I

THE DAUGHTER OF COLONEL GRAND

Snuggling down in a nest built of certain westward hills in fair Virginia, near the head of a valley long noted for healing waters that spring, warm and cold, from subterranean alchemies into picturesque pools and steaming rivulets, lies the ancient village of Hollandville, with its quaint, galleried facades; its flower gardens and its mill- race; its ambient clouds and drowsy sunshine, and the ever-delicious somnolence that overcomes the most potent vigor with an ease that mystifies. Beyond Hollandville, less than half a league distant, against the mountainside, facing the great ridge opposite, stands a time-honored, time-perfected hostelry inside whose walls and upon whose galleries the flower and chivalry of Virginia have clustered for generations. Names historic are to be found on the yellow pages of venerable and venerated ledgers and day-books, names of men and women known and cherished before the dauntless settler had turned his footsteps toward the territories of the Middle West. Here had come the famed Virginia and Maryland beauties of an ancient day, and here still came their great-great-granddaughters to create envy among the flowers that steal from the earth to bloom in this valley of delight. Here came Washington and Jefferson and others whose names will never die so long as there is an American heart-beat among us; came with their coaches, their servants, their horses and—their livers: for they had livers even in those good old days. If one were to call upon the sweet night air, and spirits were allowed to respond, the fair face of Dolly Madison would emerge from the shadows, attended by all the wits and beauties of her luxurious day. Betty Junol, too, held court in this primitive Spa. Here duels were fought for ladies fair, and here the hearts of the noblest women of our land were won by gallants who will live forever.

Beaten roads that stretch off down the valley and wind through the hills could tell countless tales of those who, in one glorious century, rode hand-in-hand and unarmored to the lists of love and fell together in the joyous combat. To this very day the lists are open and the contenders as resolute, as gentle and as brave as in the ages when Washington was a boy and men wooed with a sword at their hip.

Still stand the narrow, thatched cottages, immersed in honeysuckle and ivy, that sheltered the fathers of the Constitution; still wind the beaten roads over which rolled their coaches in days before the American historical novel was more than a remote probability. Heroes of a later war than that which gave us our freedom come now to this sequestered spot, men whose grandfathers fought with our George against the George of England. But, as their forefathers came, still come they, and will come for generations, for this is the ancient Mecca of Virginia gentlefolk to whom tradition is treasure and companionship wine.

Late in the spring of 1880, when the dogwood was repainting the hillsides and wild-flowers were weaving a new carpet of many hues for the feet of wandering lovers, the company of guests assembled at the Springs—as yet numerically small—included no fewer than a dozen girls whose beauty was famed from one side of the Southland to the other. Attendant upon these dainty American princesses, there were again as many young men, rivals all for favors small.

A chill, moist wind of a certain evening blew down from the mist-shrouded ridge, driving all guests to the glow of the fireplaces or to the seclusion of coveted nooks in shadowy halls, where staircases held secrets as tenderly inviolate now as on the nights of a dim, forgotten past. About the great fireplace in the general lounging-room a merry crowd of young people were gathered, discussing the plans for a projected trip to the Natural Bridge, quite a two days' journey by coach.

A tall, lean-faced young man of twenty-three or four stood beside the fireplace, his elbow on the ancient mantel, his shapely legs crossed. There was a moody expression in his handsome face, albeit he smiled in quiet enjoyment of the vivacious conversation that went on around him. Half a dozen girls chatted eagerly, excitedly, in response to certain arguments advanced by young men who had the expedition in hand. Arrangements were being discussed, approved or set aside with an arbitrariness that left no choice to the proposers. From time to time disputed questions were referred to the tall young man at the mantelpiece. He appeared to be a person of consequence in the eyes of all; his decision was accepted, even by the most arrogant of rebels. Not one of these fair girls looked into his dark, steady eyes without hope that the thought which lay deep in them was of her and of no other, and yet each was painfully certain that he thought of some one else, whether present or absent they could not conceive.

He gravely twisted the point of a small, dark mustache, then in vogue among the fashionables, and proffered his suggestions with the quiet assurance that comes from a thorough appreciation of the deference due the man who is "real quality" in the Southland, and yet without the faintest suggestion of superciliousness or conceit in his manner.

This man was born to it; it had come to him through the blood of unnumbered ancestors. He was an aristocrat among aristocrats, as fair Virginia produced them. Notwithstanding he had arrived at the Springs no earlier than the forenoon of the day at hand, without knowledge of previous plans regarding the expedition, he was nevertheless established by common though unspoken consent as the arbiter of all its features. He had come among friends who knew him of old—last year, the year before, and the years before that.

For this tall young man who leaned so gracefully against the mantelpiece was the master of Jenison Hall—the last of the Jenisons. And that was saying all that could be said, so far as a Virginian was concerned.

Their council was disturbed by the arrival of the belated night coach that came over the mountains from the nearest railway station. The shouts of the driver and the darky hostlers, the pounding of horses' feet in the bouldered yard below, the rush of footsteps across the broad veranda, and the sudden opening of the door by an ebony porter, —all went to divert the attention of those who waited eagerly by the fireplace to catch a glimpse of new arrivals.

Preceded by bags and satchels and rugs, there came two women out of the drenched night into the glow of the firelit room. Two of the girls in the circle stared for a moment, and then, with sharp cries of surprise, rushed over to the desk where the newcomers stood, having been conducted by the porters: two pretty girls from Baltimore. The group looked on with interest while greetings were exchanged.

The arrivals were persons of consequence. Two French maids followed them into the room and stood at the foot of the staircase, respectful but with the composure which denotes tolerance. In those days few people in the South presented an opulence extending to French maids. The younger of the two women at the desk was tall, slender and strikingly attractive: of the dashing, brilliant type. She was not more than twenty, but there was an easy assurance in her manner that bespoke ages of conquest and not an instant of defeat. The elder was an aristocratic woman past middle age, the possessor of cold, aquiline features and smileless eyes. Her hair was almost snow white, but her figure was straight and youthful.

Presently they were conducted to their rooms by an obsequious porter, and the young girls returned to the group at the fireside. There was a common, ridiculously casual movement among the older people in the room; the newcomers were barely out of sight in the upper hall before the first of the curious ones was looking over the register. Inside of three minutes a score of persons had glanced at the freshly written names and passed on to the water cooler, thence back to their seats, a fresh topic for conversation well in mind.

"Who is she? " demanded an eager young man from Richmond.

The Baltimore girls were visibly excited.

"I didn't know they had returned to this country, did you, Nell? They've been living abroad for several years. Goodness, how that girl has blossomed out. I'd never have known her if she hadn't been with her mother. "

"Do you think she's so very pretty? " enquired the other, quite naturally.

"She's a dream! " cried the Richmond young man, before the other could give her opinion. "But who is she? "

"Roberta Grand. She's a Baltimore girl and—"

"What name did you say? " asked the tall young man beside the fireplace, suddenly interested.

The name was repeated. He listened to a long discourse on certain school day friendships, succeeded by a period of separation in which the subject of all this interest had traveled abroad with her mother, completing an education that, if one were to judge from the descriptions volunteered by her former classmates, gave small promise in the beginning of attaining much beyond the commonplace.

"She was a dreadfully stupid girl at Miss Ralston's, " proclaimed Miss Baltimore. "Wasn't she, Nell? "

"Indeed she was. She —"

The master of Jenison Hall was staring across the room in the direction of the register. He interrupted again.

"Grand? Are there many Grands in Baltimore? " he asked.

"Why are you so interested, Dave? " demanded one of the men.

"I once knew a man from Baltimore whose name was Grand, that's all. I'm wondering if she can be —"

"Her father is Colonel Robert Grand. He's the great racehorse man. Every one knows *him,* " said one of the Baltimore girls.

"Colonel Bob Grand? "

"Yes. Of course he and Mrs. Grand don't live together any longer. They were divorced about five years ago. Didn't you see the account of it in the Richmond papers? It seems that he ran off with an actress—to London, they say. Oh, I don't remember all the details. Mother wouldn't let us read the stuff in the papers. But I do remember that he bought a house in London for the woman and he never even fought the divorce. He treated Mrs. Grand shamefully, I know that much. Father says he is a terrible man. "

David Jenison was very pale and very still. He did not take his eyes from the face of the speaker.

"Who was this actress? " asked some one. He went very cold. He tried to close his ears against a name he dreaded to hear on the lips of the fair gossip.

"I don't know. Some one you never heard of. Just a common, ordinary actress, as I remember. "

Jenison abruptly left the group and strode out upon the porch, leaving the others to puzzle themselves over his unexpected defection.

In the five years that had passed since his brief but ever green experience with the circus he had not come upon a single trace of Mary Braddock and Christine. With all the impulsiveness of boyhood he had at first made feverish efforts to find them. Detectives in his employ followed the circus for several weeks, keenly alert to discover anything that might put them on the track. Others shadowed the disgruntled Colonel; while Blake, his old pursuer, went to New York and, reinforced by agency men of Gotham, watched the home of Albert T. Portman. But they had disappeared so completely that every effort to unearth them proved futile. David was in college the following winter when he heard, through Dick Cronk, that Colonel Grand had sold out the circus to P. T. Barnum, with whose vast enterprises it was speedily amalgamated. As the concern was sold at private sale, by actual premeditation, Mary Braddock's interests were undefended. There was talk among the circus people, however, to the effect that Grand, after certain judgments had been satisfied, advertised throughout the country for Mrs. Braddock, conveying to her notice by this means the fact that he held in his possession many thousand dollars belonging to her. Whether this tempting bait found her in such dire distress that she could not remain in hiding while it was being offered, no one seemed to know. If she had come forth to claim her portion of the proceeds, the fact remained unknown to the old friends.

Tom Braddock, so David learned, forsook the show soon after his wife's disappearance, and went to the Middle West. From time to time news of him reached David in roundabout ways. He had developed quite naturally into a common street loafer in Chicago, preying on the generosity of his old acquaintance and living the besotted life of a degenerate. Of certain cheerful wights who made up David's secret circle of intimates we may expect to hear more as we go along. Suffice it to say, he kept in close touch with them during his years at the University and subsequently as the recognized "lord of the manor, " excepting a rather lengthy period devoted to travel abroad. On more than one occasion he responded generously to diffident appeals for help, coming from one or the other of his old friends. He never failed to contribute from his store of wealth, for young Jenison was the richest as well as the kindliest planter in all Virginia.

Jenison farm lands stretched far and wide; Jenison town property was to be found in no less than five cities of importance; Jenison securities, as sound as Gibraltar, were piled up in New York vaults, and the Jenison collection included more than a score of the rarest paintings ever developed under the magic of Rembrandt, Franz Hals, Turner, Gainsborough, Velasquez, Stewart and others.

He was more than a person of landed importance, however. His story was so well known that wherever he fared he was hailed as a hero. In his own sunny land he was a hero-prince with as many retainers and loyal subjects as ever bent knee to an Eastern medieval potentate. Rich in fair looks as well as in worldly possessions, the owner of a distinctive charm of manner, combined with the poise of good breeding, a certain interesting reticence and a wonderfully impelling smile, he was more than a hero to the young, and little short of an idol to the old.

Countless assaults had been made against his heart. Every wile known to beauty had been employed in a hundred sieges. But the Jack Snipe of eighteen was still the lonely Jack Snipe at twenty-three: his heart was sheathed in a love that harked back to a rough, picturesque development and was strong by virtue of its memories.

At no time in all these spreading years had Christine Braddock's flower-face and girlish figure faded from his vision. On this misty night in early June, while others were thinking of him, he was thinking of her and the promise made five years before. In five years, they both had said. The term of probation was drawing to an end. He was waiting now for the redemption of that promise.

Once, and once only, had he heard from them, and then in the most mysterious way. Soon after his return to the University an envelope containing four hundred dollars in crisp new bills was delivered to him by Jeff, his body-servant, who came all the way up from the plantation to say that it had been left at the Hall by a man who offered no explanation except that his master would understand.

No day passed that he did not look for some sign from Mary Braddock. She had promised, and he knew that she would not fail him. His mind was charged with the wildest speculations. What would be the nature of the resurrection? What word would come from the present to greet the past? From what mysterious hiding-place would come the call? Even now, at this very instant, from some far-away spot in the great wide world a voice might be winging its way to him. What tidings were in the air?

What word of the girl he loved?

And now, like an icy blast, came the appalling possibility that the world knew more of Mrs. Braddock's whereabouts and actions than he, who was so vitally interested. The word "actress" as supplied by the contemptuous Baltimore girl conveyed to his soul a sharp, sickening dread. Was Mary Braddock the one? Had she given way under the strain? Had circumstance cowed her into submission? Was she the one who occupied the little house in London-town?

If so, what of Christine?

He smoked as he paced the long veranda. In a dark corner at the lower end, sheltered from the mist by trailing arbutus, a group of three persons from the inexperienced, uncouth North, were drinking juleps served by an impassive but secretly disdainful servant bent with age and, you might say, habitual respect. Jenison did not notice them in his abstraction, but his ears would have burned if he could have heard the things the two women were saying about him to their male companion.

As he passed the broad office door in one of his rounds it was opened and in the full glow of light from within appeared the tall, graceful figure of Roberta Grand. She remained there for a moment, looking out into the sombre night. Their eyes met as he passed. She was exceedingly fair to look upon, golden-haired and *spirituelle*, but he could see only the repulsive, hated features of Colonel Bob Grand, destroyer.

When he returned to the group at the fireplace, half an hour later, she was sitting with the others, her back toward him as he approached. He was at once presented by the girl from Baltimore.

Miss Grand looked up into his face with cool, indifferent eyes.

"I have heard so much of you, Mr. Jenison, " she said. Her voice was soft and pleasant.

"We live in a very small world, Miss Grand, " he said. "One's reputation reaches farther than he thinks. "

"It depends on the method by which it is carried, " she responded enigmatically. He started.

"I trust mine has been delivered by kindly messengers. "

"Both kindly and gentle, " she said.

"Some girl, I'll bet, " remarked one of the young men.

"Not so singular as that, Mr. Priest. The plural is 'girls, '" said Miss Grand.

"I am relieved, " said David. "It's much easier to understand the plural of girl. Girl in the first person singular is incomprehensible. "

"Do you really think so? " asked Miss Grand calmly. He bowed very low and said no more. It occurred to him in a flash that this fair girl knew more of him, in a way, than any one present.

Later on, at the foot of the stairs, she came up with him. Without the slightest trace of embarrassment she remarked:

"I think you knew my father, Mr. Jenison. "

He flushed in some confusion. "Your father is Colonel Robert Grand? "

"Yes. It was he who told me your story, long ago. I have always been interested. "

David hesitated for an instant, then boldly put his question: "May I ask where Colonel Grand is at present? I hear you no longer live in Baltimore. "

It was a very direct attack, but he justified himself through the impression that she invited it.

"We live in Washington, Mr. Jenison, my mother and I. My father's home is in New York. Some time, while we are here, I hope you won't mind telling me something of your experiences with the—the circus. My father often spoke of you. He said they called you—was it Jack Snipe? "

David was taken aback. The girl's frankness amazed, unsettled him.

"A name given me by one of the performers, " he murmured.

"The proprietor's daughter, Christine Braddock. Oh, you must not be surprised. I know her. "

"You know her? " he asked quickly.

"That is, I once knew her. She came out to my father's stables years ago to practice her riding. I used to envy her so! You see, I wanted to be a circus rider. " She laughed very frankly.

"Do you know what has become of her? " he asked, risking everything. He watched carefully to catch the expression in her face.

"No, " she replied, hesitating. "I have not seen my father since our return from Europe. "

The words were ominous. He experienced a sinking sensation.

She continued: "I supposed that you knew something of *our* family history, Mr. Jenison. " He looked sufficiently blank. "My father and mother lead absolutely separate lives. It happened four years ago. Perhaps you have forgotten. "

"I did not hear of it at the time, Miss Grand, ' he explained.

"We have lived abroad ever since. So, you see, I have had little or no opportunity to talk with my father. We write to each other, of course, but letters are not like talks. I am to visit him next month in New York. I can hardly wait for the time to come. " She was now speaking rapidly, eagerly. "I—I don't believe that all the things they said about him in the newspapers were true. My mother's lawyers brought up everything they could think of, whether it was true or not. You see— Oh, you don't mind hearing me talk like this, do you? " She interrupted herself to insert this question.

He hastened to assure her that she might speak freely to him, and with perfect confidence in his discretion. But, he suggested, it would be better if they were to continue the conversation in a place less conspicuous. He led her to a distant corner of the room, where they might be quite free from interruption. Her peculiar attitude interested and disturbed him. It was quite plain, from a single remark of hers, that her sympathies were with her father, although she had remained at her mother's side.

"You knew my father quite well, didn't you, Mr. Jenison? He has often told me of the close friendship that existed between you in those days, how he tried to help you and how appreciative you were. "

David concealed his astonishment.

"They were wretched days for me, " he said evasively.

"I am sure you wouldn't believe all the horrid things they said about him, knowing him, as you did, for a kindly, honorable gentleman. My mother was desperate, Mr. Jenison. She believed everything the lawyers put into her head. Of course, I understand now why it was so necessary to blacken his character. It was for the money—the alimony, they call it. And, more than that, it was to compel the court to give me into her custody. I had no choice in the matter, it seems, in spite of the law which says a child may elect for herself after she is fourteen. They made it so dreadful for him, that he could not take me, although I would have gone with him, oh, so gladly. I—" She stopped short.

He waited for a moment, appalled by this undisguised antipathy to the mother, who, as he knew so well, had been wronged beyond measure by the beast whom the girl, in her ignorance, defended. "My dear Miss Grand, " he said, "I am more than sorry if any rude inquisitiveness on my part has led you to—"

"Oh, I want to talk about it to you, " she interrupted with a directness that made him more uncomfortable than ever. "I know that you knew my father for what he really was. You knew how kind and good he was, and how nobly he befriended the Braddocks and all those wretched show people. You know how they treated him in return for his generosity. I feel as if I had known you always. "

"It's very nice of you, " he mumbled helplessly. "You say the show people turned against him. Do you mean at the—er—the trial? "

She lifted her brows, a sudden coldness in her manner.

"Not at all. I refer to what happened afterward. "

"I am quite ignorant, Miss Grand, " he said, a certain hoarseness creeping into his voice.

"He was actually compelled to pay something like twenty thousand dollars on the complaint of Mary Braddock, who set up the claim that she owned part of the show. It was a blackmailing scheme, pure and simple, but he paid it. He is a man. He took his medicine like one. "

David glowed. He felt the blood surge to his head; he grew warm with suppressed joy.

"When did this happen? " he asked, the tremor of eagerness in his voice.

"Oh, I don't remember—three or four years ago. It really never came to a public trial. He settled her infamous claim out of court. Her lawyers hounded him as if he were a rat. "

"I happen to know that Mrs. Braddock was part owner in the show, " he said quietly.

"But he had already bought her out, " she exclaimed. "He wrote all of this to me, after it came out in the papers. I had the whole story from him, just as it really happened. No, Mr. Jenison, he was compelled to pay twice. "

He was half smiling as he looked into her face. The smile died, for he saw in the features of Bob Grand's daughter a startling resemblance to the man himself, hitherto unnoted but now quite assertive. A moment before he had thought her pretty; now he realized that he had scarcely looked at her before. There was the same beady, intent gleam in her dark eyes, which were set quite close to each other over a straight nose with rather flat nostrils. Her mouth and chin were unlike Grand's. They were perfect, they were beautiful. The eyes were unmistakably his, and therefrom peered the character of the girl as well as that of the man.

David was sharply cognizant of a feeling of repugnance. Much that had puzzled him a moment before was perfectly plain to him now.

She championed the father because he had been stronger in her creation than the mother.

"Did Mrs. Braddock prosecute her claim in person? " he asked, subduing the impulse to set his friend right in the eyes of this girl.

"Not at all. She kept out of sight. Lawyers did it all. "

"Did your father say where she was living at the time? "

"Oh, I know where she was living in London. "

"London? " he said, suddenly cold.

"Yes. We saw her there, Centennial year. She had a home in one of those nice little West End streets. Of course, we could have nothing to do with her. "

"Of course not, " murmured he dumbly. "And Christine? "

"She was at the Sacred Heart Convent in Paris, —at school, you know. Father wrote me about her. "

He could not ask her the sickening question that was in his mind: was Mary Braddock the woman in the case? But his heart was cold with despair. He could not, would not believe it of her, and yet the circumstances were damnably convincing.

"In a month, Mr. Jenison, I will be of age. I am sure that you, having been such a friend to him, will be glad to know that I am going to him. If he wants me, I shall stay with him. "

"You—you will leave your mother? " he demanded, unconsciously drawing back in his chair.

"Just because my mother cast him out is no reason why I should do likewise. I love my father—I adore him! What did you say? "

Under his breath he had uttered the word "God! "

"I beg your pardon, " he said hurriedly He felt like cursing her. "I just happened to think of something, " he explained.

"I am sorry to have bored you. I thought you'd like to know about father after all these years. Pray forgive me. "

"You intimated awhile ago that perhaps he could tell me where Mrs. Braddock is living, he said. His forehead was covered with moisture.

"I've no doubt he knows, Mr. Jenison. She is living in New York. "

She was perfectly calm and matter-of-fact about it. If there was more that she could have told him, her inscrutable smile signified plainly that it should be left for him to find out for himself.

He looked into her eyes for a moment without speaking. A feeling of loathing such as he had never known before welled up in his heart against this girl. He hated the sight of her face. He almost imagined he could see its soft, warm tints changing subtly into the gray, putty-like complexion of his oldtime enemy. A beastly jowl seemed suddenly to spread from her smooth round cheek and sag heavy over her neck; her smile, bewitching to other eyes than his, took on a mysterious breadth that horrified him. He was seeing visions. He knew that there was no change such as his mind pictured, and yet he could not cast out the illusion. He arose abruptly, fearful that she might see the repugnance in his eyes. He could not sit there an instant longer, facing this reminder of Bob Grand. Something atavistic in his nature urged him to strike out with all his strength at the fantastic face that forced itself upon him.

"I beg your pardon, " he said, and his voice sounded queer in his own ears, "but I must get off some letters to-night. May I take you to the stairs? "

A few minutes later he was lying flat on his back, fully dressed, on the bed in his chamber, staring up at the ceiling, his brain a chaos of anguish, dread, pity—and faith, after all, in Mary Braddock. The walls seemed papered with the faces of Bob Grand and Roberta Grand. He was haunted by them.

At daybreak he arose, without a single instant of sleep behind him. His mind was made up to one purpose. He could not stay in the same house with Roberta Grand.

Before going in to breakfast at eight o'clock, one of the young men in the party of the night before asked the clerk at the desk if Mr. Jenison had come down.

"Mr. Jenison left by the morning stage, Mr. Scott. He had a letter calling him back to Jenison Hall. Something very important, sir. He left a note for Miss Beaumont, I believe, to tell her he can't be back in time for the trip to Natural Bridge. "

CHAPTER II

THE STRANGER AT THE HALL

The letter that called David to Jenison Hall came, by curious coincidence, at a most opportune time. He had decided to leave the Springs within a day or two, cutting short his proposed stay of a month almost at its beginning. The advent of Roberta Grand, heretofore an unknown quantity, brought with it new and unpleasant complications. Her revelations disturbed him, her attitude angered and disgusted him. It was from this girl, so amazingly like her father, that he would have fled in any event. His nature revolted against the possibility of constant association with her, he scarcely could have maintained even a perfunctory show of consideration for her. And then something told him that her confidences would grow, that she would go farther in the effort to justify her father. He realized that he could not stand by and hear the things she doubtless would feel called upon to say in respect to Mary Braddock. His sleepless night had drawn many ugly pictures for him to efface before he could be at peace with himself.

All through that dismal night he had given his thoughts to these people, and to three cities, —London, Paris and New York.

In the last of these, Mary Braddock was living. Staring up at the dim, flickering shadows on the ceiling, he traveled in horrid conjecture from one to the other of these immense wildernesses. Ahead of him stalked the ugly figure of Robert Grand, who *knew*—who perhaps had known all the time; at his side was the knowledge that the five years had come to an end. Was Mary Braddock, after all, in a position to redeem her promise?

The candle sputtered and went out. But he was no more in the dark than he had been all along. If there was to be light, he must make it for himself. He would not wait for her to speak out of the darkness. He would search her out, come what may; he would claim Christine.

With his mind full of the decision to go to New York as soon as possible, where it would be an easy matter to find Colonel Grand, at least, he hurried down to an early breakfast, successfully evading his body-servant. There were two letters in his box, products of the night mail.

One of them caused him to start and almost cry out aloud. It was from Artful Dick Cronk. The envelope bore the Jenison crest and it had come from Jenison Hall. A year had passed since he had heard from the pickpocket.

The missive was brief, as were all of Dick's communications, written or oral. It said: "Just stopped off on my way north. Niggers say you are at the Springs. I'll wait here till you come back, if it ain't too long. Hope this reaches you prompt, because I am in a hurry to get up to New York. Don't write. You can get here just as quick as a letter. Maybe quicker. "

Except for the schoolboyish signature, that was all; but there was a world of importance between the laconic lines. David caught the early morning stage and was on his way over the ridge to the railroad with old Jeff, before eight o'clock.

He reached home that night, surprising the housekeeper and servants. To his amazement, they knew absolutely nothing of Dick Cronk. He had not been there, nor any one answering to the description. David was thunderstruck. He carefully examined the letter, which he had retained. There could be no mistake as to the stationery or the postmark. He went to his room, gravely mystified by the circumstance. A messenger was sent post haste to the village hard by, with instructions to find Dick if he were at either of the boarding-houses. The master of Jenison Hall could not help chuckling to himself in contemplation of the crafty tricks the writer of the letter had employed in securing his information and in appropriating stationery.

It was nearly eleven o'clock when the darky boy returned with the word that no one fitting the description had been seen in the village.

"But he must be there, " said the young master, vastly perplexed and not a little annoyed.

"Yas, sah, " agreed the darky, not for a moment questioning the assertion that fell from his master's lips. If "Marse David" said he was there, he *was* there; that is all there could be to it. "He suttinly mus' be thah, sah. But I 'spec's he mussa fo'got to tell anybody 'bout hit, sah. "

"Ask Jeff to call me early in the morning, Pete, " said David. "Good night. "

"Good night, Marse David. "

The boy went out, gently closing the door behind him. Almost instantly it was reopened.

"What now, Pete? " demanded David, who, with his back to the door, was advancing to the mahogany bureau across the room. He came in line with the tall mirror that surmounted the chest of drawers. His fingers stopped suddenly in the light task of removing a pin from his scarf.

Just inside the door stood Artful Dick Cronk, a genial smile reflecting itself in the mirror which confronted the other. David stared unbelievingly for a few seconds and then whirled to face the— but it was not an apparition.

The lean, cunning visage of the pickpocket was illumined by the never- to-be-forgotten smile of guilelessness that so ably stood him in hand in moments of peril. The humor of it gradually succumbed to the satirical leer that always came to translate his strange sophistry into something more expressive than mere words. He was plainly enjoying the effect of his magic invasion. To make the puzzle all the more startling, Mr. Cronk was attired in one of David's loose dressing-gowns. He wore a pair of comfortable slippers and he smoked David's picturesque Algerian pipe. A picture of domestic contentment was he. You might have taken him to be the owner of the house, and not the sly intruder.

"What are you doing in my room? " Dick demanded, assuming an air of severity.

David's astonishment gave way to a hearty laugh. He advanced with his hand extended.

"Well, you *do* beat the world, " he exclaimed. "In the name of heaven, where did you come from? "

They shook hands. Dick's sprightly face presented a myriad of joyous wrinkles.

"Where did I come from, kid—I should say, Mr. Jenison? I—"

"Call me David, " interrupted the other.

"Sure! Come from? Take a seat, kid. You are my guest for the evening. Make yourself at home. I've got a couple of toddies planted here behind the dresser. You see, I was expectin' you. " He went over and, reaching down behind the bureau, came up with two toddy glasses in which the ice clinked cheerily. "I made 'em just before you came in, " he explained. David passed his hand across his brow. Then he accepted one of the glasses from the pseudo host.

"Do you mean to tell me that you were in this room all the time I sat over there waiting—"

Dick put his finger to his lips. "Sh! Not so loud, please. I'm not really supposed to be here, you know. Just think what heart disease would do to the wooly old boy that runs the front door if he heard you talking to me at this time o' night. I'm glad to see you, David. You got my letter, I see. Well, well, it's wonderful what a two-cent stamp'll do sometimes. A postage stamp is the greatest detective I know of. I've had 'em find me time and again, right off the real, when twenty plain-clothes men couldn't get a smell of me to save their souls. Sit down, David. Make yourself at home. It's good to see you here, old chap. I'm sorry you must be leaving so soon. "

"Leaving so soon? "

"Yep. You're going away to-morrow. " He was sitting now, with his long legs crossed, leaning lazily back in the lounging chair at the end of David's desk.

"Don't talk in riddles, Dick. What's up? And how do you happen to be here, occupying my house without the knowledge of my servants? "

"A simple question, with a simple answer. I've been here two days and two nights, right here in the house. My bedchamber is down the hall there, and this has been my lounging room. Of course, I had my meals in the dining-room—my after-the-theater suppers, you might say. It's been good fun, foolin' the servants. I hope you don't mind my fakin' grub from your larder, kid. I used to sit around, unbeknownst to the niggers, and listen to them talk about spirits and ghosts and all that sort of thing. It was most amusin'. They couldn't account for the disappearance of pies and cakes and Sally Lunn—say, how I do love Sally Lunn. And jam, too. To say nothin' of fried chicken. Say! I've been living like a prince, kid. Sleepin' in a real bed and hangin' around in swell togs like these. Say! You *do* know how to live, David. You'd have been very much entertained half an hour ago if you could have seen me swipe a Washington pie and a quart of milk right out from under the nose of old Aunt Fanny. Milk is my favorite beverage, David. You notice I'm not drinkin' this fire-water. I made two of 'em for company's sake, but I still turn my back on the wine when it's pink. Not for me—not for little Dicky-bird. "

"I don't see how you do it, Dick, " cried David delightedly.

"That's part of my game, kid—not letting people see how I do anything. But it's as simple as rollin' off a log, as the jays say. I must confess—and that is something I make it a rule never to do—that this high living is not good for me. I'll get into awful habits, if I keep it up. I won't be satisfied with pretzels and bologny sausages. Seems to me I feel a touch of the gout coming on now. "

"You will have breakfast with me in the dining-room to-morrow morning, Dick, " announced the master of the house. "It won't be necessary to swipe it, as you call it. "

Dick grinned. "My dear chap, " he mimicked, "I have my breakfast stowed away in the garret at this minute. Never put off till to-morrow what you ought to do to-day. In time of plenty prepare for famine. Still, if you insist, I'll join you at some ham and eggs—and coffee. I *do* miss my coffee, old chap. We take a train for Richmond at nine A. M."

David's patience gave out. "What does it all mean, Dick? I must know at once. It must be important or you wouldn't—"

"Maybe it's important and maybe it ain't, " philosophized Dick, relighting the long pipe.

"Well, let's have it. "

"Tom Braddock's out. "

"Out? I don't understand. "

Dick's surprise was genuine. "You don't mean to say you never heard what happened to him? "

"Joey wrote me that he had gone completely to the dogs in Chicago. "

"Joey's off his nut. Brad's just out of Sing Sing. "

"Sing Sing! The penitentiary? "

"The sure-enough cooler. He's been there for nearly three years. "

"Christine's father a convict! " groaned David.

"As I said before, he's out. It may interest you to know that I spent a year's vacation up there in '78. I needed the rest, old chap. Brad came in shortly after I got settled. He *had* been in Chicago for two years, boning his friends and living like a gutter-snipe. We spent most of our evenings at Sing Sing on the same piazza. During the day we sauntered back and forth between our apartments and the academy for physical research. Just to amuse ourselves we learned to make barrel staves between times. It was two months before we managed to speak to one another. After that we corresponded quite reg'lar. I had notes from him, and he from me. I soon got on to Brad's troubles. Seems that Bob Grand owed him several thousand dollars. He had owed it for more 'n two years. Some deal in connection with the show. You remember Brad was froze out soon after his wife left the aggregation in '75. He says Grand bulldozed him into duckin' the—I mean, leavin' the show, all the time owin' him the long green. Seems that Brad hadn't delivered all the goods mentioned in the bill of sale. Bob wouldn't settle until he got the goods.

"Well, Brad hung around Chicago, fightin' firewater and always gettin' licked at it, for two years or more. Then he up and sashayed to New York for a show-down with our old friend Robert. He had blood in his eye, Brad had. He'd been buncoed bad, and a bad man hates that worse than the thought of hell. When he got to New York he hunted up Mr. Bob Grand, who was just leavin' for England. It seems that Brad's wife and girl had been located over there by the Colonel, who had never stopped lookin' for them. Which is more than you could say for Brad. Mrs. Braddock, through her father and a firm of lawyers, had forced old Colonel Dough-face to fork over a big wad of greenbacks. Her share in the show, you understand. Brad heard of it in some way. So he concludes he'll get in his little graft.

He goes to the Colonel's rooms in a hotel on Broadway, but misses him. Then he lays for him on the street. They have it hot and heavy, back and forth, and it all ends with the Colonel puttin' over a job on Brad that lands him in the cooler. Charge of highway robbery. Brad gets three years in the pen. I'll say this for him, though; I'm dead sure he wasn't guilty. "

Dick paused to relight his pipe.

David was trembling with eagerness. "What did he have to say of Mrs. Braddock and Christine? I am interested only in them, Dick. "

"He's up a tree regardin' them. They never peeped, so far as he's concerned. He never heard from them after they dusted that time. Of course, he thinks it was a put-up job, that gag of the Colonel's, payin' her all that money. He argues that it was all understood between 'em, and that it wasn't a squeeze on her part. The Colonel denied it, mighty strong, sayin' he had never heard from Mrs. Braddock until her lawyers and old man Portman came down on him, just after his own wife had got a divorce from him. "

"I have heard, " ventured David, "that Mrs. Grand based her complaint on the fact that her husband was mixed up in some way with an actress. "

"She had to have *something*, Davy, " said the other. "They faked up an imitation—that ain't the word—an imaginary actress for the occasion. Joey Noakes told me all about that. She first tried to get some of the old crowd to swear that Mrs. Braddock was the one, but she got a terrible throw-down there. They was all for Mary Braddock, strong. Then what do you think her lawyers up and does? They actually went to Joey and offered him ten thousand if he'd let 'em use Ruby's name. "

A spasm of rage transfigured the face of the imperturbable rascal. His hands were clenched and the veins stood out in his temples.

"What a cowardly, outrageous thing to do! " cried David.

Dick did not speak for several minutes, but sat staring at his hands, his thoughts five hundred miles away. At last his lips spread into a dry, crippled smile.

"Joey told 'em to go to hell. And he rather helped the guy along the route by kickin' him half-way down stairs. If he hadn't caught himself against the railing half-way down, he'd 'a' been in the bad place these last four years. I wish to state at this point, Davy, that for the past four years I've made it my business to make that guy wish he was there a hundred times over. It's mighty hard to do a lawyer, but I've got that feller so's he sits up nights, looking like a ghost, waitin' to see what's going to happen to him if he should accidentally fall asleep. But, 'nough of that. After I got out of the pen I dropped in to see Joey. He was just organizin' that road pantomime show of his. He told me all about Mrs. Grand's proposal, and I was for cutting the dame's throat, only he wouldn't hear to it. You been in Joey's home in Tenth Street, haven't you? I mean the old one, just a little ways off Broadway. Well, you remember *them* stairs? Can you imagine bein' kicked down them stairs? Gee whiz! How I'd like to ha' been there! Well, you know all about Joey's pantomime fizzle. It almost busted the old boy's heart. He went stony broke the first year. Him and Ruby had to go over to live in an awful place on the east side, just off the Bowery. It happened to be right near the joint where Ernie and me hang out in the winter time. Our palatial residence then was back of a cobbler's shop, two flights off the sidewalk. I can't say that it's as sunny and as nicely aired as your joint here, kid, but it's harder to get inside of. And it would be impossible to get out if you once got in, unless you had a recommend from one of the gang. Seven of us hangs out there now. Maybe I'll show you the joint some time, if you can keep your jaw shut about it.

"But I'm gettin' off the trail. After Joey's bust up, Centennial year, who comes along and offers him a stake but old Colonel Grand. Offers to lend him money enough to start all over again. That's where Joey made his mistake. The old jay took the money and started all over again with—"

David started to his feet. "Impossible! " he exclaimed. "Why, I—I myself, Dick, lent him the money three years ago to get on his feet again. "

"Sure you did. I haven't come to that yet. I said he took a couple of thousand from the Colonel. That was before you come into it, and he was so ashamed of it he never told you. Well, out they go on the road again, with him as the clown, Ruby as the columbine, Casey as harlequin and a guy named Smith as pantaloon. They had a show something like Humpty Dumpty. But you know all about that. "

"Perfectly, " said David, smiling reflectively. "I was with the show for a week on the road in '78. I must say I liked the rough old tent days better than the life they led in those abominable country town opera houses. "

"Umph! " was the other's comment. "That's originally the way the Colonel's wife took it into her head to drag Ruby in if she could. Well, what does the Colonel do, after the show gets to going well, but drop in occasionally just as he did to Van Slye's circus, and proceed before long to make love to Ruby. Yes, sir! That's what he did, the hell-rotter that he is. Soon as Joey finds out his game, he up and takes a fall out of him. Then the Colonel threatens to put him out of business. Right then and there is where Joey writes to you for help. You fork over proper-like, as you should, and he pays back what he owes Grand, preferring to owe you. So he got rid of the devil for more than forty days. That's about the time I goes to the pen. I carelessly lets myself get nabbed, actin' on Ernie's advice. He's a slick kid, that boy is. He ain't goin' to let me get hung if he can help it. You see, I'm booked for hangin', sure as fate; he knows it as well as I do, only he's smart enough to want to put it off till I'm so old I won't mind it. So I goes to the pen just to keep from killin' Bob Grand. A year in the cooler makes you see things most sensible-like. I knowed that when I went in. If I'd waited a week after hearin' Joey's story of that dog's attentions to Ruby, I'd ha' been in Kingdom Come long ago, and so would he. We'd both been down below to welcome Mrs. Grand's lawyer when he arrived. So, actin' on Ernie's advice, I gets pinched the second night after hearin' about it. Ernie's a humane cuss. He saved two lives, then and there. "

"You deliberately put yourself in prison? " cried David.

"Just to postpone the hangin', kid, that's all. "

"It's all rubbish, this talk of hanging, " protested the other. "You're too kind-hearted, Dick, to kill a fly. "

"There'll be a rope around my guzzle some time, Davy, just as sure as you're sittin' there, " said Artful Dick, and, notwithstanding his careless laugh, a perceptible gleam of terror showed in his eyes for an instant. "But I'm wandering again. When I was up to Sing Sing I tumbled to what was on Brad's mind. He thinks she turn him down for Grand. The more he thought of it, the more full of the devil he got. Just before I left the place he wrote me a long letter and slipped it to me in a hunk of bread. He said he'd made up his mind to kill her and Grand as soon as he got out. You can tell by a convict's looks whether he's bluffin' or not. I tell you, Davy, I sees it in Brad's face. He meant what he said. He's going to do it, as sure as fate. He ain't got anything to live for and he ain't going to let the two of 'em live any longer than he does. "

"And you say he's out? Dick, we must do something to prevent this awful—"

"Sit down, Davy. You can't get a train till tomorrow. Besides, there's time enough. The first thing I does after I leaves the coop was to hustle down to see Joey. I put him on to Brad's bad talk, and he promised to keep a sharp lookout for him. At that time Mrs. Braddock was livin' in London, but Joey didn't know it. I found out later on through Ernie. He got her whereabouts by pumpin' a coachman who worked for her father, old man Portman. It seems that while she wouldn't take money from the old man, she appealed to him to help her in gettin' what was due her from the sale of the show. She went to Europe a couple of months after she left the show, a school friend puttin' up for her, I understand. Her dad was willin' to forgive her, after she'd tied the can to Brad, but she says nix. She changed her name and took charge of this school friend's children who were being educated in London, givin' their mother a chance to chase around Europe without bein' bothered by kids. When she got the dough out of old Bob Grand she puts Christine in a school some 'eres and—"

"Thank God, and you, Dick, for this news, " cried David fervently. "I knew that she could do nothing but the right thing. Go on! "

"Well, about six months ago, her stepmother up and dies. The old man promptly sends for her to come back and cheer his declinin' years, as the novel writers say. Ernie writes all this to me and I gets the letter a couple of months ago down in New Orleans, where I was attendin' Mardi Gras, a sort of annual custom of mine, don't you know, old chap, by Jove! I'm terrible careless about my correspondence, which accounts for my neglectin' to write this to you. However, I'm not so careless that I neglected to write this to Ruby—a thing I do reg'lar every month, some months. Four days ago, in Looieville, I gets two letters, one from her and one from Ernie. Ernie knows everything. He's seen Christine nearly every day for three months, but she ain't seen him. Poor devil of an Ernie! I made him what he is—I banged him up for life. "

"It was an accident, Dick. Don't take it—"

"Nix. It ain't no accident when you kick a four-year-old kid down a flight of stairs. Well, anyhow, they both write me that Tom Braddock is in New York and actin' terrible ugly. He's layin' for Bob Grand. As luck would have it, the Colonel is off attendin' the races along the spring circuit, and Ernie says he won't be back in New York for three or four days. Mrs. Braddock has got her father down South some-'eres, but the servants are expectin' 'em back this week. "

"Then we may be in time. We must not lose a minute, Dick. If Tom Braddock carries out his threat, we'll be to blame—you and I. Christine, —where is she? What is she like? What do they say of her? "

"Ruby's been on the road, so she don't mention having seen her. And, say, Davy, don't be sore at me for what I'm going to say now. It's this way: Ernie made me promise never to tell you anything about her— how she looks—how she acts, where she is, or anything. I've only told you where her mother is, mind you. You'll have to guess about Christie. You see, Davy, that boy's sure jealous of you yet. I—I— guess you understand. "

David nodded his head without speaking. He understood. There was nothing for him to say. "I'll find her myself, " he said, beginning to pace the floor in his excitement. "She must be beautiful. She must be all that her mother promised. But, Dick! "

He stopped short, struck by a sudden thought. "Why hasn't Mrs. Braddock written to me? She promised. The five years have passed. We were to see each other at the end of five—"

"Well, maybe you will, kid. Don't get peevish. I guess Mrs. Braddock knows her business. Has it ever occurred to you that there might be another Romeo lookin' at Christie? Five years is quite a spell. Girls are fickle brutes. "

"For God's sake, Dick, if you *do* know of anything like that, tell me. "

"Cross my heart, Davy, I *don't* know, and that's straight. "

"We *must* catch the first train in the morning. "

"Don't hop around like that, Davy; you'll upset something. You can't hurry a train, kid. We'll catch it, all right. Sit down. Get a pipe and take a smoke. Keep cool. That's our game, kid. If you go bumpin' into old man Portman's house without bein' sure you're wanted, you might get—well, I won't say what! "

"You're right, Dick. She may have forgotten me. She may have asked her mother not to write to me. I've waited and hoped and counted on having her—I've checked off the weeks and months and years. I wonder if you can understand how it is when you care as much as I do, and always have? No one knows. It's all in a fellow's own heart. It—"

"Oh, I've had a case or two myself, kid. It ain't nothin' new, this crimp you've got, " said Dick, putting his heels on the desk. "Adam had it. So did Solomon, only he had it in so many places he got so he didn't mind it. Think of them guys that have harems. Think of Brigham Young. Why, kid, you don't know the first thing about love pains. Think of the guy with the harem and *his* guesswork! He's got something to worry about, he has. It's awful when you've got to love a couple of hundred of 'em at once, and them all hatin' you like poison. And old Brigham—think of him settin' up all hours of the night, wonderin' whether she loves him as much as she used to, and not being able to remember just which *she* he's thinkin' about. Brace up, kid. It's only a rash you've got. If Christie has given you the shake just remember how easy it was for Brigham to collect 'em. The woods are full of 'em. "

"But, good Lord, Dick, " cried David, laughing in spite of himself, "I'm not a Mormon. "

"Kid, every man's a Mormon at heart. Just cram that in your pipe. And every woman, no matter how ugly she is, thinks she's a siren. It's in the blood of both sexes, this Mormonism and sirenism. Oh, don't look so surprised, kid. I got some of my views out of the dictionary, but most of 'em came from observin' people as they look to me from my own level. I have a way of bringin' everybody down to my own level, kid, and I find, except for that commandment about stealin', we all have about the same amount of cussedness in us some'eres. It's human nature to be bad, or to want to be bad. We'd all be a little bit bad, from time to time, if we wasn't afraid of being found out. Course, it comes in different size doses. Some girls think it's terrible bad just to wink at a feller, but they do it because it's bad and not because it's sanctimonious, you bet. Then there are other girls who'd cut your throat with a razor while you're asleep. You bet they wouldn't be doing that if it was considered good. All men have got deviltry in 'em, and all women mischief. The women like the men for the deviltry, and it's the mischief in women that plays the devil with the men. It don't appear on the surface, but it's there just the same. "

"What amazing philosophy, " laughed David.

"I've been gettin' philosophy up in your attic, Davy, " said Dick with a quaint grin. "I read some'eres that all philosophers get in their real work in attics. Now, I guess we'd better turn in. I don't think you'll do much sleepin' to-night, so you'd—"

"First, Dick, " interrupted David, rising to pull the old-fashioned bell cord in the corner of the big chamber, "we'll have a bite of supper. I want to introduce you to my servants. "

"Hold on! " Dick came to his feet quickly. "It's my treat. You wait here. I've got a fine supper goin' to waste up in the garret. I copped it out early this evening. Poke up the fire there, Davy, and don't try to foller me. "

He was gone, the door to the hall closing gently behind him. There was not a sound to be heard in the house. Outside the frogs were chattering, and a nearby owl hooted dolefully. David stood still in the center of the room, his gaze fixed on the hall door. He counted the minutes, expecting, in spite of his preparedness, to be startled when the door opened with ghostly ease to admit the lank figure of the "dip. " There was a certain sense of dread in the knowledge that somewhere off in the dark, silent halls a stealthy, noiseless, almost sinister thing was moving—moving with the swiftness and caution of a weasel, but with all the merry purpose of a harlequin. David experienced a grewsome, uncanny desire to shiver. He remembered Dick's admonition and was about to turn to the fireplace, in which the logs were no longer blazing.

Suddenly the door opened. He could have sworn that the knob had not turned. There had not been the faintest sound, and yet Dick

Cronk stepped quickly, confidently into the room, a grin on his face. In one hand he bore a fair-sized package, done up in a napkin.

"You are the ghostliest thing I've ever known, " said David with a nervous laugh of relief. "How do you do it? "

"Simple twist of the wrist, " said Dick, employing a phrase of the day. "Gee, how tired you must be, after pokin' up the fire like that! "

David hastened to do his part of the pantomime. When he turned from the replenished fireplace a cold supper was spread on the desk, the napkin serving as a tablecloth. There were knives, forks and spoons, and a china plate apiece. A pitcher of milk stood at one end, a bottle of claret at the other, with tumblers beside them. In the center of the board was a plate of fried chicken, some young onions, freshly baked bread, salt, pepper, and, most wonderful of all, —Aunt Fanny's newest marble-cake, huge and aggressive.

The master of the house stared open-mouthed at this amazing feast. Where had it all come from? How had it been transported?

"Well, I'll be hanged! " he gasped.

Dick shuddered. "Don't say that! It gives me the Willies. Sit down, friend, and make yourself at home. Ah! This is real comfort! Don't you think I'd make some woman a fine husband? I'm no slouch as a provider, am I? "

It was after two o'clock when Artful Dick Cronk whispered good night and slipped out into the hall. He carried with him all the plates, cutlery and remnants of the midnight feast, having remarked in advance that a careful operator never left anything "half finished. " It was his purpose to restore every article except the food, to the place from which he had taken it. He and David chuckled joyously over the fresh amazement of Aunt Fanny in the morning; she had been living in a state of dread for three appalling days, as it was.

The next morning Dick appeared at breakfast with his host. He rescued Zuley Ann's greatly prized silver watch from the steaming coffee urn, and picked Jeff's pocket-book from the mouth of a lamp chimney, afterwards restoring the thirty-eight cents it contained. Strangely enough, he took the coins from the wool on Jeff's head. If ever a negro's wool undertook to stand on end it was at that moment. Zuley Ann's eyes were permanently enlarged. I have it on excellent authority.

At eight o'clock they were off for Richmond and the New York express.

CHAPTER III

THE MAN WHO SERVED HIS TIME

Long before the train reached the station in New York, David and Dick parted company. The shrewd but whimsical scamp presented at considerable length the problem of virtue and vice stalking arm in arm, as it were, through the streets of New York; he pictured, with extreme unction, the doleful undoing of virtue and the practiced escape of vice.

"Kid, " said he, "the first cop that laid eyes on us meanderin' down Broadway would land on us like a rat-terrier. Being a clever devil, I'd hook it and give him the slip. But you, kid! Where would you be, little innocent? How far would virtue and justice carry you up an alley with a cop at your coat tails? Nix, kid. We go it alone after we leave Newark. That's the trouble with this world. Nothing's plumb square. Now, here's the point: Virtue's all right if it trots alone. But just let Virtue hook up with Vice for ten minutes, unsuspecting like, and see what the world says. Kid, that little ten minutes of bad company would upset a lifetime of continuous Sundays. 'Specially in the eyes of a cop. A cop ain't acquainted with virtue. My advice to the young and innocent is to avoid evil companions and cops. It's a long ways to heaven, and lonesome traveling at that, but it's only a step to hell, and the crowdin' is something awful. It's mighty nigh impossible to turn back once you get started, on account of the mob. I'm not saying you won't run across worse guys than I am at the swell hotel you'll stop at, but they ain't on speaking terms with the police. "

David went to one of the big hotels patronized by all well to do Southerners of the day. At the railway station he looked about for the philosophic jailbird, but he was not to be seen. The Virginian drove to the hotel, conscious of a strange loneliness, now that the resourceful rogue was not at his elbow. He found some consolation in Dick's promise to communicate with him before the close of the following day, when doubtless he would be able to furnish news of interest, if not of importance.

The next morning saw David on his way to the home of Joey Noakes, far down town and to the west of Washington Square. He knew the house. He had been there before. A narrow, quaint little place it was, reminiscent in an exterior sort of way of the motley gentleman who solemnly called it his castle. You climbed a tall stoop flanked on either side by flower boxes, and rattled a heavy knocker that had all the marks of English antiquity, —and English servility, —and then you waited for the trim little housemaid, who betimes was a slavey below stairs and not permitted to answer the knocker until she had donned her cap and apron and rolled down her sleeves—and slipped on her cuffs, for that matter. If you were an unpleasantly long time in gaining admittance, you might be sure that she was also changing her shoes or perhaps brushing her hair. In any event, after you knocked it was some time before she opened the door, and then you were immediately impressed by the conviction that her brightly shining face had scarcely recovered from the application of a convenient "wash rag, " and that she seemed deplorably out of breath. But she was neat and clean and quite English.

As for that, everything about the establishment was English. The window-boxes, from basement to garret; the way the curtains hung in rigid complaisance; the significant name-plate on the middle panel of the door: "Joseph Grinaldi, Esq. "; the minute plot of grass alongside the steps that led to the basement, with a treasured rose-bush in the corner thereof. You were positive, without looking, that Joey had a back yard which he called a garden, and that it possessed everything desirable except a vista—and he would have that if it were not for "the houses in between, " to say nothing of the high board fence he had built to keep out all prowling beasts—including humanity—with the double exception of cats and sparrows. Although it was a typical, hemmed-in New York house, you wouldn't have thought of calling the chimneys anything but pots, nor would you have called the shingles by any other name than slates.

Joey was at home. He was expecting David, which accounts for the prompt appearance of the sprightly maid, and the genial shout of welcome from the top of the stairs.

"Come in, my lad, " called Joey, bounding down the steps with all the resilience of a youth of twenty. "My crimes, I'm 'appy to see you. "

They shook hands warmly, the little maid bobbing her head in rhythmic appreciation.

"You knew I was coming? " asked David, following the old man into the "drawing-room. "

"I found a note under the door this morning, David, left there mysterious-like during the night. It was left by the fairies, I daresay, although the 'and-writing was scarcely wot you'd call dainty. " Joey pulled a knowing wink.

"Dick Cronk, " announced David. "He came up with me. Braddock is in the city, Joey. "

"Sit down in that chair by the winder, David. So! Wot a 'andsome chap you've got to be! My eye! Ruby will be proper crazy about you. I beg pardon: you mentioned Tom Braddock. Well, he was a setting right thore where you are not more than twenty-four hours ago. "

"You don't mean it! "

"Ruby will be in before long, " rambled the old clown, thoroughly enjoying himself. "She's off to the market. Do you know, Davy, she's a most wonderful manager, that girl o' mine. We've been in from the road for nearly a month now—closed the most prosperous season on record at Rochester, New York, on the 17th of May—and Ruby 'ad the 'ouse running like it 'ad been oiled inside o' two hours arfter we got off the cars. She's a—Oh, we was talking of Brad, wasn't we? Well, let me see. Oh, yes, he was 'ere yesterday. And now you're 'ere to-day. It's marvelous 'ow things do go. Brad asked arfter you. "

"I suppose so, " said David impatiently. "But, tell me, Joey, what is his game? What is he in New York for? "

The old clown did not answer at once. He pursed his lips and stared in a troubled sort of way at the leg of David's chair. Then he began to fill his pipe. His hand trembled noticeably.

Saving the snowy whiteness of his hair, Grinaldi did not appear to be an hour older than in the days of Van Slye's. His merry, wrinkled face was as ruddy, as keen, as healthy as it ever had been. No one would have called him sixty-five, and yet he was beyond that in years.

"He's 'ere for no good purpose, I'm afraid, " said he, at last. "In a way, I'm kind o' sorry for Brad, David. He'd 'a' been a different sort o' man if it 'adn't been for Bob Grand. If ever a chap 'ad an evil genius, Brad 'ad one in that man. I suppose Dick told you Brad's been up for two or three year, doing time. Not but wot he deserved it, the way he treated Mary, but it don't seem just right that Bob Grand should be the one to send 'im up. Mary 'ad nothink to do with it, but you can't make Brad believe that. He's got it in 'is 'ead that she's been working with Grand all along. I talked to 'im for two hours yesterday, but I couldn't shake 'im. He's a broken man—but he's a determined one. The time served up at Sing Sing 'ad one benefit to it: it dried up all the whiskey that was in 'im. He came out of there with 'is eyes and 'is mind as clear as whistles, and he's not the feller you used to know, David. He's twenty years older, and his face ain't no longer bloated; it's haggard and full o' lines. His hair is nearly as white as mine. And 'ere's the great thing about 'im: he ain't drinking a drop. He says he never will drink another drop, so long as he lives. Do you know why? "

The old man leaned forward and spoke with a serious intentness that sent a cold chill to the heart of his young friend.

"He says he ain't going to take any chances on bungling the job he's set out to do, " went on Joey slowly. "He wants to be plumb sober when he does it, so's it will be done proper. "

"You mean—murder? "

"That's just it, David. He's going to kill Bob Grand. "

"Joey, we must prevent that! " exclaimed David, rising and beginning to pace the floor. "There is time to stop him. Grand is not in the city. We must get Braddock away. Think what it would mean to—to Christine and her mother! Why, it's—"

"Brad ain't going to stop to think about 'ow it will affect them. He's only got one idea in his 'ead. He'll 'ave it out with Mary beforehand, if he gets the chance, but he won't do 'er bodily injury. He swears he won't do that. He admits he's done 'er enough 'arm. Do you know wot he told me? —and he cried like a baby when he told me, too. David, he actually sold 'is wife to Bob Grand when he gave up the show. "

"Good heaven, Joey! "

"He told me so 'isself, sitting right there. But he says he 'ad sunk so low in them days, pushed along by Grand, that there wasn't anything too mean for 'im to do. He told me he stole your pocket-book—and a lot of other cruel nasty things he did besides. But he said it was whiskey—and I believe 'im. You see, David, I knowed 'im when he was as straight as a string, and a manly chap he was, too—even if 'is father was an old scamp. He ain't making any excuses for 'isself—not a bit of it. He says he's a scoundrel. "

David sat down limply, stunned by the news of Tom Braddock's depravity.

"But if he is sober and in his right senses, he must feel the most poignant remorse after that one terrible act, " cried the young man. "He surely must know that she did not fall into the trap—that she actually fled to escape it. He knows all this, Joey. I think he loved her—in his way. I know he loved Christine. We must get at him from that side—the side of his love for the girl, the side of fairness. If he feels remorse, as you say, all is not lost to him. Where can we find him to-day, Joey? To-morrow may be too late. "

"Wot does Dick say? " asked the old clown, puffing at his pipe. His calmness served its purpose. David stared and then relaxed.

"To tell you the truth, I'd forgotten Dick. Before we parted yesterday, it was understood between us that I was to do nothing until I had heard from him. He promised to find Braddock and report to me— by letter. Of course, he did not know that you had seen him, or he would have come last night to talk it over with you in—"

Joey held up his hand and shook his head. "Oh, no, he wouldn't, David. Dick thinks too much of me to come 'ere. You see, it would never do for him to be seen frequentin' this 'ouse. I've *invited* him 'ere, I'll say that; but he's too square to come. He says it would injure me, and my 'ouse would be watched as long as I live in it. And, besides, it wouldn't be right to Ruby. Once or twice he 'as sneaked in as a peddler or a plumber, by arrangement, poor chap, but never openly. "

To David's annoyance, Joey went into a long dissertation on the inscrutable virtues of Dick Cronk, concluding with the sage but somewhat ambiguous remark that it not only "takes a thief to catch a thief, " but that an honest man is usually a thief when he is caught in the company of thieves.

"You see, Davy, we ain't with the circus now. We're at 'ome in our own 'ouse, and things is different. A circus is one thing and a man's castle is another. Leastwise, that's wot Dick says. He says I'm too old to be caught in bad company. I'd die before I could live it down. He's an odd chap, he is. And now, in regard to Brad, just you keep cool until you 'ears from Dick. You can't afford to stir up a row. Old man Portman and Mary and Christine won't thank you for stirring things up. They're not anxious to 'ave a scandal. If you go arfter Brad too rough, it will percipitate matters instead of 'olding them back. And he'll know to onct that you are acting for his wife—a sort of go-between, don't you see. That will make it the wuss for 'er. So, just 'old yourself in, David. Now, let's talk about somethink else. Yourself, for instance. "

David resignedly settled back, and was at once involved in an exchange of personal narrative.

"I 'ave retired from the stage, " remarked Joey, putting his thumbs in the armholes of his velvet waistcoat. "I am too old to go clowning it any longer. This was my last season. I've got a comfortable income, thanks to you, David, and I'm going to spend the rest of my days in peace and quiet—if you call New York quiet, wot with the church bells and the milkmen. Three seasons in the pantomime, doing all the one- night stands in this bloomin' country, is enough for Joey. If you 'adn't staked me when I was stony broke three years ago, Davy, I'd be in the poor 'ouse now, I daresay. You saved the show for me and I'm properly grateful to you, even though you won't let me mention it. Next season Ruby will go out with the show, but I'm getting a new clown. That is, she'll go unless something important 'appens to pervent. "

He screwed up his eye very mysteriously.

"What is likely to happen, Joey? "

"Well, " said he, "girls do get married. "

"You don't mean to say Ruby's going to be married! " David's thoughts ran to Dick Cronk, although he knew there was no possible chance for him.

"Well, there's a chap mighty attentive to 'er these days. You never can tell. She's a 'ansome girl and—but I daresay it's best not to count chickens before they're 'atched. I don't mind saying, 'owever, " he went on rather wistfully, "I'd like to see Ruby 'appily married and retired from the stage. It's wuss than the circus, my lad. The temptations are greater and there ain't so much honor among the people you're thrown with. The stage is surrounded by a pack of wolves just as vicious as Bob Grand ever was, and a girl's got to be mighty spry to dodge 'em. "

"Is—her best young man a desirable fellow? " asked David, feeling very sorry for the outcast who had not so much as asked for a chance.

"Capital chap. He's a newspaper man, but I can't say that it's anything very damaging against 'im. He seems a very sober chap and thrifty. You wouldn't believe it, but it's quite true. "

"I'm sure I wish her all the happiness in the world. "

"She can't quite make up 'er mind to leave the stage, " mused Joey. "And he won't 'ave 'er unless she does, for good and all. So there you are. "

"If she loves him, she'll give it up. "

"She loves 'im all right, " said Joey. "I know it, because she never talks about 'im. I don't see wot's keeping her. She could ha' gone to market and back five times—Hello! " He was peering through the little front window. A huge smile beamed in his face. With a chuckle, he called his visitor to the window. "Sh! Don't let 'er see the curtain move! She'd take our 'eads off. See that chap? *That's* why she's been so long to market. "

Ruby was walking slowly down the opposite sidewalk, attended by a tall, strong-featured young fellow whose very attitude toward her bespoke infatuation. They crossed the street and stood for a long time at the bottom of the steps, laughing and talking, utterly unconscious of surveillance. Then she shook hands with her courtier, tapped his cheek lightly with the grocer's book which she carried, and ran lightly up the steps. The tall young man, his face aglow, stood motionless where she left him, his straw hat in hand, until she entered the house and closed the door behind her. David's last glimpse of the suitor presented that person, with his chest out, his hands in his pockets, striding off down the street, very much as if he owned it. The young Virginian barely had time left to turn away from the window before Ruby swept into the room.

He had noted, as she stood below, that her figure was a trifle fuller; she was a bit more dashing, and a great deal handsomer than when he had seen her last. Somehow, David, without intending to do so, found himself mentally picturing her ten years hence: a stout, good-natured matron with a double chin and a painful effort to disguise it.

He was not taken aback when she rushed over, with a little scream of delight, and kissed him resoundingly. After which she shook hands with him. It was what he expected. You could have heard the three of them talking if you had been on the sidewalk, but you could not have made head or tail of the conversation. Joey repeated a single remark four times, without being heard by either of his companions. It referred to a joyful reunion and a mug of ale.

At length Ruby gave over rhapsodizing on the tallness, the broadness and the elegance of their visitor, and rushed to the hall door. Raising her voice, she called out to some one down the hall:

"Millie! "

"Yes, Miss Ruby, " came the instantaneous response, suggesting a surprised propinquity.

"Goodness! I thought you were downstairs—But never mind! Don't forget what I told you about the new radishes. "

"No, Miss Ruby, they shall not be forgot, " said the trim little maid, bobbing in the doorway.

"Mr. Jenison likes his waffles crisp, " added Miss Noakes. To David she said: "I love waffles and honey for lunch, don't you? "

"I do, " responded David. "But I didn't know I was to stop for lunch. "

"Father, didn't you tell him? " demanded Ruby.

"I surely did, " prevaricated Joey; "but you were both talking so 'ard he didn't 'ear me. "

During luncheon, which was blissfully served by Millie, David took occasion to compliment Ruby on her good looks, her success and her prospects.

"Don't guy me, David, " she cried, turning quite red.

"If every girl I know could enjoy such improvement in five years, I'm sure—" began David gallantly.

"I suppose you're thinking of Christine Braddock when you say that, " said she shrewdly.

He had the grace to blush.

"Well, let me tell you, David, she's the prettiest thing on two legs— I should say, on two continents. Goodness, a girl does pick up such awful expressions on the stage! I'm just perfectly awful. "

"She is beautiful? " asked David, his heart-beats quickening.

"She's what you might call ravishing, " proclaimed Ruby. "And she's very elegant, too. "

"She don't forget 'er old friends, though, " said Joey hastily. "She sent me that geranium over there larst month and she—"

"Never mind, dad. David isn't interested in her or what she does. Tell me about Colonel Grand's daughter. "

"How do you happen to know—"

"Oh, a little Dicky-bird told me, " she said. "It was in the newspaper I take that you and she were at the Springs at the same time. Oh, I read the society news. Is she pretty? "

"She reminds me of her father. "

"Then she looks like that African gazelle we had with Van Slye's! Poor girl! "

"I don't like her, " said David. Then he related his experience with the young woman. His hearers were disgusted but not surprised.

"They're all alike, " commented Joey. "They're bad, them Grands—father, mother and daughter. First one, then the other tried to bribe me and Ruby. I sometimes believe the wife's as bad as he is, only in a different way. "

They were still seated at the table, discussing the Grands, when a heavy knock came at the front door.

"Who can that be? " said Joey, glancing at his daughter, who was suddenly quiet. The knock was repeated before Millie was instructed to go to the door.

She admitted some one, after a moment's parley. The husky, low-toned voice of a man came to the ears of those in the dining-room. As Joey arose to investigate, the maid came in.

"It's the same man who was 'ere yesterday, Mr. Noakes. He says as he's 'ungry. "

"Braddock, " said Joey in a half whisper.

The man was standing just inside the front door; his dim figure was silhouetted red against the narrow, colored glass window in the casement. Something told them he was fumbling his hat and that his head was bent.

"Ask him to come in here, father, " said Ruby promptly. "I can't bear to see a man hungry. I don't care who or what he is. "

Joey looked at David in doubt and perplexity. David, who had clutched the back of his chair with tense fingers, nodded his head. The old man, obeying the second but unvoiced entreaty of his daughter, strode out into the hall. They heard the low mutter of masculine voices, one in evident protest, the other cordially insistent.

"He's changed quite a bit, " whispered Ruby,

David rose to his feet and stood staring blankly at the man who followed Joey into the dining-room, the man who had struck the never- to-be-forgotten blow. Could this gray, lean, shuffling creature be the leonine, despotic Tom Braddock of other days?

The man stopped just inside the door and fixed his sullen gaze steadily upon the face of the Virginian. Without glancing at Ruby, he uttered a curt "Howdy do, Ruby. "

"I guess we ain't expected to shake hands, " said Braddock, a twisted smile on his lips.

"I can't shake the hand that struck me as yours did when I could not defend myself, " said David coldly.

"'Ere, 'ere, " remonstrated Joey nervously. "We can't 'ave any old quarrels took up in my 'ouse. "

"*I'm* not quarreling, Joey, " said Braddock, still watching David's face. David had the feeling, quite suddenly, that he was looking into eyes he had never seen before—intent, hard, steady eyes that were full of purpose. They were no longer blood-shot and protruding: they seemed to slink back under the pallid, bony brow, looking forth with a sort of cunning that suggested a hiding animal, nothing less.

The change in Tom Braddock was astounding. David had always thought of him as the bullying, bloated giant, purple-faced and blear-eyed. His face was thin and gray—with the pallor of the prison still upon it; his cheeks were sunken, and the heavy stubble of beard that filled the hollows was a dirty white. One would have guessed this apparition of Tom Braddock to be sixty years of age, at least. His hair, still rather closely cropped, was no longer black, but a defiant, obtrusive gray. The heavy neck was now thin and corded; the broad shoulders drooped as if deprived of all their youthful power. His aggressive mustache of the old days was gone, laying bare a broad, firmly set lip. The cheap jeans clothing that fell to him when he left the penitentiary hung loosely on his frame, for he had lost many pounds; the coat was buttoned close about his throat, albeit the day was warm. He wore no collar. His "hickory" shirt was soiled. He had slept in these garments for many nights.

The contrast was appalling. That this cadaverous, prideless individual could once have been the vain-glorious showman was almost inconceivable. It is no wonder that David stared.

"Well, I guess you've changed about as much as I have, " said Braddock, reading the other's thoughts. He uttered a bitter laugh as he turned to drag a chair up to the table, with something of the assurance of old.

"I hope I've changed as much for the better as you have, Braddock, " said David, and he meant it.

Braddock whirled to glare at him in wonder. He was silent for a moment. Then he flung himself into the chair, his jaws setting themselves firmly, no trace of the sarcastic smile remaining.

"I guess you have, David, " he said shortly. "You're not what you were when you joined us five years ago. " A sneer came to his lips. "What a high and mighty chap you've come to be. No wonder you won't shake hands with a jail-bird. "

"Stop talking, Tom Braddock, " said Ruby, a gleam of anxiety in her eyes. "Here's what's left of the lamb and here's—"

"Wait a minute, Ruby, " said he. With his elbows on the edge of the table and his chin in his broad, sinewy hands he leaned forward and spoke again to David. "I've been out three weeks. I was up there for two years and a half. I'm just telling you this so's you'll know why I've changed. The whiskey's all out of me. There never will be any more inside of me, do you understand that? Ten years ago I was a man— wasn't I, Joey? I was a dog when you knew me, Jenison. Now, I'm a man again. See these hands? Well, they've been doing honest work, even if it was in a convict barrel factory. I'm ten times stronger than I was before. There isn't a soft muscle in my body. What you miss is the fat—the whiskey fat. I'm gray-headed, but who wouldn't be? But that is not what I'm trying to get at. I saw Dick Cronk this morning. I don't know how he found me. He told me you were up here to take a hand in my affairs. What I want to know, right here, Jenison, is this: Where is your friend Bob Grand and where is *she?* "

He spoke quite calmly, but there was a deliberate menace in his tones. David was startled. An angry retort leaped to his lips, but he choked it back.

"You are very much mistaken, Braddock, if you consider me the friend of Colonel Grand. I hate him quite as bitterly as you do. I—"

"Oh, no, you don't, " snapped the other. "No one in all this world, from its very beginning, has ever hated as I hate. "

"He is no friend of mine, " reiterated David. "I think you know me well enough to believe that I do not lie. I have not seen him in five years. "

Braddock stared hard at him. Suddenly he leaned back with a deep breath of relief. "I believe you, " he said. "You don't know how to lie. Well, what are you doing here, then, mixing in my affairs? "

"We'll talk about that later on, " said David. "Here is food, man. Eat. You are half-starved. Have you no money? "

"Money? Say, do you think they pay you up *there*? I *am* hungry. Not a mouthful since yesterday noon. Before I touch this grub, Joey, I want to say to you that I don't deserve it of you. I sold you all out. I wasn't square with you. But it was drink and—and that devil behind me all the time. I took your pocket-book that night, David. I stole it. I guess I was crazy most of the time in those days. I don't say I'll ever pay it back. I'm not apologizing for it, either. I'm just telling you. I meant to get all you had, but—well, I wasn't mean enough to crack you over the head. It would have been the only way—"

"Don't speak of it, Braddock, " interrupted Jenison painfully. "That's all past and gone. "

"I've paid for some of my sins—but not all of 'em, " said Braddock. "Not all of 'em. "

He fell to eating ravenously. The others sat back, stiff and uncomfortable, watching him. His sunken but powerful jaws crunched the food with some of the ferocity of a beast. It came forcefully to the minds of the two men that they were looking upon a man whose great sinews were of steel, who could have crushed either of them in the long, hard arms that stretched forth to seize the food Ruby had placed before him. They were slowly coming to realize the bent of this man's mind during its savage development in prison. He had slaved to a purpose. The same thought grew in the mind of each observer: what chance would Robert Grand have in the naked hands of his enemy?

Joey was the first to broach the subject.

"Brad, " he said soothingly, "you want to think twice before you do anything desperate. "

236

Braddock gave an ugly laugh as he jabbed a fork into a piece of meat.

"Joey, " he said, "I've already thought ten thousand times. "

"What do you intend to do? " asked David.

"I'm going to get square with Bob Grand, " said he very quietly. "I'm not going to be rash about it. I'm going to take my time and be *sure*. "

"We'll have to do something to prevent—" began David.

"You can't do anything. I'm not saying what I'm going to do to him, so don't get fidgety. "

"You intend to kill him! "

"He sent me up, didn't he? Without cause, too. He swore me into the pen. Said I tried to kill him. I never tried it. He owed me money. I asked him for it. " He suddenly sprang to his feet. "By Jove, I try not to think that *she* had anything to do with it. I don't want to believe it of her. "

"She didn't 'ave anything to do with it, " cried Joey. "Get that idea out of your 'ead. You treated 'er like a dog, Brad, but she never turned on you like that. I can swear it. "

Braddock went over to the window and stared out upon the little garden. A long interval of silence ensued before he turned to face the others.

"Don't look so scared, Ruby, " he said, noting the girl's expression. "I'm not going to hurt *her*. I guess I've hurt her enough already. She's living as she'd ought to live, and so is—so is Christine. I'm not going to begrudge *them* anything. But I'm going to have a talk with her. " His manner was ugly.

"I'm going to ask her two questions. She'll tell me the truth, I know. That's all I ask. "

"She has always hated Bob Grand, " cried Ruby, "if that's what you mean. "

"That's what I mean. But I'm going to ask her just how much he has pestered her since—well, since that time with the show. I'm going to ask her if she knows what I did to her in the sale of my interest. I'm going to find out if he told her. Oh, you needn't worry! I won't do anything to hurt her or Christine. If she don't know already what I did to her, I'm going to tell her myself. If I get a chance to see my girl, I'm going to tell her just what I did to her mother. "

"Braddock, you must listen to reason! " cried David. "No good can come of this. They are happy and contented. Don't spoil it all for them. Go away, man. Try to forget your grievance against Colonel Grand. God will punish him and—"

"I'll tell you what I came here for to-day, Jenison, " said Braddock levelly. "Dick says you're still crazy about my—about Christine. He swears you haven't seen her in five years—some kind of a promise my wife made, he says. I came to ask you this question: will it make any difference in your intentions regarding her if I—if her father should happen to end his life on the scaffold? I don't say feelings, mind you, —I said intentions. "

"I mean it. Would you still want her if—if it turned out that way? "

David looked helplessly from Joey to Ruby and then at the set, emotionless face of the questioner.

"Braddock, I can tell you this from my soul: nothing you may do will alter my feelings or my intentions. Christine is in no way responsible for your transgressions. I am only sorry that she has such a father. If she still cares for me, I shall ask her to be my wife, even though you are strung up a hundred times. But this is beside the question. *You* should think of her happiness, her peace of mind. All her life she will have to think of you as a—a—well, I won't say it. You—"

"I'll say it for you, " interrupted the gray-faced listener: "as a gallows bird—as scaffold fruit. "

"Please don't, Tom, " cried Ruby.

"You would better a thousand times shoot yourself than to bring that black shadow into her life, " said David. "Suicide is bad enough but— ugh! " He shuddered.

238

"Look here, Jenison, I might have been a good man if it hadn't been for Bob Grand. I always would have been a showman, I reckon, but I'd have been fairly self-respecting. Today, instead of being what I am, I'd still have the love of my wife, the respect of my girl, and—oh, well, you can't understand. You all are against me—and have been for years. I don't blame you—not a bit of it. I deserve it. Grand deliberately set out to ruin me—to pull me down. You know why. We won't go into that. I happen to know he afterwards paid her a lot of money for her interest in the business. When she tells me it was a square transaction I'll believe it, but not before. "

He paced the floor, his hands in his coat pockets, his brows drawn down in a thoughtful scowl.

"You can stop me, I suppose, by having me locked up—but you can't keep me there forever. I'll get out some time. I don't say I'm going to shoot Bob Grand. I want you all to bear witness to this statement: whatever I do to him will be with these two hands. See 'em? Don't they look competent? He didn't use weapons on me, and I'm not going to use 'em on him. It's just a case of who has the best hands in this little game. "

"Why, man, it would be cowardly in you to put your strength against his. You could crush him, " groaned David.

Braddock smiled, almost joyously. "Won't it be a pretty sight? My hands on that fat neck of his! Ha! "

"And the 'angman's rope on that neck of yours, " put in Joey, wiping his moist forehead.

"That's not the point, " said Thomas Braddock.

He picked up his hat, which he had cast upon a chair, and, without another word to either of them—no word of thanks to Ruby, no word of appreciation to David, no word of gratitude to Joey—he strode out into the hall, through the door and down the steps.

They sat still looking at each other for a long time.

"He can't do it to-day, " said Joey in hushed tones. "The man's still out o' town. "

CHAPTER IV

THE DELIVERY OF A TELEGRAM

On David's return to the hotel he found a hastily scrawled note from Artful Dick Cronk. He had remained at the Noakes' until mid-afternoon, discussing the sinister attitude of Thomas Braddock. Joey stubbornly maintained that it was worse than useless to have the man locked up; it would merely delay the consummation of his purpose, and it would add fuel to the fierce flames that already were consuming his brain. He was for temporizing methods, attended by shrewd efforts to keep the enemies apart. It was his opinion that Braddock would listen to reason before many days. Certainly there could be no immediate danger with Grand out of the city. Jenison at last came to his way of thinking, although not without a twinge of misgiving. He had no respect, no sympathy for Braddock. It was his firm opinion that the man had in no way reformed; that he was as bad, if not worse, than ever, for now he was himself and not crazed by drink.

Dick's note bore the disturbing news that Colonel Grand had returned to town, and that Mrs. Braddock was expected the following day. Ernie had obtained this information through the friendly Portman servant, who (to quote Dick) affected the hunchback's society because he believed that the "touching of a hump would bring good luck! " Old Mr. Portman, it was given out, was on his way to his summer place in the Adirondacks, Naturally he would be accompanied by his daughter and Christine. They were due to arrive at four o'clock, and expected to remain in town for ten days before going up to the cool hills. The closing sentences of the pickpocket's note were quaintly satirical: "Brad says he can't afford to be seen in my company. You know how politely he would say it, don't you? He says he can't take chances now. But I staked him to a bed for to-night and I told him I'd give him grub money. It seemed to tender him up a bit. He's hanging round with Ernie to-day and I'm going to see him to-night. Did I tell you that Ernie has a little apartment all to himself over on Fourth Avenue? He's some elegant. Of course, it won't do for me to be seen around his shack much. I might accidentally give the place a bad name, see? Well, I'll close, but will write again to-morrow. DICK. P. S. They come in on the Pennsylvania. "

David spent a miserable night. He was obsessed by the fear that Braddock would seek out Grand that very night, and that it would all be over in the morning. At breakfast he scanned the newspapers closely, half expecting to find the dreaded head-lines. As the morning wore away his spirits lifted. He had made up his mind to go to the railway station. From an obscure corner he would see her without being seen. It was his whim to see her first in this manner, to stare to his soul's content, to compare her in the flesh to the glorious picture his brain had painted. He made no doubt that she would far surpass the portrait in his mind: did not Ruby say she was ravishingly beautiful? His heart leaped fiercely to the project in hand; more than once he found himself growing faint with the intensity of yearning and impatience.

He took Joey and Ruby to luncheon at Delmonico's. All through the meal he was busy picturing to himself the girl who was whirling northward, nearer and nearer to him with each minute of time. She would be tall and slender and shapely. His mind's eye traveled backward. Her hair would be brown—But, even as he constructed her to please his eager imagination, he quailed before the spectre of doubt: was the heart of the girl of fifteen unchanged in the woman of twenty?

Ruby was glibly telling him of the young men who paid court to the granddaughter of old Mr. Portman. Both she and Joey found rich enjoyment in the fact that these sprigs of gentility knew nothing of the circus-riding epoch in Christine's life; they wondered what the effect would be when the truth came out. Joey ventured the opinion that "the devil would be to pay, " and Ruby added the prophecy that "they would drop her like a hot poker. " Strange to say, David found considerable satisfaction in these dolorous predictions.

He caught the ferry soon after luncheon, and was in the station on the other side of the river long before the train was due.

Buying a newspaper, he took a seat in a far corner of the concourse. He read but little and that without understanding. His mind was quite fully occupied in peering over the top of the sheet in the direction of the sheds. Finally he became convinced, by certain psychic processes of the mind, that some one was staring at him. He looked about in all directions. At last his eyes rested on a squat, misshapen figure far over by the ferry entrance.

He had no difficulty in recognizing Ernie Cronk. His presence there was disquieting in more than one sense. Dick had said that Braddock was "hanging 'round" with his brother. This, of itself, was sufficient to create alarm in David's mind. He searched the scurrying throng for a glimpse of the drab, sinister figure of Christine's father, all the while conscious that Ernie Cronk's baleful gaze was upon him. The beady eyes seemed to penetrate shifting obstructions, never changing, never wavering.

David considered briefly, and then decided to consult the cripple. As he made his way over to him he noted that Ernie was flashily dressed, almost to the point of grotesqueness. One might have forgiven the vivid checked suit on the person of a buoyant barber, but it was grewsome in its present occupation. Its gaudy, insistent cheapness leaped out at the observer with much the same appeal for favor that one imputes to the garments of a clown. One might have read the envy in Ernie's soul as his eyes swept the tall, straight, simply clad Southerner who approached. He stood his ground defiantly, however; there was no smile of friendliness on his thin lips.

"Hello, Ernie, " said David. Ernie's arms were folded across his breast. As he gave no sign of unfolding them, David did not proffer his hand.

"You don't have to speak to me if you don't want to, " muttered Ernie, his eyes snapping.

"Where is Braddock? " asked the other, imperturbably.

The rat-like eyes glittered with a cunning smile. "Don't ask me. Got you worried, eh? "

"We are trying to keep him from hurting Christine, that's all, " said David tactfully.

"He ain't going to do that, " said Ernie quickly. A shadow of anxiety crept into his face, however. "He's after Grand. "

"Just the same, we are afraid. Is he here? "

"No. He's asleep at my place, if that'll do you any good. I'm not going to turn against her father, which is more than the rest of you can say. You can tell her, if you want to, that I'm still his friend. " It was plain to be seen that he was adopting this pitiful policy as a means of gaining the attention of the otherwise unapproachable Christine. " He was up all night—*looking!* "

"For Grand? "

"I didn't ask, " leered the hunchback. Suddenly his eyes flew wide open. He was staring past Jenison. "Say! Speaking of angels, look behind you. "

David turned. Not twenty feet away stood Colonel Grand, twirling a light walking-stick and surveying the throng with disinterested eyes. He had seen and ignored Ernie, but had failed to recognize the young man whose back was toward him.

David experienced a sickening sense of disappointment. His heart sank like lead. Grand's presence in the station could have but one meaning. A great wave of revulsion swept through the Virginian. He forgot the anticipated joy of the moment before in contemplation of this significant proof of an understanding.

His lips were dry. He moistened them. Ernie, observing the movement, concluded that he was muttering something to himself.

"Say it to his face, why don't you? " he recommended sarcastically. Before David could interpose, the hunchback called out to Colonel Grand. The latter turned quickly. For a moment he stared intently at the face of the tall young man. Suddenly light broke in upon him.

"Why, it's Jenison, " he exclaimed, and advanced, an amiable smile on his lips. David ignored the hand that he extended; he could only stare, as if fascinated, at the puffy face of the speaker.

Grand had altered but little in appearance during the five years that had passed. He seemed to have grown no older, nor was he less repulsive to look upon. As of old, he was carefully, even immaculately dressed.

Ernie Cronk moved away. They might have heard him chuckling softly to himself.

"Let me see, it's five years, isn't it? " went on the Colonel suavely. He did not appear to resent David's omission. "You've changed considerably. The mustache improves you, I think. "

His voice was as oily as ever, his eyes and his nose as sheep-like. Something arose in David's throat, bringing a certain hoarseness to his voice.

"Time has not affected you, Colonel, " he retorted.

"So they tell me, " said the other. "Are you waiting to meet some one? "

"Yes, " said David, and nothing more.

The Colonel twirled his stick. "My daughter is arriving by the four-twenty, " he announced. "Beastly old station, this. What a godsend a destructive fire would prove if it took it from one end to the other. "

"Your daughter is coming? " asked David. The note of eagerness and relief in his voice caused the other's eyes to narrow suddenly.

"You've met her, I believe, " he said, studying David's face.

"Once, —at the Springs. "

"She's coming rather unexpectedly to make me an extended visit. I should deem it quite an honor, David, if you would give us the pleasure of your company some evening for dinner—"

"My stay here is to be very brief, Colonel Grand, and my time is entirely taken up, " said David coldly.

"I'm sorry, " said the Colonel, shrugging his shoulders in self-commiseration.

It was on the tip of David's tongue to ask him if he knew of Thomas Braddock's presence in town, but timely reflection convinced him that it would be unwise. The Colonel, in his alarm, might set about to have Braddock hunted down and confined without delay; and there was no telling what crime he would lay at Braddock's door in order to secure long imprisonment.

"I met your wife, also, at the Springs, " said David, coolly substituting the thrust.

The Colonel frowned slightly. "You are doubtless aware that my wife and I are no longer living together, " he said, his lips straightening.

"I have heard something to that effect, " said David easily, —so easily that the other could not mistake the insolence of the remark.

Grand flushed. "I am happy to say, young man, that my train is pulling in. I must therefore deny myself the pleasure of conversing with you any longer. Good-day, sir. "

He did not bow as he turned away. A moment later he was threading his way through the crowd. David sauntered over to his first place of waiting, a smile on his lips. He was immensely relieved now, and not a little ashamed of a certain unworthy suspicion.

He fixed his eager gaze on the throng of people that came up from the train, pouring into the big waiting-room. First, he saw Roberta Grand as she came rushing up to her father. He was struck by the swift change that came over the Colonel's face, who stared in amazement over the girl's shoulder, even as he embraced her. David allowed his gaze to return to the oncoming crowd.

Mary Braddock approached, apparently unconscious of the presence of either of her old associates. She walked beside a decrepit old gentleman whom David at once surmised to be Albert Portman. A maid and a male attendant followed close behind. Christine was not in sight.

Mrs. Braddock saw Grand when not more than half a dozen paces separated them. She almost stopped in her tracks. David detected the look of surprise and dismay in her face. She and Grand were staring hard at each other, but neither made the slightest pretense of anything more than visual recognition. She averted her gaze after a moment of uncertainty, and, with her head erect, passed close by the Colonel and his daughter, both of whom were scrutinizing her with brazen interest.

She did not see David Jenison, although he might have touched her by moving two steps forward. Disconcerted by the rude, insolent stare that was leveled jointly by her old enemy and his daughter, a vivid flush mantled her cheek and brow.

Time had made few changes in her appearance. Her face was softer, gentler if possible; her carriage was as erect and as proud as ever. She was modestly, unobtrusively attired, as David expected she would be.

After she had passed, the young man turned his attention again to the crowd, his nerves jumping with eagerness. Christine was sure to be not far behind her mother.

He saw her at last, a laggard at the end of the hurrying procession. She passed close by him. He stood motionless, seeing no one else, thinking of no one but this slim, adorable girl who had no eyes for him. At her side strode a tall, good-looking fellow whose manner toward her could be mistaken for nothing short of simple adoration.

She was smiling brightly, even rapturously up into the eyes of this eager swain. In another instant they were lost in the crowd that rushed to the ferry, but David was never to forget that passing glimpse of her—not to the day of his death.

She was all that his fondest dreams, all that his fairest prophecies, had promised—nay, she surpassed them!

The pure, girlish face—the one of the deep, earnest eyes and tender lips—had been toned and perfected and rechiseled by the magic hand of Time. She was taller by several inches; a lissome creature who moved with the sureness and grace of an almost exalted symmetry.

His dazzled, gleaming eyes followed her into the vortex below. A vast wave of exultation suddenly rushed over him. He had held her in his arms—he had kissed this beautiful, joyous creature—this product of enchantment! Now, more than ever, was he resolved to claim her for his own. It was as good as settled, in his enraptured mind! Nothing could keep her from him now. He had loved her, he had waited for her, and he would have her in spite of everything.

What could it matter to him that she was coveted by all the men who knew her? He rejoiced in the fact that they were at her feet. It was left for him to look down upon them in the end, and smile with all the arrogance of triumphant possession!

Even as he exulted, a dissolving element was flung upon the crystal in which he saw his own glorification. A harsh, discordant voice was speaking at his elbow. He turned. Ernie Cronk was standing beside him. It required a moment of concentration on the part of the infatuated David to grasp the significance of a certain livid hue in Ernie's face. The hunchback was looking up at him. His eyes were bleak with unhappiness. There was no anger in them: only despair.

"That's the fellow, " he was saying, his voice cracking hoarsely. "He's the one she's in love with. "

David started. "You mean—she's in love with him? " he demanded blankly.

"That's Bertie Stanfield. He's a great swell. He was here to meet her. I saw him. It's—it's no use, David. No one else has got a show. " His inclusion of David in his own misfortune, though by inference, would have been amusing at another time. Somehow, at this moment, it struck David as tragic. Was it possible that he was to find himself in the same boat with this unhappy, uncouth worshiper?

He pulled hard at the end of his short mustache, and swallowed hard with involuntary abruptness.

"I—I have heard of him, " he said, a sudden chill creeping into his veins.

"Did she—did she speak to you? " asked Ernie. The hard look was creeping back into his eyes.

"She didn't see me, " muttered David.

"She spoke to me. She always does, " said Ernie, twisting his fingers. "But, " he went on, almost in a wail, "it's because she—she pities me! "

David's heart was touched. He laid his hand on Cronk's shoulder and was about to speak kindly to him. The other drew back, shaking off the compassionate hand.

"None o' that, now. I don't need any pity from you. Keep your trap closed about me. " He jammed his hands into his coat pockets and allowed his gaze to travel toward the ferry entrance. The despondent note returned to his voice. "Shall we take this boat or wait for the next? " he asked. It was as if he had said: "We are companions in misery, you and I. Let's make the best of it. "

David looked at him for a moment oddly. The humor of the situation struck him all at once; but the smile of derision died on his lips. After all, perhaps he was in the discard with Ernie Cronk.

"I'm going to catch this boat, " he said decisively. He started off, followed by his unchosen comrade, and caught the boat almost as it cast off in the slip.

Mrs. Braddock and Christine were far forward. They were chatting gayly with the blonde Mr. Stanfield, who appeared to be giving them the latest news of the town. Old Mr. Portman sat against the deck house.

David watched the little group at the rail from a safe distance. He allowed his fancy full play; his hopes rebounded; his confidence revived. By the time the ferry-boat was locked in the Manhattan slip he was buoyant with the hope and resolution of unconquered youth. He would win her away from them all.

All the way across the river he had been aware of Colonel Grand's close proximity to the little party of three. He stood, with Roberta, across the forward deck, leaning against the rail, his arms folded. At no time did he withdraw his gaze from the figure of Mary Braddock. Her back was toward him, —resolutely, it seemed to David, —and she must have been conscious of the carnal eyes bent upon her. Somehow David had the feeling that she was battling against the impulse to turn in response to the hypnotic command.

He hung back, biding his time, until the party had disappeared inside the ferry building. Then he hastened toward one of the exits, intent on securing a cab. He had made up his mind not to accost them; he would not present himself unexpectedly at a time and place when embarrassment to them might be the result.

From somewhere at the edge of the crowd a thin, sardonic voice called out to him:

"So long, David. You know how it feels yourself now, don't you? "
He knew who the speaker was without looking.

Mrs. Braddock was standing at the counter of the telegraph office
near one of the street doors. He did not see her until he was almost
upon her. She was alone and engaged in writing out a telegram. His
plans were altered in an instant. A moment later, he was at her side,
his face flushed and eager.

For many seconds she stared wonderingly into his smiling eyes.
Before uttering a word she glanced at the message she had finished
and was about to hand it to the clerk; then her gaze returned to his
face.

"David Jenison, " she said, and there was something like awe in her
voice, "is it really you? How strange—how very strange! "

"I'm not a ghost, " he cried. "You look at me as if I had crept out of
my grave. "

She looked again at the telegram. "Why, David, " she began
falteringly. Then her face cleared. A glad smile broke over it, and
both her hands were extended. "It really *is* you? I am not seeing
visions? Yes, you are flesh and blood! You dear, dear David! I am *so*
glad to see you. How does it happen that you are here? Where do
you come from and —" She went on with the eagerness of a child,
asking more questions than he could remember, much less answer.
"And how wonderfully you have grown up! "

"I have seen Christine, " he said eagerly. "She is perfection—she is
marvelous. "

"Seen her? Where? But we cannot talk here. We must have hours and
hours all by ourselves. Come to my father's house to-night. We are
living with him, you know. There is so much that we have to tell
each other—all that has happened in the five long years. "

"I am here solely to remind you that the five years are ended, Mrs.
Braddock. Mahomet has come to the mountain, you see. "

Her face clouded. She glanced quickly through the window. His
gaze followed hers. Christine and young Stanfield were driving

away together in a hansom. He read her thoughts. "I'll take my chances, " he remarked confidently.

"I know that she has not forgotten, David, " she said after a moment of deliberation, "but—well, I will be frank with you. She has suddenly shot past my comprehension. It is the privilege of a girl to change her mind, you know, when she changes the length of her frocks. "

"You haven't changed, have you? " he asked bluntly. She stared. "I? "

"I mean, you are still my champion? "

"Of course, " she replied readily. "

"Then, as I said before, I'll take my chances with the rest. I'll not hold her to that girlhood bargain. That would be unfair. But, if you'll permit me, I'll go in and win her as she is to-day—if I can. "

She smiled at his ardor. "I hope you may win, David. But you must win for yourself. Do not look to me for help. She must decide for herself. "

He did not refer to the young man who had taken her away in the cab. Mrs. Braddock noted this and was not slow to divine the well-bred restraint that lay behind the omission.

"That was young Stanfield, " she observed. "He is delightful. My father is devoted to him, "

David smiled. "I hope to have the pleasure of meeting him soon. "

"You may meet to-night. "

If she expected to see a trace of annoyance in his face, she was disappointed. He gracefully confessed his interest in the prospective meeting.

"I shall be more than delighted to come, " he said.

"And I am glad he will be there to engage Christine's attention while I devote myself to you, Mrs. Braddock. "

"You nice boy! "

She extended her hand. "I must not keep my father waiting out there. You don't know how glad I am that you are here, David. " Suddenly a wave of red mounted to her cheek; an expression of utter loathing came into her deep eyes. In some alarm he glanced over his shoulder.

Colonel Grand was standing at the door through which she would have to pass. He was not looking at her, but his motive in placing himself there was only too plain.

"Confound him! " involuntarily fell from David's lips.

"If he dares to address me—" she began, her face going white. "David, I have not seen that man since the day I left the show. Why is he here to-day? Is it to annoy—to torment me in—"

"He won't do that, " announced David firmly.

"I have a strange foreboding, David, —of evil, of something dreadful. Perhaps it is due to the unexpected sight of—his horrid face. I—"

"That's it, " said he promptly. Nevertheless, a slight chill entered his heart. There was Tom Braddock to be considered. "I'll come early to-night, if I may, " he said, more soberly than he meant. "There are some very important things to discuss. Now I'll take you to your carriage. "

During their talk she had absently folded the telegram. He observed it in her hand and said:

"The telegram—don't forget that, Mrs. Braddock. "

Her smile was enigmatic. With a diverted smile for the waiting clerk she said: "I shall not send it, after all. "

David walked with her to the door. They passed so close to Colonel Grand that David's elbow touched his arm, but neither of them looked at him. She hastily entered the waiting carriage, a sort of panic overtaking her.

Thrusting the crumpled bit of paper into David's hand, her eyes steadfastly held against the impulse to look at the satiric figure in the doorway, she said in a half-whisper:

"Take it, David—and come to-night. "

He stood there with his hat in his hand as the carriage drove off, sorely perplexed by her action. Suddenly a light broke in upon his understanding. He spread out the small sheet and read:

"The five years have passed. I redeem my promise. You are not obliged to keep yours, however. " It was signed "Mary Braddock. "

Colonel Grand was smiling sardonically in the doorway.

CHAPTER V

THE LOVE THAT WAS STAUNCH

"I shall depend on you, David, to bring my husband here to see me. Search for him until you find him. "

The white-faced, distressed woman said this to David Jenison a few hours later in the Portman library. They sat alone in the half-light. Stanfield's married sister had taken Christine off earlier in the evening, to a concert. Mrs. Braddock, in a spirit of whimsicality, forbore mentioning the appearance of David to the girl, planning to surprise her when she returned from the concert. If David was disappointed at not finding her, he went to considerable pains to hide the fact from the mother. As a matter of fact he was secretly relieved, strange as it may seem, after the first shock of disappointment. Christine's absence was providential, after all. He had ugly news for Mrs. Braddock; he could wait on the opportunity to see Christine, but what he had to say to the mother could not be put off for a moment.

He had gone at once to his room in the hotel after leaving Mrs. Braddock at the ferry. He was startled almost out of his boots by the discovery that Dick Cronk was there ahead of him, calmly occupying the easiest chair and reading the evening paper. A skeleton key had provided the means of admission to the room; a brave heart and cunning brain did the rest.

Dick's news created great unrest in David's breast. Braddock, it appeared, had gone, early in the afternoon, to the apartment hotel in which Grand lived. Fortunately the Colonel was not about the place. Dick, on missing the ex-convict, had hurried at once to Grand's hotel, finding his man there, seated in the small lobby, a sinister example of respectability, waiting patiently for the return of his enemy. The self-appointed guardian coaxed him away from the place, conducting him to the cheap, ill-favored thieves' lodging-house where he had taken a single room for temporary occupancy. Braddock, after a show of obduracy, finally had consented to make an effort to see his wife before visiting his wrath upon Colonel Grand.

Dick informed David: "He's set on doing something nasty, kid, that's all there is to it. He *won't* be turned aside. Those years in the pen have put something into his backbone that never was there before. Maybe Mrs. Braddock can talk him out of it, but I dunno. She always had influence over him, but that was before he took to getting tight. It's different now. If we can't do anything else we'll have to warn Grand, that's all. I hate to do it, but—I guess it's the only way left. "

For the first time in their acquaintance David saw Dick lose control of himself. His face was convulsed by an expression so violent that the Virginian drew back in alarm.

"David, I hate the sight o' that man. I'd go to hell to-morrow if I thought I could have a place where I could look on and see him burn forever. I never see him now without wanting to stamp that face of his to jelly. It's growing on me, too. Oh, to kick that white, putty face until there was nothing left of it! I'd give—" But David had grasped his arm, to shake him out of his frenzy, speaking to him all the while. He grew calm as abruptly as he had gone to the other extreme. His brow was moist, but the old, quizzical smile beamed beneath it. "I'm going on like a crazy man, ain't I? Well, forget it, kid. I'm off my nut, I guess. Get back to business. You got to fix it up with her to see Brad. " He paused and eyed David's face narrowly. "Say, are you still worryin' about what I said about trampin' on his face? "

David had cause afterward to recall the ugly sensation that this extraordinary burst of rage created in his mind.

Before leaving, Dick announced that he was eager to start West to connect with Barnum's circus, complaining of the unprofitable idleness that had been forced upon him. He expressed the confident hope that Braddock might be persuaded to leave with him.

"I can't afford to be loafin' around New York this season of the year, " he reflected in the most *degage* manner imaginable. "It's expensive, the way Ernie and me are living nowadays. I got to get out and round up the rubes. Now, kid, don't preach. Oh, by the way, has Joey told you the good luck that's happened to Ruby? Going to marry Ben Thompson, a newspaper man. I'm mighty glad she's gettin' a chap like him, and not one of them rotten guys that hang around the op'ry houses. She's—she's a fine girl, Davy—a plum' daisy. "

Jenison once more impulsively offered to provide a refuge and employment for life on his plantation for the delectable scalawag, but Dick laughed at him in fine scorn. He departed a few minutes later, sauntering down the hall with a complacency that fairly scoffed at house detectives and their ilk.

David went to the Portman home in a state of suppressed eagerness and anxiety, one emotion topping the other by turns as he was being driven toward Washington Square. He expected to see Christine. He was counting on it with all the pent-up fervor of a long-denied lover. The brief glimpse he had had of her in the afternoon drove out all doubts as to his own state of mind concerning her. She was incomparably beautiful; she had the air of the high-bred; she was worthy of the attentions of the well-born; she possessed poise, manner—all that and more: the indefinable charm that radiates in some mysterious way from the superlatively healthy.

His admiration for her, instead of suffering the shock that might have been anticipated—and which was secretly dreaded, to be quite candid— had grown more intense under the test. What would be her attitude toward him? That was the question. What had the five years and new environment done for her?

Eager as he was to discover the state of her feelings, he recognized, however, the more pressing matters that were to be considered. The peace and welfare of the girl herself demanded his first thoughts, his most devoted efforts. Tragedy stalked close beside her. He was afraid to think how close it was, or when it would make its ugly presence felt.

He lost no time, therefore, in apprising Mary Braddock of the true state of affairs. She sat before him, a great dread in her dark eyes, the pallor of helplessness on her cheek, listening to the direful tale he told. He did not make the mistake of minimizing the situation. He spared her not the details, nor softened the stubborn facts. As clearly as possible he drew for her the picture of Thomas Braddock as he had seen him. He repeated faithfully all that Dick Cronk and the Noakeses had told him, neglecting no particular in the known history of her husband since the old circus days.

She was very still and tense. Her eyes never left his face while he was speaking, except once when she looked toward the door in response to a sound that led her to believe that Christine was returning. There were times when he imagined that she was not breathing. After the first few minutes she asked no questions, but mutely absorbed the story as it fell from his lips. The light of joy and gladness in her eyes that had been his welcome was gone now. In its place was the dark gleam of dread and anxiety.

She interrupted him once, to ask him to tell her again how Braddock looked and how he had acted. As he repeated the description, her perplexed, even doubting, expression caused him to hesitate, but she shook her head as if putting something out of her mind and signified that he was to proceed.

"I would not have known him, " he concluded, "he was so unlike the man I knew. "

"He had not touched whiskey, you say—not since—"

"Not in three years. It has wrought an unbelievable change in him. "

"I knew him, David, before he drank at all, " she said, staring past him. "Perhaps the change would not be so great to me. "

"He has aged many years. There are hard, desperate lines in his face. You *would* see a change, I am afraid, Mrs. Braddock. "

She was silent for a moment. "Go on, David, " she said, suddenly passing her hand before her eyes in a movement as expressive as it was involuntary. "Dick Cronk has a certain amount of influence over him, you say. "

"It will not last. When Colonel Grand hears that he is back in town his first step will be to have him thrown into jail on one pretext or another. Braddock realizes this. He has made up his mind to strike first. I think he believes in you, Mrs. Braddock—in fact, I am sure he does. I know he loves Christine. But he hates Colonel Grand even more than he loves her or—you. He—"

"Oh, he does not love me, David. You need not hesitate, " she said drearily.

"As I have already said, he gave Dick a half-promise that he would try to see you. He has two questions he intends to ask, I believe. I think, Mrs. Braddock, you will be doing a very wise thing if you see him—of your own free will. He will probably insist on seeing you in any event—even in the face of opposition. You can avoid a great deal of trouble by—well, by not barring him out. I know how it must distress you. I wish I could take all the worry, all the trouble off your shoulders. But there would be only one way in which I could do it—and that would be a desperate one. "

It was then that she laid her trembling, icy hand on his, and said, "Search for him until you find him. "

David hesitated a moment before putting his next question. It touched on a very tender subject.

"Have you thought of divorcing him? "

"No, David, " she said quietly. "I made my bed years ago, as Joey would say. Tom is Christine's father. He is my husband. You may well say, God help both of us. But, David, while I cannot live with him, I intend to remain his wife to the end. I am ready to promise anything to him if he will go away. I will give him all of the money I received for my share of the hateful business. He must accept it quietly, sanely. It is for *her* sake, and he must be made to see it. The world knows that I ran away to be married, but it has forgotten the circumstances. The general belief is that my husband died years and years ago, and that I have lived abroad ever since. There is one thing to his credit, David. I shall not forget it. When he was arrested, he thought of Christine and—and—well, he gave an assumed name, an alias, to the police. Colonel Grand kept his own silence, and for years he has held this over me as a threat. I have had many letters from him, believe me. Christine is no longer the little, unheard-of circus rider. She is—well, she is a *personage*. Do you understand? "

He nodded his head. She went on hurriedly.

"Tell Tom I *want* to see him. Tell him I am ready to discuss everything with him. Tell him that nothing must happen that can injure her. "

"He may insist on seeing—her. "

"She does not know that he has been in prison, " she said miserably.

"But if he should insist? "

"I should have to prepare her, David. She knows that he is alive —
but —Listen, David! " She leaned forward to give emphasis to her
words. "If he comes to her now with the story of his—his wrongs, of
his sufferings, she will forget all that has gone before. Her heart is
tender. I am afraid of the stand she may take—and she may compel
me to take it with her. "

"I'll do all that I can, Mrs. Braddock, to—" he began. The sound of
voices in the vestibule came to them at that moment. Good nights
were being called from the steps to the street below. Then the door
was opened and closed quickly. Some one came rapidly down the
hall. There was a swift rustling of skirts, the low humming of an air
from "Pinafore. " David was on his feet in an instant, visibly excited
by the impending encounter.

Christine came into the library. She was half-way across the room
before she realized that the tall young man beside her mother was a
stranger... She stopped. Her questioning gaze lingered on his face.
His smile puzzled her. Her eyes narrowed, then suddenly they were
distended; her lips parted in amazement, tremulously struggling into
a smile of wonder and unbelief. No one had spoken.

"It—it is David, " she said, a quaver of breathlessness in the soft
tones.

He sprang forward, his hands extended.

"Yes, " he cried, transported by the new aspect of loveliness.

She stood straight and slim before him, still unbelieving. Slowly her
hands were lifted to meet his, as if impelled by a power not her own.
He clasped them; they were cold. Something in their limp
unresponsiveness chilled him as if he had been touched by ice. He
gently released them and drew back, dismayed within himself.

"Why—why didn't you tell me, mamma? " she cried, the flutter in
her voice increasing. A swift wave of color rushed to her cheeks. She
suddenly held out her hands to him again, an eagerness in the action
that caught him unawares and lifted his spirits to dizzy heights. "Oh,
I am so glad—so glad to see you, David, " she cried. Her firm little
hands were warm now, and trembling.

"Christine, " he half whispered, "are you—are you truly glad to see me? Do you mean it? "

She was looking straight into his eyes. In her own glowed a dark appeal; she seemed to be delving in the secret recesses of his heart.

"David, " she cried, forgetful of everything else in the world, "does it mean that you—you still care for me? You haven't changed? I have been wondering—oh, how I have been—"

The plaintive note drove all doubt from his mind. He was suddenly exalted. Speech was beyond him. His dream had come true. She was incomparably fairer than his waking hours had pictured her during the five years of probation; only in fond dreams had she appeared to him as she now appeared in reality. He could only look down into her face, mute under the seal of wonder. All that he had longed for and prayed for was here revealed to him; he could have asked for no more. He went suddenly weak with joy.

"My little Christine, " he murmured.

"I have been so afraid, " she was saying, still searching his soul through his eyes. "I am still afraid, David. It has been a long time. So many things may have happened. We were such young, foolish things. Oh, David, you don't know how I have worked and planned and striven to make myself what you would like, if you were ever to come to see me again. I—"

"You are perfect—you are divine! " he cried, all the passion of his soul ringing in the tender words. "I can't believe it! You really care, Christine? You have not changed? It has always been the same with you? "

"Changed, David, " she whispered, her lip trembling, a sudden mist swimming in her sweet young eyes. "Changed? "

"You *do* love me? I am not dreaming? It is really *you?* "

She suddenly lowered her eyes, the warm flush spreading to her throat, her neck, her ears. She caught her breath in a half-sob.

Both had forgotten the tall woman who stood over there by the window, her hands clasped, her heart in the eyes that looked upon them. They did not see the beatific smile that came to her colorless lips. Nor were they aware of the fact that she turned away, to gently draw aside the curtain that she might look out, unseeing, upon the gloom of the night beyond.

He quickly lifted the girl's hands to his feverish lips. There he held them for many minutes while he steadied his rioting senses, regaining control of his nerves. He looked down upon the dark, soft hair and worshiped. A red rose rested there. He bent over and kissed her hair— and the rose.

Then she looked up.

"I do love you, David, " she said softly, "are you—are you sure that you—Oh, David, are you sure? "

For answer, his eager arm stole over her shoulder and she was drawn close to his breast. She raised her lips to greet the kiss. Her little hand clutched his with a sudden convulsive ecstasy. He felt the warm, quick breathing—and then their lips met.

"I am very sure, " he murmured, his voice husky with emotion. "There never has been a minute in which I was not sure, Christine, my darling. "

"You have forgotten—you can overlook those old days when I was Little Starbright? " she whispered wonderingly. "They will make no difference —now? "

"I loved you then. You and I and my love have grown older and stronger and dearer with the years that have—"

She broke away from him, putting her hands to her cheeks in pretty confusion. Her eyes were shining brightly as she looked beyond him.

"Oh, mother! I—I forgot that you were there. I forgot everything. " She ran to her mother and buried her face on her shoulder. "I told you it would come true, mother. I knew it would. Oh, I am so happy! Have I been ridiculous? Have I been silly, mother? "

It was the ecstatic David who reassured her on that point. In his unbounded joy he rushed over and enveloped the two of them in his long, eager arms.

Later on, after Mrs. Braddock had gone to her father's room, he sat with Christine on the low, deep sofa under the bookshelf gallery. Her hands were clasped in his. They had but little to say to each other in words. Their eyes spoke the thoughts that surged up from their reunited hearts. She had thrown aside the light, filmy wrap, and the sweet, velvety skin of her neck and shoulders gleamed in the soft light; her perfectly modeled, strong young arms were as clear and white as marble.

He was lost in admiration—in marveling admiration. For long stretches at a time he permitted himself to fall into silent, rapt contemplation of this perfected bit of womanhood. Every childish feature that he remembered so well had been subtly vignetted by the soft touch of nature; he was sensing for the first time the vast distinction between fifteen and twenty—the distinction without the difference; for she was the same Christine, after all. It was unbelievable. A delicate bit of magic was being performed before his very eyes; the slim, girlish sweetheart of other days was being effaced. The soft, insinuating loveliness of young womanhood, with all its grace, all its charms, was being revealed to him as if by some wonderful process in photography— new shades, new lights, new tints, all ineffably joyous in tone. He could not remember that her hair was so soft and wavy at the temples, nor had it ever seemed to caress her ears so adorably. Why was it that he had never noticed the delicate arch of her eyebrows? Why had he failed to see the limpid sweetness in her eyes? And her hair, too, seemed to cling differently above the slim, round neck. What magic sculptor had chiseled her lips into their present form? Her chin; her nose; her broad, white brow—why had he never observed them before? And what was this strange, new light in the dark eyes? This look that was no longer childish, no longer inquisitive, but steady with understanding!

The girl of fifteen was gone. This was the perfect, well-blown human flower, the woman. The woman! Slender, beautifully molded, sinuous, incomparably fine—the woman! He closed his eyes in sudden subjection to that thing called rapture. He held her close, strained to his own triumphant, vigorous body. She was his! The woman! Ah, it *was* different!

"How beautiful—how wonderful you are, Christine, " he whispered. "I can't believe that you are *my* Christine. "

She could only smile her confirmation. No words could have told so clearly the sensuous delight that stilled her tongue. There was joy in her soft breathing, in the gently spreading nostrils, in the half- closed eyes. She was experiencing the unspeakable thrill that comes but once in the dream of love.

When he spoke, at uneven intervals, his voice was husky with the passion that consumed him.

Once he was saying: "It is too good to be true. I came unbidden, determined to learn how I stood with you. I could not wait. When I saw you to-day, I said to myself that you had grown away from me. I told myself I should have to win you all over again. You seemed unapproachable. You were so wonderful, Christine—so utterly beyond anything I had expected to find. I was alarmed, I was actually dismayed. But I told myself that I would win you; I would begin all over again and I—"

"You saw me to-day? " she interrupted in surprise. "Where? "

"I was waiting for you at the station—far back in the crowd. I wanted to see you in that way first. Your mother and I met there. She did not tell you. She asked me to come to-night, but she was careful to give me no hope. You will never know the doubts and fears that have beset me all this long evening. And then you came in. I was dazed. I was all a-tremble. And then to find that—that I had had all my fears for nothing! Why—why, I could have died for joy! You did not hesitate. You swept me off my feet. When you kissed me, Christine, I—I—it was as if night had turned to day in—"

"I have gone on loving you, David, from the beginning. There never has been a moment in which I have ceased to do so. Ah, you had nothing to fear. But I! Oh, my dear one, I was never free from doubt—never quite certain. You were so far above me that I—"

"Don't say that! "

"That I was sure you would not take our—our love dream seriously. When you came to be a man, with all that manhood meant to you, I felt somehow that you would forget the little circus girl who—"

He kissed her. Then she was silent for a long time.

"Your mother was telegraphing me to-day to come, " he said after a time. "Did you know that she intended to do so? "

"No. I only knew that she would do it—soon. She had promised—both of us, you know. "

"Have you never asked her to send me the message? "

"Never! How could I? I would not have held you to the compact. Nor would she. "

"And have you not told her that you cared for me all these years? Didn't she know? "

"Listen, David, " she said seriously. "My mother has never spoken of our compact. She did nothing to influence me. She was content to let time take its course—and nature, too. Ah, how wise she is! But all this time I have been conscious of a strange feeling that she was making me over anew with but one object in view. She wanted me to be all that you could expect, demand, exact, if you were to come some day to—to look me over, to see if I was—was worth the effort. Yes, David, she prepared me against this day. She worked with me, she planned, she denied herself everything to give me all that you might wish for in a—"

"My dear, you had everything to begin with, " he began gallantly, but she checked him with a shake of her head.

"No, I did not. True, I had not been brought up as other circus children were. But I had a point of view that required years of training to destroy. We won't speak of my father. I don't like to think of him. David, as we used to know him, you and I. There was a time when he was different—and I loved him. But that was long before. I—I think he has gone out of my life altogether. "

David realized then and there that she should not be kept in the dark regarding her father's whereabouts and designs. She was sensible, she was made of strong timber. She could face the conditions, no matter what they proved to be.

The thought was responsible for the irrelevant remark that followed. "I must have a word or two with Mrs. Braddock before I leave to-night. "

263

She looked up quickly. "A word concerning—you and me? " she asked.

"Yes. "

Her eyes were lowered again, this time with some of the life gone from them. A shadow crossed her face.

"David, " she said, "I trust you, I know you are staunch and true. But, dear, are you considering well? Are you sure that you will never regret—this? No, don't speak yet, please. We must be frank with each other. I am not a silly, romantic girl, believe me. I have faced and can still face the real things of life. You are not driving yourself to forget or to overlook all the conditions that surround me, are you? I was a rider. My father was a rider. Oh, you are going to say that my mother was different. But what has that to do with it? What does it matter that she has brought me here, to this home of plenty and of respectability and—well, let us say it, of position. I am the granddaughter of Albert Portman. That may stand for something— yes, it *does* stand for a great deal. But do not forget, David, dear, that I am the daughter of Tom Braddock. I am the granddaughter of old Stephen Braddock, who was a—a—"

"Don't say it, dearest! Why should you be saying all this to me? You, an angel among—"

"I must, David, " she went on resolutely. "You have come here to ask me to be your wife—to hold me to a promise. You must think all this out in time, David. Please don't laugh in that scornful way. It hurts. I am very serious. Your friends, your people, will welcome me gladly as the granddaughter of Albert Portman, but will they take me, can they accept me, as the granddaughter of Stephen Braddock? As the product of a fashionable convent they may rejoice in me, but as the pupil of the sawdust ring, —as Little Starbright, a thing of spangles! Ah! How about that side of me? Who were my childhood friends and associates? Don't misjudge me. I loved them all—I love them now. They were the best friends and the truest. But could they ever be the friends of your friends? "

"They are *my* friends, " he said simply, struck by her earnestness. "Are you forgetting what they meant to me in the old days? And what was I? A fugitive with a price on my head. A—"

"Ah, but you were different—you always had been different. You were a Jenison. What are you going to say when some one—and there always will be the miserable some one—reminds you that he saw your wife when she was Little Starbright? What—"

"Don't look so miserable, Christine! If any one says that to me I shall congratulate him. "

"Congrat—Oh, do be serious! It doesn't matter what I am to-day, David; it's what I was such a little while ago. I am not trying to belittle myself. *I* am proud of what I am. Don't misunderstand me. I am a Portman! *Her* blood is in me—her mind, her soul. But I am not all Portman. Suppose, David—suppose that my father were to come back some day. We know what he is—what he was. Perhaps the world may have forgotten, but suppose that he reminds the world of the fact that he is my father—"

"Christine! You are working yourself into a dreadful state over all this—"

"Am I not calm? Am I excited? No; you see I am not. "

"Dearest, I want you to be my wife. You urge me to think in time. Haven't I thought it all out? What more is there for me to think about, save my love for you? You are not presenting new conditions to me, sweetheart. They are old ones. I do not intend that either of us shall sail under false colors. When you go to Jenison Hall as my wife, it shall also be as the daughter of Thomas Braddock, the showman. "

"But, David, he may have fallen so low—he may have sunk to the very lowest—oh, you must understand. We have heard nothing from him. We don't know where he is, nor what his life has been. Suppose—oh, I can't bear to think of it. "

He put his hands on her cheeks and turned her face so that he could look squarely into her eyes. He saw the trouble there, the agony of doubt.

"Look at me, Christine, " he said gently. The light in his eyes held her. "It doesn't matter what he was, what he is or what he may become. I love you, as I have always loved you. You are going to be my wife. That is the end of it all. "

His heart was sinking, however, under the weight of the thing he knew, the thing she was yet to know. He would have given all he possessed in the world for the power to shield her from the blow that was yet to fall.

There came swiftly to mind the hazy, indistinct interior of a dressing-tent, with its mysterious lights and strange people, just as it had appeared to him on that first, never-to-be-forgotten night. He felt himself again emerging from that state of insensibility to look upon the queer, unfamiliar things that were to become quite real to him. And out of the phantasmalian group of objects there grew a single slim, well-remembered figure in red, to dazzle him with her strange, unexpected beauty, and to soothe him with an unspoken faith that began then and had not yet faltered in her lovely eyes. She had given him food. She had said he was no thief. It all came back to him. He had looked upon her as an angel then—a strange, unfamiliar angel in the garb she wore, but an angel, just the same.

Now he knew that love began with the first glimpse he had of her. It was as if she had been revealed to him in a vision. His mind swept along over the rough days that followed. He saw her again in the ring, in the dressing-tent—everywhere. Then there was that night under the grocer's awning—that sweetest of all nights in his life!

And now she was here, with him again, but amidst vastly different surroundings. She was here, and she would need him now as he had needed her then. It was for him now to present himself as the bulwark between her and the fickle, disdainful world of which she had become a part. She was no longer the self-reliant, petted creature of the circus, where environment and adversity formed a training-school for disaster, but a delicate, refined flower set out in a new soil to thrive or wither as the winds of prejudice blow. In the other days she could have laughed with glee at the vagaries of that self-same wind, but now, ah, now it was different. She was not Little Starbright.

He drew her closer. She trembled in the clasp of his arms. Her firm, full young breast rose and fell in quick response to the driving heart-beats. Again his thoughts shot back to the prophetic, perfect figure of the girl at fifteen. He fought off a certain delicious, overpowering intoxication, and forced himself to a bewildered contemplation of her present powers of resistance to the hard problems of life. She was strong of body, strong of heart, strong of spirit, but was she strongly fortified with the endurance that must stand unshaken through a period of sorrow and shame and—disgrace?

Again he looked into her half-closed eyes. He saw there the serene integrity of Mary Braddock; the light of that woman's character was strongly entrenched in the soul of Christine Braddock. He experienced a sudden sense of relief, of comfort. She was made of the flesh and spirit that endures. Product was she of Thomas Braddock in his physically honest days, and of Mary, his wife, in whose veins flowed the strain of a refinement elementally so pure that the bitterest things in life had proved incapable of destroying a single drop of its sweetness.

"What are you thinking of, David? " she asked, impressed by the look in his eyes and the unconscious nodding of his head.

"Of you, " he said, catching himself up quickly. "Always of you, dearest. "

"You were thinking of what I said to you a moment ago, " she said steadily.

"Yes, " he agreed, "and of what you said to me five years ago. "

Soon afterward he prepared to depart. She ran upstairs to tell her mother that he wanted to see her. She had kissed him good night. He did not see her again. Later on, she stood straight and tense, in the center of her bedroom floor, her hands to her breast, waiting for her mother's return. Vaguely she felt that something harsh and bitter was to be made known to her before she slept that night.

In lowered tones David Jenison was saying to Mary Braddock: "She must be told everything to-night. It isn't safe to put it off. She is strong and she knows that I am staunch. Nothing else should matter. We don't know what to-morrow may bring, but she must be as fully prepared for the worst as we are. It isn't fair to her. Tell her everything. "

"Yes, " she said steadily. "And you will try to find him to-night? "

"I will, " he said.

CHAPTER VI

DOOR-STEPS

David hurried off toward the car-line, bent on reaching Joey's home before that worthy retired for the night.

At the top of a flight of stone steps leading to the doors of an imposing mansion across the street from the Portman home a motionless figure sat, as bleak as the shadows in which it was shrouded. Like a malevolent gargoyle it glowered out upon the deserted street; a tense, immovable chin rested in a pair of clenched hands, knees supporting the elbows. This desolate, forbidding figure had been there for an hour or more—ever since Christine's return from the concert. Not once were the burning eyes removed from the lighted windows across the way. At last, long after the footsteps of the anxious Virginian had died away in the night, and the lights were extinguished in the house opposite, the silent watcher moved for the first time. Slowly he came to his feet, his eyes still upon the solitary window in which a light had lingered long after all the others were gone.

"Well, they're through discussing me, " muttered Tom Braddock, thinking aloud. Shivering, as if from a mighty chill, although the night was warm, he stalked down from his perch and went swiftly up the street, a gaunt, broad-shouldered figure whose step seemed to suggest purpose more than stealth.

As he slunk past the approach to a basement hard-by, a stealthy figure slipped out from the recess and kept pace with him, not twenty feet behind. A block farther up the street this second watcher quickened his pace. He came alongside the man ahead.

"Hello, Brad, " fell upon the ears of the stalked. He betrayed no surprise, no sign of alarm. He did not check his pace, nor look around.

"Confound you, Dick, " he said, as if pronouncing sentence, "if you don't quit dogging me like this I'll kill you, so help me God. "

"You might have known I'd be somewhere around, " said the other quietly. They were now side by side, gaunt, slouching figures, both of them.

"I thought I'd given you the slip. "

"Umph, " was the expressive comment.

"What did you follow me over here to-night for? " demanded Braddock fiercely, after thirty steps.

"You know why, Brad. Don't ask. "

"This is my affair, " went on the big man. "I was doing no harm, sitting across there. Can't a man sneak off for a single look at his own child—in the dark, at that—without being hounded by—Say, you must stop dogging me, d' you hear? I'm not a rat. I'm a human being. I've got feelings. I wanted to have a look at her. She's my girl and— "

"Not so loud, Brad. Remember who you are with. You are in bad company, old man. Don't draw attention to the fact. Take a word of advice from me. Keep away from that house. Don't—"

"I don't want to hear anything more out of you, " grated Braddock. "I know what I'm doing. I'm living up to my promise, ain't I? Didn't I say I'd see Mary before I—Say, " he broke off incontinently, his thoughts leaping backward, "that was my girl that said good night to the swells back there—mine! Did you see how prettily she was dressed? Did you hear how sweet her voice was? I—I—" Something came up in the man's throat to cut off the words; and a long silence fell between them.

Not until they were turning into Fourth Avenue did Dick Cronk speak again. Somehow he felt the emotion that struggled in the breast of the man beside him. For the first time in his life he was sorry for him.

"Where are you going now, Tom? " he asked, knowing full well what the spiritless answer would be.

"To that hell-hole of a place you call home, " said Braddock. Dick slipped his hand through the other's arm; they turned oft into one of the cross streets, wending their way through the sodden community, one with his head erect, the other with his chin on his breast, his hands in his coat pockets.

Half an hour later a cab stopped at a corner not far from a Pell Street intersection. Two men got down and picked their way through the vile street, searching out the house numbers as they progressed. They passed the all-night dives and brothels, whence came the sounds of unrestrained and unrefined revelry, and came at last to a spot beneath a huge wooden boot that hung suspended above the door of the most unholy structure in the narrow street. A man in his shirt sleeves sat back in the shadow of the tumbledown stoop, smoking a pipe. At his left a narrow, black passage led down between two squalid buildings, one of which was dark, the other lighted so that the vicious revelers within might see and be seen.

The uncertain, timorous actions of the strangers in Thieves' Alley brought a fantastic smile to the lips of the smoker. He watched them as they looked up at the boot and compared notes in rather subdued tones.

"This must be the place, " said one of the men. There was no mistaking the note of disgust in his voice.

"Looking for some one, gents? " demanded the smoker, without rising from the stool on which he sat leaning against the wall.

"Is this No. 24—Hello! It's Dick! "

"Ain't you afraid to be seen down here, Joey? " asked the man on the stool, chuckling.

"It's worth an honest man's life to be seen 'ere, " said Joey Noakes, in hushed tones. "God 'elp 'im as can't 'elp 'isself if he ever strolls in 'ere unawares. "

"It's rather late in the night for any one to be about, " said Dick Cronk. "Still, I've been expecting you, gents. That's why I'm sitting out here, takin' things easy—and makin' things easy for you. If you don't mind I'll keep my seat, David. It ain't wise to be seen hobnobbin' with swell gents at this time o' night—in Hell's Kitchen particularly. I know what you're here for. *He's* back there asleep. Don't worry. I've got him safely sidetracked. "

He jerked his thumb over his shoulder to indicate the narrow passage. The others looked down that filthy corridor and shuddered.

"What a place! " muttered David Jenison.

"Wot 'as Brad been up to to-night? " demanded Joey.

Without changing his position, Dick Cronk, in as few words as possible, told them of Braddock's vigil.

"Don't hang around here a minute longer than you have to, " he said in conclusion. "There are a hundred eyes on you right now. You don't see 'em, but they're looking, just the same. I thought you'd be blame' fools enough to come, so I waited up. Something told me you would go to Joey's when you left her, kid, and you'd make him come along to hunt me out. Brad's safe, and he's not going to do anything just yet. So go home and go to bed. I'll see you to-morrow and we'll arrange for a time when she can talk with him. She'll see him, won't she? "

"Of course. She is eager to see him. I am to bring him to her as soon as—"

"We've got to handle him carefully or—" began Dick.

Joey interrupted him. "The devil's to pay in another direction, Dick, " he said. "Bob Grand 'as 'eard that Brad's out and that he's been 'anging around his 'otel, nasty-like. Who should come to my 'ouse in a cab at nine o'clock to-night but Bob Grand 'isself. He finds me alone, Ruby being off with 'er young man. When I sees who is coming up my steps, I almost keels over. The first words he says took my breath away. I was getting ready to kick 'im into the gutter when he puts a check on my leg, curious-like, by remarking that he's looking for Tom Braddock. He came to arsk me where he could be found. I told 'im I didn't know, and, if I did, I'd be hanged if I'd tell 'im. We 'ad some pretty sharp words, you may believe. But he took all the impudence out of me by announcing most plainly that he understood Brad wanted to kill 'im and that I'd best 'ave a care how I acted, because my 'ouse was being watched by secret service men. There was a lot more, but I 'aven't time to tell you. The upshot of it is, he's going to 'ave Brad nabbed and put where he can't do any 'arm. And, see 'ere, Dick, I don't want to be mixed up in this business. You've got to get Brad out of town to-night. He's done for now and—"

Dick Cronk interrupted his old friend with a snarl of impatience. "Get him away yourself! I'm doing the best I know how. He won't leave of his own free will. He's here to do that man and he won't be put off. And what's more, Bob Grand ought to get it good and hard. Somebody ought to spike him, and who's got a better right than Tom Braddock? I'm ashamed of you, Joey! If you'd been half a man you'd 'a' beat his head off to-night when he put his foot on your doorstep, after what he put up to Ruby. I—I wish I'd been there! "

The bowl of the clay pipe dropped to the bricks. He literally had ground the stem in two with his teeth.

"Go home now—both of you, " he said, a moment later, following his own awkward laugh. "You can't afford to be seen here. I'll look out for Brad. The Colonel won't come here a-lookin' for him, you can bet your life on that. You'll hear from me to-morrow. Maybe you think I ain't sick of this business? If it wasn't for you, Davy, I'd cut it in a minute and dig for the wooly West, where Mr. Barnum and Mr. Forepaugh are dying for my society. Move along now! Don't block the sidewalk! Can't you see the ladies want to pass? "

Two maudlin women of the underworld lurched by, with coarse, ribald comments on the "swells. " David felt himself grow hot with shame and disgust. After their laughter had died away he turned to the grinning Dick.

"But we must do something to-night—" he began imploringly.

Dick lifted his hand. "Correct, " he said. "We must do some sleeping. " He strode to the mouth of the forbidding passage. A light from a saloon window shone out upon a long flight of rickety steps at the farther end, leading up to the darkness above. "See that stairway? Well, I wouldn't advise you to follow me up there. It ain't a Romeo and Juliet balcony, gents. Good night! "

He turned into the passage with a wave of the hand. They saw him pass up through the shaft of light from the window and disappear in the shadows. Then they hurried away from the foul place, almost running to the cab at the corner.

David did not sleep that night. He tossed on his bed, beset by the direst anxiety and dread, his eyes wide open and staring. He dozed off at six, but was wide awake before seven, when he arose and partook of a hurried, half-eaten breakfast. It was not likely that he would hear from Dick Cronk before the middle of the forenoon. Until then he was to be harassed by doubts and fears that would not be easy to suppress in his present unquiet frame of mind. While he was obliged to stand idle and impotent, the very foundation of all the future happiness of the girl he loved might be irreparably shattered. Silent, deadly, purposeful forces were working toward that end. Her mother would, no doubt, prepare her in a way for the crash, but there always would be the memory of the cruel blow that might have been prevented.

He crossed into Madison Square, taking a seat where he could watch the entrance to his hotel, though the hour was so early that it seemed sheer folly to expect Dick Cronk. A dozen times in the first half-hour he looked at his watch. Would the hands never reach nine o'clock? He knew that Dick would make his approach slyly. Perhaps if he returned to his room he would find him there. It would not be an unusual circumstance, he recalled.

Had Colonel Grand's detectives swooped down upon Tom Braddock? Was Christine's father already in jail? Was Grand in a position to hold a new club over the heads of the two women? Were the newspapers preparing to revel in the great story —

He was in the midst of these direful questions when some one tapped him lightly on the shoulder from behind. He turned and glanced upward, his nerves a-tingle.

"Dick! " he exclaimed, leaping to his feet.

"Sit down! " commanded the pickpocket warily.

David dropped to the bench, his eyes fastened on the white, drawn face of the pickpocket. A thick, white bandage was wrapped around his forehead, partially hidden by the slouch hat he wore. The man seemed faint and unsteady on his feet.

"I say, Dick, " cried David, " what has happened? You are hurt. Who—"

With a rigid grin Dick put his hand to his head.

"Braddock, " he said succinctly.

"You don't mean—Tell me what has happened? Wait! Do you require the attention of a surgeon? "

"Sit still, kid. I'm all right. You might pass me a quarter or something, just to make people think I'm boning you for a breakfast. Thanks! Well, Brad's gone. "

"Gone? "

"He cracked me good and hard, that's what he did. I told you he wouldn't be held down long. He's in no mood to be kind to them that are trying to be kind to him. He's past all that. He means business, Brad does. This morning about six he got up. I was watchin' him. He said he was going over to see his wife. He said he wanted to see her before Christine was awake, or out of bed. I told him they wouldn't let him in at that time of day. He said he'd get in or know the reason why. Then he opened up on me about all of us trying to manage his affairs for him. I tried to quiet him. But the devil of it was he was quiet enough. He was *too* quiet. It looked bad. When he started for the door I took hold of him. He—well, he shoved me off. When I jumped in front of the door he picked up a chair and let me have it over the head. I didn't know anything for a long time. When I came to he was gone. Jimmie Parsons, who was in the room with us all the time, also tried to stop him after he biffed me. Jimmie's got two wonderful black eyes as a result. "

"The man must be insane! " cried David, aghast. Dick shook his head. "Not a bit of it. He's the sanest man I know. "

"Where has he gone? You said he started for Mrs. Braddock's? Great heavens, Dick, he may do her bodily harm! He may have shot her down in cold—"

"Easy, easy! He ain't likely to do anything like that until after he's got Bob Grand. "

"Then he will shoot Bob Grand this morning, mark my words. He—"

"He won't shoot anybody. He hasn't any gun. He says he don't need one. If he gets Grand, it won't be with a weapon of any kind. That's what he says, and he means it. If Bob Grand dies from a bullet, you can bet your life it won't come from Tom Braddock. But all this can wait. I stopped off at Joey's. He sent Ruby down to Mr. Portman's at once, and he's gone over to keep watch around the hotel where Grand stops. The thing for you to do is to make tracks for Portman's. I'm going to—"

But David did not wait to hear what Dick intended to do. He was rushing off to hail a passing hansom.

Dick followed him to the curb. "If you see Brad tell him there's no hard feelings, Davy. It was a dirty smash, but I deserve it for not ducking. And say, be careful how you tackle him. Remember that thing about wisdom being better than—what's the word? Nerve? "

The hansom turned and sped down Fifth Avenue with its nervous passenger. Dick shook his head wearily. Then he smiled. From his coat pocket he slyly extracted a shining revolver. Three minutes before it had been in David Jenison's pocket. "He's better off without a thing like this, " mused the clever philosopher.

Thomas Braddock rang the door-bell at the Portman home shortly after eight o'clock. He was perfectly calm and in full possession of himself. A brisk manservant opened the door and faced the strange caller.

"I want to see Mrs. Braddock, " said the man in the vestibule.

"Call again, " said the servant curtly.

"Just a minute, please, " said Braddock. He did not offer to resist the closing of the door in his face. There was something in his tone, however, that caused the footman to hesitate. He took a second, surprised look at the gray, set face of the caller.

"Mrs. Braddock is occupied, " he announced.

"You mean she isn't up yet. I'll wait, " remarked Braddock, still very quietly. The man stared hard at him, suddenly struck by the pallor of his face. His eyes swept the grim figure in the ill-fitting suit of jeans.

"What do you want? Can't you leave a message? "

"Want? I want to see her. " The footman glanced back over his shoulder as if searching for some one on whom he could shift an amazing responsibility. Recalling his dignity, he essayed to close the door in Braddock's face.

"I am her husband, " announced the caller, his hands still in his pockets. The servant's hand was stayed.

"Won't you call again? " he temporized. "I don't quite understand. It don't go down very easy, I'll say that. At any rate, you can't see her now, no matter who you are. She was up all night with Miss Braddock, who took sick suddenly. Mrs. Braddock has just laid down for a—"

"Christine sick? " demanded Braddock. The new note in his voice commanded attention. "It—it can't be serious. She was all right when she came in last night. What's the matter with her? Speak up! What does the doctor say? "

"They didn't call a doctor. "

He was surprised to see the ominous glare fade from Braddock's eyes. They wavered and then fell. An uneasy, mirthless laugh cracked in his throat; then his lip quivered ever so slightly—Brooks could have sworn to it. His hand shook as it went up to fumble the square chin in evident perplexity. For a moment Thomas Braddock stood there, reflecting, swayed by an emotion so unexpected that he was a long time in accounting for it. Indecision succeeded the arrogant assurance that had marked his advances. He looked up quickly, suspecting the lie that might have been offered as an excuse to get rid of him.

"Are you lying to me? " he demanded.

"Sir! "

Braddock's mind, long acute, worked swiftly. He went back of the servant's statement with an intelligence that grasped the true conditions quite as plainly as if they had been laid bare before him. Christine was ill. No physician had been called. He knew what the servant could not, by any chance, have known. He knew why Mary

Braddock sat up with her daughter. A doctor? As if a doctor could prescribe for the affliction that beset her! Too well he now understood what had transpired in that upstairs room. A thing of horror had come to rack the soul of that happy, beautiful girl—had come suddenly because the time was ripe. She was suffering because *he* was near! *He* understood.

A tense, bitter oath struggled through his lips.

"Well, it's time she knew, " he muttered in self-justification. Impelled by a strange anxiety—perhaps it was apprehension—he strained his eyes in the effort to penetrate the depths of the unfriendly hall at the servant's back. His ear seemed bent to catch the sounds of sobs or moans that he knew must reach him if he listened closely.

He again questioned the servant with his eyes, a long, intense scrutiny that confused the man.

Then he turned away.

"All right, " he said sullenly, putting his hands into his pockets once more and drawing up his shoulders as if he were cold. "I'll come again. Tell Mrs. Braddock I was here and that I'll be back in a couple of hours. " Another glance through the half-open door, over the footman's shoulder, and he stalked off, his jaw set, his hands clenched in the pockets of his coat. At the foot of the steps he shot a quick, involuntary glance upward, taking in the second story windows. The wondering servant looked after him until he turned the corner below.

Brooks had seen men with the prison pallor in their faces before.

He was not long in apprising Mrs. Braddock of the stranger's visit. She was with Christine when he made the unhappy announcement. If he expected a demonstration of concern or surprise, he was disappointed.

"I will see Mr. Braddock when he returns, " said his mistress quietly. Brooks blinked two or three times, his only tribute to the stupendous shock he had experienced.

Thomas Braddock walked to the Battery. There he sat down on one of the benches and glowered out upon the blue waters of the bay for an hour or more. No muscle moved in his face. He waited with a patience that was three years old.

When David drove up to the Portman place, Mrs. Braddock herself arose from one of the chairs in the narrow stone porch at the top of the steps. She, too, had been waiting, but not for the young man who dashed up the steps.

"He has been here, " she said, as she gave him her hand. The tenseness of the clasp revealed the strain that was upon her. He noted the pallor in her cheek, the dread in her eyes. The hot glare of the June sun seemed to bring out gray hairs he had never seen before. He had not thought of her as growing old until now.

"Yes? " he cried anxiously. "Where is he? I tried to get here in time. Did he—"

"Sit down, David—here, please, behind the balustrade. I am waiting out here for him. He went off in that direction. I've been watching for nearly an hour. He is coming back. "

She resumed her chair, facing the direction which Braddock had taken.

"You—you sent him away? "

"I did not see him. You must not think, David, that I am afraid to see him. I am nervous, upset, but it really isn't fear. Christine— Christine knows everything. I told her last night. She is—well, you can imagine, she is very unhappy. Everything looks black to her. I did not hide anything. She is crushed. "

"Where is she? I must see her. I can comfort her, Mrs. Braddock. Let me see her before he comes back. " He was standing over her, his face working.

"She will not see you, David, " she said in dull tones. He started. "What do you mean? She *must* see me. " "Her father was in the penitentiary. " That was all; but it told all there was to tell.

It required a moment or two for comprehension. Then he cried out reproachfully: "Does she think that will make any difference in my—"

She held up her hand. "She knows it won't. That's what distresses her. I am afraid, David, after all, you have brought your honor to a wretched market. We are what we are, we Braddocks. We can't look beyond our environment. You cannot marry a convict's daughter. It was bad enough before. I should have seen all this. But I was blind only to her happiness. We can't—"

His jaws were set. "Mrs. Braddock, " he said, his voice quivering with decision, "I am not going to be put off like this. You may as well understand that, first and last. I love her. I want her. She loves me, thank God. It won't be so hard to make her understand how impossible it is for anything to come between us. She is going to marry me, Mary Braddock. "

A great light leaped into her eyes, even as she shook her head. The words of protest she would have uttered failed to pass her lips. She reached out as if to clasp his hand, a movement as involuntary as it was instinctive. He had turned and was facing the closed portals behind which his heart's desire was beating all joy and hope out of her poor tormented soul. The tears rushed to his eyes.

"I can't stand it, " he cried. "She must hear the words *now*— this is the time for me to go to her and say that I love her better than all the world. Nothing else matters. "

In his eagerness he was starting for the door when a sharp cry fell from her lips. He hesitated, struck by the note of consternation in the cry.

A carriage had drawn up at the curb in front of the house. A face appeared at the open window of the vehicle, a never-to-be-forgotten face that brought to mind the African gazelle in Van Slye's.

David turned. For a moment he could not believe his eyes. He stood rigid in the paralysis of stupefaction. Then a cold perspiration started from every pore of his body. He sprang to Mrs. Braddock's side. She was even then peering down the street, a great fear in her heart, every fiber quivering with alarm.

Colonel Grand was assisting his daughter to the sidewalk. Already he had lifted his hat and sent a nauseous smile to the woman above. David's gaze followed hers in quest of a more sinister actor who might even then be coming upon the scene for the tragic climax.

The young man recognized the necessity for quick action. Colonel Grand, whatever his motive for appearing so unexpectedly at the Portman house, must be turned away without ceremony or consideration. At any minute Thomas Braddock might return. A tragedy would be the result; that was inevitable.

David started down the steps, passing the rigid, staring woman at the top. He was vaguely aware of Roberta Grand's bow and of the look of annoyance in the Colonel's face. Half-way down he called out:

"Colonel Grand, you must not stay here—not a second longer. I will explain if you will let me ride with you for a couple of blocks. "

Grand advanced.

"Young man, " he said coldly, "I am here to see Mrs. Braddock on a matter of importance. You will do well to subside. "

David flushed angrily. "But Mrs. Braddock does not care to see you. She—"

Grand came on up the steps, ignoring Jenison, addressing himself to Mary Braddock.

"I have come to discuss Tom with you, Mary, " he said. She started at the use of her name, a hot wave of anger rushing over her.

"Go away! " she cried, in low, intense tones. "How dare you come here, Colonel Grand? Go! "

He stopped, raised his hat, shrugged his shoulders in a deprecating manner, and then quickly lifted his free hand to check the approach of the young man who was ominously near at hand.

"I fancy it will be best for all concerned if we avoid tableaux. Still, I will go away if you see fit to send me—"

"I do see fit! Go! "

Roberta Grand was staring at the speaker from the bottom of the steps.

"Don't haggle with her, father, " she cried venomously. "Bring her to time! "

"You have met my daughter, Mrs. Braddock? " said Grand in his most suave manner. "What are you looking at, Jenison? " he demanded, suddenly noting the young man's frozen stare, directed down the street.

David passed his hand over his damp brow and turned to look helplessly into Mary Braddock's face.

Tom Braddock was standing across the street at the corner below, clutching a lamp-post for support. He was staring with wide open eyes at the group on the steps.

CHAPTER VII

TOM BRADDOCK'S PROMISE

She had seen Braddock turn the corner. Her eyes were closed now, as if to shut out the disaster that must rush down upon them in the next instant; her thrumming ears waited for the sound of running footsteps and the crack of a revolver. David started up the steps toward her.

"It will be best for you to hear what I have come to say, " observed Grand, ignorant of the peril that lay behind him. He resumed his progress up the steps, Roberta following close behind.

"For Heaven's sake, man, go while you can, " cried David hoarsely. "Don't you see—"

"Mary, will you listen to me? We've got to come to an understanding concerning Tom. He's in town. We must come to some agreement, you and I, as to whether a scandal is to follow his arrest—a scandal which will blast you and Christine forever in New—"

"Is there no way to stop him? " groaned Mary Braddock, opening her eyes to look again upon the sinister figure across the way. She had not heard a word of Colonel Grand's minacious overture.

"By this time Braddock has been taken by the police, —as Sam Brafford, the ex-convict and yeggman. Is he to go up this time as the father of Christine—"

David sprang to his side, seizing his right arm in a grip of iron. In the same movement he whirled the older man about and pointed toward the figure at the corner.

"It's Braddock! " he hissed. "Now we're in for it. By heaven, he ought to kill you! "

"Braddock! " gasped Grand. "Why, he is in jail—" The words died on his lips. He recognized the man. His eyes bulged, his grayish face seemed to freeze stiff, with the lower lip and tongue hanging loose.

Transfixed, he saw Thomas Braddock straighten up, relinquish his grip on the iron post, and start diagonally across the street, his head bent forward, his lower jaw extended. His unswerving gaze never left the face of Robert Grand.

"Get into the carriage, Roberta, " shouted Grand, suddenly alive to his peril. He trembled, but he was not the man to run from an adversary, nor was he likely to sell his life cheaply. With a quick, desperate tug, he jerked himself free of David's grasp. His hand flew to his inside coat pocket.

Thomas Braddock had reached the curb. Miss Grand stood directly in his path, petrified by terror. Like a cat he sprang forward, cunningly putting her body between him and Grand, making it impossible for the latter to shoot without imperiling the life of his daughter.

A revolver gleamed in the hand of the man on the steps.

David's wits worked quickly. It may have been that he was inspired. Instead of attempting to grasp or disarm Colonel Grand, he decided to let the situation take care of itself for the moment. Neither of the men could make a move to attack the other.

"Here, I say! " gasped the Colonel. "He can shoot me down like a dog. Stop him, Jenison! Don't you see I can't protect myself? "

David took advantage of the knowledge that Braddock was unarmed.

"Colonel Grand, " he cried out sharply, "if you attempt to kill that man I'll see that you suffer for it. "

"But, damn it, he is here to kill me! I have the right to kill in self-defense if—"

"Then why doesn't he kill you? He has you in his power. He is not here to attack you. That must be plain, even to you. Mr. Braddock has come to see his wife before leaving the city. "

He caught the cunning gleam in Tom Braddock's eyes. His heart gave a great bound of relief. The man was not so mad as to court certain death by attacking his enemy under the present conditions.

Christine's father was perfectly cool; he was absolute master of himself. Nothing could be farther from the mind of Thomas Braddock than the desire to be shot by Robert Grand. It was his one purpose in life to kill, not to be killed. He realized that he was powerless. Grand could shoot him down like a dog—an inglorious end to the one spark of ambition left in him. The workings of Braddock's mind were as plain to Jenison as if the man were expounding them by word of mouth.

"Before leaving the country, " David substituted. The ghost of a sneer flickered about Braddock's lips. He spoke for the first time, hoarsely, but with wonderful calmness.

"I came to see Mary, " he said. "You'd better go, Grand. I don't want anything to do with you. It won't be healthy for either of us if we see too much of each other. "

"Stand out from behind my daughter, you coward, " shouted Grand.

"Don't shoot, father! " screamed the girl, terror-stricken.

"Go ahead! " said Braddock grimly.

The driver of the cab was looking wildly about in quest of a policeman. Two women had stopped on the opposite side of the street, and were staring at the group in front of the Portman mansion.

"Shall I call a cop? " called out the cabby, addressing himself to the one person who seemed to belong on the premises—Mrs. Braddock.

"No! No! Take them away! " she cried. "That's all I ask of you! "

"Wait! " said Colonel Grand, master of himself once more. "We may just as well understand each other. I had an object in coming here. It concerns this man. He—"

David broke in peremptorily. It was time to bring the distressing scene to an end, if it were possible to do so without inviting the actual catastrophe. He realized that he would have to act quickly in order to anticipate the curious crowd and to be ahead of the police.

"Colonel Grand, you have put yourself in an unpleasant, uncalled-for position, " he said. "I am of half a mind to hold you here until the police arrive. Cabby, I call upon you to witness, with all the rest of us, that Colonel Grand has drawn a revolver with the design to kill an unarmed, unoffending man. You have seen everything. Mr. Braddock saved his life only by—"

"Unarmed! " shouted Colonel Grand. "Why, he is armed to the teeth. He's after me. He's going to kill me on sight, I swear—"

"What is to prevent him from doing so now, Colonel? " demanded David. "You are in a position where you cannot shoot. He could drill you full of holes if that were his intention. Mr. Braddock, are you armed? "

"No, " said Braddock. "Do you suppose, if I had a gun, I would be standing behind this girl? "

"Do you hear that, cabby? Do you, Colonel? Now, I want to say just this to you, sir; I am going to the nearest police station and swear out a warrant for your arrest. I can't hold you myself, but I can do the next best thing. I can land you in jail for attempted murder. "

Colonel Grand stared at him with uncomprehending eyes, a sickly smile on his lips.

"You know better than—" he began.

David cut him short with an exclamation. Then he walked out to the curb, opened the cab door and coolly motioned for Colonel Grand to step down and enter.

Mary Braddock waited no longer. She sped down the steps, passing the slow-moving, stupefied Colonel, and ruthlessly shoved Roberta Grand to one side, taking her stand in front of her husband, facing his foe.

"It isn't necessary for my husband to shield himself behind your flesh and blood, Colonel Grand, " she said, her head erect. "Now, if you care to shoot, you have both of us at your mercy. "

"I came to propose a peaceful—" began the Colonel, baffled.

"Step lively, Colonel Grand! " commanded Jenison. "Permit me, Miss Grand. "

"Don't touch me, " hissed Roberta, disdaining his assistance. The look she bestowed upon her father, as she passed him, was not a pleasant one. He had promised her a different reception at the Portman home, secretly depending on his power to force Mrs. Braddock to welcome an armistice, no matter how distasteful it may have been to her. He had not anticipated the outcome. Miss Grand accompanied him, meanly it is true, in the hope that she might gloat over the Braddocks in their humiliation.

She entered the cab, frightened and dismayed. Her father, still grasping his pistol, followed her. He cast a defeated, almost appealing glance at the uncompromising face of the young man who held open the door.

"You can't obtain a warrant for me, " he said nervously. "I have the law on my side. I can prove that this man threatened—"

"Drive on, cabby, " said David relentlessly. "I've taken your number. You will be called on as a witness. Don't argue! I mean it! "

Muttering excitedly, the driver, without the customary "where to? " started off down the street. Colonel Grand leaned forward to send a menacing scowl toward the group on the sidewalk. He smiled sardonically when he saw that Mary Braddock still kept her place in front of her husband, evidently afraid that he would fire from the window of the departing cab. Then he called out his instructions to the driver and settled back in the seat.

The gritting of Tom Braddock's teeth did not escape the tortured ears of his wife. She looked up quickly. He was glaring after the cab, a look of appalling ferocity in his face.

"Come into the house, Tom, " she said quickly.

He turned on her with a snarl.

"I won't keep you long, " he grated. "I've got other business on hand. " It occurred to him to tender David his meed of praise. "That was pretty sharp in you, David, staving him off like that. I owe you something for doing that. "

"I knew you were unarmed. You would have had no chance. "

They were going up the steps, Braddock between the others. Brooks, the footman, was holding the door open. He had been a politely interested witness to the startling encounter.

Braddock seemed to be studying each successive slab of stone as he ascended. The muscles of his jaw were working. He seemed to have formed a habit of jamming his hands far down into his coat pockets.

"That was the only chance *he'll* ever have, " was his sententious remark. No other word was uttered until they were inside the house, Mrs. Braddock's gasp of relief could not have been called a sigh.

"Thank God! " she breathed, sinking upon the hall seat and clasping her clenched hands to her breast.

Braddock shot a quick glance up the broad stairway. The surroundings were strange to him, —he had never been inside the home of his father- in-law before, —but he knew that Christine was somewhere overhead.

"How's Christine, Mary? " he asked roughly.

"She is wretchedly unhappy, Tom. "

"Umph! " was the way he received it, but a close observer might have seen the flutter of his eyelids and the sharp, convulsive movement in the coat pockets. "I don't want her to see me, " he said.

"She wants to see you—"

He faced her angrily. "No! I've got to take care of my nerves. I can't take any chances on having 'em upset. See here, David, " he said, lowering his voice and speaking with deadly emphasis, "that talk of yours about swearing out a warrant for Grand don't go, do you understand? I don't want him to be arrested. I don't want him locked up. I want him to be *free*. He'd be too safe behind the bars? "

The sound of a door opening above came to them at this juncture, followed by the swift rush of feet and the rustle of skirts. Braddock looked up and instinctively drew back into an obscured recess at his left.

Christine's face appeared over the railing above. She leaned far forward and called out in the high, tense tones of extreme nervousness:

"Father! Is it you? Are you there? "

There was no response.

David, standing on the lower step, permitted his gaze to swerve from the sweet, eager face of the girl above to that of the man in the corner.

The effect on Braddock was astounding. Signs of a great convulsion revealed themselves in his face. His lips were parted and drawn as if in pain; his eyes were half closed, screening the emotion that groped behind the lids. It was the face, the figure of a man mightily shaken by an unexpected emotion. Slowly his eyes were opened. An expression of utter despair and longing had come into them. Mrs. Braddock was staring at her husband as if she could not believe her senses.

Words came hoarsely, unbidden from the man's lips, spoken as if from the bottom of his soul after years of subjection and restraint, so nearly whispered that they came to David's ears as if from afar off.

"Oh! How lonesome I've been all these years, just for the sound of her voice! "

His wife's hand went out to him involuntarily. He looked at it for a second, then into her eyes, waveringly, uncertain as to the impulse that moved her. He suddenly regained control of himself. He grasped the slender hand in his great, crushing fingers; the sullen, repellent glare leaped back into his eyes; alert and shifty, he held up his free hand to command the silence of David. Then, like a hunted creature at bay, he glanced over his shoulder. Seeing an open door almost at his elbow, he resolutely drew his wife after him into the room beyond. As he turned to slam the door with vicious energy, the tense, incisive voice called out once more from the head of the stairs:

"Father! "

The door banged as if propelled by the added energy of sudden fear.

An instant later, David was dashing up the stairs, three steps at a time. She had started down. He met her at the bend.

"Not just now, dearest, " he cried. "Wait! He wants to see your mother first. "

She clutched the rail, putting one hand out as if to ward him off. The dread in her eyes went straight to his heart. Her lips were stiff, her voice was low with anxiety.

"Is—is she safe, David, —is he himself? Oh, I must go down there. I know I can reason—"

He stopped her gently. "Please, Christine, " he commanded. She suddenly put her hands to his face, and looked into his eyes.

"If anything were to happen to her, " she whispered in agony, "I would—"

"She is perfectly safe, " he broke in. "Your father will not mistreat her. " He clasped her hands and held them to his breast. "My poor darling! "

Her head dropped, her lip quivered. Then she quietly withdrew her hands and sank to a sitting posture on the step, leaning her head wearily against the banister.

Ruby Noakes, a discarded wet towel in her hand, came into the hallway above them. She saw them, hesitated for a moment, and then quietly returned to Christine's bed-chamber.

David dropped to his sweetheart's side. His arm fell about her shoulders. She did not offer to remove it, but sat listless, unresponsive, her eyes lifted to a narrow window beyond which the hot sky gleamed.

He began by whispering words of encouragement and sympathy, his soul in every syllable. She was so quiet, so hurt, so forlorn; never had she been so precious to him as now.

"David, " she interrupted, closing her eyes as if through faintness, "it is so good of you to say these things to me, but—but—oh, can't you see how impossible it is now? Don't stay here! Go away, David. Do you think that I can marry you now? It was bad enough before—but now! What am I that you should take me to be your wife! You must go away and forget—"

Her drew her head to his breast, smothering the heartbroken cry by the fierceness of his embrace.

"Open your eyes, Christine! Look at me. " She looked up, utter desolation in her eyes. "Nothing on earth can keep you from being my wife—nothing! I couldn't give you up. What am I for, if not to cherish and protect and comfort you? What is the real meaning of the word 'love'? Husband! What does that stand for? A stone wall between pain and peril and trouble; that's what it means. And I'm going to be all of that to you—a stone wall for all your life, Christine. It is settled. The strongest man in the world is not strong enough for the weakest woman. I will never cease being proud of the fact that you are my wife. Don't speak! Lie quiet, dearest. Nothing can change things for you and me. "

"It cannot be, David, —it cannot be! " she moaned, covering her face with her hands. He held her there, sobbing, against his breast.

Meanwhile Thomas Braddock was pacing the floor of the library almost directly beneath them. His wife watched him in silence; her eyes followed the tall, bent figure as it swung back and forth with the steadiness of a clock's pendulum. He had not spoken since they entered the room, nor had she moved from the spot where he left her when he released her hand. All this time she had been holding the wrist he had grasped so cruelly. It pained her, but she was only physically conscious of the fact; her mind was not comprehending it.

It was the first time she had seen him in five years. A curious analysis was going on in her perturbed brain. The change in him! She could not take her eyes from the haggard, heavily-lined face, so unlike the blithe, youthful one she had loved, or the bloated, bestial one she had feared and despised. The coarseness, the flabbiness, the purplish hues were no longer there. The bulging, bleary eyes, on which the glaze of continuous dissipation had once settled as if to stay, were not as she remembered them. Instead, they were bright and clear, and lay deep in their sockets. The lips, now beardless, were no longer thick and repulsive. She marveled. This was not the vacillating, whiskey-willed man she had known for so long; here was a determined character, swelling with force, fierce in the

290

resources of a belated integrity of purpose. No longer the careless, handsome youth, nor the honorless man, but a power! Whether that power stood for good or evil, it mattered not; he was a man such as she had never expected him to be.

She was sensitive to one thing in particular, although the realization of it did not come to her at once, she was so taken up with the study of him as a whole: she missed the cigar from the corner of his mouth.

He stopped in front of her.

"This is the first time I have ever been asked into this house, " he said, his lips curling in a bitter, unfriendly smile. "Where is your father? "

"His rooms are in the other end of the house, upstairs. He sleeps till noon, " she answered mechanically.

"Umph! " he grunted, resuming his walk.

"Tom, " she said, taking a firm grasp on her nerves, "let us talk it over quietly. Sit down. "

He halted. "I can talk better standing, " he said grimly. He came up close to her. She stood her ground, looking him squarely in the eyes. "There isn't much to say, Mary. You know me for what I am, and you know who made me so. He's got to pay, that's all. We won't go into the past. It's not easily forgotten. I guess we remember everything. "

"Everything, " she said.

"I'm not excusing myself. I'm past that, and besides it wouldn't go down with you. You know where I've been, and you must give me credit for trying to shield Christine a little bit. I took my medicine, and nobody but you and Grand knew that her father was up there until now, excepting Dick. I want to say to you, Mary, I was railroaded for a crime I didn't commit. I was jobbed. He was at the back of it. He was afraid of me—and well he might have been. I did a lot of rotten things while you and I were ploddin' along through those last two years with the show—you know what they were. But it was whiskey! I took money that didn't belong to me—yours and Christine's, and Grand's, and Jenison's. I did worse than that, Mary.

I sold you out to Bob Grand—you knew that, too. But I'm going to try to pay up all my debts—all of 'em, in a day or two. I owe you my ugly, worthless life. I'm going to pay you in full by ending it. I owe Colonel Grand for everything I was, for what I am. I'm going to pay him, so help me God. Don't interrupt! My mind's made up. Nothing above hell can change it. I came here to ask you just two questions. I want you to answer them. I'm going to believe you. You never lie, I know that. "

"I will answer them, Tom. "

He hesitated, his gaze wavering for the first time. "I—I hate to ask you this first one, Mary, " he said.

"Go on. Ask it. "

"It's a mean question, but I've just *got* to hear you say no. Did you go to England with Bob Grand? "

"No. "

He breathed deeply. "That's one, " he said.

"Here's the other. Did he give you money to live on, to educate Christine with, abroad? "

"No. ",

"I'll ask still another. Where did you get the money? "

"Some of it from my father. Afterwards I brought suit against you and Colonel Grand for an accounting. He was compelled to pay into court all that was due me as part owner of Van Slye's. I had my own money in the show. I could not be robbed of that. "

"I'm glad you did that. It must have been a nasty dose for him. "

"His wife tried to make trouble for me. You heard that? "

"I knew she would, sooner or later. "

"You knew it? "

"She wasn't blind. "

"But how could she dare to think that I—"

"She knew her husband's reputation, that's all. He was careless about women. " His face went black as a thundercloud. "But he's had his day! "

"Tom, " she cried, clutching the lapels of his coat, "you shall not leave this house until you've promised me to do nothing—"

He shook off her hands. "Don't come any of that, Mary. It won't do any good. He made me what I was, he would have prostituted you. I was just bad enough to fall, you were too good to even stumble. Then he landed me in the pen. Maybe you won't believe it, Mary, but I'd stopped drinking and was earning fair wages—well, I was tending bar in Chicago. Barkeepers *have* to be sober men, you see. I had not touched a drop for nearly three months. The temptation was too strong there, so I got out of it. Then I looked up Barnum to get a job as ringmaster. I was going under the name of Bradford. Somehow nobody would trust me. They knew me. Joey Noakes came through the West with a pantomime show about that time. He told me you were in Europe. First thing I'd heard of you, that was, Mary. Then he told me you'd got your money out of Grand, legitimately, he swore. I didn't believe him. I thought there had been some shinanigan. I stood it as long as I could, and then I broke for New York. You see, girlie—I mean Mary, I'd done for you in a nasty way. I practically handed you to him. You—well, we won't go into that. "

"No, " she said, very pale, "we must not go into that, Tom. You sold me with the show. I—I can never forgive you for that. "

"I'm not asking forgiveness, am I? " he cried harshly. "I'm just tellin' you, that's all. Well, I came down here to kill him three years ago. I knew you hated him. If you gave in it wasn't because you wanted to, but because I'd fixed it so's you couldn't very well get out of it. There was only one way for you to be rid of Bob Grand after that—and only one man to do it for you. So I came down here to do it. Ernie Cronk ran across me on the street one night. He began filling me up with stories of how Grand had also tried to hurt Christine, and all about how you were living like a princess abroad. I waited until Grand came back from England, a couple of weeks later. Ernie had got me clear off my head by that time, nagging me day and night. He tried to get me to drink, but I was too wise for that. Well, I found Bob Grand and, like a fool, started in to tell him what I was going to do to him instead of doing it first. All of a sudden he pulled a gun. I had no chance, so I bolted. He fired twice and yelled for the police. They— they caught me in an alley—and I had a gun in my clothes, too. The next morning he came to see me in the station-house—to identify me, he said. Then he told me he was going to send me up for highway robbery—but he was willing, for your sake and Christine's, to say nothing about the past—or anything. He did swear me into the pen, and I kept my mouth closed. But, Mary, I am not a thief at heart, I never was one. Whatever I did that was crooked in the old days was due to whiskey. It's a habit men have, I know, blaming everything on to whiskey, but—but, oh, say, Mary, you *know* I wasn't that sort of a man when I married you. I was straight, wasn't I? I never had done a crooked thing in my life. I don't think I'd ever told a lie. I had a good mother, just as Christine has. But what the devil am I doing—talking like this! " The eager, rather appealing note went out of his voice; he almost snarled the bitter sentence. "I didn't come to explain, or to beg, or to excuse myself. I won't keep you any longer. Remember, I'm not asking anything of you, Mary, — not a thing. I'm not that low. "

He was out of breath. No doubt, it was the longest speech he had made in years. Perhaps his own voice sounded strange to him.

"You are not to leave this house, Tom, until you have promised, " she said firmly. All the time he was speaking, she had stood like a statue before him, never taking her eyes from his distorted face.

"Oh, I'm not, eh? We'll see! "

"What are you going to do to Colonel Grand? "

"I'm going to—" he checked himself. "I'm going to beat him to a jelly! "

"You mean, you are going to murder him? " She shuddered as she said it.

"No, " he said, with grim humor; "I'm only going to help him to die. You see, Mary, Bob Grand committed suicide the day he sent me up.

The final death struggle has been a long time coming, but it's almost here. He took a very slow, but a sure poison. "

The time had come for the strong appeal. She laid her hands on his shoulders.

"Tom, have you thought of what it will mean, not to me, but to Christine? "

"She knows, by this time, that I'm an ex-convict. It won't hurt her to know I'm even worse. "

"She does not believe you were guilty. She always has said you could have been a good man if you had let whiskey alone. You see, Tom, she understood — she understands. Isn't it worth your while to think of her? You are not drinking now. Can't you think of something good — something kind to do? Must you go to your grave — and such a grave! — knowing that you never did a really big thing for her in all your life? Have you no desire to make her think of you as something except the unnatural beast you were when she knew you best of all? I see the change in you. Don't you want her to see it? What do you gain by killing Colonel Grand? He has wronged you, but do you help yourself by making matters infinitely worse now, so many years afterward? Do—"

"He told me, over there in the police station, three years ago, that he had won your love, that you lived for him alone. He lied. I could kill him once for that lie. He told me, in the next breath, that you and he were going to sell Christine to a certain French nobleman, who already had a wife and family. He lied again. I could kill him once more for that lie. He told me—"

"Don't! Don't! For God's sake, don't tell me any more, " she groaned, horror-stricken.

He went on. "He taunted me, he laughed at me. I was up there for three years. In all that time his damned sneers and laughter were never out of my mind. He laughed at me because the drunken bargain I had made with him had turned out to his credit, after all. "

"The sale? "

"Yes. "

He looked away. The expression in her eyes cut him like a knife.

"I ought to have been shot for that, Mary, " he said.

"Yes, " she agreed mechanically.

His hand went to his mouth suddenly, as if to steady the lips.

"I'm not asking you to overlook it. Maybe you'll spare Christine the knowledge of it—not for my sake, but for hers. "

"Tom, don't you feel that you owe *me* something? " she asked steadily.

"Everything. I'm going to pay, too. I took you from a home like this and—Oh, well, it won't do any good to bring it all up again. Let's—"

"You owe me a little happiness and peace, Tom, after all these years. "

"Oh, I'll go away all right. This is the last time you'll ever see me. "

"It isn't that that I ask. There was a time when we were happy, you and I. I do not forget the old days, before you—I mean, when we were working together, you and I, to get control of the circus. Not that I liked the life—God knows I did not! but that we were striving for big, good things. I—"

"You got your money back, " he broke in weakly. "That's more than I did. "

"What had I ever done to you, Tom, that you should sell me as if I were a concubine to—"

"Didn't I tell you it was whiskey—and cards? " he cried fiercely.

"True. You *did* tell me that, " she admitted, closing her eyes. He looked at the lowered lids for a moment and then swore softly to himself—not an oath of anger but of despair. She opened her eyes and caught the fleeting look of shame and remorse. "Ah, " she cried, "you *have* a heart, after all. I saw it then. Tom, you *did* love me, years ago—you were fine and strong and true. You were yourself. You have changed, but I can still see something of the strong, manly Tom Braddock *I* loved in those wonderful days. "

He was scowling again, but she had seen through the mask. She went on eagerly: "You are obsessed by this idea of vengeance. What can it mean to you, after all is said and done? You say you are going to end your own life, as well. You will escape the consequences, as any coward would, and you are *not* a coward. Who stays behind to suffer all the pain and anguish? Not you! Oh, no! I am the one — as if you had not already done enough. Christine and I! We —"

"I won't listen to you! " he cried, his breast heaving.

"You are listening! You can't help it. Come! You must sit down here beside me. This is the one, great, solitary hour in your life. "

He drew back and permitted an irrelevant question to break from his lips: "Why didn't you divorce me? "

"Because I married you, Tom, that is why! I'll always be your wife. I — I can't live with you — but I —"

"Mary, you are the grandest woman in all this world, " he cried, amazement in his eyes. "And to think of it! I am the one to have married you, — a thing like me! "

She was trembling all over. "Will you do this for me, Tom? "

"Do what? "

"You know what, Tom. "

"You mean, give up the one thing I've lived for all these awful years? "

"Yes. "

"I — I can't do it, Mary. It's got to be, sooner or later. That man and I can't live on the earth at the same time. "

"Oh! Won't you give me something to thank you for after all I've —"

"Wait a minute! Let me think! " He began pacing the floor again. She watched him with bated breath, a half-hope in her heart. He stopped before her once more. His eyes were bright with a new, strange light. "I'll tell you what I'll do, Mary, — for you and Christine. I'll put an end to myself. That's the best way out of it. I can't live if he does.

Wait a minute! It's the simplest, surest way. Don't breathe a word of this to any one. I'll go down to the river to-night. That will be the end of it all. I swear to you, I won't hunt up Grand, —on my word of honor, if you will believe that I have any honor. There is some sort of integrity in a man who can fight the battle I have—and without wavering or whimpering. I'll do that for you, Mary. It's the safest way. "

She had heard him at first with a sickening horror in her soul. It was a frightful compromise that he proposed. She knew he meant it, that he would keep his word. She understood how great the sacrifice would be on his part, how bitter the defeat; and she realized that he was doing it to justify himself in her eyes. As he got deeper into his amazing proposition, her clearing brain began to discern the rift in his armor. Not that she saw a sign of weakness beyond, but that the humanness of his strength was being revealed to her. There was an authority in his offer that dispelled all doubt as to the cloudiness of his mental vision. He was seeing things clearly. His sacrifice lay in the willingness to forego the joy of killing another man before he carried out his original design to make way with himself. She studied his face for a moment before speaking. There was something like gladness there—a truly bright glow that told of the relief he had found in at last doing something to please her!

"Is there no other way, Tom? " she asked, so quietly that his eyes narrowed with a curious intentness.

"It's the only one, " he said grimly.

She walked over to the window and looked down into the area-way. Her heart was throbbing loudly.

"To-night? " she asked in muffled tones.

"If I don't do it to-night I'll do something worse to-morrow, " he said.

"You promise me, —on your word of honor? "

He started. "Certainly. I'll do it. "

She turned to face him, her back to the light. He could not see the expression in her eyes.

"You will do this for me, Tom? "

He nodded his head, that was all.

"Take your own life? "

"I was going to do it anyway. Before they could hang me. "

Both were silent for a long time. Neither had changed position.

"You won't tell Christine that I did it, will you? Just say that I went away—to South America, I guess. "

"I will not tell her, Tom. "

"Is she going to marry David Jenison? "

"I hope so. "

"Well, she'll feel easier in her mind if she knows I'm gone for good, then. Maybe you'd better tell her I'm dead. "

He said it as calmly as if he were announcing the time of day, but he was none the less earnest.

"There is one alternative, Tom, " she said, at last coming to the plan she had had in mind from the beginning.

"You're not thinking of—of taking me back, " he said, aghast at the very thought of it.

"No. I'm going to make an offer that will give you greater satisfaction than that. Will you go away from New York forever, if I pay over to you every cent that I received for my share in Van Slye's—"

"No! " he almost shouted. "You can't *buy* me off. I was willing to do the right thing a minute ago. Now, you've gone and spoiled it all. " He clapped his hands to his eyes; his big frame shook with rage.

She went quickly to him.

"Now, I *know* you are a man—a big man, Tom. I am prouder of you now than I ever was in all my life. "

He looked bewildered. "You mean, you did that to *try* me? "

"To try myself, " was her enigmatic response,

"Well? "

She stood back and looked at him intently.

"I still have your promise. You *will* do it to-night? "

He stared at her as if he could not believe his ears, but he said resolutely:

"Of course, I will. "

CHAPTER VIII

COLONEL GRAND AND THE CRONKS

She walked away from him and sat down in one of the big chairs, as if her limbs suddenly had lost the power to support her. He pulled his crumpled hat from his pocket and fumbled it for a few moments. She sat there, looking at him, her lips parted.

"Well, " he began, "I guess I'd better be going. "

"Going? Where are you going? " she demanded, suddenly alert.

"Oh, out somewhere. I've got ten or twelve hours to kill. "

She struggled to her feet.

"Tom, you are not going to leave this house until to-night. "

He drew back, amazed.

"What? "

"I am going down to the river with you. "

Comprehension was slow in filtering into his brain. A ghastly pallor spread over his face.

"What did you say? "

"I am going to the river with you. But you must stay here until to-night. You are not to go out into the streets. Do you understand? "

"You can't mean that—Why, you must be crazy. You? Why—why, I'm doing it so that you can *live*. You can't mean what you're thinking of—" He could not complete the sentence. A heavy sweat broke out on his forehead.

She forced a miserable smile to her lips. "You do not understand me, Tom. I am going down to the river with you, but I am coming back alone. "

He slowly grasped the meaning of it.

"You—you're going down to see that I do make an end of it? " he cried.

"I want to be sure, for Christine's sake, " she said, quite steadily.

He was glaring at her now. "Oh, I see. You don't trust me, " he exclaimed bitterly. He put out his hand to steady himself against the library table. "I can't say that I blame you, either. But I won't stay here. I would, if it would do any good, but how can it? The police are likely to pile in here any minute with a warrant for me. That would be fine, wouldn't it? " He strode to the window and tried to look through the passage into the street. "I don't want to be pinched now. Go and look out of the front windows—go on! See if there's any one out there. "

She did not move.

"Ain't you going to look? " he demanded.

"The police? " dropped from her lips dully. She had overlooked the danger from that direction, although her mind had been so full of it a little while before. "He won't send them here, Tom—"

"Of course, he will, " he broke in irascibly. "He's crazy mad, and he'll act quickly to head off Jenison's warrant. I can't stay here— not another minute. Can't I get out the back way? They may be laying for me in front. Don't look like that, Mary! I can give 'em the slip. It won't do to have them nab me here. Just think of the newspapers! Wake up! Don't you see? And listen: I'll do what I said I would—to-night. I swear it. You can trust me, Mary. Now, quick, show me the way out—and don't let me bump into Christine. I—I couldn't stand that. I don't want to lose my nerve. "

She left him and ran into the next room to look out into the avenue. He followed rapidly.

"There are two men standing at the corner, " she whispered in alarm. He would have looked out if she had not dragged him away.

"It would be terrible if they were to come in here, " she was saying distractedly. "Yes, you must go. " She grasped his arm. "Tom, you may go if you'll promise to come back tonight. "

"What's that for? "

"Because I insist. At ten o'clock—or any time you may choose. Only you *must* come back. "

He studied her face curiously. Something stirred in his heart, but it had been so long since anything had touched that organ that he failed to credit himself with an emotion. Whatever it was, it impelled him to submit to her demand.

"I'll come, " he said uneasily. "I don't see any use in it, though. We can say goodby now. "

"No! " she exclaimed. "It must be to-night. "

"All right, then. I'll come at ten, —*the back way.* "

Without another word she hurried him through the intervening rooms to the servants' entrance. They passed Brooks in the rear hall. He bowed stiffly to Braddock. Brooks had been listening at a keyhole.

She opened the door and pointed the way with a trembling hand.

"There is the alley, Tom, —through the little gate. Be very careful. "

He did not respond. Turning his face away resolutely, he stalked down the narrow steps, and, without so much as a glance behind, hurried off toward the alley-gate. She watched him pass through it, a strange cramp of disappointment in her heart because he had resisted the temptation to look back at his judge. How long she stood there stark and silent she did not know.

Brooks, the footman, was speaking to her.

"Miss Christine is ill, ma'am, " he said, from somewhere behind her. "The housekeeper thinks she has fainted, ma'am. "

Colonel Grand was in a quandary. He was not afraid of the Braddocks, but he was distinctly alarmed over the intervention and attitude of David Jenison. That aggressive, determined young man had made a threat which struck something like terror to his heart. The more he thought of it, the more insistent became the conviction that Jenison held the whip hand over him. It was not altogether incomprehensible, this amazing turn of affairs. He *had* drawn a revolver, and he had put himself in a decidedly uncomfortable position, with at least four witnesses against him, three of whom he could not hope to buy off in case of an inquiry.

His first thought on driving away from the Portman house was to rush over to the nearest police station and set the officers of the law on the track of the man he feared and hated, in the hope that he might forestall any action on Jenison's part. On second thoughts, he decided that it would be wiser to make haste slowly. He was in the unhappy position of having to consider his own daughter as one of the witnesses. His brain was working rapidly despite the fact that his daughter was doing all in her power to distract it by an unrestrained flow of invective against—not the Braddocks, but David Jenison!

To her surprise and subsequent rage he suddenly broke in with the announcement that she was to take the first afternoon train out of the city. He had some difficulty in making it plain that her speedy departure was necessary to her own as well as to his personal comfort. While she was still arguing and pleading to be allowed to stay and fight it out with him he stuck his head through the window and instructed the driver to take them to his hotel instead of to the police station, as first directed.

With characteristic decisiveness he directed Roberta to begin her packing as soon as she reached her room. She entreated him to come away with her before Jenison could carry out his threat, but he sharply refused, already having in mind a plan of action, desperate but effective. His first step, however, met with an unexpected rebuke. On the arrival at the hotel he took the cabman aside and deliberately offered him a large sum of money on condition that he would swear that Braddock drew or attempted to draw a revolver. The cabman thought it over. Then he refused.

"Money won't tempt me, " he said doggedly, "although God knows I need it. You pulled a gun on him, and he didn't have any that I could see. That young feller took my name and number. He'd catch me in the lie, sure as shootin'. And, say, they sent a couple of guys up for perjury just last week, pals of mine, they were. Not for me, guv'nor. I'll stick to the truth, just to see how it feels. "

"But the man has sworn to kill me! "

"You pulled a gun on him, " retorted the driver surlily. "I don't like that kind of business. And I guess, if they happen to ask me, I'll just mention that you tried to buy me off, too. Ta-ta! Maybe I'll see you later. " And away he went, less virtuous than nature intended him to be, but wholly satisfied that he possessed a conscience, after all.

The Colonel, grim and furtive, accompanied Roberta to the station and saw her safely off. By three or four o'clock in the afternoon he began to feel reasonably certain that Jenison had failed in his attempt to secure a warrant, or had been turned from his purpose by that cool- headed, far-seeing woman, Mary Braddock. He remained in his rooms, disdaining flight or subterfuge. All through the long, hot afternoon, he paced the floor or sat in the windows, nervously awaiting the descent of the officers. They did not come. His spirits took wing again as the close of the day drew down upon him. He had waited, with all the stoicism of the born gambler, for the crash and it had not come; he had taken the chance; to use his own expression, he "stood pat. "

At six o'clock he threw away his half-smoked cigar and sauntered forth from the hotel. The Colonel was very punctilious in that respect: he made it a point not to smoke in the street.

Although he was now quite comfortably sure that there was no immediate danger of arrest, he still was confronted by the ugly certainty that Tom Braddock was hard upon his heels and that no amount of persuasion could have turned him from his purpose. His blood went cold from time to time when he permitted himself to recall the set, implacable expression in the man's face, and the tigerish strength that marked every repressed movement of his body. Robert Grand knew that Braddock's sole object in life now was to kill him. He knew that the meeting could not long be deferred; and when it came, he would not have one chance in a thousand against this wily, determined giant. Braddock would accomplish his end, of that he was as sure as he was certain that the sun would rise in the morning. It was in the cards. He knew. He was a true-born gambler, with all the instincts, all the wiles, all the insight of one who courts

Chance and fights it at the same time. Such men as Robert Grand go on defying Fate to the bitter end, but they know that there will be an end, and in the end they are bound to lose.

This man, a lifelong tempter of Fate, had learned early in the game that the gravest errors in the category of crime came under that lachrymose heading, "wasted energy. " Men of his stamp make it a point never to do anything that may be safely left undone, nor are they guilty of overlooking the act that should be performed. They think quickly and soundly, and they act at the proper time: never too soon, never too late.

He had an object in remaining in his rooms during the afternoon, just as he had a purpose in venturing forth at six. That was the hour when the streets were crowded to their capacity by restless homeward-bound pedestrians, and the saloons, by those who paused in their haste. His tall, slightly stooped figure moved through the hurrying throng until he came to one of the most famous of the sporting bars. He entered, and, without looking to right or left, made his way to the small cafe in the rear. A man seated at one of the little tables looked up and nodded. Grand took the chair opposite to this person and, after an exchange of greetings for the benefit of the waiter, ordered oysters and a pint of musty ale. The Colonel had his principal meal at midnight.

"Do you know where Braddock is? " he demanded as soon as the waiter had left the table.

"Sure, " said the man opposite. "He's laying low in that dive over on— "

"Nothing of the kind, " interrupted Grand sharply. Fixing him with his cold, steady eyes, he went on: "You are a wonderful spotter, you are. So you've been watching that place over there all day, have you? And you are sure he's there, eh? Well, let me tell you how damned worthless you are. I expected you'd have him behind the bars before ten o'clock, but—"

"Say, Colonel, on the square, the police here are the slowest bunch of—"

"Never mind, " snapped the Colonel. "He's still at large, and he's not over there at Dick Cronk's. So much for your fine detective work. "

The man was an operative for one of the biggest private detective agencies in New York. It was his duty, and had been for years, to *watch the police* in order that Colonel Grand's *sub rosa* interests might be preserved from the fatal inconstancies of a greedy department.

Just now he was devoting his time to Tom Braddock, laying the trap for the one man his employer feared more than he feared all the laws of the land and all the authorities behind them.

The Colonel related his experiences of the morning. The private detective perspired freely. He realized how near his employer had been to death, and all through him. All efforts to explain his unhappy mistake met with curt interruptions from the Colonel.

"Now, " said that worthy, in conclusion, "I want you to find out if Braddock has returned to Cronk's place. Naturally the police could not find him this afternoon. He wasn't there. But he may go back to-night. His wife won't be able to hold him under her thumb. Find this Cronk fellow—the deformed one, I mean—and tell him I want to see him. Tell him it is worth just one thousand dollars to him, and possibly five times that amount. Send him up the rear stairway at Broadso's. I'll be in room five until twelve o'clock to-night. Any time after eight he will find me there—alone. You know where he lives; go and find him. Then make sure that Braddock is at Dick Cronk's room. That's all. "

At half-past eight o'clock that evening Ernie Cronk stole up the stairway in the rear of Broads's saloon. He slunk down the narrow, dimly-lighted hallway until he came to a door which bore the numeral five. For a full minute he stood there irresolute, held inactive by the two mental elements that bear such close kinship to each other— apprehension and greed. At last, with a stealthy glance at the lighted transoms down the hall, he tapped on the panel of the door. Colonel Grand himself opened the door and held it ajar that he might enter.

The hunchback glanced quickly around the room. He had never been there before, but he knew in an instant where he was and what manner of traffic was carried on in this small, close room with the green- covered table in the center, over which was suspended a fully lighted chandelier. The door closed gently behind him and a key was turned in the lock. Like a trapped rat, he whirled at this ominous sound.

Colonel Grand, smiling suavely, stood between him and the door.

"Don't be alarmed, Ernie, " said he in his oiliest tones. "Sit down, my lad. We're quite alone and we won't be disturbed. I am master of the hall, as they would say in England. "

He motioned to a chair beyond the table, and, bowing politely, settled himself in one nearer the door.

"What's the game? " demanded Ernie Cronk, his long, bony fingers fumbling his flat derby hat. "Brown said you wanted to see me. "

"Where's your brother Dick? " asked the Colonel irrelevantly, leaning forward a trifle.

"Dick? Why, he's—he's—I don't know where he is. He's got a place of his own somewheres. I don't see much of him these days. I can't afford it, to be honest, Colonel. "

"His reputation, eh? Well, I don't blame you. He didn't come over here with you, did he? "

Ernie started. His gaze wavered ever so slightly, but the Colonel noted the change.

"I haven't seen him in a week, " said the hunchback steadily.

"You are lying, Ernie. He's across the street now, waiting for you. "

"So help me God, Colonel—" began Ernie, but the Colonel checked the denial without ceremony.

"I am just as sure that he came over here with you to-night as I am sure that you are sitting there. I thought you'd bring him. That's why I sent for you. I knew it was the easiest way to get him here. He wouldn't come if I sent for him, but he'd go anywhere on earth if you asked him to. We'll wait a quarter of an hour, Ernie, before we proceed to business. At the end of that period I'll open the door suddenly and we'll find Artful Dick Cronk standing in the hall. To make it all the more interesting I'll present you with ten dollars if he isn't there. "

Ernie's ferret-like eyes blinked in sheer amazement. Down in his mean little heart there always had been a dark fear of this rather imposing man; in his mind there was a no uncertain estimate of the Colonel's almost supernatural power to read the thoughts of others.

"If he's outside there I don't know it, " he said doggedly.

"You told him I had sent for you, Ernie. Don't lie. I know you did. It's all right. So, you see, my little strategy worked out beautifully. I want to see Dick quite as much as I do you. We'll wait until he comes up to see what's happened to you. "

Ernie hesitated, then broke out with an uneasy note in his voice. "You said it would be worth a thousand and maybe more to me. Well, I'm square with Dick. He divides with me. I want to let him in on anything good that comes my way. "

"I see. You are willing to divide with him, so you are going to let him in on condition that he will do *all* the dirty work while you sit back and boss the job. I see. You are a great financier, Ernie. "

"You ought to see my new flat over in Eighth Street, " said Ernie proudly, quite taken in by the Colonel's none too gentle sarcasm.

"You don't share that with Dick, I imagine. "

"Well, hardly! " ejaculated Dick's brother. Suddenly his uneasiness developed into a sort of whining protest. "Say, if you got anything to say to me, say it. I got to be moving along. If I can make a thousand honestly, I'm on the job. What's—"

"We'll wait for Dick, " observed the Colonel coolly. He took his time to light a long cigar, the hunchback looking on with curiosity and doubt in his shifty eyes. Then he handed a cigar to his guest. "Have a cigar. I'd offer you a drink, only I don't believe in drinking between friends. Only enemies drink to each other, Ernie. Bear that in mind. Unconscious enemies. "

"I don't drink, " was the surly rejoinder.

Precisely ten minutes later Colonel Grand got up from his chair. In three strides he was at the door; he turned the key and—

There was Dick Cronk leaning against the wall on the opposite side of the hallway, his hands in his pockets, his long legs crossed, his "dicer" on the back of his head. There was no evidence of surprise or confusion in his face; he was as composed, as serene, as if the expected had occurred. A bland smile greeted the triumphant Colonel.

"Evening, Colonel. Have you seen anything of a lost boy around here? "

The other stood aside, giving him a fair view of the room. "Come in, Dick. I've been expecting you, " he said quietly.

Dick stared for a second or two longer than he might have done under less trying conditions.

"No, thanks. I'll wait out here, " he said dryly. He did not change his attitude in the least.

"We've been waiting for you, " said the Colonel. "We can't proceed without you. Do me the honor to step into my parlor. " He bowed very deeply.

"'Said the spider to the fly, '" quoth Dick, shifting his foot.

Ernie appeared behind Colonel Grand. He indicated by a significant motion of his head that Dick was to enter, and without delay. Slowly the long pickpocket unwound his legs. He then removed his hands from his pockets, after which he coolly strode into the room. The door was closed quickly after him. There was an inscrutable smile on his face, even before the sharp exclamation of concern fell from the lips of Colonel Grand.

"I've got the key here in my hand, Colonel, " he observed, with his gentlest smile. The older man glared for a moment and then broke into a short, even admiring laugh.

"You are a wonder, Dick. You must have wished it out of the door. I'll swear my hand hasn't been off the knob since I opened it a minute ago. How do you do it? "

"Simple twist of the wrist—*presto visto*, as the feller'd say. Don't worry. I'll leave it in the door when I depart. And say, while we're exchanging compliments, allow me to hand you one. You're something of a wizard, too. I don't wonder you always win at poker if you can see through an oak door as easy as all that. "

"We'd better lock the door, " urged the other, paying no heed to the remark.

"All right. But, if you don't mind, I'll keep the key. " He locked the door and then turned toward Ernie, sudden comprehension in his face. "Oh, you told him I came over with you. That explains it. " Ernie protested. He would have repeated the entire conversation that had taken place if the Colonel had not stopped him with considerable acerbity.

"You can talk that over afterwards, " he said sharply. Ernie winced. Grand did not observe the ugly gleam that flickered for an instant in Dick Cronk's eyes. "I've got a proposition to make to you fellows. "

"What has it got to do with Tom Braddock? " demanded Dick bluntly. He sat on the edge of the table, one foot touching the floor.

The Colonel came to the point without delay.

"There's no sense in beating about the bush with you, I see, " he remarked. "I want to get this man Braddock out of the way for good and all. He's a menace to me and I'm willing to pay to have him completely blotted out. You fellows are out for the coin of the realm. You, Dick, get it in dribs by plundering the unwary. It's slow work and dangerous. Ernie lives off of you with something of the voracity of a leech—no offense intended, Ernie. Now, why not turn your hand to something big and definite and safe? " He paused to let the idea sink into Ernie's avaricious soul.

Dick drew a long breath. "Why don't you kill him yourself? " he asked, shooting a quick, apprehensive look at his brother's face. Ernie's eyes were glistening.

"I didn't mention a killing, did I? " retorted Grand, momentarily disturbed. "If I had that in mind, Dick, I daresay I could accomplish it without calling on you for aid. What I want is to see him landed in Sing Sing for a long term of years—the limit, you might say. "

"See here, Grand, you've called in the wrong stoolpigeon this time. I'm not in that kind of business. Never in all my life have I put up a job on a pal, never have I done a trick as dirt-mean as that. I guess you'll have to count me and Ernie out. "

"Don't go off half-cocked, Dick, " admonished the Colonel easily. "You're no fool, nor is Ernie. It's worth just ten thousand between you if Tom Braddock is landed to-night, with the goods on him, so to speak. Two thousand down, the balance—"

"You infernal beast! " snarled Dick, standing squarely in front of him and glaring into his eyes with a scorn so shriveling that the other drew back with an oath. "So that's what you wanted with Ernie, is it? Through him you hoped to get me to do the trick, eh? Well, you've slipped up good and hard on *me*. I—"

Ernie, his lips twitching, his fingers working, seized his brother's arm and pulled him back.

"Wait a minute, Dick, —listen to me, " he fairly croaked in his excitement. "Let's hear what his plan is. Maybe we can see a way to help him. Le' me talk, Dick. Leave it to me. I'm smart and sensible. You're off your nut to-night. Just le' me do the talking. "

"That's right, " cried the Colonel quickly. He recognized an asset in Ernie's despicable greed.

Dick shook off his brother's hand. "No! This is no business of yours, Ernie. I'm the one he wants to dicker with. You can't put up a job on Brad and he knows it. He's just using you to land me. Not for ten million, Grand. Do you get that? "

"Don't shout so that they can hear you in the street, " cried Grand, scowling deeply. "Let me have a few words with Ernie. "

"Yes, Dick, you'd better shut up, " added Ernie eagerly. "I'll just talk it over with the Colonel. If we find we can't do it, why, we'll tell him so, that's all. I tell you ten thousand's a lot of money. We could open the nicest kind of a cigar stand with that, and live like honest, respectable men ever afterward. "

Dick sank back against the table and studied his brother's livid face with the darkest despair in his eyes. His shoulders drooped suddenly.

"Honest and respectable? " he said, passing his hand over his eyes. "You mean, *you* could be all of that, but where would I come in? Would you let me stand behind the showcase in your fine store? Would I ever get so much as a pipeful of tobacco out of it? No! Don't try to argue with me, Ernie; my mind's made up. I came here to-night just to save you from a game like this. I knowed you'd be for it strong, and I'd just have to do it if I wasn't here in the beginning to cork it. Look here, Grand, I don't know just what your plan is, but I'll tell you this: I'll blow on you as sure as I'm alive if you try to carry it out. Tom Braddock is an honest man these days. He's not a whiskey-soaked bum any longer. He cracked me over the head this morning—you can see the plaster there—but I don't hold it up against him. He considers me his friend because I swore I'd stand by him if he'd hold back on getting you right away. He trusts me and he thinks you're all right, too, Ernie. Now, once and for all, I'm not in on this dirty work. *And neither is Ernie!* "

Colonel Grand sat motionless before the angry young man, quietly tapping on the table with his long, white fingers, a faint smile on his half-crescent mouth.

"We'll see, " he said deliberately. "Perhaps you'd better let Ernie do the talking. I don't believe you are as wise and discreet as you might be, Dick. "

Dick whirled upon Ernie, who stood behind him. The hunchback was staring at him with a strange, unfamiliar expression in his face. It was a look of combined wonder and awe.

"Come on, Ernie. Let's get out of here. "

"Just a moment, Ernie, " interposed the Colonel. "Sit down and listen to what I have to say. "

But, for the first time since it entered his body, Ernie's soul arose above the sordid flesh. It came as from a great distance and slowly, but it came to take its frightened, subdued stand beside its kin.

"I guess I'll be going, " he said, and even as he uttered the words he wondered why he did so. "Ten thousand's a lot of money, but if Dick thinks it's too dirty for us to touch, why, I'm with him. You can count me out. " He put on his hat and started toward the door.

Dick could hardly believe his ears. "Great Scott, Ernie, you—you— Well, you're just great, kid! "

"Just a minute, " said Grand, arising slowly, an ominous glitter in his eyes. He towered above the hunchback, who was near the door. "I don't intend to let you go until you've heard *all* I have to say. "

"Get out of the way, Grand, " said the pickpocket, his fingers clenched so tightly that the backs of his hands were white.

"There's only one way to handle swine of your breed, " sneered Grand; "and that is with a club. You are a fine, virtuous pair, you are. I've got a job for you to do to-night, and I have the means of compelling you to do it. You must not get it into your heads that I did not prepare myself for either view you might take of the matter. I'm not such an idiot as all that. Now we'll indulge in a little plain talk. You are a couple of low-down sneak thieves, both of you. Of the—"

"Hold on, Grand! " snapped Dick. "None of that! "

"Of the two, Ernie is the lower. You miserable, misshapen scoundrel, you are worse than the vilest thief that ever lived. Dick is an angel compared—" "I'll get you for that! " quavered Dick, so shaken by rage that he could scarcely hold himself erect.

"No, you won't, " squeaked Ernie. "I'll get him! I'll cut his heart out! "

Grand reached out with his left hand and touched a button in the wall. In the other hand gleamed a revolver.

"If I press either the button or the trigger it will mean the end of you, you dogs. Now, listen to me. At the foot of the stairs are two policemen and a couple of detectives. They were duped into coming here by the word that a sucker was to be fleeced in Broadso's rooms to- night. All I have to do is to press the button and call for help. This hallway will swarm with waiters and men from all the rooms, and the cops will come on the run. I have nothing to do but to turn you over to them as a couple of thieves who came here to rob me. Trust me to make out a case against you. "

"I'm no thief! " shouted Ernie. Dick was looking about, like a rat in a trap, his teeth showing in the desperation of alarm. "You fellows will come to terms with me inside of two minutes or I'll land you both in the pen so quickly you won't know it's been done. I want this man Braddock put out of the way. I've got two men waiting to go with you, so don't imagine that you can play me false after you leave this room. It is all cut and dried. You are to carry out a plan I have for landing Braddock. The police will—"

"I'll see you hanged first, " grated Dick Cronk. "You are the king of crooks, you are. "

"Don't let him call the police, Dick, " whined Ernie, shrinking back against the wall. "I'm no thief. I won't go to jail! I won't! "

"Well, that's just where you'll land, my handsome bucko, " said the malevolent Colonel. "Dick won't mind it, but it will be a new experience for you, your reverence. 'Gad, you toad! "

"Let me go! " cried Ernie. "Keep Dick here, but let me out. Dick will help you, honest he will. I'm no thief. You wouldn't send me to jail! "

"Oh, I wouldn't, eh? " snarled the other. "You'll look fine in stripes, you will. And nothing under the sun can save you if I push this button. Ten years, that's what it will be. The Cronk brothers! The *sick* brothers! Why, a jury would give you the full limit. It will please your brother, after all these years, to see you doing time—Here! Drop that, curse you! "

There was a deafening report, a blinding flash and a cloud of smoke. Then a gurgling groan, the scraping of a heavy body against the wall, and Colonel Grand slid to the floor, his arms and legs writhing in the last tremendous spasm of death.

Neither of the Cronks moved for a full half-minute. They gazed as if stupefied at the bloody face of the great gambler; they saw his legs stiffen and his chest swell widely and then collapse.

"Give me the key! " It was a whispered shriek that leaped from the lips of the hunchback. "Good God, he's dead! They'll hang us! "

He sprang to Dick's side and snatched the door key from his stiff fingers. As he leaped toward the door, through the powder-smoke, he stumbled over the body of the dead man. He crashed to the floor but was up again in a flash, gasping, groaning with terror. An instant later he was in the hall. Like a cat he sped past the still closed doorways beyond and reached the stairway before a human being appeared in sight.

Half-way down stairs he met men rushing upward, attracted by the pistol shot. He actually tried to clear their heads in a frantic leap. He was caught in the air, struggling and kicking furiously, to be borne down and held by strong arms. Shrieking with rage and terror, he fought like a wild cat.

"I didn't do it! " he screamed, over and over again, foaming at the mouth. "It wasn't me! It wasn't me! Oh, God! Oh, God! "

Some one struck him a violent blow on the mouth. The foam was red from that time on. In the hallway above there were shouts and the sounds of rushing footsteps. Loud oaths of amazement came ringing down the corridor. A man in his shirt sleeves appeared at the top of the stairs, his face livid with excitement.

"Hang on to him! " he shouted. "Don't let him get away. We've got the other one! "

"What's the matter up there? " grunted one of the two officers holding Ernie, whose feet were now braced against the steps in the effort to keep them from dragging him upward.

"I didn't do it! " he panted between his teeth.

"Search me! See if I have a revolver! I never carry a gun. Dick always carries one. Let me go! Let me go! Why don't you go and get Dick? "

"Shut up, you! "

They dragged him to the door of No. 5. He caught sight of his brother standing between two men near the body of Colonel Grand, beside which a coatless man was kneeling. Another man was going through the pockets of the tall, glassy-eyed prisoner.

From an inner pocket the searcher drew forth a revolver. With nervous fingers he broke the weapon. A cry fell from his lips.

"Here's the gun. One shell empty. Barrel still hot. You low-lived scoundrel! "

Dick's eyes never left the bloody face of the murdered man. He was breathing heavily, as if in pain or extreme terror.

"Is he dead? " he whispered through his bloodless, motionless lips. Just then he looked up and saw Ernie at the doorway, bloody-faced, cringing, wide-eyed with dread. Two burly policemen were dangling his ill-favored body almost clear of the floor.

"Dead as a door-nail, " said the kneeling man. "Here's his gun with all the chambers full. He didn't have a chance to shoot. Say, this is the worst thing I've ever heard of. You'll swing for this, you dog! "

Ernie sent up a shriek. "Swing for it! I didn't do it! You can't prove anything on me. Can they, Dick? What are you holding me for? Let go! I'm an honest, respectable citizen of New York. I'm—"

"Call a wagon, " shouted one of the officers to a newcomer. "Nasty job here. We've got the murderer all right. " Dick straightened up at this. He turned to look at the condemning pistol in the hand of the man who had taken it from his pocket. A great shudder shook his frame.

"You got me all right, " he said. "You won't believe it, of course, but he pulled a gun first. I had to shoot. Get me out of this. If you don't I'll kick his face to a jelly. I've always wanted to. " He glanced at Ernie, a crooked smile on his lips.

"Well, Ernie, I guess it's going to come true. I always said it would. "

CHAPTER IX

IN THE LITTLE TRIANGULAR "SQUARE"

Jenison did not seek the warrant for Grand's arrest. He remained in the Portman house until the middle of the afternoon, vastly exercised by the fainting spell that had come over Christine. The household was considerably upset by the occurrences of the morning; old Mr. Portman was the only person about the place who appeared to be in ignorance of impending peril and disaster. He went out for his drive at two, but was not accompanied by his daughter, a defection which surprised and irritated him not a little.

Christine was herself again in a little while. She stayed in her room, attended by the entertaining Miss Noakes, who struggled manfully, so to speak, in her efforts to shatter the depression that surrounded the young girl like a blank wall.

Downstairs Mary Braddock listened to David's earnest eager plea for an immediate marriage. Now that Braddock had promised to leave at once for the far West, never to return, it seemed to David that all of their problems were solved. She had told him that her husband was to depart by the midnight train, and that it was her intention to go with him to the depot. David begged her to take him along with her, but she was firm in her determination to go alone. Braddock had made it a condition, and she could not break faith with him.

Shortly after the noon hour she drove up town to the bank. On her return she informed David that she had drawn out a sum of money to be delivered to Braddock before the train pulled out. She would not say how much she had drawn, except that it was sufficient to start the man out afresh in the world, and to keep him comfortable for a long time to come, if he should adhere to his decision to eschew drink and cards for the remainder of his life.

"Where is he going, Mrs. Braddock? "

She shook her head. "I will not tell you that, David. Only he and I are to know. "

"And you are to send him money from time to time? "

"No, I am not to send him a penny. "

"He goes to-night—positively? "

"He goes to-night, positively. "

"And he refuses to see Christine? "

"Why should he see her? "

"Well, I don't know, " said he dubiously. "It seems rather hard, don't you think? "

"Yes. He worships her, David. Yes, it is hard. He is going in this way because it makes it easier—for both of them, he says. You see, David, he is doing it for her sake, not for his own. If he were to do things just now for his own sake, he would kill Grand instead of running away from him. "

"He's a good deal of a man, after all, Mrs. Braddock. "

"A good deal of a man, " she repeated.

"He wishes Christine to be my wife. He told you so, but she won't consent until you tell her that it is all right. It's silly of her. I'm never going to give her up, and she knows it. "

She faced him suddenly. "You ask me why the marriage cannot take place to-morrow, David. Would you be just as eager to have it take place if her father decided to change his mind and remain here, with all the consequences such an act might create? "

"Certainly, " he replied promptly.

"You do not forget what he is, what he has been, what he may yet become? "

"That has nothing to do with it. I love Christine. "

"Would you be willing to stand at his side, the husband of his daughter, and say, 'I am content to be called your son'—would you? "

David stared hard at the floor for a moment. "I think that is rather an unfair question, Mrs. Braddock, when we stop to recall the fact that both you and Christine have denied him for years. I will call myself his son when you call him husband and Christine speaks of him as father—to the world. You can hardly expect me to be proud of what you are ashamed to own. "

She bowed her head in sudden humility. "I was wrong, " she said. "I deserve the rebuke. "

"I have hurt you. Forgive me. "

She placed her hand on his. He observed that it was as cold as ice. "While it is true that we have denied him, my dear David, nevertheless we do belong to him. She is his daughter. That is what I am trying to make plain to you. "

"If she chooses to call herself his daughter, I am perfectly content to call myself his son. "

"I wanted to hear you say that, David. You must take her as Thomas Braddock's daughter, quite as much as you do as Albert Portman's granddaughter. "

"I am not deceiving myself, " he said with a smile.

"Then I am ready to give my consent to an immediate marriage, " she said. For the first time since their interview began she spoke hurriedly. A feverish light came into her eyes, burning bright and dry.

He sprang to his feet, triumphant. "Come with me to her! She will name the day if you—"

"I shall name the day, David, " she said evenly. "It must be to-night, —this very night, —before her father goes away. "

"Are you in earnest? " he cried, scarcely believing that he heard aright.

"She loves you with all her soul, and you love her. You are her protector, the stone wall between her and all the unkind things of life. She needs you now. Tomorrow may bring the hour of trial. It is

320

best that she should have you to lean upon. It must be to-night. Come; we will go to her. It is nearly three o'clock. There is much to be done between now and the time that your train starts for Richmond. I want her to be in Jenison Hall to-morrow. "

Together they went to Christine. Half an hour later he hurried away from the house, a dozen imperative duties to be performed between that time and seven o'clock. He went with a joyous spirit, a leaping heart, and with the will to accomplish all that was required of him in that short space of time.

At seven Christine and he were to be married in the huge, old-fashioned drawing-room; at eight-thirty they would be on board the train, bound for Jenison Hall. He was to take her away with him, far from all the ugly possibilities that crept up from all sides to threaten her. Mary Braddock refrained from telling Christine even so much as she had told David concerning the plans of her husband. The girl was allowed to believe that the man was already on his way to the far West. There was a rather trying scene when Christine learned that it would be impossible for her to see her father. She broke down and wept, crying out bitterly that she might have been able to comfort him if she had been given the opportunity. It was with some difficulty and the exercise of considerable patience that her mother convinced her that they had acted for the best.

"Some day I shall go to see him, mother, " she had said with a resoluteness that brought a strange gleam to the eyes of the older woman. "I am sorry for him. He needs some one to love him. I am sure he is not so wicked as—"

"You must be guided by what David says, my child. Remember that you will have more than yourself to consider, " was the evasive remark of Mary Braddock.

Brooks was sent off with a letter to Dr. Browne, the rector, requesting him to conduct the marriage ceremony. Maid-servants packed Christine's trunks, all enjoined to secrecy. Ruby Noakes and old Joey attended to a few of the many preparations that were being hurried through with such nervous haste.

All through the long afternoon Mary Braddock lived under the most intense strain of suspense and apprehension. Uppermost in her mind was the question: had he succeeded in eluding the watchers who were on his trail?

At four o'clock she went to her father, prepared to tell him all that had transpired during the past thirty-six hours. She held nothing back from the old man, not even Braddock's gruesome design. They were closeted together for more than an hour. That which passed between father and daughter went no farther than the walls of the secluded little room that he called his study. She came forth from the trying interview with her head high and her heart low.

The old man's last tremulous words to her were these: "Well, Mary, God shows all of us the way. Sometimes the way is hard, but we reach the end if we look neither to the right nor the left, —nor behind. What you have just told me is terrible. Is it the only way? "

"Yes, it is the only way. "

He bowed his head and said no more. She kissed his gray hair and passed out from the room, closing the door gently behind her.

David and Christine were married at seven o'clock. The shadow which hung over the household, the grievous exigency which made haste so imperative, did much toward suppressing the joy and gladness that under other conditions would have filled the house and the hearts of all therein. Mr. Portman, gray-faced and taciturn, gave the bride in marriage. There were but three witnesses outside of the family. Joey Noakes and Ruby were there and a single college friend to whom David had gone in the stress of necessity.

Mother and daughter said their farewells in private. Christine sobbed in her mother's arms, imploring her to come away with them at once, to be happy forever. Mary Braddock's eyes were dry and burning, her hands were cold, her heart like ice.

"I will come some time, my darling, but—not now. You must make your home before I come to see you in it. I shall go abroad, as I told you this afternoon. Father agrees with me that it is the thing to do under the circumstances. When I return, my child, I will come to see you in Jenison Hall. You will be its true mistress by that time. You will have discovered the true happiness of life. Until then, my darling, you will not have lived. Even I found joy and happiness in their fullest estate before I came to know bitterness and unrest. You are to be very, very happy. I will come to you in the midst of it all. "

After they were gone and the lights were out Mary Braddock, wide-eyed and tense, stole down to the stables and waited for the father of the bride. She was there a long while ahead of the appointed time— hours, it seemed to her.

He came at last, slinking up from the mouth of the alley where a single street-light spread a dim glow in which he resolved himself for a moment in transit, only to be blotted out again as if by some magic process. With narrowed, anxious eyes and alert ears she waited, standing there in the half-open door of the carriage-house. Suddenly he grew up out of the darkness, almost at her side.

"Tom, " she cried out softly.

He came straight to her. His eyes, used to the darkness and made keen by the ever-present sense of danger, had seen the faintly white splotch in the night that marked her face for him. He had seen and had waited to make sure that it was she who stood there peering forth.

"Well, I'm here, " he said in a hoarse, restrained whisper. "Have you heard what's happened? "

"They are not pursuing you? What is it, Tom? "

"Grand has been murdered, Mary! "

For a full minute they stood as motionless as statues, he listening for the footstep that had been in his ears for days, she stunned by the appalling news. Her voice was shrill with agony when she finally broke the silence—agony, despair, horror, all combined in one bitter cry.

"You promised me you wouldn't do that! "

"Sh! Be careful, " he whispered, coming close to her side. "I *didn't* do it, Mary, —so help me, I *didn't*! Wait! Listen to me! I'm telling you the truth. " She had fallen back against the wall of the building. Her breathing was quick, as if horror was strangling her. "They caught the murderers, —a couple of gamblers at Broadso's, I heard. I didn't hear much about it. The newsboys were shouting it over in Broadway half an hour ago. I bought a paper, but it gave no details, —except that he is dead. "

"He is dead? Oh, Tom, Tom, you *do* swear to me that you had no hand in it. I couldn't bear that now. " Her arms were spread out against the building, her hands clenched. In the darkness he could see her eyes, wide and staring.

"I swear it, Mary. I was not within a mile of Broadso's. I am as innocent of that murder as you are. You will know the truth to-morrow, even if you don't believe me now. I'll never hear the true story. Oh, I don't mind saying I would have given my very soul to have been the one to do it. Maybe you think I'm pleased that he is dead. Well, I'm not! I begrudge those fellows the pleasure they had in killing him. But, this is not the time or place to talk. Let's say good-by here, Mary. You go back to the house. Let me go and do it alone. "

She swayed toward him. He caught her on his arm, —an arm of iron. She put her hand to his face.

"Tom, " she whispered, "God has taken a hand in our affairs—in yours. You must believe in God! You must give yourself to Him to-night. "

His voice broke a little. "I—I guess you'll have to do the prayin', Mary. Go back to the house now and send up a little prayer for me. That's all you've got to do. I can't stay here. It's dangerous. There is the chance that the police may try to connect me with this murder. It's known that I was after him. Don't you see? Good-by, Mary, I—"

"I am going with you, Tom. "

She grasped his arm tightly. He breathed heavily once or twice; a groan broke in his throat.

"All right, " he said. She felt the great muscle in his arm swell and relax again. "Do you know the way, Tom? " she asked.

"That next street below takes us to the docks. I walked down there this morning. By heaven, Mary, I think you might spare yourself all this. It's too horrible to even think of. Why—why, I just can't do it with you looking on. What do you think I am? "

"You said you would do it, Tom, " she insisted dully.

"Bob Grand is dead, " he reminded her. "I said that he and I couldn't live on the same earth. It's hard to think of going straight to hell with him not more than two hours ahead of me. "

"Come, " she said, starting off resolutely. He caught up with her, and they hurried through the alley side by side.

"*I'll* do it, all right, " he said, after they had traversed nearly two blocks in silence. The words came as an epitome of the struggle that was going on in his mind.

"Don't walk so fast, Tom. You are tiring me. "

"Tiring you? " he exclaimed. He looked at her bent head and laughed, —a short, mirthless chuckle. "You'll have to forgive me, Mary. You see I've been thinking of something else. Men walk fast when they're in a hurry. "

"Is it much farther? " He could scarcely hear the words.

"Six or eight blocks, if I remember right. "

She did not speak again until they were in the middle of the second block beyond. From time to time he turned to look at her, his benumbed soul trying to get in touch with the spirit that moved her to come with him to the very brink of the grave. He was puzzled, he could not understand it in her. If there was a hope of any kind lying buried under the weight that was in his breast, he neither recognized nor encouraged it. There was an awful, growing dread that she did not intend to let him go in alone. He tried to put down the ghastly fear. His glances at her became more frequent, less furtive. The thought of this splendid, noble, beautiful creature going down into the black waters after him was almost beyond his power of comprehension, and yet he was slowly allowing it to take a hold on his senses.

He came to an abrupt stop, rigid with horror. His hand fell upon her shoulder, roughly, regardless of the physical pain it was sure to inflict.

"Mary, how can I be sure that you won't jump in after me? You act so queerly. I don't understand you. For Heaven's sake, go back! Don't do anything like that. I can't bear it—I can't bear the thought of you down there in the water, under the hulls, covered with—Ah! " He covered his eyes with his hand.

She listened for a tense moment to the labored breathing of the man. He had thought of her at last! An odd, mysterious smile flickered on her lips. With a sudden convulsive movement she drew the long shaker cloak closer about her shoulders.

"Tom, there is a little park over there, with benches. Let us sit down for a moment. "

"You won't do it, Mary, will you? " he pleaded, now completely in the grip of that terrible dread.

"I am not as brave as you are, Tom, " she said. He caught a new, vibrant note in her voice. He misconstrued it.

"I call it pretty brave to be able to go down and see a man jump into the river. Not many men could do it, let alone women. It's like seeing a man hung. "

She led him, unresisting, to a bench in the corner of the dark little triangle that was called a "square. " People were passing by, but no one had stopped there to rest, or to reflect, or to make love. They had the green little park all to themselves.

"Christine was married to-night, " she said after they had been seated for a few minutes.

He remarked lifelessly: "Hurried it up on my account, eh? It's bad luck to postpone a wedding, even for a death in the family. Well, I'm glad. She's sure to be happy, God bless her! "

"Yes, she will be very happy. "

"I suppose she—and you, too—had a notion that I'd turn up some day to spoil the whole business. So you got it over with, eh? "

"I wanted everything to be settled, that's all. "

He was silent for a while, breathing heavily.

"Did she ask about me? "

"Yes. "

"You told her I was going away—that I'd probably never see her again? "

"I told her you were gone. "

"I suppose she was relieved. "

"She cried because you were not there to see her married. "

He was fully half a minute in grasping the full meaning of that wonderful sentence.

"Did she? " he asked, lifting his head suddenly. "Honest, Mary? You're not saying it just to—to make me feel—"

He stopped and waited for her to reply to his unuttered question. She shook her head.

"Then she does care a little for me. She hasn't lost all the feeling she used to have—"

"She cried because she was not given a chance to talk with you. She thought she could comfort you, could help you. That was why she cried, Tom. "

He allowed his chin to rest in his hands, his elbows on his knees.

"I wonder if I could have—Oh, say, there's no use talking, " he ended bitterly.

"What were you about to say, Tom? "

"Nothing. "

"Yes, you were. Tell me. "

"Oh, " he cried, with all the bitterness of a lost, hungry soul, "if I had only known! She *could* have comforted me. What a fool I was not to see her. I've been cursing myself all day. Now I know why I cursed. It was because I wanted to see her—" He struck himself a violent blow on the mouth, as if that were all that was needed to crush the great longing that was in his breast.

"Yes. Go on, Tom, " she said quietly.

"I can't, Mary. I can't talk about it. I guess I'd better say good-by now. I'll lose my nerve if I get to thinking and talking. I don't want to think that I might still get some happiness out of life if—if I went after it right. "

She put her cold hand on his big, clenched fist. He looked at her. The faint light from a near-by lamppost struck his face. It was heavy, leaden with despair and misery.

"Almost the last thing she said to me before she went away was this, Tom: 'Some day I shall go to him. He needs some one to love him. I am sure he is not so wicked as—' She got no farther than that. I stopped her. "

"She said all—Mary, why did you stop her? Why didn't you want her to say it? Why did you begrudge me a little thing like that? " He was trembling violently. There was misery, not anger or resentment in his voice.

"Tom, are you ready to go to the river? "

He shrank away from her, shuddering, appalled.

"It's hard to die, after all. I—I ought not to have let you tell me all this. It's made it harder. I never thought of it before. Somehow, Mary, I—I think I might have turned out a better man if—if I'd known just how Christine felt. " He got to his feet suddenly. "I said I'd do it. You want me to do it. Well, I will! "

She clung to his hand. He turned upon her with an oath on his lips. The light now struck her face. What he saw there caused him to catch his breath and to choke back the imprecation.

"I am convinced that you would do it, Tom, for her sake and mine. You would do it, not because you are weak, but because you are strong. I am satisfied now. "

"Satisfied? " he murmured, wonder-struck.

She arose. "Tom, I am not going to say that I love you. You cannot expect that. There is a feeling within me, however, that may develop into something like the old love I once had for you, if you give it the right kind of encouragement—and care. "

"What are you saying to me, Mary? " he cried hoarsely.

"You would have given up your life so that Christine might be happy. I am willing to do as much, Tom, toward the same end. I will give up the life I am leading. You want another chance, Tom. Well, you shall have it. I will go where you go, live where you live. "

"Mary! " he gasped.

"Christine said you needed help. Well, I will try to give it to you. You have her love. You didn't quite kill that, as you did mine. " She took his limp hand in hers and looked up into his eyes. "Perhaps, if both of us try hard, you and I together, Tom, we may be able to make her forget the ugliest part of her life. "

"Together? I don't understand. "

"I am still your wife, " she said, a shrill note creeping into her voice despite the effort she made to be calm.

"You—you mean I won't have to go—to go to the river? " he cried, unable to think beyond that awful alternative.

"I never meant you to do that. "

He suddenly took a long, deep breath and lifted his face, to stare about as if trying to convince himself that he was really there, alive and awake.

"I guess I don't quite get your meaning, Mary, " he muttered, but his fingers were beginning to tighten on hers. "Of course, I understand you are still my wife, and—You don't mean you—you are going to take me back! "

"No. I am asking you to take *me* back. "

He could not speak for a full minute or more.

"You'll give me another chance? That's what you mean—that's what you're really saying, isn't it? " He was fairly gasping out the words.

"Yes, Tom. "

"Oh! " He turned and flung himself on the bench, bursting into tears. "I don't deserve it—I don't deserve it! It's too much to hope for. " These and other sentences fell in broken disorder from his lips.

She did not speak, but sat down beside him, laying her hand on his shoulder. After a time, he grew quieter, —then almost deathly still. She shook him gently.

"Will you come home with me now, Tom? " she asked. She too had been crying softly.

He looked up. They were so close together that she could detect the humble, wistful look in his face. His lips moved, but the words did not come at once.

"Home with you? "

"Yes. We have our plans to discuss, Tom. "

"To your father's house? " he persisted.

"Yes. He understands. I talked it all over with him this afternoon. It was hard to do, Tom, —it was very hard to hurt that poor old man all over again. But I had it to do, and he understands. He asked me to bring you back with me. I told him I would. He wants to talk with you in the morning. "

"Mary, " he began, fingering his hat in the extremity of an emotion that almost benumbed him, "I don't know whether you want to hear me say it, but I've never stopped caring for you. It isn't all Christine with me. I just want to tell you that. "

"I understand, Tom, " she said, still more gently.

"I can't take any help from your father, " he managed to say after another long period of silence.

"He will offer nothing but his hand and his well-wishes. "

"This is all so unexpected. I'm trying to get too many things through my head at once. Let me think for a minute or two. "

She was silent, looking off into the gloomy little street below. A man was whistling gayly near by. From afar came the sound of rumbling street cars. She had not noticed these or any other sounds before. A policeman came up to the corner, stopped and looked at the huddled twain for a minute or two, and then moved off. The sight of that uniform created a sudden chill in her heart. Tom Braddock began speaking again, in low, steady tones in which there was not only a sort of bitter determination but something like defiance.

"What's more, Mary, I won't accept anything from you. Whatever you've got, put it aside for Christine or against the time when you may need it yourself. I'm not going to live off you. I'm not what I was back in those rotten days. I believe I'm going to be I happy again—I think life's going to be sweet to me after all. Half an hour ago I had but a few minutes to live, as I believed. I don't know just how to take this new grip on life. Maybe I'll be able some time to tell you all that I can't say now. I'm all befuddled. The main point is: I'm going to have a chance to be a man again, a real man; to be your husband and to make Christine forget she was ashamed of me. That's it. That's what I'm trying to say. So, you see, I can't afford to be ashamed of myself. Do you get what I mean? "

"You would be ashamed of yourself if you accepted money or help from me? Is that it? "

"Yes. I can work, Mary. I can support you, if you'll come with me. I know where to go. But you'd better think it over carefully. I can go alone, Mary dear, —I can go alone, if you feel you can't stand being with me. "

331

She hesitated, weighing her words. "I have a plan, Tom, that I want to talk over with you. I'll tell you about it when we get home. I want to know what you think of it. Perhaps you will consider it a good one. It occurred to me this afternoon while I was making preparations to leave the city with you to-morrow. "

"You—you had it all thought out before you—"

"I had it all thought out. In fact, Tom, I have the railroad tickets at home in my desk, —two tickets, one way. "

"You are the most wonderful woman in all this world, Mary, I'd die for you a thousand times, " he cried. It was almost a sob.

She smiled. "I wouldn't allow you to do it even once for me. Come! We will go back the way we came, only we will go in by the front door. "

As they turned onto the sidewalk he cast a swift, involuntary glance, as of terror, in the direction of North River. She distinctly heard the quick intake of his breath and the involuntary chatter of his teeth.

"You will sleep in a good, clean bed to-night, " she said, reading his thoughts.

He reached forth and touched her arm, timidly at first, as if he were afraid that ever so slight a sign of affection would be repulsed. Finding that she did not shrink or draw away, he ventured to draw her arm through his. His figure was still bent, but the slouching, furtive movement was gone. Mechanically she fell into his stride and they moved swiftly up the street. A clock in a house across the way banged out the hour. Far away, in the neighborhood of Broadway, a raucous- voiced newsboy was crying his "extra. " They knew that he was shouting:

"All about the murder! " in that unintelligible jargon of the night.

"We will get it all in the morning papers, " she said.

"I hope they don't try to connect me with it—Mary, I'm afraid of that! You'd better let me get out of town to-night. "

She shook her head.

He walked with his eyes set straight ahead, trying to understand, trying to get control of his new emotions. Always there was the sharp, ugly little notion that she still despised him, that she was sacrificing herself that he might be drawn as far away as possible from the child she was so anxious to shield.

"I'm going to try my best to make you care for me again, " he said, a vast hunger for sympathy and love taking possession of him.

"I hope you may, Tom, " she said drearily.

"You're doing this for Christine, " he said resentfully. "Just to get me away, so's I can't trouble her. That's it, isn't it? Tell the truth, Mary. "

"I would not expect you to do anything for her sake if I were not willing to do a great deal myself, " was her enigmatic rejoinder.

"Don't hate me, Mary, " he burst out.

She pressed his arm. "I am giving you a chance, " she reminded him. There was still a dreariness in her voice, but he did not detect it. He returned the pressure, half hopeful that the beginning already had been made.

Brooks let them in. He had been waiting up for them.

"Mr. Braddock will be here over the night, Brooks. "

"Yes, Mrs. Braddock. " He opened the door into the library for them, and then silently hastened upstairs.

"You must have been pretty sure of yourself, " commented Braddock, in no little wonder. She threw off the shaker cloak.

"There is a cold supper for you in the dining-room, Tom—and a piece of a last-minute wedding cake. You must be hungry. While you are eating we will talk over my plan. "

He went about it as if in a dream. For an hour they discussed her plan for the future. In the end he fell in with it.

"I'd be a dog if I didn't give in to you in a matter like this, " he said. "You're doing everything for me. "

333

"Our room is at the head of the stairs, the first door to the left, Tom, " she said, rising. Her face was very pale; she looked old. "The bath adjoins it. If you don't mind I'll stay downstairs awhile. I have many papers to look over and some letters to write. "

He went upstairs to the wide, high bed-chamber with its azure walls. For a long time he stood in the middle of the room, looking around in dull amazement and doubt. Was it really true that he was there, in the midst of all this elegance and comfort? He glanced at his big hands and started with shame. They were not very clean. The soiled cuffs of an ill-fitting "hickory" shirt came down over his wrists. Involuntarily he pushed them up. The greenish-gray of the coarse jeans garments he wore, clumsy and crumpled, was sadly out of harmony with the delicate, refined colors that surrounded him. It seemed to him all at once that he *jarred on himself.*

Suddenly his gaze fell upon a neatly folded suit of clothes lying across the foot of the bed. The garments were dark blue, with a thin stripe running through the cloth, and they were new. On the center table there was a straw hat. Shoes stood beside the chair at the head of the bed. An immaculate white shirt hung over the back of the chair, while on the seat were undergarments. He rubbed his eyes. Then he sat down on the chaise longue and stared, with growing comprehension. The coverlet on the bed was neatly turned down; a night-gown was there, clean and white. Beside it was another, soft and filmy.

Braddock put his hands to his face and sobbed dry, choking sobs that were not of anguish, but of bewilderment.

At last he pulled himself together and arose to make a tour of the room. On the dressing-table there were collars and neckties and cuffs. His own old-fashioned silver watch lay there before him, with its heavy gold chain attached. He remembered with a pang that he had given it to her for preservation long ago, because it had once belonged to his grandfather and he was sentimental about it.

He looked again at the clothes he wore, the clothes the state had placed on him when he left the penitentiary; he looked at his soiled hands; in the glass he caught a glimpse of his haggard, unshaven face and the dirt streaks that the tears had made. With a cry of disgust he began tearing off the hated garments.

She had done all this for him! She had known all along that he was to come home with her.

Half an hour later he came from the bath, scrubbed until his skin was red. He was clean! He was shaved! His hands were amazingly white.

Like a boy, he tried on the fresh, new, clean-smelling clothes. Even to the shoes the fit in all cases was perfect. She remembered everything—the size of his collars, the size of his shoes, the length of his sleeves: the measurements of Tom Braddock as she had known him when they were young together. He picked up the filmy night-dress and kissed it a dozen times. Then he looked at the other one. A grim smile touched his lips. How long had it been since he had slept in a thing like that? It seemed like centuries.

He sat down on the side of the bed and dropped his chin to his hands, suddenly a prey to widely varying thoughts, desires and emotions. For many minutes he drooped there, thinking, wondering, doubting.

Over in a corner stood a small new leather-bound trunk. He did not get up to look at it, or into it. He knew without looking.

"It's like a fairy story, " he murmured over and over again. "I'll do anything in the world for her, as long as I live! "

Suddenly he started up. He would go down to her. He would renew his pledges, his promises. As he opened the door to pass out to the stairs he heard her moving in the hall below. She tried the front door. Then the lower light went out. He heard her mounting the stairs slowly. She was coming up to him!

When she got to a point where she could see the streak of light from the partially open door she came to a stop. A slight shudder went over her body. Her steps were slower after that, dragging, dejected, with one or two complete pauses. Braddock understood. He had been listening to that pitiful approach of the woman who was his wife. He could almost see the expression in her face.

A sudden wave of pity swept over him. He gently closed the door and locked it on the inside.

She came on and turned the knob, feebly, timorously.

"Good-night, " he called out from the most distant corner of the room.

Fully ten seconds passed before she responded. He felt somehow that she held her breath during that time.

"Good-night, " she cried, a vibrant note in her voice. He heard her as she went down the hall. She was running.

CHAPTER X

THE BLACK HEADLINES

Christine had been mistress of Jenison Hall for three days when the expected and anxiously looked-for letter came from her mother.

A sensation of dread, of uncertainty, had been present during those three wonderful days, lurking behind the happiness that filled the foreground so completely. She could not divest herself of the vague, insistent fear that disaster hung over the head of the mother she idolized. David, supremely happy, used every device that his brain and a loving heart could present to set her mind at rest, to drive away the unvoiced anxiety that revealed itself only in the occasional mirror of her telltale eyes.

When no word came on the morning of the third day, she timidly suggested that they run up to New York for a short visit. He laughed at her and playfully accused her of being tired of him, of being homesick. Nevertheless, he was troubled. He had seen the newspaper accounts of the murder of Colonel Grand, and he had been horrified, immeasurably shocked, to find that Dick Cronk was the self-confessed assassin.

There was no mention of Braddock's name in the dispatches, yet he could not banish the fear that ultimately the man would be implicated.

Dick Cronk's story of the crime, as presented by the newspapers, was clear and unwavering. He said that he had shot the man in the heat of a quarrel over money matters. The newspapers professed to be unable to secure a statement of any kind from the brother, Ernest Cronk, who was in jail as an accomplice, despite the vigorous protests of the principal figure in the case. The newspapers went into the history of the Cronk boys, from childhood up, devoting considerable space to the excellent reputation of the cripple and the unsavory record of the noted pickpocket. In summing up the case, there seemed to be no question of the innocence of the cripple, although it was stated that the district attorney intended to put him on trial for complicity in the crime. The men, held without bail, were to be given a hearing in the trial court at an early day.

Letters from Joey Noakes and Ruby to the Jenisons set forth the details of a visit to the Tombs on the day following the murder. Both were constrained to remark that, in the view of Dick's confession, it would go very hard with him; they could see no chance of escape for him. Joey, however, urged David to contribute something toward engaging the services of a clever lawyer who at least might save him from the gallows. He stated that Ernie, after stubbornly maintaining his own innocence, refused to pay out money for an attorney, preferring to let the state provide counsel for him, under the law. There was no mention of Braddock in either letter, for obvious reasons.

Then the letter came from Mary Braddock. It was addressed to Christine. The mother's heart cried out in the opening pages. David, at least, could read between the lines. There were the tenderest protestations of love and the most confident of prophecies, uttered with a buoyancy of spirit that convinced and delighted the girl, who had been so hungry for reassuring words. A new   radiance enveloped her. But he saw beyond the wistful, carefully considered sentences. He saw the shadow of Thomas Braddock at the elbow of the woman as she wrote.

Near the bottom of the second page she abruptly took up the subject which was, after all, uppermost in the minds of these anxious young people.

"Your father, " she began, "has changed his mind about going to the mines in the Southwest. I saw him after that dreadful thing had happened at Broadso's. He was afraid I might think he had a hand in it, so he came at once to reassure me. Of course, he was not implicated in any way. It will please you, Christine, to know that my father had a long talk with him on the day following the murder, and that he was more than merely impressed by the change in him. He firmly believes that your father means to lead an honorable, upright life. I, too, believe that he can work out his own redemption. Perhaps David will bear me out in this. He saw him, and he noted the wonderful change. Time, however, will tell. I ought not to be too rash with my prophecies.

"He loves you. He wants to reclaim your love and respect. That is all he has to live for, I firmly believe. For this reason, if for no other, I am confident he will make a brave, a wonderful effort. What he needs most of all is encouragement, sympathy, the promise of ultimate reward. If he realizes that the time may yet come when he can stand before you without shame on his own part, and be received without shame on your part and David's, I am sure it will mean everything to him in the struggle he is to make in the next three or four years.

"He is now on his way to your grandfather's ranch in Montana, of which he will assume the management next fall. The present manager is most unsatisfactory to my father. He recognizes Tom's great ability in handling men; his training in the school of hardship and adversity has given him all the requisites necessary to the conducting of a large ranch. You remember the name of the post-office where the mail for the ranch is always sent. I implore you to write to him often. It will mean so much to him, and, in the end, so much to you and yours. He insists that you are to make no effort to see him. You can well understand how he feels about it. Let *him* come to you in his own good time. That is best, I am sure. I strongly advise you to respect his wishes in this connection.

"As for my own plans, I am going to the ranch with him. He needs me. "

That was all she had to say of herself or her plans.

In the next sentence she spoke of Dick Cronk:

"I suppose you have read of that unhappy boy's arrest. Joey is trying to raise means with which to employ capable counsel for him. I have sent him a check for a thousand dollars, with the understanding that my name is not to be mentioned as a donor. Your father says he cannot conceive of Dick committing a murder. Nor can I. I have a strange feeling that he did not do it, but, of course, that is silly in the face of all that has come out. I am sorry for Dick. If David can find it convenient to befriend him in any way, I am sure he will not hesitate to help that poor, unfortunate boy who once did him an unusual service.

"We are leaving at 5.30 for Chicago .... "

The weeks passed rapidly for the blissful young Jenisons. The letters from the far West were full of promise. Even the skeptical David was compelled to admit to himself that the silver lining was discernible against the black cloud that Mary Braddock had so deliberately set herself under.

With his fair young wife he journeyed to New York toward the end of their first month of married life. It had not required the advice or suggestion of others to rouse in him a sense of duty. He owed more to Dick Cronk than he could have hoped to repay under the most favorable of circumstances: now it seemed utterly impossible to lift the obligation. His first act was to send a large check to Joey Noakes. This was followed by numerous encouraging letters to Dick Cronk, in each of which he openly pledged himself to do all in his power to help him in his great trouble.

Dick's replies were characteristic. They were full of quaint, sarcastic references to his plight, glib comments on the close proximity of the scaffold, and bitter lamentations over the detention of his brother Ernie, whose misery and unhappiness seemed to weigh more heavily with him than his own dire predicament.

On his arrival in town David went at once to the office of the great criminal lawyer who had been engaged to defend the Cronks. There he was met by Joey Noakes, Casey (no longer a contortionist but the owner of a well-established plumbing business descended from his father) and young Ben Thompson, the newspaper man who was soon to become Ruby's husband. The man of law was brutally frank in his discussion of the case. He had gone into it very thoroughly with the two prisoners. In his mind there was no doubt as to the outcome of the trial. The men had elected to be tried jointly. Richard Cronk did not have the ghost of a hope to escape the extreme penalty; Ernest would be discharged. There did not seem to be the remotest chance of saving Dick from the gallows.

The testimony of the two prisoners would have but little weight with a jury, and there were no extenuating circumstances behind which he could go in support of his plea for leniency. The prisoners had revealed to him their motive in visiting Broadso's place, going quite fully into the details of the interview which ended in the shooting. David's surprise and horror on learning these hitherto unmentioned facts can well be imagined.

"Personally, " said the lawyer, "I am inclined to the opinion that Dick Cronk tells the truth when he says Grand drew a revolver on him and that he shot in self-defense. If we can make the jury see it in that light there may be some chance for him. That is the defense I shall offer, in any event. The state, however, is in a position to make light of the plea, and with tremendous effect. It is just as plausible a theory that Grand himself drew in self-defense. The fact that Cronk fired and Grand did not will go far toward substantiating that theory in the minds of intelligent jurors. It is not at all likely that Grand, who knew the character of his visitors, could be forestalled in a shooting affair, especially if he had been the first to draw. Gentlemen, I shall do my best, but I must say to you that it is a hopeless fight. Young Cronk is perfectly indifferent as to his own fate. He seems only anxious to have his brother acquitted of complicity in the actual crime. Ernie Cronk says that he saw a revolver in Grand's hand, but, you see, he is so vitally interested that it is doubtful if his testimony will be credited. It is very black for Dick Cronk. You may as well understand the situation. We have one chance in a thousand of getting him off with a life sentence, one in a million of securing an acquittal. "

The next day David and Joey went to the Tombs to see the two men. Dick came down to the visitor's cage, but Ernie stubbornly refused to see the callers.

"He's in a terrible way, David, " said Dick, in explanation of his brother's attitude toward them. "You see, I'm an old hand at the business, and I advised him to talk with no one except the lawyer. It's bad policy, gabbing with everybody that comes along. Keep a close tongue in your head, that's my motto. Ernie's followin' my advice right up to the limit. He's so cussed stingy with his conversation that he won't talk to himself. I don't believe he has said fifty words out loud in the past two weeks. It's getting to be quite a joke among the other guys in here. I never knew any one to be so careful as he is. But, as I said before, he's in a bad way. It's telling on him, poor kid. He can't see anything but the rope for both of us. And then, Davy, my boy, he's got a particular reason for not seeing you. I guess you know what it is. He's a terrible proud feller, Ernie is. Not a bit like me in that respect. Now I'm willing to thank you for putting up the coin for us, and all that, and I do thank you; but Ernie—well, he's a curious kid. He can't bear to—well, you understand. "

"Dick, " began David as soon as the complacent rogue gave him the opportunity to break in, "I want you to tell Joey and me just how it happened. We are your best friends—"

The prisoner held up his hand, palm outward, shaking his head slowly as he spoke. "I'd be a poor example for Ernie if I blabbed after tellin' him to keep his trap shut. Excuse *me*, Davy. My lawyer is the only one I talk to about the case. As he's your lawyer just as much as he is mine, and more so, I guess, I don't mind if you chat with him. He can tell you all he wants to. But not me. Nix, kid. Not even to you and old Joey here, the greatest close-mouth in the business. Why, I saw Joey last winter in that pantomime out West, and he never said a word from the time the curtain went up till it went down. Talk about your tight-lipped guys! Say, he's the king of them all. He's the only actor I ever saw that wasn't kickin' for more words to conquer. These gabby actors just give me a—"

"For heaven's sake, Dick, be serious! " cried David impatiently. "You *must* talk to us openly, frankly about—"

"I'm sorry, David, " interrupted Dick, his face grave in an instant. "I can't talk about it. I'd sooner not. You see, I've got to consider Ernie. He's absolutely innocent. If I got to spoutin' around, I might say something that could be twisted so's it would hurt him. So, if you don't mind, I'll talk about the weather. How is it down in old Virginia? How's old Jeff? And how is the cook-lady at Jenison Hall? Say, I wish you'd mention me to her. I'm the ghost that took her pies and cold chicken, you remember. "

It was useless for them to continue. He smilingly but stubbornly refused to be moved by their eloquence. To all of their subtly-worded entreaties he gave but the one, oft-repeated response:

"I guess you'd better discuss that with Mr. Prull, the lawyer. "

They gave it up, but not until the time allotted to them as visitors was nearly over.

"Mr. Prull has all the facts. Let him do the worrying, " quoth Dick, the philosopher. "Ernie will get off, dead sure. As for yours truly, I made my bed, so I guess I'll have to sleep in it. Joey, I'll have the laugh on you. You always said I was a crazy freak when I told you where I was going to end. Just you remember that, will you, when you read about me doing the groundless dance one of these fine days. My old man did it before me. He was seventeen minutes strangling, they say. Almost a record-breaking performance. To tell you the truth, Joey, I'd be downright disappointed if I should happen to cash in natural-like. It would be an awful jolt to my faith in Fate. "

"For the love of 'eaven, Dick, don't go on like that, " groaned Joey. A cold perspiration was standing on his forehead. "You ought to 'ave some regard for my feelings. "

Dick laughed merrily. "There you go! Always thinkin' of yourself. I've always heard that Englishmen haven't got any feelings. "

"Well, they 'ave, " was Joey's retort.

"Say, David, what's the latest news from Brad? " He listened with great interest to David's brief recital. "Good for Brad! " he exclaimed. "I always said he'd come out clean if he had a chance. I say, Mrs. Brad's a brick. She'll bring him around, see if she don't. He ain't a natural crook, Brad ain't. He's got a conscience and he can't get away from that. No man's a real crook who has a conscience. I've got my own definition of the word 'conscience': a mental funeral with only one mourner. Say, kid, I guess I saved your father-in-law's neck when I plugged old Grand—"

"Dick, don't breathe that, I implore you, " cried David. "He had promised Mrs. Braddock that he'd go away. It can do no good to drag him into all this. "

"Well, " said Dick reflectively, "I guess you'd better ask Mr. Prull about that. He knows all the facts. "

"I beg your pardon, Dick. I'm sorry I spoke so quickly. "

"It's all right, kid. No harm done. Don't worry. There won't be anything said about Brad's *original* intentions. I hope Christine—I should say Mrs. Jenison—is well. I know she must be happy. "

"She is both, Dick. She is very deeply interested in your case. "

"I hope you won't let her send me roses and sweet violets, kid. That's an awful gag they're workin' now. There's a fellow down the line here that cut his wife's head nearly off in two places—on both sides of the neck—and he's getting pink roses and lilies of the valley by the cab-load. "

"Christine is sending books and fruit, and three times a week you are to have a dinner fit for a—"

The sudden fierce glare in the prisoner's eyes caused David to stop in amazement.

"Look here, " demanded Dick savagely, "ain't poor Ernie to have any o' these things? Is he to set by and see me eat—what? "

"You are to be treated alike, of course, " cried David quickly. Dick's face cleared. He looked down in evident embarrassment.

"Excuse me, kid. I—I always get riled when I think of him getting the worst of anything. I'm sure we'll both be terrible grateful to Chris— to Mrs. Jenison. She's an angel, —as of course you know, kid. Sending me books, eh? Tell her I like Dickens, will you? And, say, there's *one* book she needn't go to the trouble of sendin' me. "

"You mean the—the Bible? "

"Yes. "

"Dick, you don't really mean that. You—"

"I've already got one, " said the prisoner simply. His eyes fell with curious inconsistency. They saw his chin and lower lip quiver ever so slightly. He scraped the floor with his foot a time or two, and his fingers tightened on the bars. "It's a little one my mother gave me when I was a kid. I've always kept it. Funny little old Bible, with print so small you can't hardly read it, 'specially that place where all them guys with the jay names were being begot. They seem to run together a good deal—I mean the names. I guess they must have run together considerable themselves, if accounts are true. Yes, my ma gave it to me for being a good boy once. "

His eyes were wet when he looked up at David's face again. His smile seemed more twisted than usual.

"Where is it now, Dick? " asked Jenison, a lump coming into his throat. Joey was plainly, almost offensively amazed.

"Why, —why, Ernie's got it. He didn't have anything else to read, so he took it a couple of weeks ago. I—I guess I'll ask him for it some day soon. Oh, yes, there *is* something I want to speak to you about, Joey. A couple o' years ago I took out a life insurance policy in favor of Ernie, and also an accident policy. I couldn't keep up the accident one, but the other's paid up to next January. Maybe I won't have to pay on it again. It's for five thousand. I want you to see that he gets the money if—if I—well, you know. The policy is in the safe over at old Isaac's pawnshop, —you know the place. I'll write and ask him to come down and see me, and I'll tell him to give you the paper, if you don't mind, Joey. "

"Sure, Dick. I'll take charge of it. You're very good to Ernie, and thoughtful, lad. "

"Well, I guess I ought to be, " remarked Dick dryly.

David from the first had been more or less certain that Dick was not the one who shot Grand. He could not drive the ugly conviction from his mind. It occurred to him at this juncture to put his theory to the test, hoping to catch Dick off his guard.

"The police are now saying that you did not do the shooting, Dick. " He watched the other's face narrowly.

There was not so much as a flicker of alarm.

"They don't think the old boy committed suicide, do they? " asked Dick, with a chuckle of scorn for the obtuseness of the police.

"No. They're working on some new evidence, that's all. "

"It's grand to have a reputation like mine, " grinned the amiable rogue. "They won't even believe me when they catch me red-handed. Once a liar, always a liar. That's their idea, eh? If I was to turn around and say I didn't do it, I suppose they'd believe me? Well, nix! I guess not! "

David and Joey left almost immediately after this, promising to visit him from time to time, and to do all in their power to aid Mr. Prull.

"Well, so long, " said Dick at parting. "Say, Joey, will you remember me to Ruby? I wish her all the luck in the world. "

The summer months wore away and toward the middle of October the case of the State *vs.* Cronk and Cronk came up. There was little or no public interest in the hearing. Two sets of friends, rather small circles very widely apart, were deeply interested, and that was all. The Jenisons and their friends formed one contingent, while the other was made up from that shifting, stealthy element of humanity known as the "under-world. "—pickpockets, cracksmen and ne'er-do-wells who had been the associates of Dick Cronk in one way or another, off and on, for years.

The plea of self-defense was ably presented by a great lawyer, but it was shattered by the State quite as easily as he had anticipated. He made an eloquent, impassioned appeal for clemency. The jury was out not more than an hour. Their verdict was an acquittal for Ernest Cronk, a conviction for murder in the first degree against Richard, with the recommendation that he be hanged by the neck until dead.

Following the conviction came the application for a new trial, which was not granted. The record in the case was so clear of error and the proof so conclusive that Mr. Prull declined to carry the matter to the higher courts, realizing the hopelessness of such a proceeding. Then began the systematic, earnest effort to induce the governor to commute the sentence to life imprisonment. He declined to interfere.

Dick Cronk was doomed.

At eleven o'clock on the morning of a bitterly cold Friday in January a grim, sullen group of men, evil-faced fellows whose eyes were heavy with dread, and whose lips hung limp with dejection, crowded around the stove in a squalid, ill-smelling basement room. They spoke but seldom; their voices were rarely raised above the hoarse half-whisper of anxiety known only to men who wait in patience for a thing of horror to come to pass, an inevitable, remorseless thing from which there is no escape.

They shivered as they crouched close to the red-hot stove, notwithstanding the almost unbearable heat of the foul, windowless room in which they were gathered. Their faces were pallid, their eyes bloodshot, their flesh a-quiver.

Occasionally one or another of them would go to the door to listen for sounds in the black passage beyond. He would resume his seat without a word to his fellows, each of whom looked up with stark, questioning eyes. Then they would fall to staring at the walls again, or at the floor, their chins in their hands. At their feet lay the newspapers, eagerly read and discarded by each and every member of this little group. There was a "noon extra, " fresh from a ten o'clock press. It had been the last to fall into their hands.

They tried to smoke, but the water of mortal terror filled their mouths. The smell of dead, dank tobacco pervaded the room.

In a far corner, huddled against the wall, there was a shivering, silent figure, a Pariah even among these under-world outcasts. He sat apart from the others, denied a place in the circle, despised and abhorred by the men he once had scorned because they were the devil- may-care companions and emulators of his brother. His beady black eyes never shifted from the low, padlocked door in the opposite end of the room. He, too, was waiting for the dread news from the upper world. His breathing was sharply audible, as of one drugged by sleep; his body had not moved an inch in an hour or more, so fierce was the suspense that held him rigid. From time to time he swallowed, although his mouth was dry and empty; there was a rattling sound accompanying the act that suggested the hoarse croak of a frog. Always his gaze was on the door, never wavering, unblinkng, fascinated by the horror that was creeping down to him as surely as the sun crept up to the apex of the day.

Noon! Twelve o'clock, midday! The hour they were dreading!

One of the shivering thieves beside the stove drew forth from a ragged pocket the plutocratic timepiece of a millionaire victim. The way his eyes narrowed as he looked at its face told the silent observers that it was twelve o'clock and after. Unconsciously every figure stiffened, every jaw was set, every nostril spread with the intake of air. Every mind's eye in that fear-sick group leaped afar and drew a picture of the thing that was happening—then! At that very instant it was happening!

"Oh! " groaned some one, half aloud.

"It's after twelve, " muttered another thickly.

"The jig's up wid Dick, kids. Blacky ought to be here wid de extry. Wot's a keepin' him? " said the first speaker, glaring over his shoulder in the direction of the door.

"Twelve sharp, that's wot it says, " shuddered a small, pinched thief. "He's a-swingin' now. "

Suddenly a wild, appalling shriek arose from the corner behind them. As one man, they whirled. Their gaze fell upon the cringing figure over there, now groveling on the floor in the agony of a terror that severed all the restraining bonds that had held his tongue so long.

They shrank back as their minds began to grasp the words he was shrieking in his madness.

He was sobbing out the thing that each man there had suspected from the first!

For many minutes they listened to his ravings, stupefied, aghast. Then a stealthy glance swept round the circle as if inspired by one central intelligence. It crept out of the corners of rattish eyes, reading as it ran the sinister circle, and hurried back to its intense, malevolent business of transfixing the quarry in the corner.

A hand reached down and grasped the leg of a short, heavy stool. Another went lower and clutched a long, murderous bar of iron that served as a poker. Savage eyes went in quest of deadly things, and purposeful hands obeyed the common impulse.

Then they advanced....

Later, the stealthy, shivering group stole forth from the room and down the black hallway that led to the street. The last man out cast a terrified glance at the still, shapeless object in the corner as he closed the door behind him and fled after his fellows. When they came from the passage into the full light of day, each skulker looked at his hands and found that they shook as if with a mighty ague.

Even as they blinked their eyes in the glaring sunlight, an excited young man came rushing toward them from the opposite side of the street. They paused irresolute. The newcomer was white, excited — yes, jubilant. In his hand he carried a newspaper, the heavy black headlines standing out in bold relief.

"He's got a reprieve! " he was shouting eagerly. "Look 'ere! See wot it says. "

Fascinated, they slunk back into the dark passage, to listen in stupefaction while the joyous Blacky repeated the astounding news from the prison.

"Mr. Jenison and his wife done it, " cried Blacky, his eyes gleaming. "It says so here. They went to the gov'nor this morning and put it up to him in a way that made him grant a reprieve for thirty days, so's Mr. Jenison can get the real facts before him. That means a pardon sure, kids. Say, Jenison's all right! He's the kind of a friend to have, he is. He never quit on Dick. Say, where's Ernie? We'd better put him wise. "

"It won't make any difference to Ernie now, " said one of the rogues, wiping his wet brow with his hand.

Blacky fell away with a great look of dread in his eyes. He understood.

"We'd better duck out o' this, " he muttered vaguely. "It says here that the cops are going to question Ernie. They're out huntin' for him by this time, kids. "

"They know he was here wid us, and they'll find him sure, " cried one shifty-eyed fellow. "Me to the woods. "

"Hold on. Spike, " interposed another grimly. "We got to stand together on this. We got to stick by Dick, now he has a chance. We got to stay here and tell 'em what Ernie said to us in there. It's the only way. We'll do time for it, but what's the dif? Dick was doin' more for Ernie. We're sure to get off light, when it all comes out. "

They drew back into the passage and waited for the police to come.

An hour went by, and not one faltered. There came at last to their ears the sound of heavy footsteps on the narrow stairway. Spike heaved a deep sigh and said to his comrades:

"We've seen the last of Dick, kids. This Mr. Jenison will take care of him from now on. He'll have a good chance to be honest, lucky dog, just as he's always wanted to be. "

The fellow with the plutocratic watch took it from his pocket and gazed at it with the eyes of one who is contemplating a great sacrifice.

"Jenison's all right, God bless him. I'm going to see that he gets his watch back, too. I was a dog to have pinched it in the first place. "

THE END